LOST
IN THE
WIND

CALLE J.
BROOKES

LOST RIVER LIT PUBLISHING, LLC
SPRINGS VALLEY INDIANA
EST. 2011

Other books by

Calle J.
Brookes

Denying the Devil

SMALL-TOWN SHERIFFS

Holding the Truth

SUSPENSE/THRILLER

PAVAD: FBI CASE FILES

PAVAD: FBI Case Files #0001
"Knocked Out"
PAVAD: FBI Case Files #0002
"Knocked Down"
PAVAD: FBI Case Files #0003
"Knocked Around"
PAVAD: FBI Case Files #0004
"White Out"

Calle has several free reads available at
www.CalleJBrookesReads.com

For my grandfather, the best man I have ever known.
You will be missed.
Oct. 2015

For my grandmother, who gave me the courage to try. Without you and your love of
romance, I never would have made it this far.
Feb. 2016

For my papaw, whose children loved him deeply, and will always
miss him.
Oct. 2017

Calle J. Brookes is first and foremost a fiction writer. She enjoys crafting paranormal romance and romantic suspense. She reads almost every genre except horror. She spends most of her time juggling family life and writing while reminding herself that she can't spend all of her time in the worlds found within books. CJ loves to be contacted by her readers via email and at **www.CalleJBrookes.com**. When not at home writing stories of adventure and wrangling with two border collies and a beagle puppy, CJ is off in her RV somewhere exploring the beautiful world we live in, along with her husband of she can't remember how many years and their child.

FCI102019

Then took the other, as just as fair,
And having perhaps the better claim
Because it was grassy and wanted wear,
Though as for that the passing there
Had worn them really about the same,

—Robert Frost

LOST
IN THE
WIND

FINLEY CREEK: DISASTER
BOOK   1

Chapter 1

DR. NIKKIE JEAN NETORRE felt like the biggest fool when she walked into the Barratt County Hospital, her bloodied hand wrapped in a cartoon-owl-printed kitchen towel. The towel had been a housewarming gift from her friend Jillian when she'd bought her small house just inside the Barratt County line three months earlier.

Jillian had so helpfully pointed out that Nikkie Jean resembled that owl. With the mud-brown hair, hazel eyes, and prism-laced glasses *plus* contacts, she couldn't deny it. When she blinked, she probably did look like a cartoon owl.

Now she was just a bloody owl. A bloody, stupid one. Had it not been her dominant hand that she had injured, Nikkie Jean could have set the stitches in her own wound. Stitching herself up would have been a wee bit difficult. She'd stopped before she'd compounded the stupidity.

Barratt County Gen was closer to her new home than FCGH, the hospital where she spent most of her days. She'd never been to this smaller hospital before.

No time like the present.

Nikkie Jean stepped up to the intake desk and said *excuse me* to the man bent over the desk, rifling through a drawer, muttering and cursing.

Well, Nikkie Jean said it to his back.

He spun. Glowered.

Nikkie Jean took a step back. She hadn't expected *this* particular glowering giant. "Dr. Holden-Deane! I…"

Nikkie Jean looked closer at the behemoth of a man in front of her as the scowl deepened. Well.

She had just left Rafael Holden-Deane ninety minutes ago at

FCGH, when he'd excused the surgery department from a meeting he'd called to address an upcoming surgical department audit. Every file, every report, every lab request, every bill, every supply request going back ten years. The COM was being thorough. No real surprise; people had died because of hospital lies lately. Rafe was now responsible for cleaning up those messes. He'd just need a really big broom for it.

The man glowered down at her. Not that surprising; Rafe was usually glowering at someone. She tried to stay out of his orbit when he looked just like this.

Nikkie Jean looked closer.

This man's eyes were darker, harder, and even more terrifying. That made her take a step back.

Rafe was almost a big softie under his hot warrior exterior. She doubted she'd ever be able to say the same about this guy.

"You have me confused with someone else. May I help you?"

She blinked up at him—Dr. Rafe Holden-Deane was at least six foot six with three-feet-wide shoulders—and she was a ninety-eight-pound, barely five-foot small fry.

Dark hair, the eyes so brown they looked black, and the slightly olive skin tone. The muscular body of absolute perfection. Check, check, check, and check—this guy had all that, too.

That was kind of hard to miss. Nikkie Jean hadn't missed admiring it at all a time or two with her own boss.

She might have a *no-doctors* policy for her personal life, but that didn't mean she was blind. She pulled her glasses off her face and rubbed the rain off them as best she could one-handed. Just to make certain she wasn't seeing something that just wasn't there.

Nope.

She might be half-blind—at least without the glasses, anyway—but she wasn't wrong. The hair was possibly a little longer. A little shaggier than her neat-as-a-pin boss. Wilder. Far more untamed.

This guy looked like…power. Strength. Threat.

He could ride a dragon easily. More than that, he'd tame one without breaking a sweat. The scar over his eye was *definitely* different. It was noticeable and gave him a sexy pirate look.

No, she wasn't wrong completely. It wasn't Rafe, but it sure looked like him.

Rafe didn't have a dragon tattoo on one strong arm. And maybe, maybe Rafe's arms weren't quite as well defined.

The doctor standing in front of her was a dead ringer for the FCGH chief of medicine. Freaky. "I...I'm sorry, but you look just like my boss at FCGH. Dr. Holden-Deane. Enough to be his identical twin."

Here fishy, fishy, fishy. She wanted information. She'd take it right back to Jillian—Rafe's wife.

If possible, his expression darkened even more. Yeah, he really did resemble her cantankerous boss right down to—almost—the last eyelash. Except maybe his eyes *were* just a shade blacker. Which was impossible—they had to just be dark brown. Nikkie Jean was staring but well...she stared at Rafe sometimes, too.

The way one would a very handsome, very beautiful, very dangerous beast.

"Is that why you've come here today, Miss..."

"Dr. Nikkie Jean Netorre. And no—" He had her there. Most definitely not. Her hand was really starting to hurt, too. Time to get back down to business; Nikkie Jean had things to do tonight. "I came here because I have...this little problem here. And I need stitches. Barratt County is closer to my home than FCGH. I figured the sooner the better. And the less my people at FCGH get of me, probably the better. There was a *tiny* issue of one thousand containers of chocolate pudding being delivered today that I may or may not have been responsible for. I'm hiding from the head of surgery until he settles down. He's doing a shift in the ER tonight to keep from getting rusty."

And she didn't want the people at her hospital hovering. Hovering was something she wasn't exactly used to.

Cherise would practically coddle her, Wanda would make her cookies, and Lacy and Jillian would personally take care of the wound. She'd feel grateful and stupid and...weird. Embarrassed that such a fuss was being made. Nikkie Jean had survived thirty years without being hovered over. She wasn't comfortable changing that now. She held the bloody owl up for him to see. "I could have dealt with it myself, but it's my dominant. I can't set the stitches. And...it's really starting to hurt."

She'd tried. But stopped. So here she was. At Barratt County. FCGH's country cousin.

Nikkie Jean took her first real look around.

Barratt County looked like the hospital she had just left. Only smaller. Even the wall decor was the same.

"It's like FCGH in here, in miniature." With the Holden-Deane clone in the middle of the intake desk glaring at her, it was like she'd entered the Twilight Zone. Freaky.

"I believe we share the same decorator." He beckoned to a nurse. "Chloe, take Doctor—"

"Netor-*uh*. Pediatric surgical resident. I'd shake hands, but…well…" She did not want to touch him. Touch a tiger wrong and he'd bite off your hand.

"Take Dr. Netorre into exam room one. I'll be with her shortly."

"Sir?" the nurse shot him a questioning look. No kidding. The COM usually didn't treat patients in the ER.

It must have been Nikkie Jean's lucky day.

"I'm filling in for Curtis tonight."

"Of course."

Nikkie Jean obediently followed the young nurse, surprised the Rafe clone hadn't bitten the nurse's head off yet for questioning him.

She thought about him to distract herself from the inevitable. Nikkie Jean hated the thought of metal instruments going through her skin. A weird hang-up for a surgeon to have, but she had it nonetheless. No problems with metal in other people's skin, but her own? Nope.

Probably from when she'd been sixteen and an inept phlebotomist had left her with a three-quarter-inch scar across the back of her hand. That metal needle ripping through her flesh…Nikkie Jean shuddered mentally at that memory.

She was a big wimp. And she knew it. Another reason she'd chosen the neighboring hospital over her own.

So her friends didn't see her turn into a big baby.

She'd been in exam rooms millions of times now. No big deal. She'd spent thousands of hours in exam rooms and hospital rooms—on both sides of the equations. She could deal.

She'd never like it from *this* side, though. Being vulnerable like that to other people. Nope. She'd never liked that. Far too many bad memories.

She distracted herself with thoughts of the man she'd just found—first chance she had, she was going to text Jillian about the pirate with Rafe's face.

She'd always had a thing for pirates. Something about the rebel had always appealed to her.

Too bad she wasn't into other doctors, though.

—

Dr. Caine Alvaro glared at the little feminine tornado as she followed Chloe into the exam room.

She hadn't said anything he hadn't heard before.

Eventually, he would have to address the source. He wasn't an idiot. He'd seen photos of the man she had said he resembled. The man had been all over the news a few weeks ago.

Caine had known about his brother for seven years—a year before his father had thrown it in his face that he had a twin of his own out there. Before the old bastard had died six years ago from too many years of booze and stupidity. Known who he was, where he was, and what he was doing.

Caine could have found him at any time.

What he hadn't known was what he was going to do about it. He'd spent six of those years in the military, paying for medical school the hard way. Six weeks ago, he'd taken the job in little Value, Texas, after spending a year in Abilene and a year in Amarillo. He needed the peace of a small town again. To see children running, shrieking with laughter.

To see *his* children making the roots he'd never had. In the cities, he'd been so busy with working, he'd had little time for his children. They'd spent more time with sitters and his uncle than they had with him. He hadn't liked that.

Caine was hoping to change that in a smaller setting. A smaller hospital meant more of a life for him with the people who mattered most.

Caine wanted to spend more time with his family. The last two years since his wife's death had gone by in too much of a blur for him. He wanted time with his children.

This woman wasn't the first to mention his resemblance to the man now running FCGH. There were several physicians on staff at both hospitals, as well as several nurses who did part-time work at both locations.

Caine and his brother's paths would cross eventually. Of that, he had no doubt. It was just a matter of time. Their paths would cross, but he wasn't about to seek it out himself.

He had other problems to worry about. Like medical-billing fraud rumors going back years. Not to mention HIPAA—the Health Insurance Portability and Accountability Act—violations they were still investigating.

He wasn't lost to the irony—he'd spent the last seven years avoiding even thinking about his mother's family and the brother he knew was out there.

Only to end up less than forty minutes away, working the same damned position—for the same damned medical group.

Fate obviously had plans for him.

Caine had never let fate dictate his future. Far from it.

He hadn't appreciated being stared at like he was a damned monkey in a circus, either. She had blinked up at him like he was a mirage she was trying to make certain was real. He scowled again and tossed the file he had been studying on the counter for JoLyn to put away.

He'd deal with this Dr. Netorre himself and then get her out of his hospital and on her way back to the larger, better, more wonderful world Finley Creek Gen.

And Dr. Rafael Holden-Deane.

Then he'd forget all about her and how she'd somehow brought the wind in with her.

He stalked into the exam room as the woman was giving Chloe her pertinent medical history. She spoke clearly, with the tiniest bit of an East Coast accent. Her hair was loose around her shoulders, long brown streaked with honey and stick straight. She wore dark-pink-rimmed glasses that made her hazel eyes look far too big for her face. There were Disney characters on the glasses. Caine looked closer to confirm it. Yes. Tinkerbell, to be exact.

It fit.

She moved. Constantly.

She barely came up to his shoulder. Maybe. She may have been even shorter than that. Five feet or so. Maybe one hundred pounds. He listened as she gave her birthdate again for their records.

Thirty. She'd just had her thirtieth birthday a few weeks ago.

She didn't look it. He would have put her far younger, had she not said *doctor* earlier.

Dr. Netorre pushed the glasses up her small nose, and he was struck by how thick the left lens was. Most surgeons had near perfect eyesight. This one didn't. "How well do you see?"

She turned toward him. He might have been mistaken, but he almost thought she rolled her eyes at him. He'd bet *this* resident was the trouble-making kind. He didn't envy his brother working with this woman at all.

"Very well—with the glasses and contacts simultaneously. I'm not blind. Just half—in my left eye. The right one is just so lazy; it's never bothered to keep up. I've scolded it and scolded it. It never learns. It works, but it's only ever been a C student. How well do you see me?" She held her arms open, almost inviting him to study her, dressed as she was in candy pink scrubs.

She shot a smile filled with perfect teeth and dimples right at him. This woman was no pushover. He respected that.

He just grunted, then turned toward the injury. "So how did you hurt your hand, Dr. Netorre?"

"Tree branch went through the attic window. I cut my hand on the glass. It was wet and slippery. The glass, not the branch."

"Let's take a look. How long have you been at Finley Creek?" Caine asked the same type of questions he would have anyone. Sometimes the power of distraction was an effective tool.

"Eight months. I attended med school there, then went home to Pennsylvania for a few years. Now I'm back here. Studying under Allen Jacobson. He's a wonderful surgeon and teacher. Hopefully, he'll forgive me for the chocolate pudding order. But really, the cafeteria has no decent desserts. Rafe should really get around to fixing that. I was only trying to help."

Caine bit back a laugh. If she'd pulled that stunt in his hospital, he'd have a problem. But FCGH wasn't his circus. Barratt County was.

He took the edge of the dish towel wrapped around her hand and started pulling gently. She hissed out a small breath. He shot a quick look at her face.

She was cute, more than beautiful. Attractive, if a man went for wholesome, girl-next-door.

Caine never had.

She was unmarried, or so she'd told Chloe. Lived alone, didn't smoke, or use alcohol to excess. She spoke easily about what had happened—even how she had tried to treat the injury herself, but stopped. She and Chloe fell into a discussion of shared acquaintances. She was apparently a chatterer. No doubt her patients all adored her.

Caine examined the three-inch gash across her palm. Any deeper and she could have had trouble performing surgery in the future. He didn't tell her that. He suspected she knew. If she was a resident at FCGH, she had to have the skills to get herself there. FCGH didn't take just anyone. It was highly competitive, especially the surgical department. FCU, the university the hospital was affiliated with, had a hefty price tag. "Three weeks. No using it for at least three weeks."

"I think a week or so is more than appropriate, don't you?"

Hazel eyes met his. He scowled. He did not like to be second guessed. Especially by little surgeons in training like this one. He'd seen hundreds of residents come and go. He was reserving judgment on this one for the time being, FCGH or not.

"I am being cautious, Dr. Netorre. You've injured yourself more than I think you realize. Three weeks, not a moment before. Are you certain you removed all the glass?"

"It was just the one piece, but I flushed it thoroughly. I just couldn't suture it myself."

It didn't surprise him that she'd tried. Not in the least. He'd bet she was the type to try everything at least once, to think she could do it all herself. This woman was no doubt a handful of trouble waiting to happen. "No. You couldn't."

It took him fifteen minutes to get a row of tiny stitches across the delicate flesh of her palm. Luckily, the injury was to the outer edge of her hand. That would make it easier for her to regain full range of function. Her skin was pale, delicate, her hand small beneath his. She shouldn't scar too badly, at least. And she'd be able to use it for the delicate work surgery required.

Although he couldn't see this little tornado standing still for more than five minutes. Definitely not for the hours that surgery could require.

When he looked up, she was staring at him. "What?"

"I'm sorry. You really do look like Rafe. Same scowl, too. Although you look far more like a pirate than he does. I think it's the hair, and your pet dragon there. You're definitely more of a dragon. Rafe's like a tiger. Beautiful and deadly before he pounces. I've seen him pounce before. Does he have a name? The dragon. Not Rafe."

Rafe. Caine's scowl deepened. "You always call your boss by his first name?"

"He's a friend, so I do when off the clock. Well, he's married to a good friend of mine. And his sister Ariella is a friend, too. I handled the guest book at Rafe's wedding recently." She said it softly, her face not that far from his. "I studied genetics. Rafe has a smaller scar on his forehead. Your hair is a lot longer. That's about it."

"My scars aren't all visible. And there's plenty of damned differences between us."

"So you know him?"

He waved Chloe out of the room. Nothing got under his skin faster than someone butting into his personal life.

Someone needed to put her in her place. Even as he thought it, he chased that thought up with the knowledge that she'd just pop back out of that place in the next instant. Then go about doing whatever she wanted to satisfy her curiosity—nonstop. "I'll finish up here."

When his nurse was gone, he turned back to the woman in front of him. And glowered. "I don't want to know him. I have no need."

"Why?"

"I've known about him for years. And it's none of your business. I don't choose to know him. Or any sister he may have."

"Well, I kind of figured that. Although that's your loss; I certainly understand about estranged families. Mine's as estranged as it gets, too." She shot him an absolutely perfect smile, complete with dimples. "But the two of you would make an interesting case study for a nature-vs-nurture debate."

Caine bit back a surprised laugh. There was something so guileless in her eyes, her smile. He hadn't been expecting that.

All traces of his earlier irritation with a staff member who'd called off disappeared. Even the irritation with her interference lessened. He covered the stitches with a bandage and motioned toward the curtain.

"Get out of here, Dr. Netorre. May you never grace my ER again."

"That sounds like a plan to me. Catch you later, Alvaro. See you around sometime. Want me to say hi to your brother for you? Just to see what happens?"

"Go."

Chapter 2

"HE LOOKED JUST LIKE him, Lace. only crankier." Nikkie Jean's stitches came out easier than they'd gone in. One week to the date after the incident, she stood patiently in the midst of one of the now-empty ER exam rooms while her friend and surgical colleague, Lacy Deane, snipped the silk. Lacy had had questions. Nikkie Jean was doing her best to answer them.

"Is that even possible?"

Dr. Holden-Deane was her brother-in-law, and Lacy was fiercely protective over the man—but no one was blind to the truth. Dr. Holden-Deane had been very snarly when he first came to FCGH. Now that he had met and married Jillian, it was a slightly different ballgame.

He was still snarly, but only about half as much as he used to be. Jillian had definitely tamed that particular tiger.

Jillian was a brave, brave girl. Far braver than Nikkie Jean would ever be. Nikkie Jean was allergic to tigers—and male doctors.

At first, Rafe had terrified Nikkie Jean. She wasn't too wimpy to admit it. But he'd terrified everybody then. He'd been hurting, Jillian had told her privately, from horrors he'd seen in his relief work in Africa.

Nikkie Jean could definitely understand that. She'd had her own share of horrors to heal from. Nikkie Jean wasn't certain she ever would fully. Trauma could do that to a girl. Or boy. Or anything, really.

Lacy finished with the stitches and then looked at Nikkie Jean. "Rafe doesn't want to meet him yet. Neither do the rest of his brothers and sisters. They did contact Dr. Alvaro, but he sent a not-so-polite reply back. Not all that different than Rafe's original reply, but Rafe doesn't like to hear that. Dr. Alvaro has no interest in reunification. He made that bluntly clear. And Rafe and the others don't want to push. But...*just* like him?"

"Just like him. Even the same scowl. Longer hair and looks like a pirate. He has a scar from here, to here. More muscly and perfect, if that's possible. Harder. Still, a very pretty man."

"Weird. Two Rafes in the world. Hard to believe it."

"I know, right?" She shot Lacy a grin. "I'm not sure Texas is big enough for two."

"Neither am I. Neither am I."

—

He was on her mind as she trekked across the parking garage toward her car after Lacy finished removing the stitches. The garage was reasonably better lit than it used to be, but after everything that had happened in the parking garage in recent months—a woman had been murdered just outside the door, Cherise had been mugged by a drugged out mugger, Dr. Lanning had committed suicide and almost killed Lacy, and a few other things she didn't want to think about—Nikkie Jean was always going to be leery back there.

Even if she wasn't a card-carrying member of the Cowards' Club.

Usually, she walked out with someone, but her usual crowd was still on the clock. Everyone else had left while she was having Lacy remove the stitches.

She had two choices—wait until the next person left and walk with them, or ask the security guard, Creepy Ray, to walk with her.

Neither option held much appeal.

Ray freaked her out. She'd caught him staring at her before; in ways that definitely didn't make her feel safe and secure. Far from it. Nikkie Jean always followed her instincts when it came to matters of her own personal safety.

The second door opened, and Dr. Henedy stepped out. He smiled when he saw her, revealing a handsome if somewhat insincere smile. But at least he was better than Ray. Her fingers tightened on her phone, just in case. Predators wore all different disguises—including lab coats. Nikkie Jean knew that to the bottom of her toes.

"Dr. Netorre, beautiful evening, isn't it?"

"For now. Storms are supposed to be coming."

"Where are you off to so late?"

She fell in next to him, careful to keep some distance between them. She didn't know him well, but he was a real human being. That mattered. Nikkie Jean wasn't stupid—she looked like an easy victim. Her lack of height, slighter build, glasses, the fact that she was a woman—they all added up to a great big bullseye.

She'd already been assaulted once.

That more than doubled the likelihood it would happen again. Even though she was triply safety conscious. A woman had to be careful. She made that very clear to every support group and trauma talk she gave at the women's charity across the street.

"Annie Gaines is organizing a protest on Boethe Street at six. I'm joining her there to help."

"Annie is? Surprising. It must be a cause dear to her heart."

"It is. The mayor's *Clean Up Boethe Street* initiative. It's evicting Annie and thirty of her neighbors soon. She's organizing the neighborhood into a protest to stop it. But she'll need help." Lots of it. This deal was being touted as the way to solve all of the city's worst problems.

Annie was fighting a definite uphill battle.

Annie wasn't much of a *fighter,* either.

Boethe Street was directly behind the hospital, and it was the worst neighborhood in the city of around fifty thousand people. A smart woman didn't walk down that street alone. Nikkie Jean had driven Annie home many times and it still made her shudder. She wasn't about to let Annie walk home or ride the bus. Not if she could help it.

"Interesting. My nephew and wife own several properties in that area. I'm not sure if the initiative affects them or not. Well, I wish you and Annie good luck." He stopped near his Lincoln, then hesitated. "I would love to meet with you and discuss the results of Annie's protest. Perhaps over coffee, or dinner, sometime?"

Nikkie Jean just blinked. She might not know the man well, but she did know one thing.

He was married to a city councilwoman. A very prominent, very publicity-driven, prettily coifed councilwoman.

His invitation hadn't been platonic. Nikkie Jean wasn't stupid.

"I...don't think that will be a good idea. I don't have much time for socializing, outside of work. Perhaps I can meet you and your wife some other time? I could bring Annie with me; she would love your wife's help with this."

His smile hardened. She finally understood what that expression meant. That didn't exactly make her feel secure.

Her car was just in the distance. Nikkie Jean was never happier to see it.

—

She was still irritated long after the protest had fizzled—very few people had actually shown up to help Annie. Nikkie Jean was trying not to grumble over him as she drove home.

The highway was long and straight between Value and Finley Creek, and her turn off was just north of the small town of less than a thousand people. The road wound through the countryside for another seven miles before she made it to her house. It was a long, solitary drive, and she usually used it to think.

She normally didn't mind the drive, but tonight was different. Tonight she felt more vulnerable than she had in a long, long while.

Dr. Henedy brought back far too many memories she had battled long and hard to forget. What a giant piece of middle-aged man-scum.

Not going to happen. It was because of men like him she'd instituted her *no-doctors* rule in the first place.

Chapter 3

NIKKIE JEAN ALMOST missed the man waving her down from the middle of the road. He was large and strong and angry. The exact opposite of what Nikkie Jean liked.

Her breath hitched. Alone, deserted street, sun beginning to set. Small, single woman. Big, strong, angry man.

Yep, this was a recipe for disaster.

Or a bad horror novel.

But if someone needed medical assistance—she had to step up to the plate.

She slowed until she got close enough to see who it was. Some of her tension lessened. Just some.

The dragon tattoo told her which doctor twin it was glowering at her in the rain. "Oh, goody. Another man doctor! Just my luck."

Basic human decency meant she couldn't just keep going. Not now. That was Jillian's brother-in-law out there, after all.

She instructed her phone to send quick voice texts to both Izzie and Jillian—telling them to call her in half an hour for a safety check, that she was giving someone she didn't know well a ride somewhere.

Nikkie Jean wasn't stupid, after all. Helpful, but not stupid.

She'd just texted Jillian exactly who she was picking up alongside the highway.

She rolled down the passenger window. "Out for an evening constitutional, Alvaro?"

Dr. Alvaro had a cross look on his face that was extremely familiar. She'd been on the wrong end of his twin's ire *once*. Her own fault, but not an experience she wanted to repeat. His resemblance to Rafe had some of the tension leaving her.

Some. Not all. Rafe would never hurt anyone. But she had no

idea if this man would.

Thunder echoed over them, and Nikkie Jean tried not to jump. She'd always hated storms. "Get in. I'm going your way. I think."

"Thanks. A fan broke on my truck, and I don't have the parts to fix it."

With the approaching storm, he wouldn't be able to do much good with it anyway. She heard the frustration and irritation. No doubt everything always went the way he wanted it in his world. He'd command just that.

And he was very angry about that, no doubt. "Sorry. Well, you're lucky I had to do my part in civil disobedience tonight. No one else will come down this road for hours." It was one of the things she liked about living out there. Solitude.

Sometimes that was all she longed for. Solitude, quiet, freedom—behind her five deadbolt locks.

"Probably not." He climbed into her little Jeep, dwarfing it. The doctor twins were some seriously well-put-together men. Snarly, but so nice to look at. "You always pick up men you don't know on the side of the highway, Dr. Netorre?"

"Nope." She pointed to her phone just as a photo of Jillian popped up on the screen, and the phone vibrated. "That's *your* new sister-in-law Jillian texting. Isn't she so pretty? Your twin brother just adores her. He even jumped out a window to save her when a bad guy tried to kill her. I helped put him back together again afterward. I texted her and another friend to let them know I was picking you up. Jillian knows exactly where to find you if you cause me any trouble. She'd cause you trouble in return—and would enjoy it. She did not like the letter you sent her husband and your sister Ariella last month. Jillian's very protective, and Ariella is her best friend. That letter came at a really bad time, you know?"

Jillian had told Nikkie Jean all about it when she'd asked her about Dr. Alvaro. The picture Jillian had painted in confidence had not been super pretty.

Nikkie Jean had imagined she could understand some of his hurt. Families were just so complicated sometimes. Hers certainly had been.

He just grunted as she sent a quick voice text back to Jillian telling her she was fine and would call back as soon as she was finished with Rafe's doppelganger.

"See, I'm a helpful neighbor, but I'm not stupid. I'm going to trust you, Dr. Alvaro, not to be a homicidal maniac, ok? I really need you not to be one of those, ok?"

Because male doctors were the stuff Nikkie Jean's nightmares were made of. Even Rafe, and his look-alike.

That was a lesson she would never forget.

"I'll do my best. Turn here."

Chapter 4

CAINE FOUGHT THE IRRITATION the situation caused and studied his unlikely rescuer. Her scrubs had frogs in spaceships printed on them. The hair was pulled into two braids that hung down over her breasts. There were cartoon characters—frogs—on her glasses. Did she have a pair of glasses for every outfit?

She looked like a kid playing dress-up, not like the gifted surgical resident he'd learned she was.

His nursing supervisor had raved about her, the wunderkind of FCGH, with a gifted touch. Several of the staff at Barratt County also worked at Finley Creek. All had spoken highly of her. Nikkie Jean Netorre had been the topic of hospital gossip for half a day.

Hell, she even had freckles over her nose.

She couldn't have been cuter if she'd tried.

She shifted a bit; the frogs pulled over her chest, revealing more curves beneath the scrubs for just an instant.

A heat of a different kind burned through him, surprising him at the intensity of it.

He'd never been attracted to the cute, super-short, girl-next-door, mosquito-irritating, hyperactive type before.

April, his children's mother, had been sleek, sophisticated perfection. She had epitomized what he'd always thought he'd been attracted to. Before.

He'd lost his taste for women in general after April had taken off with the fifty-eight-year-old chief of oncology to continue their two-year affair, two days after she'd revealed she was pregnant. And the baby most likely hadn't been his.

Caine had lost his taste for women in general after that.

"So…where exactly am I taking you?"

"Two miles down Bracker's Mill Road. The old Larson place."

"I'm not familiar with that particular landmark. You just point where I need to turn; I'm on Old McGareth Road, six miles before the turn off to the Deane Ranch Road. A friend in my department recommended the little house to me when it came up for sale. Her husband owned it originally. He kept the land surrounding the house, but sold me the cottage at a great deal. Well, he's Rafe's brother. But what are you going to do once I get you there? Someone can drive you where you need to go?"

"My uncle. He'll drive. It means getting my children out, but it can't be helped." She talked; the woman just talked constantly.

"I didn't know you had kids." She shot him a look filled with curiosity. He had the feeling this woman lived by curiosity. And meddling.

"I have three children."

"How many wives?" Another grin, this time.

"I'm…widowed. I'd prefer you not mention that to your little friend when you call her tonight."

He glowered at her. She'd probably talk to his brother's wife about him for hours. She seemed the type. No doubt she was glued to her cell phone at every opportunity.

"Girls or boys?"

"Two boys, one girl." He wasn't going to go into detail about his children. He never did. His family was private. They'd had enough of gossip three years ago. He wasn't about to expose them to more.

She shot him a wistful look. "Fun."

"You don't have any children." He remembered that from her file. Too bad; he had no doubt children just loved her. It was no wonder she'd chosen a pediatrics field.

"No. I'm afraid that's not in the cards for me. But I like kids. Maybe someday I'll adopt."

"No man in the picture?" The words slipped out, and he cursed himself. He didn't want to encourage her to keep prattling on. Or asking something personal he didn't want to answer.

He pointed to the road she needed to take; she turned, faster than he would have. She had a bit of a reckless streak, apparently. No surprise. The woman was probably very dangerous. In more ways than one.

"Not at the moment." Another cheeky grin came at him. "You offering? I have to say, glowering chiefs of medicine *really* aren't my thing. That's Jillian's answer, and I never copy off my friends' papers. That would be so overdone."

She drove up to his front porch, nimbly skirting around the pink bike in the center of the drive.

"I'm sorry about that. My daughter has a tendency to leave her stuff lying everywhere."

"It's easier to see stuff when you leave it out. This is your stop, big guy. That'll be two dollars and twenty-eight cents." She held out a small hand, then shot him a wicked grin, revealing the dimples—which racked up the heat flooding his gut. "Pay up, Alvaro."

"I'm flat out of cash." An uncharacteristic bolt of humor hit him. To mingle with the sudden lust that apparently was going to hit him every time this woman smiled in his direction. "I'll have to give you an IOU."

"I'll take you up on that. Someday. You...have a greeting committee."

He turned, and there they were. His life. Keller held the baby by the hand as all three of them watched the unfamiliar car. "Every night."

"You're a very lucky man, Dr. Alvaro. I hope you realize that." Her words went soft, and the teasing quieted. That quiet had him answering more than anything else.

"I do. Each and every minute of the day." Words couldn't adequately describe what his children meant to him. They were his world and had been from the moment Everett had taken his first breath in the world, to be followed fifteen minutes later by his sister.

"I've got to go. Water the plant and all. He gets cranky if I'm late. And I've had my fill of doctor men tonight. I'll tell you about the sixty-year-old surgeon who asked me out to coffee tonight—without his wife—some other time. See you around."

He almost commented on the other man but didn't. It wasn't his business. Her personal life was her own problem. "You, too."

She blew him a cheeky kiss, then waved to the three children on the front porch. She called out a hello to them and then put the Jeep in reverse.

He was going to do his best to stay far away from this woman—before he did something stupid. Like seeing if she tasted as sweet as she looked. Or asking her out for coffee himself.

The last thing either one of them needed was *coffee*.

He forced himself not to look over his shoulder as she pulled away. He didn't have time for Nikkie Jean Netorre right now.

No matter that she'd turned him on faster than any woman had—in years. He'd honestly thought April had broken that part of him completely

Chapter 5

NIKKIE JEAN WAS SUCH a pretty little thing.

Dr. Wallace Henedy watched her as she finished scrubbing up before their next surgery and laughed to himself when the surgical nurse Dominique tied her into the sterile gown and helped her glove up.

Nikkie Jean Netorre looked like a child, barely bigger than the eleven-year-old boy on the table behind them. It was a routine surgery on a hernia, one of the most common types of surgeries on children.

Nikkie Jean had a steady hand. Wallace felt privileged to be one of the ones to instruct her on the technique, along with Allen Jacobson. Jacobson was one hell of a surgeon, and an even better teacher.

He was glad to see the younger man back after that little bit of trouble he'd had with a pharmacy tech.

She'd been mercenary; he'd known that from one look at her when she'd hired on to the hospital over a year ago.

He'd thought Allen Jacobson was smarter than that. The man should have known how to keep his private business outside of the hospital.

Wallace had plenty of practice himself. His body still ached in the most delicious places from his latest with Connie.

She was getting quite demanding. Pushing him in ways he wasn't comfortable with.

He'd told her at the beginning that he loved his wife.

That wasn't going to change from a little recreational sex to blow off steam.

Wallace was on staff at all three hospitals in Finley Creek—Finley Creek Gen, Finley Creek County, and a smaller Catholic hospital near the northern boundary of the city. Not to mention his home office at Barratt County General in the next county south.

He faced a lot of pressure. He needed an outlet. He always had. Wallace needed that stimulation. The excitement of the chase. Being made to feel important.

Nikkie Jean brushed in front of him. She barely hit his shoulder. That didn't stop her from being a force of nature.

She brought laughter wherever she was. She was making quips about feeling like a burrito in the white surgical gown.

Wallace shot her another look. The gown might be shapeless, and Nikkie Jean might be a thinner woman, but there were enough curves for him to know that she was all female.

Pretty. Bubbly. Gifted.

He'd been fascinated by her for months.

Yes, it was time to cut Connie loose and move on.

Nikkie Jean would do quite nicely for what Wallace needed. It would just take some planning on his part to make it work for the both of them.

Chapter 6

DR. ALLEN JACOBSON WATCHED the women dancing around the small children's ward cafeteria as they did their best to entertain the dozen children two hours after surgery ended.

No doubt it had been Nikkie Jean Netorre's idea.

She was becoming more than incorrigible. He was glad he wasn't acting chief of medicine any longer. Dealing with Nikkie Jean's antics could end up being a full-time position.

As it was, Allen would be eating chocolate pudding cups in his lunch bag for the next three years after Nikkie Jean's little stunt to welcome him back last week.

He'd kept some of the pudding and planned to donate the rest to the food bank three buildings down from his medical office.

But as Nikkie Jean wiggled and giggled along with Lacy Deane and Jillian Deane to a familiar theme song from a children's program—one Jillian had starred on when she'd been younger—he had to smile, then flat out laugh.

The three of them had a way of making everyone do that lately. Patients and hospital staff alike.

The children were mostly slated to go home in the next few days, none were seriously ill at this point. Nikkie Jean and her friends had done this show a few times before. That he knew of.

He'd only been back at the hospital himself for a couple of days. He'd taken a month or so to get his thoughts back in order after everything that had happened lately.

There had been a lot of changes to this the place since Rafe had been injured. The other man ran a tight ship, but the atmosphere was far more welcoming to its employees than it had been under his friend Logan, or the men who'd run the place before.

Including Allen himself, who'd done a stint as a temporary chief of medicine. He'd tried, but as a temporary COM, his hands had been tied by the board. Repeatedly. Deliberately.

He bit back the disloyalty to Logan. The man hadn't been a good COM; Allen wasn't blind to that. But he'd been a good friend. At least until the last part of his life.

He distracted himself by looking at the crowd gathered for the show.

Jillian, Lacy, and Nikkie Jean held center stage, of course. They had a handful of the second-shift nurses helping do crowd control before their shifts started.

It looked impulsive and impromptu, but he easily sensed that it wasn't. There had to be some careful planning involved in order to get something like this going so smoothly.

He suspected he knew exactly who had done that planning.

He shot a look toward the back of the room. Rafe and Fin, his assistant, were in the back, watching. With approval.

No surprise. Just about everything that Jillian did lately was approved.

A bittersweet pang went through him. He'd been attracted to Jillian once. But he was glad she'd found Rafe. The two just sparked something almost visible with each other. They were well-matched. No one could argue that.

The crowd laughed, and he looked back at the trio in the center. Nikkie Jean held a water gun now.

A poor unsuspecting second-shift nurse took a shot right to the chest and hair. The woman wiped the short, dark-chocolate hair off her face and laughed, her big, dark eyes lighting. For a moment, she looked like an elf or a fairy with sparkling eyes and a mischievous grin.

Talk about a false impression.

Allen smirked. She was far prettier when she was laughing than shooting fire at people. That nurse had a real problem with men. Especially physicians. Especially those in authority.

He couldn't even remember her name. They'd had at least two disagreements over patients in the last three days. He'd been tempted to complain to HR, but he'd heard from Lacy that Logan had had a habit of writing up nurses over the most trivial things.

He was determined that no one viewed him like they'd viewed Logan. Not any longer.

Allen had his reputation around the hospital to repair.

How much he'd let money and friendship blind him to reality wasn't lost to Allen. He'd been blind to Logan, blind to Banks.

And he'd been blinded by another dark-haired, dark-eyed woman he'd wanted.

Allen liked to think he'd learned his lessons.

He'd stood over Banks's coffin, Banks's two sisters next to him. There hadn't been many more people at Banks's funeral than there had been at Logan's. Not even Allen's younger sister had gone. Not like she had Logan's.

Banks was a criminal. Logan had been hurting. There was a difference. A massive one.

Allen ruthlessly shoved that hurt away.

The nurse hadn't been wrong; not exactly. They just had different styles of treating patients.

He'd tried to remember that.

He was just straightening, turning to head to the cafeteria to wait for Nikkie Jean—she owed him lunch for that pudding fiasco—when a spray of cold water shot him right in the chest.

Allen sputtered and looked at the culprit.

Nikkie Jean shot him a wicked look, complete with a dimpled grin and laughing hazel eyes.

Allen looked at her, as genuine humor burst out.

It had been a while since he'd felt *genuine* happiness with anyone other than the younger sister who had been hovering over him. "You'll pay for that, Dr. Netorre. Just you wait."

The audience laughed, exactly as Nikkie Jean had no doubt intended.

She spun away, singing the next words to the children's song, as he watched. She tossed the toy gun to Lacy and did a cartwheel between the other two women without missing a step.

Choreographed. Well-planned. Nothing impulsive about it at all.

Things were starting to feel *genuine* again. Thanks to Nikkie Jean.

Chapter 7

WALLACE WATCHED THE three women as they danced, and he fought the urge to dance along with them. That wasn't dignified; and no other physicians were moving to the music. Still, Wallace couldn't look away.

This was the first time he'd ever seen a show in pediatrics.

Jillian, the COM's young pretty wife, was a decent performer, as was her sister-in-law Lacy Deane. But it was Nikkie Jean who held his attention.

He had news that was going to shatter the girl.

Wallace wasn't looking forward to it at all. The patient hadn't even been Nikkie Jean's. After their hernia patient, she'd moved on to a teenager with bone cancer, and Wallace had had an emergency appendectomy to perform. But she'd asked him to take good care of this one for her.

She was drawn to the children; no surprise, considering her chosen field. This was going to shatter her.

She danced around now with a young preschooler riding on her hip from her eyes. Wallace felt sick as he played it over in his head, figured out what words he was going to use with her. It wasn't going to be easy. He was about to take that joy he saw in her eyes.

Someone touched him on the arm, and he looked over to see Amy, the head surgical nurse. Her eyes were damp. She'd been the one to cover the child's face after Cage Ralstone had called the child's time of death. It had been a solemn moment for all of them. One that would never get easier for any of them. If it did, then medicine was the wrong field of choice. Wallace turned his attention back to the laughing children in front of where he stood.

He needed to see their faces for a moment. He just needed to. *These* children were going home soon. Thank God.

"I'll tell Nikkie Jean. She asked specifically that I tell her when the surgery was over. I think she was planning to come back after her shift ended and sit with him. She promised to bring him some chocolate pudding."

"She sat with him last night for a while, I think," Wallace said quietly. Dr. Ralstone and Dr. Patel had mentioned it. When they'd spoken of how alone the child had seemed. Only a lone, young social worker had paid much attention to the child at all. After social services had been called in.

Of course, that would be the kind of pediatric patient Nikkie Jean would be most drawn to. Wallace had wondered before why she seemed so alone. If she longed for the connection to others that he himself had been missing—since Jennifer had finished her real estate classes and started on her on upward trajectory more than a decade ago now. It was like Wallace wasn't as important. Or Reggie and Raymond.

He shook thoughts of his family away and looked at the nurse next to him. She was a pretty brunette in her late forties, with a pleasant body and a calm demeanor. He'd never been attracted to her, but he could see where many men would be. She had compassion. Her eyes, big and dark, were her best feature. He'd never gone for pleasingly plump—with the notable exception of his wife.

But what they had was so much more than physical. "She's going to be upset."

"No doubt," Amy said with compassion in her tone. "I'll tell her. When she's finished here."

"Thanks, Amy." He just hadn't wanted to be the one to destroy the joy in her today. Wallace watched the show until he couldn't stand it any longer. He turned and walked away, heartbroken over the child he hadn't been able to save.

Chapter 8

NIKKIE JEAN KNEW THE instant she saw the expression on Amy Hailer's face that the surgery hadn't gone well. After she and Lacy and Jillian finished their little skit in the children's cafeteria, Amy was waiting.

Watching.

With tears in her big brown eyes. She'd led Nikkie Jean into the small chapel next to the cafeteria. Nikkie Jean stayed silent until they were alone.

"He didn't do well in surgery," Nikkie Jean said.

Amy shook her head. "He had an anaphylactic reaction to the anesthesia, Nik. We did everything we could. But we lost him. I'm so sorry."

Nikkie Jean's breath caught. "I—"

The older woman hugged her lightly. Nikkie Jean resisted the urge to just cling. Amy smelled like her grandmother used to. The same shampoo or laundry soap, or something. Whatever it was, it brought back memories.

Memories she just wasn't equipped to deal with right now. She stepped away, not used to physical comfort from someone else any longer.

Even those times her mother had comforted her had been few and far between. Nikkie Jean had barely tolerated it then, either.

It was hard to count on something you only had half the time.

She pulled in a deep breath. She'd lost patients before. She would lose more in the future. It was as inevitable as breathing.

She tried to tell herself that. Tried to remember that this was what she'd signed up for.

It didn't help. All she could see was his face as she'd promised to sit with him after her shift ended. As he'd had hope that she wouldn't let him down like so many in his life already had.

Her eyes filled. "Amy...I..."

"I know, honey. It sucks." Amy already had tissue ready.

Nikkie Jean cried. Big, fat tears. Amy just patiently sat with her until she was finished. "Go home, Nikkie Jean. Take a warm bubble bath. Kiss a cute guy. Pet a cat—"

"I don't have a cat. Or a cute guy." She wiped her eyes. Forced herself to breathe again. "I have my house, and that's it. Other than Annie and Izzie and this place."

It was more than she usually shared, but it just slipped out. Nikkie Jean turned away from the compassion in the other woman's face.

"Then you go home and take that bubble bath. And remember: there is a time and place for everyone. Young or old. We here don't get to pick and choose who goes when, understand me? Only God knows when and where, not us."

Nikkie Jean found herself nodding. That was a lesson she knew very, very well.

She stood. She'd have to get her things out of her locker. Then she was getting out of this hospital and doing whatever she had to in order to forget a little boy who hadn't had a chance to live.

She went through the motions of gathering her bag, saying goodbye to everyone around her. She just shook her head when Allen asked if she was okay.

At least, she thought it was Allen. It could have been Virat.

Nikkie Jean just knew she had to get out of there before the hospital itself suffocated her.

Chapter 9

NIKKIE JEAN DIDN'T KNOW how she'd ended up at the diner. She didn't remember the drive or the road or the getting into her car. All she remembered was a little boy's face. Her heart hurt in every way imaginable.

She just wanted to grab dinner and go home. But she wasn't all that hungry. If she hadn't promised Bailey she'd drop off a stack of flyers for W4HAV's official grand opening, she would have just gone home. Bury her head in her pillow and let it all out. Scream, cry, rage for a while.

She'd spoken with him before he'd gone under the knife. Promised him chocolate pudding and a vampire role-playing game on her tablet.

None of it made any sense to her.

She placed her order and waited on a stool by the counter.

People passed around her. Some said hello. She smiled or waved, but in general, she just sat there, waiting. Trying not to think. Trying not to remember a sweet little boy who'd deserved better.

Finally, her order was ready and she stood.

Her left foot tangled in the edge of the rug. She hadn't seen it. Nikkie Jean felt herself going down. But it was like she was lost in a cloud and couldn't stop it from happening.

Strong hands caught her before she hit the ground. Caught her and lifted her right up off the floor.

Nikkie Jean blinked at the man holding her as he finally came into focus.

Caine Alvaro had her caught between his large paws like a rabbit. "Dr. Netorre, how are you tonight?"

"I've had better. Far, far better." She focused on the dragon tattoo that covered most of his arm. He kept it covered when he worked. The dragon watched her back now. Nikkie Jean just could not look away.

The dragon looked like he was watching her right now.

He lowered her to the ground, his hands tightening on her. Then he let her go. "I'm sorry."

"I...I...rough day at the office, that's all. I need to be going." She paid for her food and then hurried out to the parking lot.

She just couldn't deal with people right now. Couldn't deal with reminders of the hospital or anything resembling it.

And he definitely resembled her hospital. In a big, Rafael-Holden-Deane-clone kind of way.

She started across the parking lot, ignoring the rain as it fell down around her.

An old red truck drove by, splashing her. It barely registered in her mind.

Nikkie Jean didn't care. She just kept walking.

—

Caine had seen that look before, and he guessed at what had happened. He'd seen plenty of residents and interns with that exact same look in their eyes before—especially overseas.

And she'd made it clear she lived alone. No one should deal with what she most likely had tonight, not alone.

Caine paid for his food and followed her outside.

She'd barely noticed the old red truck, and that told him all he needed to know. The woman didn't need to be driving—or she faced the threat of ending up in his ER the hard way. The idea of her driving as upset as she was didn't sit well. At all.

She hadn't even chattered at him. That told him all he needed to know. He caught up with her in the midst of the parking lot. "Dr. Netorre."

"Don't call me that tonight. It's Nikkie Jean. Or Nik. I don't want to be *doctor* anything tonight." She turned toward him, and he knew the drops on her face weren't just the rain. "I...don't feel like talking tonight, Alvaro. So just...go away, ok?"

"I know."

She turned back to her girly purple SUV. And moaned. The sound was so unexpected Caine just stared at her.

Then he looked at the car.

At the almost completely flat tires on both the rear and front driver's side. "You have spares?"

"*Spare*. Not spares." She shot a wild look of despair at him that hit him straight in the gut. "I can't do this. I just can't do this. Not tonight."

She was right on the edge; he could sense it. Caine made a quick decision. "Then don't. I'll give you a lift."

"You don't have to do that." But there was hope in those eyes. A need for him to step in and rescue her. To just fix everything.

Caine wanted to do just that.

"But I will." It would settle their debt. He'd just drop her off at her home, then head on to his. Where he belonged. She could call a friend for a ride in the morning, or something. Caine was used to making split-second decisions. He made one now, with a hand on her elbow to get her where he wanted her.

It was all too easy to just lead her to his 4x4. She was almost docile. Broken. Going along with him without thought or protest. "Do you need anything out of your car? Is it locked?"

"My bag is in there. And I didn't lock it. I forgot."

He closed his eyes. One thing he'd learned in the military and in living in larger cities, *anything* could happen to anyone at any time. It was never a good idea to take chances.

But he kept the lecture to himself. It wasn't his place. He'd learned to mind his own business long, long ago.

Although she had no business just letting him take her home like this. If he hadn't come along, what the hell would she have done? He hated to think of the possibilities.

Anything could have happened to her out here.

She was still crying when he returned from grabbing her bag from the passenger seat and locking her doors.

He didn't say anything until they were on the highway north of Value. "You lost a patient today."

He thought she hadn't heard, but after a moment, she started speaking. The chatter was missing; her tone was flat. "Ten years old. Parental inattention leading to ruptured appendix. He had a reaction to the anesthesia, and by the time they got him back from that…a simple procedure that he should have recovered from easily. He wasn't even my patient, but I prepped him. Talked to him. Promised him I'd play video games with him once he woke up.

I...sat with him from about seven last night until almost midnight. He was afraid...and alone. I called social services. I saw bruises that shouldn't have been where I saw them. And I knew. He'd been neglected and abused. I...Rafe and I decided together to call last night. The social worker came this morning. She sat with him until it was time for the surgery. And then he was just...gone. I didn't even know for two hours. It was a known allergy—the foster parent just hadn't bothered to tell anyone. If he had, that child would have been just fine. And I'd be eating chocolate pudding and chasing vampires. He...everyone let him down, Caine. And I can't make it better now."

"I'm sorry." It was why he hadn't gone into pediatrics, sticking with general surgery. And administration.

There was no way in hell he wanted to do what she did. He'd researched her. A few times since she'd driven him home that night. He'd had a hard time getting her out of his head.

He hadn't been that attracted to a woman in over eight years. And never had it been that intense.

What he'd learned had made him admire her more.

Nikkie Jean Netorre was one hell of a pediatric surgeon—or she would be in a year or so, once she finished her training under Allen Jacobson. That was another name he recognized.

Google was full of articles about Dr. Allen Jacobson.

Top schools, full-ride scholarships, top surgical department in the region—Nikkie Jean Netorre was beyond brilliant. Any hospital would be lucky to have her. Her career was only just beginning.

When she finished her training, there would be headhunters looking in her direction.

Yet what she did had an emotional price. It always would. One he knew too well. The toll it could take on a physician personally— he doubted this little elf would ever be strong enough to pay that toll without it leaving some scars. People like her cared just too damned much.

Caine knew it from personal experience. It took a while for the callouses to grow.

"He suffered for three days with stomach pains. And his foster father, a cousin on his mother's side who admitted to me that he took him in for the money, hadn't even noticed. Ten years old. In immense pain, and no one noticed. Fever of 103. No one noticed. Not the foster parent, anyone. Three days."

"I don't know what to say. *I'm sorry* doesn't seem to cover it."

"Sometimes I wish I had picked any other specialty than pediatric surgery."

"You could still change your mind." Somehow he doubted that. You didn't choose that field without a damned good reason. It wasn't a choice; it was a calling. "Why did you pick pediatric surgery?"

"I had surgery. When I was sixteen. The woman who operated—she kept me sane at the time. Got me through the darkest time in my life, and she didn't have to. When I decided on surgery, I remembered the difference she'd made in my life. And I wanted to do that for others. For the most vulnerable in our world. Kids…they have no real choices. I didn't. But she… talked to me. Made me see that I wasn't completely alone. She saved me back then. Emotionally. She was all that did." Her words trailed off at the end. He wanted to ask more, but didn't.

He hated that she was so alone. He had his uncle to help him when needed. He always had had that one lifeline. It had made a difference.

"Sounds like you are where you are meant to be." Just like he was. He enjoyed being a physician, but running the hospital felt like a more natural fit than anything else he had ever done.

He was going to make Barratt County General the best hospital in the state if he could. It would just take him time to get it there.

"I'm in Finley Creek. That's where I'm supposed to be. I think I could belong here. Be happy."

He had to ask it. "Do you help people?"

She just stared at him, then nodded. "Most times."

"You can't win every time; we both know that. Sometimes something happens." And then you lose. Just as simple as that. She gave him directions, and he pulled off McGareth Road north of Value. The road was beginning to wash away, and he swore. She could end up stuck out there. For days. The idea of her so isolated didn't sit well with him. "Do you have another way in to town tomorrow?"

"Yes. You go up behind my place and stay on this road until it comes out, past the W-Deane Ranch. A friend of mine's husband owns that and all the fields between us. He checks on my place every other day or so, she said."

She was three miles away from his place if he took a small, little-used country farm road. She was his closest neighbor for three miles. And he was hers. "I'll come get you in the morning and drive you back to your car."

"You don't have to do that. I'll call Lacy, see if she can give me a ride. We've carpooled when we're on the same schedule. She's Rafe's sister-in-law, by the way."

"I want to." He wanted to, so he would; it was as simple as that.

"Thank you." She hesitated for a moment. "I shouldn't have gotten into the car with you tonight. I know that, you know. And I wouldn't have if you didn't look like someone I can trust. Stupid, right? You don't even know Rafe. For all I know, you're a crazy ax murderer hiding in Rafe's body."

"Possibly."

"Well, I'm glad you're not." She shot him a watery smile that didn't quite reach her eyes. "Maybe it was stupid, but it's done. So...thanks. I mean that."

He pulled into the small cottage that was hers and killed the engine. Her home looked like a damned fairy cottage from one of his children's books of fairy tales. Perfect for her. He couldn't have imagined it better. Not for her.

"Well, this is my stop. Thanks for the lift. Now we're even."

"I'll walk you to your door." He wasn't ready to leave her just yet. Not with that particular look in her eyes. "We can talk for a while."

"I'm not certain talking helps."

"I am." Losing a patient was the worst experience a physician could ever go through. That patient being a child was a thousand times worse. "You need someone to talk to tonight, Nikkie Jean. We both know that."

She shrugged. "Do we? I've lost patients before. He wasn't even my patient. Not really. I just saw him before I left last night, looking so alone. So I talked to him. Sat with him until he fell asleep. I promised him he'd...he'd be ok."

She was hurting so much. He could see it in the way she held herself. And that was why he just could not leave her to face the inevitable storm alone.

He'd been there too many times himself. The few times he'd tried to talk to April, she had cuttingly told him it was part of the job and to deal with it. Just like she did.

Unlike Nikkie Jean Netorre, April hadn't taken her patients to heart at all. It had taken him a while to see that.

This woman was as opposite from his almost ex-wife had been as a woman could get.

Chapter 10

SHE TRIED NOT TO think about the hospital. Especially considering this was the first man to ever be in her house—while she was there. Lacy's husband had been there one day while she and Lacy worked, shortly after she'd bought the place from him. He'd been replacing old lightbulbs that she was too short—and ladderless—to reach.

Lacy's husband wasn't all that frightening. Not so for the dragon next to her now.

Dr. Alvaro dwarfed her entire house. Admittedly, her house was small—a direct contrast to the towering mansion she'd grown up in—but still. Three-feet-wide shoulders in a 1920s bungalow stood out.

"You know theoretically that it's going to happen." She talked. She always talked when she was truly nervous. Silence—she hated silence. Her father and mother would go silent with each other for days after they'd argue. And they'd often glare at her during the middle of it. Well, her mother would. Her father would just go to work and stay there. For days. Sometimes, Nikkie Jean would go weeks without seeing him. They definitely hadn't done the family-dinner nights. The only time they'd all four been together was the rare occasions when her father's hospital would have functions where they'd be trotted out to look pretty and perfect.

She never wanted to go to a hospital function again.

She'd been to Jillian's father's for a family dinner once. It had somehow just happened when Lacy had car trouble. Nikkie Jean had willingly driven her friend to what Lacy referred to affectionately as "The Compound." Jillian and Rafe lived next door to her father. And across from Jillian's older sister. It was a private gated community just for their family. She'd sat at the table with

Jillian and her sisters and Rafe and Lacy, and felt completely overwhelmed.

They had talked all at once. Everyone had an opinion on everything—even the teenage boy who she thought was Ariella and Rafe's younger brother.

She'd gone home afterward and cried. From envy, and from the beauty of being a part of that family for even a little while. They'd welcomed her from the moment she'd stepped in the door.

She had a standing invitation to go there whenever she wanted. But she just couldn't bring herself to do it.

"Yes. You know it. But when it happens…"

"Tell me about your first." She busied herself with taking out her contacts.

"I was sixteen and she was seventeen…"

It startled a laugh out of her. She shoved her glasses back up her nose and looked at him.

He had set his Styrofoam container on her table. Hers was across from it.

It looked like she was about to have company for dinner.

Male company, at that.

Strangely enough, she didn't mind. It had been more than four years since she'd been alone in her private space with a man at all. Four years. She wasn't that pitiful, was she?

She still wasn't ready to be alone yet.

She grabbed the drink that came with her meal to cover the sudden awkwardness. "Not what I meant, Alvaro, and you know it."

"I was in Bosnia. A peace-keeping mission. A family of six came in, victims of a car accident. The teenage boy had been in the rear passenger seat and took a direct hit. Tall, thin, dark eyes and hair. He was awake when he was pulled out of the car. Asked me if he was going to die in broken English. I told him no, but it was obvious to everyone in the room that he was going to. Adin. His name was Adin, and he wanted to be a poet."

"I'm sorry. My first was a little girl. Terminal, genetic. Her heart. We didn't find a donor in time." Her breath hiccupped. Tears threatened again. "The little boy today was named Aidan. He liked Ninja Turtles and Chewbacca."

She was close enough for him to touch. Nikkie Jean hadn't realized that until it was happening. Warm fingers wrapped around her wrist, and he pulled her closer.

Well, he guided. There was no pulling about it.

She could smell him, could feel the warmth he exuded. He felt like a real human being next to her. She hiccupped again.

"Sit. Eat. Talk to me."

Nikkie Jean did just that.

Chapter 11

CAINE LISTENED AS she talked. Nikkie jean was one of those physicians who would remember every patient, and would remember every lost patient ten times as strongly. They finished the takeout, and she hopped up, gathering the trash as she did. He just watched her as she buzzed around.

If she stopped buzzing, then she'd have to start thinking again. He was starting to figure this woman out.

Just like him, this woman had her demons to fight.

"I...thanks for the ride. I'll get a ride to work tomorrow and get someone to tow my car. I really appreciate you driving me home." She looked everywhere but at him.

"Just returning the favor." Caine stood to go. She wouldn't meet his eyes, but some of the haze had left her. She'd be ok. No doubt she'd call one of her friends and they'd get her through the night.

She didn't need him.

And he didn't need her. He had to remember that. No matter how much he wanted to reach out and stop her. Keep her from buzzing around, fighting the grief.

Caine wanted to hold her.

Realization hit him hard. He wanted to hold *her*.

To see if her skin was as soft as it looked.

He stood, probably too abruptly.

Nikkie Jean took an immediate step back. Right into the edge of her table.

Caine's hands dropped to her waist, and he steadied her. "Sorry. I didn't mean to get in your space."

"It's the kitchen," she almost whispered. "It's a bit small. But since it's just me...you smell nice."

She leaned closer.

"And I'm not exactly small." She was. Small and built to perfection. His hands tightened as the scent of jasmine hit him. Before he knew it, he was lifting her off her feet. "And so do you."

She wasn't pushing him away. Her hands flexed on his arms.

"Dr. Alvaro, what exactly...are you doing?" Wide hazel eyes blinked up at him.

"What does it look like I'm doing?" But Caine would make one thing absolutely clear. "Tell me to stop, and I will. I'll walk out of here, and we can just forget I—oh, hell. We both know what I'm doing."

He leaned down and brushed his lips against hers.

Chapter 12

NIKKIE JEAN DID NOT want him to stop. It was as simple as that. She wanted to feel another human being. To feel that someone else out there knew she was alive. Had noticed her.

Wanted to feel that she hadn't been the one forgotten tonight. Not like she had been thirteen years ago.

Caine...he looked like Rafe. One of the few men she could trust. She wasn't stupid; she knew she was conflating the two in her head somehow.

She never would want to kiss Rafe. There wasn't even a drop of attraction between them. None at all.

Not like there was with this man.

Caine Alvaro and Rafe might look the same, but they were not the same man at all. It was important for her to remember that. To see each man for who they were. Individuals.

Seeing people as individuals instead of threats was a big thing for her. Especially now.

"I...I'm not looking for a relationship." Especially with another doctor. She'd tried that four years ago. It hadn't gone well. But Nikkie Jean didn't want to think about doctors and hospitals—or the past. She just wanted to...not feel alone right now.

Caine didn't look like a doctor now. Not in his jeans and dark T-shirt that fit him almost like a second skin. It had a Star Wars storm trooper on it.

It was so different from what she would have expected him to wear. It made him seem almost human.

His dragon tattoo stared at her, too. Telling her without words that there was so much more to this man than the title of doctor.

No. He wasn't a doctor tonight. He was a man with arms holding her tightly. Just for one night.

"I'm not either. I don't have time for anything other than my children and Barratt County."

"I've never done this before—well, the whole just jump into bed with someone thing." She'd had three lovers in thirteen years. Those relationships had been as healthy as she could make them. Never had she entered into sex lightly.

"Progressing a bit fast there?"

"Why be stupidly closed about it? You kiss me, I know what you're going to want. Open communication, honesty, and clear expectations are super big ones for me, Alvaro. I kiss you, and I...could want that same thing, too." She'd never been with a man as big and strong and forceful as the one holding her. Nikkie Jean knew the why of it, too.

Fear. She'd been afraid. Afraid of being too small to fight back again.

She'd also seen what fear could do.

She was so tired of living that way. All fear was getting her was a closed off life with barely anyone close to her.

Annie and Izzie, that was it. Jillian, Lacy, and a few others on the periphery. And she was even too afraid to get super close to them. Afraid of what would happen.

Afraid of inevitable rejection.

She was tired of feeling so alone all the time. So afraid of the world and everyone male in it. Caine Alvaro could hold back the world with his arms. That was for sure.

One of the women at W4HAV had a saying that she liked to quote during group therapy sessions that she and Nikkie Jean co-ran. *Fear robbed you of the future. Don't let it.*

Nikkie Jean suspected she'd been letting fear rob her of a present, too, lately. She'd found a safety zone and stayed there. But that wasn't living. She knew that. Years of therapy had made that clear to her.

Nikkie Jean wanted to live her life as if every moment was the last. Because she knew all too well that each moment could be.

That had been a lesson she'd learned when she'd been sixteen years old. It wasn't a lesson she was going to forget.

Her hands tightened on his arms.

Well, she was starting to feel pretty *present* at the moment now.

"I do want to be with you tonight." He almost growled it at her.

"But it won't go anywhere. Not long term. It just can't. I got my children to focus on. And Barratt County is a mess right now."

"Believe me, I know." She wasn't the type of woman men like him went for long term. No. That would be women like Lacy and Jillian who weren't afraid of their own shadow. Who went after what they wanted full-tilt. Nikkie Jean wasn't anywhere near ready for that kind of risk. If she ever was. "But there's no reason we can't...have tonight, right? Don't you ever feel alone sometimes, Alvaro?"

It was the boldest question she had ever asked in her thirty years and two months and four days on the planet.

"If you want to stop at any point, you tell me. I'll listen. Even if you have to yell it."

Somehow, he just knew she needed that. Nikkie Jean appreciated it.

"Kiss me, Alvaro. I just want you to kiss me. Then whatever comes next. I just want to forget everything for a while."

Caine could help her do just that.

Chapter 13

HAZEL EYES STARED INTO HIS. Big, wide, uncertain. It was the small bit of uncertainty that had him pausing. "You sure about this? We don't have to go up the stairs, Netorre."

She nodded, small hands tightening on his shoulders again. Somehow, he'd ended up lifting her. It was easy to do. "I'm tired of feeling so alone sometimes. Why shouldn't we...just for tonight. Tonight won't hurt anyone, will it? I won't tell; you won't tell. No one ever has to know but us. You can go in the morning, and we never have to..."

"No, it won't." But he had a feeling it would change everything—for him.

She touched something in him that he wasn't ready to evaluate yet. Maybe he'd only seen the woman twice, but that was enough for him to know she was far too dangerous for him long term. She was the kind of woman a man would change his whole world for. But Caine wasn't the kind of man who could do that. He'd done that for a woman once before; April had almost destroyed him.

She would be the first woman he'd been with since his wife's betrayal two and a half years ago. Even before that, he and April hadn't exactly had a raging-hot sex life.

Well, *he* hadn't. He would never have any way of knowing how many men his ex-wife had been with, even while they were married. She'd enjoyed throwing that up to him many times. That, and the fact that his youngest might not have been his. She'd held that over him for eight months, until Dalton had been born and there had been no denying whose son he was. He'd never taken a DNA test to confirm it; he hadn't cared. Dalton was his son, through and through. "I've been tested. I'm clean. And I have a condom."

He carried it with him, not because he'd expected to use it, but because after April, he would never take risks again.

Her cheeks turned red. "Me, too. I have a couple in the drawer. If you don't mind stripes. They were part of a gag gift for…and…I can't have children, Caine. At least, the likelihood of me ever getting pregnant even with help is less than twelve percent. I calculated it myself once. And I don't sleep around. I never have."

His arms tightened around her. He heard the hurt she no doubt hadn't meant to show. "Me, either. My wife—late wife—she was the only woman for eight years."

She shrugged, still held in his arms. Her legs had wound around his hips. "I don't want to think about stuff like that. Nothing sad or bad. Not tonight. I just want to forget and not be so alone. With you."

Caine could do that. He tightened his arms around her and kissed her. Right there in her kitchen.

And then he carried her to her bedroom.

Chapter 14

HER BREATH CAUGHT as he lowered her to her bed. Never had she slept with a man in her own bed. Her bedroom was her sanctuary. About the only place Nikkie Jean truly felt safe.

Allowing a man into that space was a major step for her.

But she wasn't going to think about that now.

Caine followed her down, looming over her. Nikkie Jean held up a hand between them. "Just...don't come at me from behind. Ever. That...I just don't like that."

He hesitated for a moment. "Understood. We don't have to rush. We...can just get to know each other now."

She nodded. "I...I'm not very experienced."

"We won't rush." He hooked an arm around her waist, and then they were rolling. Before she knew it, Nikkie Jean was straddling the man's absolutely perfect hips and looking down at him.

The scar through his eyebrow made him look sexy and dangerous and wild.

He was definitely the wildest thing she had ever done. That was for sure.

"How did you get the scar?"

"IED. I was in the military for ten years."

She brushed a finger over it, not saying a word. She had scars of her own. "It gives you a pirate look."

"So I've heard." He ran a finger down her cheek. "You have one, too."

"Yes. But...I don't ever talk about it. It was...traumatic." Her breath hitched, as she looked at him. Nikkie Jean pulled in a deep breath. She leaned down and kissed him.

Caine's hands came up and wrapped around her waist. His

body tightened beneath her. She could feel the hunger thrumming through him. The need.

For her.

Yet, even though he could, he wasn't rushing her. He wasn't grabbing and just taking.

He was letting her lead.

That was exactly what she did.

—

Caine knew something significant was happening with his partner. He just didn't know what it was. She'd lost all the confidence and snark and energy that had characterized her in those earlier encounters they'd had. In their place was a sweet hesitancy that he would never have expected.

Whatever it was had him going slower than he wanted.

Nikkie Jean needed that. And not just because of what had happened hours earlier.

It was more than that.

He kissed her when she kissed him. He touched her only after she led.

When she'd said she wasn't experienced, she hadn't lied.

That inexperience had some of his own awkwardness dissipating.

Caine hadn't had impulsive sex with a woman in more than fifteen years. He wasn't exactly an old hand at it, himself.

"Can I take this off?" she asked, almost shyly, pulling at the band of his T-shirt.

Caine pulled the shirt off and tossed it toward the floor.

"I have more scars." Scars he'd earned when a damned truck had driven into his encampment during his first deployment years ago. He had shrapnel still in one shoulder that would probably never come out.

"So do I. But they are in here." She touched her forehead lightly. "They'll probably never heal."

"I know. Trust me: I know." He had his own scars. Inside and out. They would never heal, either. "Can I kiss you?"

She nodded. "I think I'd like that. Very much."

Caine pulled her to him. One thin braid brushed against his chest. Her glasses bumped his nose. "Do we need the glasses now?"

She nodded fiercely. "I...can't see without them. I can't be that vulnerable. I need my glasses."

There was more than fear beneath her words. Caine just nodded. It made sense why she had so many pairs now. "I'll be careful with you."

He could break her far too easily. She was so small. So...vulnerable.

Even if she never wanted to admit it.

Caine pulled her closer and covered her mouth with his own, determined to go as slowly as she needed. His hands trembled with the need to touch her. To be with a woman who actually wanted to be with *him.*

April hadn't wanted to be with him for a long while. She'd never forgiven him for not getting out of the military and taking a job from one of the hospitals that had offered him positions off and on through the years.

She'd wanted him to make enough money to give her what she wanted from life. He'd wanted to save patients who needed him most.

He'd been damned good at running field hospitals for the army. That passion had fueled him.

He hadn't retired until April had been gone and buried. And that had been so he could better care for the children.

His whole life had been for the children for two years now. But he didn't think of that when he had her in his arms. Caine's hold tightened around her. He just wanted to feel her heart beating against his again.

For the first time in years, he didn't feel alone.

—

It hadn't been magical sex. Nikkie Jean knew that miracle, magical sex to cure all ills was just a stupid old wives' tale. Some people thought women who had been traumatized the way she had just needed some "good, healthy sex" to fix everything.

Yeah, right. That just didn't happen. Sex didn't fix everything.

It had still been pretty good. As far as she could tell in her limited experience.

And at least he didn't think his prowess in the bedroom would clear up all of her hang-ups associated with sex. Not like she'd come up against before.

Any minute now, she thought he'd start purring.

Now that it was over, she didn't know exactly what to do *next*. She had a three-hundred-fifty-pound dragon in her bed, looking all warm and sated.

Sex was very complicated for her. It always would be.

The last man she'd been involved with—it had started out normally. As normally as she could make it, anyway. She'd had years of therapy to that point, after all. And she'd been determined to take it slow. He'd been ok with that. At first.

He had thought she had been a virgin. When he'd learned differently, he'd expected *more* from her. When she couldn't give it, he'd gotten impatient. Blamed her.

They'd broken up because he couldn't deal with *her* baggage regarding what had happened to her when she'd been sixteen.

Her baggage she'd have always, but that didn't mean she had to take it out of the closet every time she got naked with someone. He hadn't been able to understand that fact.

They hadn't lasted even a month after that first night in bed together.

His hang-ups over sex were far more damaging to a relationship than hers.

So what if she'd had a panic attack in the middle of their last night together? He'd deliberately came up on her from behind. He'd wrapped an arm over her waist and yanked her off her feet. The one thing she would never like.

Caine slipped from the bed, one hand going between them. The practicalities of sex were about to rear their ugly head.

She almost closed her eyes to avoid the embarrassing part of what she feared was about to happen.

She didn't. Caine cursed instead.

Nikkie Jean's eyes popped open, and she looked at him as fear flooded her in an instant.

Chapter 15

THE CONDOM HAD BROKEN. Caine had had that happen twice in his years of sexual activity. The last time had resulted in Dalton, shortly before he'd learned April had been cheating on him for years. That had been the last time he'd had sex. Until tonight. The risks of that happening again were next to nil.

"It broke."

Nikkie Jean yelped. Then visibly forced herself to relax. Right in front of him. Her cheeks were flame red. "Pregnancy is not a concern. Oophorectomy and adjuvant chemo at sixteen. I *can't* get pregnant. Well, the odds of it are so slim I'm more likely to grow a beard and voice changes!"

She told him that. Repeatedly.

The nervous talking was back. As were the leery looks and the closed body language. Caine wanted to curse again but didn't.

He'd scared her. That was the last thing he wanted to do. She didn't need to worry about *his* leftover baggage from April. His ex-wife had taunted him for months. Even after they'd separated. Every time they'd communicated in the six months between separation and her death, she'd shoved the fact that the baby she carried hadn't been his.

This was far from the same situation, but in that first moment, he'd been back in their condo, with April taunting him that the baby he was so excited about hadn't been his.

"It's not like we really have to worry. I'm not even certain I've ovulated this year. Or last year. Things aren't exactly a matter of routine with me. A quarterly period and I consider that regular. You're safe, big guy. I promise. No spawn from me."

"We both know the odds, but we both also know things happen." He tried to keep his words calm, but even he heard the frost in his own words.

He just hoped he'd suppressed the fear. It wasn't the idea of a child that terrified him—though that was enough—it was how holding her, touching her, had just made him feel. Like he was where he was supposed to be—finally.

He'd been wrapped up in April at first, too.

Caine knew himself; sex would never be casual for him. He'd had emotional investment in this woman. From almost the beginning.

It was unlike anything he'd ever experienced with his wife. Even in the early weeks of their relationship. What that meant wasn't something he could process right now. If ever. But they had a more immediate concern that he *could* process. "I don't want another child. I have three. That's enough."

She froze for a moment, then slipped away from him. Caine's fist clenched. It was all that kept him from touching her again as what he'd said sank in. He hadn't meant to put it that bluntly. But she'd said she wanted honesty. And he didn't think he could ever lie to her.

Nikkie Jean huddled in the middle of her bed, just staring at him.

"I'm sorry. I shouldn't have lured you up to my lair to reproduce with you and then eat you. It was just so easy to carry you. My bad. You know, black widow spider and all that." Nikkie Jean shot him a snark-filled look.

If there were consequences, they'd deal with them—like the adults they both were. They'd known the terms going in. And now she was shutting down and her defenses were falling into place.

She was locking herself down tighter than a fortress. Because he'd frightened her.

Caine forced himself to breathe, and think like the rational medical professional that he was. "Are emergency contraceptives a possibility?"

She shook her head. "Nope. Sorry. I've taken them before for off-label issues associated with hormonal problems. Anaphylactic reaction to some of the components. Not something I'm interested in repeating. The condom broke—that doesn't mean I have your baby-making cooties inside me, you know. Neither of us are idiots. We should both know the odds here."

He nodded. If she was his patient, he wouldn't recommend it

on those kinds of odds, either.

"I have to go."

He had to, or he was going to find himself right back in that bed with her. Even if it was just to hold her.

He'd missed sleeping with someone in his arms for a long while.

He'd give his right arm to be able to hold her like that.

All night. Just once.

And after the conversation they had just had, he doubted that was what she would want at all.

He felt like a damned bastard. Or jerk. He'd had sex with her and now he was running home. Like a damned coward, afraid of a ninety-pound woman.

He half felt he'd used her; just like April had liked to use *him* whenever she had an itch to scratch and one of her lovers hadn't been available. Once he'd figured out she'd done that—by her own words—sex had been soured for him. He hadn't touched her again.

It left him feeling sick.

"I understand. And hey, it was just the one time, Alvaro. We both knew what we were getting into. Terms delivered in my kitchen. Terms we both agreed to. Curiosity satisfied." Her words were light, but he'd read that kind of body language before. She was closing herself off to rejection. From him. Because she did not trust him not to hurt her. Damn it. *He* was the last thing this woman had needed tonight, of all nights.

"Nikkie Jean, I…it's not like that." Like he'd taken what he'd wanted from her and now he was done with her. Rejecting her.

Leaving her alone.

He damned himself as her earlier words hit him.

Nikkie Jean hated being alone.

Hell, so did he. He stepped closer to the bed as he pulled his T-shirt over his shoulders.

The least he could do was hold her for a while longer; for both of them.

She held up a hand, stopping him. "It's *exactly* like that. We both agreed this was a one-time thing. And while the sex was great, best I've had in four years after all, it's not something I am interested in repeating. Ever." She grabbed a blanket off the bed and wrapped it around herself. It was just another barrier against him; Caine had no doubt of that. Nor did he blame her for it. He'd really screwed this up. For both of them. "I thought I could do the whole one-night thing, but I am starting to think I can't. So…thanks for the learning experience. I have a no-doctors policy for a very good reason. I think I'm going to stick to that rule from now on. It's lasted four years; I think it's going to last another forty-four. Thanks for being the exception that proved that rule is a good idea. So…the door is that way; please lock it before you leave. There could be homicidal maniacs out there in Value right now, after all."

Caine stared at her for a moment, knowing he'd never forget how she looked right in that moment. Knowing he'd never forget how much he had hurt her when that had been the last thing he had ever intended.

Small, naked, with a purple comforter pulled up to her chin, hair partially unbraided and tangled from his fingers, just watching him like she expected a blow. Like a glittery fairy he'd just dewinged—without anesthetic.

And a dejected look in the eyes behind her glasses as she looked at *him*.

Because of him. He'd kicked her while she was down. He felt like a total ass. He wasn't exactly liking the man he'd become since April's death.

Nikkie Jean had brought revelations he wasn't sure he was ready to face. The urge to hold her one more time slammed into him. To scoop her up again and tell her that he was just a big coward. That he hadn't meant to be a jerk. That he didn't want to leave her yet.

It wasn't the broken condom that terrified him at all. Caine wasn't stupid; a less than twelve percent chance of anything wasn't much. If something did happen, he would deal with it. As would she. What terrified him was the *woman* in front of him. She pulled him. Otherwise he never would have been there right now.

He hadn't felt this way about a woman in nine years. And even that with April had just sort of built. It hadn't been this blast of heat and chaos and…emotion. "I'm not good at relationships with women, Nikkie Jean. I never have been. It's one reason why my wife left me. Before that, she went elsewhere. On a regular basis. Because I wasn't enough. I didn't know how to give her what she needed. And once that initial trust was gone, it never came back."

"I'm sorry to hear that. You should be able to trust the one you marry." She'd pulled into herself. Started shutting him out and wasn't about to let him back in. Every door was locked. "The door? You'll lock it on your way out?"

He was going, but not before he made one thing clear. He stepped closer to the bed and looked down at her. He reached out a hand to brush the lock of hair from her eyes. He wanted to see her eyes one more time.

She flinched away. A momentary rush of real fear went through her eyes.

That had him backing away, immediately.

Caine never wanted someone smaller or weaker than he was to *ever* look at him like that. He knew far too well what it was like. He'd grown up with a man who liked his fists a little too much, after all. "If you are pregnant, you tell me. We'll figure out what to do together. You tell me. Immediately. You will not have to face that alone. Understand?"

He didn't want to leave her alone again. Yet that's exactly what he had to do.

"Sure. Loud and clear. You and I have a less than twelve percent chance of ever having a conversation again. I'm good with that, big guy. Like I said, please lock the door."

Snotty snark and frightened eyes. That was Nikkie Jean.

Hell, he wanted to kiss her and make her understand that he wasn't the asshole she no doubt thought him now.

Caine couldn't make himself reach out to her. He'd just open his mouth and screw things up even worse. He did the only thing he could. Caine left, cursing himself the entire way.

Chapter 16

JERK. SHE'D SEEN THE fear in his eyes. On some level, Nikkie Jean even understood it. She didn't want a baby by a man she wasn't fully involved with either. But Caine had gone from the best lover in her albeit limited experience in one moment to cold asshole in the other.

It was not her fault the condom had broken. It had just *happened*.

She wouldn't deny that. And he'd been an emotional connection when she'd needed one. That didn't make sleeping with him a smart decision, though.

She should have known better than to take her clothes off with Caine Alvaro. Period. What good was a no-doctors rule if she wasn't going to follow it the instant a halfway hot doctor looked at her?

Sex for her was a complicated thing. It always would be. That wasn't her fault. It had taken her a while to accept that.

Sex would never be something she just did casually. Ever.

What had happened with Caine Alvaro hadn't been casual for her. It had been more than that. As she'd lain there and thought about how he had made her feel, she'd realized that.

She'd *trusted* him. On a deeper level than should have been possible.

What a mistake that had been.

That was part of the problem. Nikkie Jean didn't understand why it had happened that way with him.

What had happened with Caine Alvaro wasn't just his fault, either. She knew that. *That* was hers; she'd chosen to have sex with that man.

Now here were the consequences.

Time to accept, and time to move on. She'd made a choice, no one else.

She'd accept that as the healthy response that it was.

Full autonomy of her body was kind of a super-huge thing for her, after all.

That didn't mean she'd processed all the emotions rolling through her head at the moment, though. *That* was going to take a while.

She slammed her locker door just a little too hard. A curse slipped out before she could stop it. Lacy and Allen both looked at her.

Lacy left to answer a page after shooting Nikkie Jean a worried look. She just shook her head at the other woman.

That wouldn't work with Allen, though.

"You ok?" He blocked her exit from the locker room with his much larger, stronger, very male body. A sliver of unease went through her, but she pushed it away.

PTSD was not going to rear its head now. Usually she was all good; but Caine Alvaro had her far unsettled for that now.

Life was sometimes all that was needed to trigger her trauma responses.

They were ingrained deep in her psyche and probably always would be. Trauma changed a person, after all.

Nikkie Jean had counseled others on that very fact many times before. Just because she knew all the ways trauma could impact her life didn't mean she was immune to it.

All it meant was that she was better able to recognize when it was resurfacing.

"As ok as I can be. Rough night yesterday."

"Rough day, too."

Allen was watching her. Nikkie Jean looked up at him. Once, it would have freaked her out to be alone with a man in the locker room, especially a physician like Allen. But that was changing. Because of Allen and Virat and Cage, mostly. They gave her the necessary space. Like they knew she needed it. And she was forcing it to change. She couldn't live like that anymore. Afraid of every man who got too close...that's what *her* therapist at W4HAV had to say about her, even if the charity hadn't opened fully yet. When it did have the grand opening, Nikkie Jean had no doubt she'd be one of their most frequent visitors.

Anyone who believed healing from trauma wasn't an ongoing

thing probably needed their brains examined.

You couldn't just get over it. Trauma changed brain patterns, after all.

Allen stepped closer, a concerned look in his beautiful gray eyes. If she was ever going to be attracted to a doctor, why couldn't it have been *Allen*? Yes, he'd been a bit of an arrogant ass a few months ago, but he'd changed since then.

All "he's my boss" aside, he was a kind man, even beneath the former arrogance that he used to wear like a cloak. Now he was different. The compassion was still there, but the confidence wasn't. Allen felt more real now. Safer, honestly.

He was as broken as Nikkie Jean used to be. Still thought she was at times. Therapy had brought her back from the edge so many times when she'd been in her early twenties and had finally had the strength to seek out the help she needed. But that didn't mean it was always going to be peachy in her life. She just had to get through this little pitfall now. Then she'd be ok. "Just a bad night with a...well, I guess I can't call him a friend. Just a really stupid mistake."

"I'm sorry." Gray eyes stared down at her. Nikkie Jean squirmed. They both knew she'd been hurt more than she was admitting. But one thing she respected about this man was that he wouldn't push.

"Well, I knew I shouldn't have been so stupid. I don't know what I was thinking. Maybe I wasn't. Aren't we all allowed two massively stupid things each decade? Well, last night was my first one of my thirties." She looked at him as she spoke, knowing she wasn't making that much sense.

Yep, there was the standard look of confusion, right there.

"Is that how many we're allowed?"

"Yep. One every five years."

"Then I've had mine. I'm not allowed another until I'm forty. Seriously? You ok? You've been quieter than I want a Nikkie Jean to be today. You should be buzzing around, making everyone smile. That's the best part of my day now, you know? Seeing you smile."

She looked up at him, and tears hit her eyes, shocking her. He reminded her of her big brother right then; Dathan had been tall and strong and had half cared about her before once, too.

Just how alone she felt sank in like lead. Oh, why couldn't she have broken her no-doctors rule with *Allen* instead of Caine? At least, she would have been left feeling like she had mattered just a little. Or like she was at least worth staying with for a little while. He'd gotten what he wanted and taken off as soon as it got a little too real there at the end. "I…damn it, Allen, I thought he…"

Gray eyes stared into hers. Nikkie Jean fought not to pull away, to close herself off from the world for a while. She couldn't do that anymore.

She also couldn't freak out every time a man with the first name "Doctor" put his hands on her.

"Nikkie Jean, did this man hurt you? Do something you didn't want him to do? Did he give you something? Because if he did—"

She shook her head. "No. What happened was *my* choice, too. I'm one hundred percent certain of that. It just didn't turn out the way I expected. And now I know. Never again. I'm just not made for casual, Allen. Or other doctors. I knew that…I just made a mistake. One I don't ever intend to repeat."

Honesty with herself was a biggie—Nikkie Jean made certain to live by that.

"Whoever he is, *he* doesn't deserve *you*. Women like you, Nikkie Jean Netorre, you're the kind a smart man grabs ahold of and doesn't ever let go. We're the lucky ones. If this guy can't see that, then you forget all about him. And find one who will." His hands squeezed her shoulders, but he didn't try to hug her or do anything more than that. "You don't deserve to be hurt. By anyone. And if anyone tries, I'll get Cage and Vir and we'll go kick his ass for you. Worse, we'll sic Rafe on him."

A vision of Rafe pounding Caine into the ground filled her head. It was exactly what he'd needed to say. "That would be a match I'd pay to watch."

He'd just reminded her that she was only a little alone. There were people in Finley Creek who were beginning to care about her.

For real.

Chapter 17

CAINE DIDN'T ALLOW himself to look at the turn off to her road the next morning. It was best if he just forgot all about Nikkie Jean Netorre and moved on.

The text response he'd gotten when he'd tried to contact her around midnight the night before had made that extremely clear. *Just fine, Alvaro. Have a nice life.*

That was pretty succinct.

She wasn't the kind of woman he could be with long term. His children would be just as baffled by a relationship with Nikkie Jean as he was. None of them were ready for him to be involved with anyone at the moment. Even if Caine himself was ready for it.

He had just now gotten his oldest son to stop resenting his youngest. Even if she would let him back in after how royally he'd screwed up last night, there wasn't room for a woman in his children's lives.

Even as he thought it, he knew that was a stretch. There wasn't any guarantee a relationship between them would have even progressed to her meeting his children. They were both physicians with highly demanding positions. He routinely put in fifty-hour weeks, and no doubt she did the same.

There was also no guarantee she would even stick around after completing her training. She could have plans to take off to any part of the country. She would be made offers to some of the best hospitals anywhere.

He wouldn't be enough to keep her here. Not long term. And she'd grow to resent him even trying; just like April had. She hadn't wanted a simple military doctor. Far from it.

She'd wanted prestige and a name for herself as Dr. Alvaro's wife.

Even though she'd been a physician and could have gone for the prestige herself. He would have supported her goals completely.

He wouldn't get the children invested in someone just for that someone to leave them. They'd been left too much already.

He would barely be able to do casual at this point—even if he'd consider it with her. That kind of a relationship would be an insult to a woman like her. She deserved all of a man. And he could not offer her that. Caine wasn't stupid. A relationship between them would be a bad idea.

But he couldn't get the sight of her out of his head.

Nor could he stop himself from the *need* to remind himself of that fact. At the least, he owed her an apology for how he had bolted. For how much of an ass he had been.

Those thoughts were heavy on his mind when he made it to Barratt County Gen.

He would find a way to push Dr. Nikkie Jean Netorre out of his head—and his life—completely. Chalk last night up to just one of those random bits of fate Caine wasn't about to let happen again. Or let control him, any more than it already had.

He had other issues to worry about. One of the fastest-growing medical groups in the country had set their sights on Barratt County Gen. The board wanted him to prepare. To ensure the hospital looked as good as it possibly could.

The board wanted that buyer. And there were hints that someone somewhere in the hospital was defrauding the insurance companies. Caine had to find that someone.

He almost snarled when he thought about it.

He hated hospital politics. And he hated curveballs in his plans. The wrong buyer could set the hospital back months, if not years, on his plans to streamline and make it more efficient. The right buyer could also be scared off by potential criminal activity. Caine was in a definite rock-hard place position right now. He couldn't afford to be distracted.

Caine motioned to his assistant when he saw her waiting by the intake desk. "I need all of those records I had you gather yesterday, as soon as possible."

"Yes, sir. I can be in your office in fifteen minutes."

Thirty minutes later, he knew he had a problem. Caine looked at the woman across the desk from him. Sleek, sophisticated, confident, Dr. Aubrey Fisher was the type of woman he had always been attracted to.

He'd even been mildly attracted to her not even two days before. He looked at her again, waiting for that twinge to hit.

Nothing.

Not anymore.

She didn't have freckles and frog-printed scrubs. Nor did she have big hazel eyes that saw right to a man's soul. Caine scowled.

Aubrey stared at him. "Is there a problem, sir?"

Caine looked at the records laid out before him. "Not necessarily, but the numbers don't match up. I am going to have an independent investigator comb through the five most-active departments. I need a baseline report for the board. By Tuesday."

"Of course. Anything else, sir?"

"Not now. But thanks."

He didn't have time for Nikkie Jean Netorre distracting him; he had a hospital to run, an annex to oversee being built, and buried skeletons to find.

It was time to put what had happened in the compartment in which it belonged so he could concentrate on what he had to do. Fixing the hospital was what he had been hired to do. Fixing it was something he would be good at. Fixing it made sense.

Fixing what he'd screwed up with Nikkie Jean was something he would never know how to do.

Chapter 18

NOT PREGNANT, HAVE a nice life. He'd received A simple text ten days after the night that had changed everything. He'd tried calling her the next morning after he'd acted like a total fool, the messages he'd left her at FCGH in the two weeks since that day hadn't been answered.

Except once. *Not pregnant, have a nice life.*

He'd gotten her hint. As far as Nikkie Jean was concerned, Caine no longer existed. He might not like how things had happened between them, but he had to respect what she'd wanted. He owed her that.

It was hard not to watch for her, though. At least three times a week, he found himself behind her on the highway by coincidence.

She drove far too fast. Like she was trying to escape him behind her.

She liked to sing to the radio. And she never even looked at him when he drove behind her.

He'd wanted to explain; he owed her that much. Honesty. They'd agreed on honesty that night. But he hadn't been totally honest with her.

For the first time in a long, long while, Caine felt like he needed to explain himself. He wasn't used to that. Especially with women.

He'd begged and bargained and tried everything with April, just to preserve his family. It hadn't worked. She'd laughed in his face. He'd made a vow never to give a woman that kind of power over him again.

Yet he was already teetering on the brink of doing just that with Nikkie Jean. After only one night.

It wouldn't stop with just casual. If he ever touched her again, Caine wouldn't be able to just walk away again.

Caine knew himself well enough to realize that. Nikkie Jean would be the type of woman to demand a man's everything. And he could not give her that now.

It was best for him to just stay away from her, like she wanted.

Otherwise, he'd just end up hurting her again. That was the last thing he wanted for that woman.

Nikkie Jean didn't deserve *him*.

He had to remember that.

So if he went to bed each night wishing she was lying there next to him chattering away about her day, wishing that he had the opportunity to fix his last idiotic mistake with her, then that was his problem.

He'd just have to get over it.

Caine told himself that as he drove the remainder of the fifteen miles into Value.

He'd passed Nikkie Jean three miles earlier. Her little purple Jeep had just sped by. His heart rate had increased just seeing her. She'd stubbornly kept her eyes on the road; she hadn't even looked in his direction.

Caine was acting like a teenager, mooning over the pretty girl who'd smiled at him once.

He was an idiot.

He'd check in at the hospital, then go home, and get the children. Take them into the city for a day of family time. Keller and Everett needed school clothes and supplies, and the baby was always outgrowing everything. Caine despised shopping, but it had to be done.

It would give Henry a bit of a break, too.

Maybe then he'd forget about her for a few hours. Surely, three children and the mall would be enough to make him forget her.

The woman was starting to haunt him, and he couldn't figure out why.

Maybe it was because for those moments with her, he wasn't thinking about the children or the hospital or anything else. He was thinking of her and him and that had been it.

April had chewed him up and spit him out—and he'd let her, for the children's sake. The last few years of their marriage had been nothing but battles and eggshells. Until he'd been split in two different directions—father and physician. Husband had been destroyed the first time April told him she'd cheated.

None of that had mattered when he had Nikkie Jean in his arms. Caine had ruined it. Now there was nothing he could do about it.

The head of the board was waiting in his office when Caine made it to the hospital. "Bryan, I wasn't expecting to see you on a Saturday. Is everything going well?"

Bryan Mostain hesitated. "I wanted to let you know. We're considering selling Barratt County Gen to the Carrington Medical Group out of Pennsylvania. They'll be here to discuss it next week. We've researched, and they have a good reputation. Especially with smaller hospitals like ours."

"We're starting an internal audit next week." And it was to take his entire focus. Not an entirely new buyer than the one mentioned before. "And breaking ground for the annex."

"I know. The board has requested that the audit be kept quiet and that you report any...uh...problems...directly to us."

"Are you expecting something?" Keeping silent on massive issues was not something Caine would do lightly.

"To be honest, I'm not certain. After all of the trouble that has happened at FCGH, hospitals in the region are on pins and needles to see what skeletons are buried in the closets. It's why Dipertese Regent backed out."

He'd always respected Bryan; he seemed genuinely honest and sincere in his work with the hospital, despite not being a physician. "I'll certainly be circumspect, but if I find anything that requires attention, I'm legally obligated to see that that happens."

"Of course."

"Why the sudden rush to sell?"

"We're hemorrhaging money. Hell, most small rural hospitals are saying the same thing. Carrington seems to be on a quest to buy out as many as possible and build regional medical centers in their place, partially funded by larger hospitals they own elsewhere. It might be good for this place. Carrington seems willing to channel funds toward the smaller hospitals, as well. I'm just asking that you keep an open mind about the situation."

Hard to keep an open mind when he wasn't fully informed on any situations going on, but Caine kept that thought to himself. "Understood. Keep me informed on your end?"

"The board just wants what's best for the hospital. I can assure you that."

"As do I."

"And…if you find anything in the audit that might make the hospital look less favorable with Carrington, will you bring it to our attention first so we can do some damage control? This hospital has been operating since the late 1800s. There are bound to be several skeletons lurking around here."

"Of course."

Chapter 19

DR. CAINE ALVARO STARED at the hospital heads of departments with a look hard and cold enough to cut glass. No diamond needed.

He looked like he'd be pretty easygoing—even sloppy—with the jeans and dark T-shirt and the hair in need of trimming.

Wallace knew it was a lie. The man was the hardest taskmaster Wallace had ever worked for.

But he was fair. He was also a drop-dead ringer for the chief of medicine at Finley Creek General. Wallace had made the mistake once of asking about the connection. That was the last time he'd ever asked Dr. Alvaro anything personal.

He'd learned that that was a boundary you just didn't cross. This meeting was unexpected. Wallace had fifty-two minutes to get to FCGH, or he would be in hot water with the man's twin.

He didn't know who intimidated him more—Caine Alvaro or Alvaro's long-lost twin Dr. Holden-Deane.

"What's this about, Dr. Alvaro? I have a consult at Finley Creek Gen in less than an hour."

"This won't take long." Alvaro didn't bark at people like his brother did. He was quieter, calmer at times.

Wallace had to admit the man seemed far slower to anger. But where Holden-Deane could burn people with his words, Alvaro could freeze them to the bone when they displeased him.

Wallace made a point of avoiding the two men as much as he possibly could.

The last thing he wanted was one of the COMs of the hospitals breathing down his neck. Wallace had a good thing going, his career was on the trajectory he and his wife Jennifer wanted. His retirement was soon. He just had one more position he needed to add to his resume. Then he'd be assisting Jennifer with her political aspirations. He didn't want to jeopardize that.

"The hospital is going to be sold," Alvaro started. "Before that happens, the board has asked that I personally check over each department for problems, inefficiencies, and discrepancies. I'll be starting on Monday. Thank you for coming. You're dismissed."

That was it?

Hell, Alvaro could have just sent it in a memo.

But had there been something in the way Alvaro had looked at him? Wallace wasn't entire certain.

Chapter 20

CAINE WAS NOT AN accountant, and he made no bones about it. But he understood profit-and-loss sheets. There were good things about Barratt County. And there were bad.

He needed money. Lots of it, if he was going to bring Barratt County up to date on medical technology and patient care. Not that the hospital ever mistreated patients. They were just using outdated technology.

It was his greatest struggle as COM. He'd heard of nightmare hospital boards before. Barratt County wasn't like that.

The problem was just a shortage of cash.

He wasn't happy about an impending sale of the hospital, but he understood the reasoning behind it. The small regional medical group that currently owned Barratt County and Finley Creek General didn't have enough assets to diversify profits. Hospitals often lost money.

Especially emergency departments.

He needed someone he trusted to go over these records for him; someone who did this sort of thing on a regular basis.

Caine made it a point to keep himself up on billing practices and the average costs of services within the industry. But the type of audit the board was wanting was specialized.

One that would potentially take months. After a quick phone call to a former military friend, he felt slightly better about the process. The man was one hell of a forensic accountant. With a medical school background. Thoreau Laughton was an enigma— but he would find the answers to any questions a paying client would have.

He'd just have to approve Thor's fee with the board.

He didn't think he'd have a problem getting that approval. Not when he pointed out the handful of discrepancies he'd already found.

Caine had a list of six physicians he had questions for. Five were still affiliated with BCGH. One had relocated to Finley Creek General.

Thor was going to have to speak directly with the head of that hospital.

And Caine would most likely have to be there.

The hands of fate were tightening around him again.

He refused to think of who else was probably in that hospital right now, working alongside the man Caine had questions for.

Nikkie Jean had cropped up in his thoughts far too often.

Caine almost growled, causing the assistant across from him to jump and eye him warily. He just shook his head. "Get me copies of everything Cage Ralstone may have billed in his last year here. By Monday. Then take Tuesday off. I need to get going." Henry should have the children up and ready. Caine needed a day with his children. For his own sanity.

"Yes, sir."

"There are far too many discrepancies in this department."

Caine had to find out why—before the hospital sold. He was going to start with Cage Ralstone.

Chapter 21

CLEAN UP YOUR OWN messes. That's what Jennifer continued to yell at him in the privacy of their own room. When they'd first married, they'd made a pact never to argue in the room where they'd loved each other. Where they slept.

That had changed.

Now she didn't want Reggie, or their nephew Ray, to hear. But the boys knew. They'd heard how she spoke to him as the years had passed. They knew.

And they never would meet his eyes when Jennifer would start.

Wallace sat in his desk and thought. Remembered. Tried to decide just what "clean up your own messes" actually meant.

He had eight surgeons who worked underneath him at Finley Creek County. He had to handle that position well. It was the only way he was going to move into position for chief of medicine. County wasn't the most prestigious hospital in the region for him to work for, but Jennifer could make it like he was doing it for altruistic reasons.

Hell, it wasn't like they needed the money. It was the recognition Jennifer wanted.

If that was what Jennifer wanted from him, then that was what he was going to do. He owed her so much for the life they had together, for their son, for all of it.

Everything he did, he did out of love for Jennifer.

He was the first in the conference room, followed shortly after by Virat Patel, Lacy Deane, and Nikkie Jean. Wallace straightened when he saw Nikkie Jean. Their paths hadn't crossed much lately.

Nikkie Jean was such a pretty girl. Smart, too. More than smart, she was beyond brilliant. She'd go far in the field of pediatric surgery. She was laughing about something Lacy had said, and Wallace bit back a smile.

He loved it when she laughed. It always brightened the room.

This wasn't the first time he'd been attracted to a young woman he worked with.

Women who understood him better than Jennifer.

He'd almost always regretted the affairs, but he was secure in the knowledge that Jennifer hadn't known. He'd always protected her from knowing, from that hurt.

Nikkie Jean was just the type of woman he'd always needed in his life. She was happy about everything. Always had a smile on her face. Uncomplicated. And it was a pretty smile, with dimples and eyes that always laughed. She was much easier to be around than Lacy Deane, who was far more acerbic.

Lacy Deane was more like Jennifer had used to be. Droll, witty, snarky, beautiful. But Nikkie Jean was a balm to a man's soul.

Her mother had been that way as well.

It had taken Wallace a while to put together who Nikkie Jean actually was. The email he'd received that morning had clarified why she'd always seemed so familiar to him. An old friend from medical school had forwarded a flyer to every physician he knew around the country.

He sent one every year around this time, but this was the first time Wallace had opened it since Nikkie Jean had transferred to Finley Creek General.

Wallace had sworn aloud when he saw the age-progressed photograph staring back at him from his screen. A missing-child flyer.

It was a highly accurate digital representation; he'd almost been convinced that it was an actual photograph of Nikkie Jean Netorre instead of a computer-generated approximation of what his former colleague's daughter would look like now.

She was Jordan Carrington's daughter; Wallace would bet money on it.

He'd heard her say before that she was estranged from her family. Wallace wasn't surprised. Nikkie Jean's mother had been a real piece of work before her death a good dozen years back.

Wallace hadn't attended the funeral, but Jennifer had.

He wondered if he should say something to her. Let her know her father was still looking for her.

Her father had been a good man, always willing to help others.

He'd helped Wallace get through some of his own med school classes, actually tutoring him at times.

Wallace couldn't forget that debt. But there was a reason Nikkie Jean didn't want her father knowing where she was. And he respected that.

He'd just have to watch and think about what he should do. If he revealed her whereabouts, that could potentially tie him to the nurse who had worked directly with Nikkie Jean's father fifteen years ago.

Something else he had to consider. The ramifications of that...could be devastating. Sweat beaded on his neck as he thought about it. He discreetly wiped it away.

"Dr. Netorre, Dr. Deane, good to see you." His path hadn't crossed theirs today. He nodded at the men behind them.

It wasn't unusual to see those men hovering around the female members of the surgical department. Wallace understood why. He suspected Jacobson was as fascinated by the two women as he was that redheaded nurse Holden-Deane was with now.

Why wouldn't the other men in the department want to spend a bit of their free time with pretty, sweet-smelling females who made a man feel important the moment they smiled at them? Wallace certainly did.

"Dr. Henedy," Nikkie Jean said, quietly. She hadn't been the same since the Henderson boy had died from an anaphylactic reaction back in May.

Wallace had gone over his notes and the file repeatedly in the few weeks since. He always obsessed over the ones he'd lost. But he hadn't made a mistake. It had just been a tragedy. Had the boy come in earlier and not in such acute distress, things might have been different. He might have been able to come back from the reaction. But it hadn't. The cards had fallen where they'd fallen.

He had been doing the job long enough to know that.

But sweet little Nikkie Jean, she hadn't grown a thick skin yet. He half hoped she wouldn't. That she would always keep the joy of who she was. Her father had been just as sensitive to the world as she was; eventually he'd closed himself off. Wallace had understood that, too.

Dr. Holden-Deane came in, like a damned force of nature. Wallace was six two and had been in good physical shape his whole life. He felt like a ninety-pound weakling next to Dr. Holden-Deane. The man was the perfect image of successful doctor. He hadn't struggled in anything, the gossip said. And there was plenty of gossip.

He was now married to one of the nurses who was good friends with both Lacy and Nikkie Jean. A beautiful woman who would help him in his career and would understand him. Not to mention was sexy as hell.

Rafael Holden-Deane was a damned lucky man.

Wallace used to think he was, too.

Now he wasn't so sure. Jennifer just didn't seem happy with him any longer. Sometimes he wondered if the only reason they hadn't divorced yet was because of the public perception and the effect a divorce would have on Jennifer's career.

He took the seat next to Nikkie Jean, pretending not to notice how she shifted subtly to put more space between them. Like she always did.

Nikkie Jean shied away from all men. Frightened, the gossip said. Though no one knew quite why.

But if she was who she thought she was, Wallace understood.

There had been some nasty scandal with her family two years after Wallace and Jennifer had relocated so they didn't have to uproot the newly orphaned Raymond. A scandal Jennifer had delighted in sharing with him. Wallace had been disgusted by it—and concerned for the teenage girl involved.

Nikkie Jean. She'd been Dannica Carrington then, three years younger than his son Reggie.

It was just one of the questions Wallace wanted to ask her. One of the things he wanted to make right for her again.

Holden-Deane started speaking. "There's a new buyer looking at Finley Creek Gen. And they're going to start in these departments—"

Sweat broke out on Wallace's neck as what that meant for him started to sink in. Dr. Alvaro was doing the exact same thing. If the two men ever got together to compare notes, Wallace could be in some serious hot water.

Hot water that could mean serious jail time if he couldn't get out of it.

That would be far more of a scandal than a divorce would. Jennifer's life would be ruined. And she would never forgive him.

Clean up your own messes.
Now he understood what Jennifer meant.
Wallace had to figure out what to do next.

Chapter 22

NIKKIE JEAN USED A cleanser to dissolve the glue from the younger woman's skin. Ariella had glued her own hand to the poster for W4HAV. "It happens to all of us."

Ariella blushed. Her embarrassment was so palpable. Nikkie Jean resisted the urge to hug her and tell her everything would be all right. It was hard not to feel protective of Ariella Avery—soon to be first lady of Texas. The woman was just so…sweet.

Unlike either of her older brothers that Nikkie Jean knew.

Neither Rafe Holden-Deane nor Caine Alvaro would ever be described as *sweet*.

"I'm not clumsy. Not really. Marc just says I get distracted— that's when these things happen to me."

"I can see where the Gorgeous Governor could be very distracting. In an extremely delicious way." Marc, or rather Marcus Deane, governor of Texas, adored his fiancée. Nikkie Jean had seen that for herself just a few weeks ago. About the same time Nikkie Jean had found herself naked with Ariella's older brother.

Ariella had the same dark eyes and the same smile. Caine's hair was a shade darker, but not by much. And where he had a seriously nice tan going on, Ariella was as pale as a ghost. But there was no denying that Ariella and Caine were related. Closely.

It was their personalities that were wildly different.

She wasn't going to let herself think about *him* today. Not today.

She had other things to think about. Like getting posters for the latest fund-raiser for W4HAV figured out. She had fifteen places in Barrattville and Value to distribute the flyers and posters.

Posters without human skin cells attached. "You need to watch for an allergic reaction to the glue—or the solvent—but you should be ok."

"Thanks. I can't believe I did this." The poor woman's cheeks were tomato red now.

"I used this same glue last week to glue Allen Jacobson's shoes to the bottom of his locker. It's how I know how to dissolve it." She shot Ariella a wicked look to distract her.

"I knew that was you!" Lacy shouted from across the room. "Rafe and Allen blamed me."

"Sorry, not sorry."

"Why did you glue Allen's shoes?" Ariella asked, sending her a wide-eyed look.

"I thought he was responsible for the jalapenos on my hamburger. I used to be able to handle peppers of any kind, but for the last few weeks, a seriously no-go on that."

"So who did the peppers if it wasn't this Allen guy?" Bailey, a deputy from the Value TSP, asked from where she was loading a mean looking gun—with staples.

"Dr. Virat He-is-Evil Patel. And I still owe him for that one."

"These are the things that go on in the surgical department?" the final woman in their group asked. Jillian was taking it easy on the nearby couch—she said she was supervising, but Nikkie Jean knew the truth.

Morning sickness had slammed Jillian with a vengeance over the last week. The redhead had been grouching about Rafe since she'd walked into the charity directly across from the hospital two hours ago. Apparently, he'd been determined to get her pregnant as quickly as he possibly could.

As Jillian put it—Rafe was an overachiever.

Jillian had probably enjoyed every minute of him trying.

It was rare that they all had a day off together—Annie, Fin, and Izzie were on duty at the hospital until six that night—but she had time with Jillian and the others.

They were serving as good distractions.

She'd gone nonstop since the night she'd been so stupid. It was easier to block Dr. Caine Alvaro out that way.

But having his sister there was making that a bit difficult.

Ariella had the same smile. Not that Caine had smiled at her much. Nikkie Jean could not get that man out of her head. No matter how hard she tried.

"Nikkie Jean and I are fighting the good fight," Lacy said, in response to Jillian's question. "We're grossly outnumbered in there. Vir, Allen, Cage, and the rest—they don't let us forget it."

The surgical department adored Lacy and had ever since Lacy had almost been killed. Logan Lanning, Allen's former friend and once an acting chief of surgery, had shot her and her fiancé. If Lacy had been anywhere else, she would have died.

Rafe had carried her from the roof himself.

Nikkie Jean still had nightmares about how her friend had looked that night. She'd assisted in that surgery and would never forget how it had felt.

It had been the first time anyone she'd known personally had ever been on her table. She'd never forget that.

"Those peppers upset my stomach for two days. Virat deserves whatever revenge I can get." She still felt a little ill from those peppers when she thought about them even a week later.

She would have said more, but Ariella's future stepchildren came barreling into the room. They'd been playing in the children's rec area in the room behind the multipurpose room.

"Mommy," the little boy said, diving at Ariella. "We're really hungry. Can we go now?"

Ariella checked her watch. "We probably should. We're having dinner with my sisters in Garrity in five hours. It's a bit of a drive, and I promised the kids we'd stop in Value to eat at the diner."

"I'd go with you guys," Lacy said. "But I'm expected across the road for a while."

"Me, as well," Jillian said with an audible groan. She was green—and it was clashing with her hair. Nikkie Jean felt for Jillian—nausea sucked. Big time. She'd had enough of that feeling when she'd been sixteen.

She was feeling a bit sick now—those peppers should not have made their way back into the conversation.

"I got lucky," Nikkie Jean said. "I'm not needed for once."

"Then you can join us?" Ariella asked quietly. "You and Bailey?"

"I can't. I'm expected at the station soon," Bailey said, genuine regret in her tone. She'd recently returned to work, and it wasn't going well. She and the sheriff were having difficulties getting along.

Nikkie Jean made a mental note to talk to the other woman privately when she got a shot. She was Bailey's unofficial sponsor at W4HAV now, after all.

"Dr. Nik! Dr. Nik! You can sit with me," the little girl said. Katie took Nikkie Jean's hand in her own. After the little girl's abduction and rescue almost two months ago, Nikkie Jean had been the one to give the girl emergency care. She'd made sure personally that Katie had not been harmed more than a mild sunburn.

It was the emotional scars that had concerned her the most that day. She'd sat and rocked the child for over an hour, just giving her the emotional connection to someone the child had needed, until Lacy's husband had taken over for her. He'd been upstairs helping keep his older brother from fracturing at the thought of losing Ariella. Nikkie Jean had helped out where she could. "I'd like that very much."

Ariella might be Caine's biological family, but she had been Nikkie Jean's friend first. And she needed friends today.

—

They'd mutinied. Caine had had no choice; even the baby was following his older siblings' leads. They hadn't wanted to go to the city to shop for school clothes and groceries. They wanted to go to the Value Reservoir to play and swim and just be children.

Basically, they'd just wanted him. They'd exhausted him long before lunch. His only recourse was to suggest a movie. There was bound to be one that the older two would sit through—that would have other toddlers in the theater, and Dalton's fussing and fits would blend right in.

There were some days he felt more than a little overwhelmed. This was definitely one of them. They were far too much for his uncle to handle alone; he'd have to get Henry help again. The older man was showing signs of the strain.

He'd be asking around at the diner for recommendations for a housekeeper to help Henry, at least through the remainder of the summer. If he couldn't find a housekeeper, there was always the hope there would be someone he trusted to watch the kids while he worked. It was summertime. There had to be a responsible teenager somewhere in this town.

The diner was packed when they walked in, with teenagers in baseball uniforms everywhere. He shifted Dalton closer when he squirmed. Dalton didn't understand why he had to be carried when his brother got to walk. There was one booth left, in the back. He waved the children toward it.

Just as the door opened behind him and a little whirlwind blew in. Caine just *knew* who it was almost before he turned.

He jerked like a damned magnet the instant he heard her laugh. He hadn't seen her in almost seven weeks. Not since the night he'd left her naked in her bed.

She'd haunted his dreams every night since.

She was facing away from him; he doubted she'd seen him yet. But he recognized her instantly. Her laugh, her scent—they were imprinted on him.

He'd regretted what had happened between them from the moment he'd stepped out of her bedroom and left her there. Not because he wished it hadn't happened, but because of how he had handled it after. He should have held and kissed her and promised that what had happened that night was just the beginning for them.

He should have known he wouldn't be able to forget what had happened between them.

He knew himself well enough to know that. Relationships with women had never been casual for him. Not from that first girl when he'd been sixteen.

He'd not touched her until he thought he'd loved her.

His uncle had taught him early on that romantic relationships required respect, caring…and trust. Caine had never trusted people easily.

April had just pounded that fact into his head.

Every muscle in his body tensed. This was not the place he had envisioned seeing her again. Far from it.

There was a dark-haired woman coming up behind her. He heard the other woman laugh at whatever Nikkie Jean had said.

And then he looked at that woman. Fully.

Big, dark-brown eyes stared back at him—and widened.

Caine bit back a curse.

He knew exactly who she was. She'd been all over the news with the governor for weeks.

He didn't know which woman bothered him the most. His stomach tightened when Nikkie Jean stopped walking and faced him.

Nikkie Jean. Definitely Nikkie Jean. He could ignore the sister he'd never met, but Nikkie Jean was a completely different story.

He would never be able to ignore Nikkie Jean Netorre again.

"Nikkie Jean, not working today?" He'd never seen her in anything other than scrubs. Or naked. Today she wore an apple-green T-shirt with W4HAV printed across her breasts. And jeans that hugged every perfect little curve.

Small but absolutely perfect. He knew exactly how perfect.

"It's my one day off this year. Hello...Dr. Alvaro."

Her eyes were carefully blank when she looked at him. Nonchalant. As if he hadn't had her naked beneath him. As if he was no more than a work colleague or neighbor. He waited for the chatter to start.

It didn't.

She finally looked at him again. "Well, this is awkward, isn't it?"

She had the dark-haired little boy by the hand. Like she knew him. He recognized the children, of course. Technically, he supposed they were his future step-nephew and niece.

The woman behind them was his sister. His younger sister, who was soon to marry the governor of Texas. She was the first of his so-called siblings he'd seen face-to-face.

The little boy Nikkie Jean held was only around five or so. He stared up at Caine. "Uncle Rafe!"

Nikkie Jean's hand tightened on the child's, pulling him closer protectively. As if she feared Caine would say something to hurt him. That...stung.

The lack of trust he'd created was hard for him to miss.

Caine shook his head. "No, I'm not Uncle Rafe, buddy. I'm...Caine."

Caine's sister shot a wary look at Caine. One just as mistrustful as Nikkie Jean's. The two of them together were enough to make him feel like a first-class slug.

"Isaac, Katie, remember how we talked about how Uncle Luc, Uncle Rafe, Aunt Zoey, and Aunt Pen are my biological siblings?"

"Tummy siblings," the little boy said. "Uh-huh."

"This is Caine. He and Uncle Rafe are twins. He's another of my biological siblings. They were in their mommy's belly together. They look the same. He's another one of my tummy brothers." His sister was quiet and calm with her children, answering the difficult question far better than Caine would have.

Then she looked up at him, and he saw the nerves. The fear.

The inner strength. "Hello, Caine. I'm Ariella."

She turned more fully toward him as she straightened. Caine felt his own eyes widen slightly.

"I know." She looked just like his daughter. That rocked him. Same pale skin, delicate jawline, long, dark hair worn in a similar style, the big, uncertain, dark eyes. Even the shy smile was an almost exact match. She looked just like Keller.

And she was scared to death of…him. He'd never deliberately scared a woman in his life—he wasn't about to start with his own younger sister. She was a good ten years younger than he was, at least. "I'm…these are my three children."

Her gaze dropped to the baby, and her eyes softened. Keller and Everett shifted to stand in front of him, strangely silent. Her smile widened, turned open and welcoming.

The resemblance between her and his children rocked him. Made him forget where they were and the fact that half of Value must have surrounded them. Nikkie Jean was watching every move he made, as if she expected him to pounce at her friend and break her. Nikkie Jean was no doubt ready to jump between them and defend against the enemy.

He was the enemy now. He didn't want to be her enemy. Far from it.

"It's nice to meet you," his sister said to the children. "These are *my* children. Katie and Isaac. She's seven, and he's five."

"We're seven," Everett said, inching closer, curiosity on his face. "We'll be eight soon. Who are you?"

He looked up at Caine for clarification.

"She's your aunt, Everett. My…younger sister, Ariella."

Keller stepped forward and gave the two women a shy smile. "Hi."

Nikkie Jean looked at his daughter, and the wariness went away for a moment. She smiled at Keller easily. "Hello, Keller. I love that necklace."

"Thank you. Uncle Henry bought it for me."

They couldn't keep blocking the aisle like they were. He motioned toward the last booth. There was a small table behind it. The four older children would fit.

His eyes met Nikkie Jean's. She wanted to escape him. He wasn't about to let that happen. Not now that he'd finally caught her again. He pulled in a deep breath.

She'd brought the wind with her again.

He shot out his free hand and wrapped his fingers around the soft skin of her elbow. Nikkie Jean had the softest skin. He'd loved touching her everywhere.

Damn it, he wanted to touch her like that again. And then again. Just how much he wanted that was sinking in—fast. She'd been in his dreams every night for weeks. Every damned night. Waiting for him with a look on her face. A look that said she was right there—waiting for him. If he was just brave enough to go to her.

Every damned night. She was driving him crazy.

"Nikkie Jean, how have you been?"

There were so many things he wanted to ask her.

"Just fine." Someone bumped her from behind, sending her closer to where he stood, surrounded by his children.

He wanted to scoop her up again, just like he had that night—almost in this very spot.

He stared down at her in challenge. He wasn't ready to let her go just yet. "Let's sit down. This place is packed."

"Ariella and the kids were headed to Garrity—where her sisters Pen and Zoey live. We spent the morning making posters for our fund-raiser. Isaac and I are good buddies. And Katie and I both love My Little Ponies." The chatter was there, but it wasn't the kind he was used to from her. She was pretending; no doubt for the children's sake.

And his sister's.

Caine was beginning to wonder just how much that chatter hid the real Nikkie Jean.

"Dr. Nik is *my* doctor. From before, when I rode the helicopter," the little blond girl said as she eyed him suspiciously. "Is she your doctor, too? You look like Uncle Rafe and a pirate."

"Do I? I've always liked pirates. I like their parrots and eye patches. But I don't have a wooden leg."

Her look told him she was reserving judgment on him. This child had been through hell recently; it had been all over the news. The children sat eyeing each other warily. His children didn't warm up to strangers quickly. Apparently, neither did his sister's future stepchildren.

He hadn't realized the woman involved in the abductions and murder had been his sister until well after reports of her being rescued had aired.

Nikkie Jean slipped into the U-bench seat. Caine followed behind her, clutching his youngest close. She still smelled like jasmine. Just like he'd remembered.

Dalton climbed out of his arms and into the booth between him and Nikkie Jean. There hadn't been any booster seats available in the crowd, but his son was a taller boy; he'd be able to reach.

Caine took a moment while Ariella was settling her two children at the table next to them with Keller and Everett to look at Nikkie Jean.

"Are you doing ok?"

"Of course. Why wouldn't I be? Although it has been a busy few weeks." She looked away from him, then smiled at Dalton.

At least, it was a genuine smile.

Dalton seemed fascinated by her, babbling at her in his own language interspersed with a few recognizable words. She laughed and talked right back at him. Dalton reached for her.

She hesitated, then looked at Caine for permission. He nodded. She was probably the one woman in the world he would fully trust with his children.

She drew him more than any other woman ever had. Even his ex-wife. After he and April had gotten together, he'd been able to concentrate. To work. Even during the ups and downs of their relationship.

But that wasn't the case with this woman next to him.

He found her creeping in when he'd least expected it.

He understood his son's fascination. Dalton snuggled onto her lap as if he'd been there a thousand times before.

Nikkie Jean cuddled his youngest son close, talking to him and rocking him. Dalton just cuddled closer, shooting her a beautiful smile and babbling. His son wrapped one hand around her braid and just held it.

His sister settled across from him finally. Hesitantly. Caine looked at her again. It was hard for him not to stare.

He hadn't wanted to meet her—or the others. But he'd kept their letter. He wasn't certain why he had. But he had.

What was he supposed to do with this woman now?

Nikkie Jean started chattering at Ariella, inane conversation including softball, fund-raisers, and some sort of choir benefit.

His sister relaxed right before his eyes.

Before long, Nikkie Jean had her responding. Easily.

It clicked. Nikkie Jean had done so deliberately. It was a definite gift she had, putting people at ease. Too bad it had the opposite effect on him. It just made him want her more.

He studied his sister's profile as she spoke.

It was like looking at an adult version of Keller. His daughter had always been so pale compared to him and Everett and Dalton, he'd wondered at it. Now he had his answer. Genetics. The shape of the jaw was the same, and the eyes. The smile. All three of his children had the same smile as this woman he did not know.

Caine didn't know what to think about that.

But he could not ignore it. Not any longer.

His daughter giggled at the next table over, and he looked at her. She was sitting with cousins now. Connections.

Keller looked so much like the aunt she didn't know. Keller kept shooting looks at Ariella, no doubt filled with curiosity.

There was a connection; one he didn't know if he wanted to foster further. But he couldn't deny it existed any longer.

The chains of fate were tightening around him.

Chapter 23

THIS WAS ONE OF the most awkward lunches of her life. And Nikkie Jean had been to quite a few, thanks to her family. Caine didn't say much, and that made Ariella even more nervous.

Caine's son sat on her lap, eating his lunch and giggling. Snuggling in that particular way children had when they were sleepy.

Having Caine Alvaro's son on her lap was a strange kind of awkward she didn't really want to delve too deeply into.

Nikkie Jean kept up the conversation as much as she could while everyone ate.

For her friend's sake, not Caine's. Ariella was so painfully shy. This awkwardness of this was not something she'd wish on anyone—especially Ariella. Ariella was the only reason Nikkie Jean hadn't taken one look at him and his little mini-Alvaros and headed straight for the hills.

Ariella needed the extra protection from a man like Caine.

By the time the meal was over, the two little girls had become fast friends, and Nikkie Jean herself was completely in love with one of the Alvaro men.

He had his father's smile and the biggest, darkest brown eyes she had ever seen. A twinge of what could have been hit her. When she had been sixteen and she'd been told the prognosis and that she'd most likely never have children, she'd been devastated. She'd lived for years daydreaming about the children *she* would have, and how she would be a far better parent to them than she had had. To lose that had been to lose…her hope. That hurt hadn't lessened all that much.

She was considering adopting eventually, after she was established in her career and could better afford to care for kids on her own. There were so many out there that needed homes. Especially teenagers.

She could make a home for teenagers, especially those with traumas. At least that was her plan, eventually. She needed to talk to Annie about that. Her friend was in the process of adopting her three foster sons soon. And her mother's foster daughter was about to age out of the system. Annie would know more about the process.

Twelve percent wasn't much of a hope, and her father had pointed that out to her very bluntly that day. Even Nikkie Jean's own research had shown that the twelve percent was a conservative estimate. It could have been as high as twenty-five percent, but not likely. And the odds of a condom failing at the exact wrong time with her particular problems made it most likely even less than that twelve percent.

The only partially unprotected sex she'd ever had in her life had been with Caine. So no possibility there. Not without a serious miracle happening.

The man had made three absolutely beautiful children, though. That shot a momentary pang through her heart. Just momentarily. Nikkie Jean had more common sense than to go for stupid wishes that would never come true.

Caine Alvaro had gotten exactly what he'd wanted out of her, and she'd given it to him willingly. Now it was time to forget all about the man pressing far too close to her side for comfort. And forget about how wonderful the man smelled and how perfect the feel of him had been that night.

There was something to be said about strong dragon-covered arms holding her tight.

It had taken her a long time to be able to enjoy spontaneous sex with even a long-term partner without having a PTSD flashback right in the middle.

Or to be able to connect with her partner at all. That mattered.

There had been a few times she'd felt like a robot going through the motions. Completely disconnected.

She'd had four years of regular therapy between that relationship and now. She'd come a long way since then.

She would just take that night with Caine as the experience that it was—and move on. Period.

Sex could be so complicated.

After the kids were finished eating, she listened as Caine gave

Ariella his email address and his cell number. As he told her gently that he was glad they'd gotten to meet today.

It was a start. He hadn't said anything rude or hateful or hurtful to Ariella; not like Rafe had at first. She'd give him that. He was almost gentle with her. Similar to how he spoke with his own daughter, who seemed shy and sensitive, as well.

Just like her aunt.

Funny how that seemed to work. Keller was like Ariella in miniature.

Now, Everett…he sat eyeing them with the same mistrust and suspicion as she'd seen in his uncle's eyes before. Everett was definitely very much like his father and uncle.

She had no doubt that Ariella and her family would make room for him and his children. All he had to do was take that first step.

They'd even made room for *her*. And she was just a work friend of Jillian's and Lacy's.

Dalton refused to let her go, so Nikkie Jean slipped him onto her hip. He was a hefty kid and looked older than she knew him to be. He was super sweet, and when he laid his head on her shoulder, she was a total goner.

He was out within seconds.

She'd always enjoyed working with children, giving them someone they could trust when they needed it. Her neighbors as a child had had much younger children. Nikkie Jean had spent as much time at their house as she could get away with until they'd moved away when she'd been fifteen.

She'd grieved them for years, but something had happened with Nikkie Jean's mother. The neighbors had cut off all contact with her family completely after that.

Keller sidled closer, asking about the plastic bracelets on her wrist. Nikkie Jean talked with her quietly, while Ariella and Caine spoke. Everett just eyed her suspiciously. Much like his father did every time she saw him.

Which, if she had her way, would be even less than she just had. No sense tempting fate, after all. It was probably best to just forget about Caine Alvaro as much as she possibly could.

Although that hadn't been easy in the last month or so. The man had a bad habit of creeping into her thoughts when she least expected it.

Or right after Rafe would walk by.

Hard to forget the very sight of a man when he had a clone in her orbit every single day of the work week.

That whole once-a-decade screwup quota had been met; she wasn't about to repeat that. She'd told herself that every time he crossed her mind—or every time she saw his clone.

She wouldn't have slept with the man if she had not have had feelings for him. Already. Sudden, sharp, intense, the attraction had been real. Even though she'd never been attracted to his twin for even a moment, she had been to Caine.

She'd trusted him. On a level she hadn't even realized until he'd been standing next to her bed telling her a future was never going to happen. That trust had fizzled in a single heartbeat.

She'd yet been able to figure out why. Or how it had happened as fast as it had. Maybe she needed to make an appointment with the psych department. Find someone to talk to about all this—besides Annie and Izzie, or the therapist at W4HAV. They knew there had been a stupid-mistake event, but she hadn't shared details. She wasn't exactly the share all the gory details type.

She never had a lot of people with whom to practice that little skill.

Twice monthly therapy notwithstanding.

Trust had never happened to her before; not like that.

She wasn't about to let him get under her skin and push her away again. Nope. It hurt too much when that happened. Best to keep the Grand Canyon between them.

She waited until Ariella had loaded her children into the limo that drove her everywhere and then turned back to Caine. His two eldest were still in the diner talking to the mayor's children, so they had a moment of privacy.

His youngest slept on her shoulder. She patted the tiny back and looked up at the grown version in front of her. "Thank you."

"For?"

"For Ariella. Not rejecting her outright. She's...healing. This is the first she's done anything without Marc or the rest of her family hovering since it happened. Jillian and Lacy, her sisters-in-law—they both had to work and asked me to stay close to her today, if I could. They don't think she's ready to be alone for too long yet." The horror Ariella had gone through still sickened her. Jillian had privately shared that Ariella was still struggling with the guilt of not being able to better protect Isaac and Katie during the attack.

Part of what Nikkie Jean had been tasked with doing by Jillian and Lacy was providing a neutral sounding board to help Caine's sister work through those nightmares.

Ariella was responsible for creating W4HAV, but that didn't mean she was exempt from the effects of trauma. Far from it. Nikkie Jean was determined to be there for Ariella however she was needed.

She and Ariella weren't superclose friends, yet. But work they'd done this morning had given them time to really talk, like they hadn't before, even with Ariella's two children running in and out of the room.

It left Nikkie Jean feeling raw, even without Ariella's older brother next to her.

If there was one thing Nikkie Jean understood, it was the value of counseling—even just talking with other survivors of trauma. After she'd transferred to Finley Creek ten months ago, she'd made certain to find a support system. She'd found it in W4HAV, which had been operating out of temporary offices at nearby Lucas Tech. Ariella and Margo had been trying to get the center going then. And struggling with the actual *needs* of the clients.

Nikkie Jean had stepped in to help with that.

She was an old hat at trauma and therapy and support groups, after all.

That made her more than a little overprotective of this friend. It would be too easy for Ariella to let down her guard with Caine; if he decided to shut her out—Ariella didn't deserve that. The rush of protectiveness for her friend that hit her didn't surprise her at all. "What happened to her was extremely traumatic. For her, Marc, and the children."

"I read the articles. I suspect a lot was left out."

"It was. Ariella's the sensitive type, too. Easily hurt. Far more than I am. I was there the day they rescued her and Katie." And she would never forget Ariella's family's pain. "I cared for Katie while she was in the hospital."

"I get your message. I won't do anything to hurt your friend. Contrary to what you believe, I'm not callous, or a monster. I don't hurt people deliberately—even if it may seem that way. An email now and then is about all I am committing to. And that is just for my children's sake. They'll eventually want to know about her, them. I don't hide from the inevitable." He reached for the toddler in her arms.

Nikkie Jean didn't want to give the sweet guy up. There was something special about a warm little body cuddled close. It was hard to let that go. "He's a sweetheart."

"Yes, he can be."

He'd dropped the curtain again, cutting her out. He'd done that before whenever she'd mentioned his children.

Message received. She was good enough to sleep with—once, in his book, but nothing more than that. Like who *she* was didn't truly matter. Especially when it came to his children.

Nikkie Jean had spent far too many years not mattering to anyone to let this man treat her that way again.

No worries, she was going to stay away from him from now on. As far away as possible.

She'd just been a bed buddy that night. She'd make certain to remember that. The man just made her feel too vulnerable. Nikkie Jean had promised herself long ago that no one would ever make her feel that way again.

She gave him back his baby and forced herself to turn and walk away. "See you around, Alvaro."

Well, she hoped she didn't, actually.

It was best to just forget all about Caine Alvaro—as fast as she could. The man was not the man for her.

She *knew* that.

Physicians like him—men like him—meant trouble. She'd learned that lesson a long, long, long time ago.

"Goodbye, Nikkie Jean. I—"

She wouldn't let herself turn around to see what he had to say. It was time to forget all about him once again.

"I'm not finished with you, Netorre. I'm coming for you. We have some things to talk about. You can count on that."

Nikkie Jean almost run to her little Jeep after that. She had no clue what he meant now. There wasn't anything the two of them needed to talk about ever again.

Nikkie Jean was just going to keep it that way.

Chapter 24

OF COURSE, WALLACE hadn't been stupid. The last thing he needed was Dr. Alvaro digging into the past. He'd never padded a single invoice or insurance billing report by more than two or three percent, he'd never misappropriated supplies to make a quick profit more than three or four times a year, but over time, that kind of money had added up. Wallace wouldn't worry about it—it wasn't like there weren't thousands of other practitioners doing the exact same thing. And he'd made damned certain not to violate HIPAA laws. There would be no reason for Alvaro to look more closely at Wallace's records. He was just being paranoid.

Most of the funds had been courtesy of Finley Creek County and Barratt County Gen. There had been a small clinic he'd been required to work at three days a month located in Garrity, as well. But it had folded more than ten years ago, due to a lack of profit.

He probably had had something to do with that. He'd taken up to a five percent service fee there.

He'd told himself that the extra charges had been legitimate. Physicians of high caliber were rare in this part of the state—and they all originated out of Finley Creek. Smaller hospitals like Garrity and Value owed it to men like him for taking the time to practice there. Over time, it had become habit. And greed. He'd bumped up the padding by another percentage point under COM Daniels three years ago. Then again under Logan Lanning. No one had noticed.

But Caine Alvaro and Rafael Holden-Deane would be the type of men who would.

Especially Alvaro. Alvaro wasn't much of a businessman on the surface. He was militarily rigid, through and through. He ran a tight ship, and Wallace had to admit things were becoming far more efficient than they had been.

In general, chiefs of medicine were not well liked at times. But Alvaro seemed fair. Just hard. Harsh. Very much like his twin brother.

Wallace had known the two men were twins the first time he'd seen Alvaro. It was hard to miss. But FCGH had been filled with rumors about Holden-Deane from the moment he'd stepped inside.

Wallace had done his best to avoid interacting with that man as much as possible. Holden-Deane was a shark in the health-care business world. And Wallace knew the other man could eat him alive.

But Alvaro was who concerned him the most. Wallace had gotten sloppy at Barratt County. Now he had figure out a way to clean that up. Jennifer demanded that.

From where she stood in the midst of the FCGH surgeons' break room, glaring up at him.

Her dark hair and eyes had always made her look like a lost little waif.

Wallace had always loved the way his wife looked in her business suits. When they'd first met, she'd been in ragged jeans and had had six-inch bangs. And such a shy smile.

From the wrong side of the tracks in Philly, she'd had no concept of marrying someone with a college degree, let alone an actual surgical intern. He'd been so proud; she'd been so pretty.

He used to think he'd rescued her from the bad home life that had shaped her.

She now liked to say she rescued herself. Wallace had always found that a tad bit insulting.

If he hadn't married her, she'd probably still be working at the Dairy Shack. Instead, she lived in one of the best neighborhoods in Finley Creek, their son and her nephew had both attended the best academy in the state, and he'd provided for her until her real estate business had grown larger than either one of them had ever expected.

Yet now she stood telling him he was a problem for her. How had that happened? When had their marriage gone so wrong?

Miranda. It had to have begun with Miranda. The nurse from Philadelphia had been Wallace's greatest mistake.

Chapter 25

SHE HAD A PROBLEM. And it had nothing to do with Virat's jalapeno peppers. No fever, no sign of infection, just nausea before noon. Every day for fifteen days.

Just like it had started with her once before. It was eerily similar.

But today was the first time she'd ever actually gotten sick.

Lacy handed her a paper towel and a bottle of water, having come in directly behind Nikkie Jean's latest mad dash to the small restroom off the rear of the surgical department break room. "Care to share? Because I doubt you're having sympathy morning sickness for Jilly. And I know you've been feeling off for over a week."

"I think I need to take a few tests. And it's fifteen days total. I've been feeling nauseated for fifteen days. Today's the first day this has happened—here." She and Lacy had shared quite a few confidences in their time in the department together. She wasn't as close to Lacy as she was Izzie and Annie—but Izzie and Annie hadn't just watched her puke her guts up, either. Again.

"Sounds like it. Anything you want to tell me?" Lacy had a knowing look in her eyes—sympathetic but knowing. Nikkie Jean closed her eyes for a moment. And then the words came tumbling out.

Confession was supposed to be good for the soul, after all.

"The condom broke. We thought it was after, and I am missing half the equipment thanks to ovarian cancer in my teens, and what's left isn't exactly in tip-top shape, Lace. Which means, it's not a pregnancy—it's worse. And I don't know if I can face that just yet. Not again." She knew she was rambling as every thought and fear came pouring out. Her friends at W4HAV knew she'd had cancer at sixteen, but she'd never told them the exact details of what had happened. "And if it's a pregnancy, what if something's wrong? Everything in there is damaged, even beyond what is normal. I'm talking like four periods a *year*. In a good year. It can't be a pregnancy. Pregnancy is not exactly a high possibility. So it's much, much worse."

Lacy put her hands on Nikkie Jean's shoulders and turned her to face her a little. Nikkie Jean just looked at her. "Don't borrow trouble. Is the timing right for a pregnancy? For morning sickness?"

Nikkie Jean did some mental math. She slowly nodded. "Yes."

"Did you have unprotected sex with a man capable of fathering children during the time frame you would have gotten pregnant?"

"Yes." He could definitely father children. She'd snuggled proof of that not even three days ago at the diner. "Sort of. I'm not exactly certain at what moment the condom broke, Lace. But it did. Never should have used a striped one. Probably would have better luck with polka dots."

"I'll keep that in mind. Is pregnancy the most likely diagnosis?"

"I don't know."

"Do you want to call him? Have him come and be with you right now?"

She hadn't even considered that it could be a pregnancy. The odds were just that long. Nikkie Jean needed to think. Needed to decide what happens next. "Not yet. I need to figure out just what to say—after I know for sure. I don't think *Hey, remember that night we did something totally stupid? Well, surprise, your kid number four is on the way!* will cut it. Especially if it's not a pregnancy." But the alternative to pregnancy was far more terrifying. "And figure out if it is a pregnancy, or more tumors."

It wasn't a diet issue. It wasn't an allergy issue, or infection, or a virus. It was more than that. Nikkie Jean knew it.

It was one of two things.

Ovarian cancer could mimic early pregnancy symptoms—Nikkie Jean had experienced that herself when she'd been sixteen. That was why she'd asked her father's partner if she could talk to him in her father's home office that night after the dinner party her mother had forced her to attend with her father's associates.

She'd been so scared something was wrong with her. And there had been.

Nikkie Jean knew her own body; even more now than she had at sixteen. She'd made a point of that after her father's partner had raped her that night.

"Probably not. But those tests? Get them done soon—or I'm tattling to Rafe and Allen." Lacy was paged over the intercom. Before she stepped out, she turned back to Nikkie Jean. "Whatever you find out or decide, you're not alone. We stick together around here: remember that. Thick and thin, beginning to end. Isn't that one of the sample slogans for W4HAV? Well, it's truth. I'll even go grab a test from the pharmacy, if you want. We'll let everyone think it's for me, if asked. That Jillian's made me paranoid. It'll be our little secret."

Tears threatened to choke her. "Thanks. It's hard to remember that sometimes. I'm really good at being alone. Been practicing my whole life. I've got it down to a science—it's kind of like my superpower. Annie, Izzie, you, and W4HAV are the first real friends I've ever had in my adult life. It takes some getting used to."

"I know exactly what you mean. I was the same way until Jillian and Ari. But things have changed for me. No reason they can't for you, too."

"Go. And…thanks, Lace, I appreciate it."

Nikkie Jean was going to bite the bullet and grab a urine test from the pharmacy half a block away. She'd take the test as soon as she got home. When she was alone and would have the time to think through every ramification of everything.

Rule out the twelve percent, before confirming that appointment with an oncologist at Finley Creek County. Something was definitely going on. Or those had been some seriously potent jalapenos.

Jalapenos didn't stay with a woman for fifteen days.

Chapter 26

SHE MET FIN AS SHE was clocking out for the day. They had to head across the parking lot to W4HAV for choir practice. Nikkie Jean had no idea how she was going to sing for the next two hours without vomiting. Either from what was going on—or from nerves.

But she had to. She had the solo on two different songs. The fund-raiser was an important one; the women of W4HAV were counting on her.

She'd be there. Her presence finally mattered to people; she would *never* do anything to let them down.

"Sorry about the letters, Fin. I know how frightened you must be." Fin and Virat had revealed what had been bothering Fin for the past month or so—someone had been stalking her while she'd been at the hospital. Virat had stepped in to help keep her safe.

Nikkie Jean had suspected something was going on with the two of them. Virat had been remarkably hard to find on his regular lunch break.

As had Fin.

Nikkie Jean had looked; she had peppers to avenge, after all.

But more important than that, her friend was hurting. And afraid. Fin had a scary past of her own to deal with; stalking definitely made that trauma resurface.

"I'm doing ok. I trust Vince's son to find the man responsible," Fin said, quietly. "Detective Acardi is at least listening to me. The previous detective wasn't."

"It doesn't have to be a man, you know. Women stalk other women."

"True. I just…I suppose it could be a woman. But I don't think so."

Nikkie Jean shot her a look. "But at least you have Virat

watching over you. And the way he looked at you…yummy."

"Yes. He is." Fin's cheeks reddened, even in the rain.

They made it to their cars. "It would probably make more sense for me to just ride with him, wouldn't it? But I'm not sure I want it hospital gossip yet."

"Yep. Because it will get out. This is Finley Creek General, remember. Best soap opera in the city. Unless you want to keep things hidden for a while?" Nikkie Jean certainly had. She was beyond grateful that no one had figured out that she had been involved with Rafe's identical twin brother. The issues that would have caused…she was so glad she didn't have to face them. "I know keeping eyes off your every move is an attractive reason to keep it secret. I…wouldn't want everyone around here knowing who I am—was—involved with. Not in the beginning. Not that I'm involved with anyone, or plan on being involved with anyone in the foreseeable future."

Nikkie Jean looked at Fin when the other woman stumbled. Movement behind Fin caught her attention. A big, dark truck was barreling across the parking lot.

Straight at them. Nikkie Jean screamed.

She dove toward Fin, years of gymnastics training kicking in.

Her hands connected with the other woman's shoulders. She shoved, as hard as she could. Fin went backward and down. If Fin had been much bigger than she was, it wouldn't have worked, but Fin was barely bigger than Nikkie Jean.

The truck was almost on them.

Nikkie Jean dove as far out of the way as she could. Her knee twisted the wrong way.

Her head cracked against the bumper of a sedan. The last thing she heard was the sound of tires screeching away…and then the sound of Fin screaming her name.

Chapter 27

NIKKIE JEAN WASN'T DEAD. She didn't think. A security guard leaned over her. Nikkie Jean blinked up at him.

"We need help, need to get inside." Fin, someone was trying to hurt Fin. Fin needed to get inside. To Rafe or Allen or Virat or Vince. She just needed to get inside. "You ok, Fin?"

"I think so." Fin knelt down next to her and started running her hands over Nikkie Jean's torso, looking for injuries. Nikkie Jean thought. All she could feel was the pain in her head. "You're bleeding, Nik."

"Hit my head." It hurt. It was going to explode. "Truck didn't hit, though…"

"I've already radioed Vincent. He'll get help. That truck came right at you. If you hadn't jumped when you did, you'd be a pancake," Tony said.

"Not something I really want to think about." She stayed where she was, shivering and fighting shock until people came running. Every bone in her body hurt now.

Virat was there first. He knelt down next to Fin. Someone's hands were at her knees, touching the rapid swelling of her left.

Nikkie Jean bit back a whimper as they all circled around her. As they closed in.

"What happened?" someone asked from behind him.

It sounded just like Caine, but she knew better. Caine wouldn't be there. Not for her, anyway. But Rafe would. Rafe would be there.

The panic threatening to clobber her receded. A little.

Jillian's husband had a way of making things just work out the way they were supposed to.

"Someone almost hit us," Fin said. "Nikkie Jean pushed me…"

Izzie was there. Peering at her like she was a bug. Izzie's hand went around hers. Some of the panic receded a bit more.

"I hit my head, Iz. And hurt my left side."

"We'll get you inside. Get you x-rayed and fixed up." Izzie leaned over her and held up some fingers. "How many?"

"Four."

"Yep. I'm not a doctor, but I think your melon got rung. You'll have to ask one of the three stooges here for certain. To x-ray?"

"No. Can't…might…" Izzie's face swam in front of her face. Nikkie Jean wrapped her fingers around Izzie's pocket and pulled her closer. There was something she had to say. To figure out. And an x-ray would be dangerous because of… "*Baby*, Izzie. No x-ray. Might be…a baby. Preg—"

"Are you saying…*Ok*."

She tried to nod. That was a stupid choice. No more nodding. She could barely talk but she forced out the words. "Yes. Keep it quiet. Blood test. Just to make sure. Only been two months since my last…twelve percent…twelve percent really isn't much."

Her head hurt. She listened to the explanations but didn't speak. Someone said her name. It sounded like Caine again. Saying her name, insisting she look at him.

Her eyes opened; she looked at Rafe as he slipped his hands beneath her back and helped Allen and Virat lift her onto a gurney that had just magically appeared.

Dark eyes looked at her from a too-familiar face.

"You just look too much like…*him*, Rafe. Too much like Caine for my sanity." Nikkie Jean looked up at him again. His eyes were just like his brother's.

And that hurt, too.

But she had never confused them. Never would.

He was Rafe, not Caine. Rafe would make everything ok. Because Jillian would make him do that.

"Do you want me to call Caine for you?" he whispered the question in her ear. "Get him here?"

"No! I don't. He doesn't want *me* at all…I'm not good enough for him, either…"

"Then he's dumber than I thought, baby. You're too good for the likes of *him*. And don't you forget it." Rafe's hand was warm and strong on hers. Comforting. Nikkie Jean tried to remember why. It had to be because of Jillian. "Just close your eyes, kid. We'll get you taken care of right now. Don't you worry about a thing."

"Isn't there a song like that…?" Nikkie Jean tried to remember as they rolled her across the parking lot, her hand wrapped in Caine's brother's the entire way.

Chapter 28 ·

IZZIE NEEDED A PHYSICIAN to sign off on the blood test. And that meant finding one circling the intake desk. The *right* one.

Lacy, bag in hand, took one look at her. "What do you need, Iz?"

She hesitated. She didn't want to blow Nikkie Jean's secret, or gossip about her friend. Lacy was completely discreet, but the only man Nikkie Jean had mentioned meeting at all had been Rafael Holden-Deane's brother. Two and two did add up to four. Or rather…one and one suddenly made three. Especially considering the timing.

"I need you to sign off on a quantitative hCG for a patient for me."

"Ok. Why me and not the attending?"

"Because the attending is now Dr. Holden-Deane and…the patient is Nikkie Jean."

"What?" Lacy took the chart and looked at it quickly. "Possible impact injuries? We were in surgery together forty minutes ago and she was fine. What happened?"

"Someone almost hit her and Fin in the parking lot. And she's concerned about X-rays." Izzie started to whisper why, but Lacy held up a hand.

There was a look in her eyes that told Izzie Lacy already knew *why*.

"Done. I'll head over there and check on her myself. Shoo any of the guys away. Nikkie Jean…won't like all those guys standing over her."

"It'll cause more trauma than she needs," Izzie said quietly. Lacy just nodded.

Nikkie Jean's hurt was a sharp one. Her friend was far

stronger than anyone Izzie had ever met. Maybe that was one reason Izzie felt so protective of the older woman. "She say anything to you about meeting a man lately?"

Lacy shook her head. "No. Not that I can think of."

She'd been hoping Lacy would confirm what Izzie suspected. But if Nikkie Jean hadn't told Lacy about Holden-Deane's brother, Izzie wasn't going to ask. "I'm going to go do the blood draw."

"Let's go."

Nikkie Jean was barely awake when they made it in. Allen Jacobson glanced at Lacy, that weird expression she'd noticed he'd get whenever Lacy or Jillian or their friend Ariella were around on his face.

The guy was seriously messed up after what had happened recently. Everyone knew it. Izzie had trouble not feeling for him; he'd been good friends with Logan Lanning before that man had gone off the deep end and almost killed Lacy.

It was hard not to feel awkward around Dr. Jacobson, though.

"Out, boys," Lacy said to Dr. Jacobson and Dr. Holden-Deane. "We're taking over from here. Go see someone else. It's girl time in here now."

"Yes, ma'am," Dr. Holden-Deane said, after sending Lacy a significant look Izzie wouldn't even hope to understand. "I'm sure you have everything in control. I have a phone call to make."

Nikkie Jean opened her eyes for a moment. "Don't call *him*."

"I won't. Unless you tell me to."

"Thanks. I'm good. I have Lacy and Jillian and Annie and Izzie and Fin and Ari and Bailey. People who have my back. *He* doesn't need to know anything. I am not his problem. Ever. Just going to stay far, far away from him."

Izzie got the feeling Nikkie Jean didn't have a clue what she was saying—or revealing—to those listening.

Dr. Jacobson moved to the left side of the bed. Nikkie Jean was facing away from him. He put his hand on her shoulder.

Nikkie Jean let out a loud, keening cry the instant his hand landed on her that had chills raising on Izzie's neck.

Everyone froze.

Lacy jumped into action, immediately moving between Rafe and the bed.

"Nikkie Jean, look at me. You look right at me." Lacy said, firmly. Nikkie Jean did. Her eyes focused on the other woman instantly. She mouthed Lacy's name and pulled in a shuddering breath. "You are safe. Safe. I'm going to take care of you. Just me, Izzie, Annie, and Jillian. No men. Not even in the room. Rafe will make them all stay out."

Nikkie Jean nodded. "Rafe can do that. I'm...I'm good, Lace. I promise. I'm *not* going to fall apart now. I'm safe here. I *know* that."

Izzie bumped her way between Dr. Jacobson and Nikkie Jean. "Ok, boys, you heard Lacy. Out."

She waited until the men were out of the room, just holding Nikkie Jean's hand. Izzie just talked to her softly while Lacy did the examination. Until Nikkie Jean's breathing leveled out and she stopped shaking.

Then in a small, flat tone she told them exactly what tests they needed to order.

And why.

Lacy's eyes met Izzie's over Nikkie Jean's gurney. Why had Nikkie Jean never told them the extent of what she'd gone through?

Nikkie Jean was good at keeping secrets, thinking she had to deal with everything by herself. Izzie knew what that was like. Izzie squeezed Nikkie Jean's hand.

Nikkie Jean was so afraid.

Izzie took the blood test to the lab herself.

And called in a favor to get the results back as fast as possible. Then she waited for those results, making it clear to the tech that it had to be kept confidential.

She looked at the results herself. She hurried back, knowing her friend was waiting, terrified.

And Izzie had the answer.

.

Chapter 29

ANNIE AND JILLIAN showed up together. Lacy had never left. They all waited for Izzie to return. The acetaminophen Lacy had ordered had started to work. A little. She was going to be really sore for a while, but she'd refused anything stronger than acetaminophen.

Just in case.

Her friends had just circled the wagons around her. Something was about to go down.

She forced herself to sit up in the bed, regardless of the pain in her head. Lacy had said mild concussion and contusions. She'd survive.

She was going to face this head-on. No matter what. She looked at Izzie. "Either I'm pregnant, or the cancer is back. Which is it?"

Izzie handed the single sheet of paper to Lacy, who read it quickly.

"HCG is through the roof; I'd say it is definitely a positive indicator of a pregnancy," Lacy said. "But with your history, we're keeping you for a while. I'm ordering a full workup, including ultrasound, just to be sure. And rule out every possibility."

Nikkie Jean nodded. She'd had two major fears since she'd been sixteen. Another assault, and another battle with ovarian cancer. She even contemplated having her remaining ovary and tube removed as a preventative measure, even though that wasn't a guarantee. She just hadn't done it yet.

Either way, what those tests would reveal would change her life completely.

Izzie wrapped a hand around hers. "Hey, no matter what, you're not doing this alone."

Nikkie Jean got her thoughts around herself enough to be able to look at the two women who'd stayed with her. Lacy and Jillian were calling for the tests Lacy wanted to run. It would take some time.

But her best friends; the closest friends she'd ever had, had *stayed* with her. So she wouldn't be there alone, no matter what she found out.

No one had stayed with her before. Not even her own mother.

Izzie and Annie knew some of the story of what had happened to her. The sexual assault that had ended with her needing surgery. She'd revealed it in group therapy sessions she helped lead for those whose traumas were newer than her own. But she hadn't told them the extent of why of the surgery.

She did, now. By the time she was done, both were in tears. For her. If she'd had them back then, *they* would have been completely on her side. That mattered. "Thanks. I...should have told you."

"No. It's yours, not ours. We're just here to support you," Annie said. "We're here to listen if you want to tell us, though."

"I...after I was attacked, I was bleeding. My mother...the housekeeper took me to the hospital. *Not* the one where my father and the man who attacked me worked. I...freaked. I didn't want any doctor near me at all. Especially the men. I equated the rape with the fact that my attacker was my father's partner in his practice. So I fought. They had to put me under. I needed exploratory surgery to find out why the damage was as bad as it was. That was when they happened to find them. I had two small tumors on one ovary. Cancerous. Dysgerminoma. Teetering between stage one and two. Laparotomy revealed it was in one ovary and had spread into the fallopian tube on the left side. I had six months of chemo and a unilateral salpingo-oophorectomy. I still have my right ovary and tube, but the chances of a pregnancy were so slim, especially after the chemo. The rate of recurrence on the cancer was about the same. I told *him* that after the condom broke."

"Who?" Izzie asked.

"None of our business, unless you want to tell us," Annie added, shooting a firm look at Izzie.

Nikkie Jean shook her head a little. "That's over. It never really *was* to begin with. Just a major mistake."

"Then he's a jerk and this kid doesn't need him."

Izzie, always Izzie, willing to fight to protect.

Nikkie Jean had never had anyone bother to protect *her* before. Just Izzie.

"The baby will have *us*. We've got your back, Nik. Remember that. No matter what," Annie added softly. Izzie and Lacy seconded that.

Izzie to protect, Annie to support. The closest friends she'd ever had.

Jillian returned, with Courtney, a supervisor from radiology. Courtney would do the actual ultrasound. The other tests would take a few days to make it back.

Lacy had already told her she wasn't going anywhere until everything was tested and back. Just in case.

Lacy was being thorough.

"I'm here to give you a lift downstairs. You ready?" Courtney asked.

Nikkie Jean looked at the friends surrounding her. This was so different from the last time she'd had procedures this terrifying done. Back then, she'd just had her mother, who'd been impatient and inconsistent, although she'd tried to be there for Nikkie Jean.

At least half the time.

Her brother had shown up sometime when she'd been under sedation, having flown in from Johns Hopkins where he'd been studying.

Her brother had punched her father in the middle of the hospital waiting room, after the older man had finally bothered to show up one afternoon. Six days after her surgery.

Her father had invited Jim to their house for the party that night, knowing the man had been having alcohol problems. Her brother had blamed her father for exposing her to Jim in the first place.

It had been the only time her brother had ever done anything to defend her in any way that she could remember. And she hadn't even been there to see it.

Her father hadn't said two words to her for six days after his best friend had assaulted her. After she'd learned she had ovarian cancer. He'd barely looked at her the two times he'd visited that first week.

He'd blamed her, for everything that had happened to Jim after the housekeeper had found him hurting her. He'd never said it, but Nikkie Jean had figured it out over time. He'd been trying to help Jim, a friend of his for more than twenty years. Nikkie Jean had gotten in the way of that.

She'd stopped trying to get her father's love after that day.

It wasn't like that now. Annie was holding her hand. Izzie was getting the wheelchair ready. Jillian was getting her a blanket from a cabinet so she wouldn't be cold. Or overly exposed to the eyes of the people she worked with.

Lacy stood at the door, like a commanding general, ready to stop anyone from entering who didn't belong.

These were her people now. *Her* tribe.

Her family.

Nikkie Jean battled back the tears.

No doubt they'd go every step of the way with her. She had a family now. She mattered to them, too.

The tears slipped free. She'd have to take her contacts out before they floated away.

Those tears flowed unchecked just fifteen minutes later, when she saw what was on the screen.

Nikkie Jean almost didn't believe what she was seeing.

It was real.

Twelve percent had just morphed into one hundred.

And she would be seeing Caine Alvaro again very, very soon.

And now they really did have something to talk about. Something that was going to change the whole world for the both of them.

Chapter 30

CAINE STARED AT THE man he considered one of his few close friends. "So, can you do it?"

"The question isn't whether I can do it. It's whether I can do it on your time frame." Thor Laughlin had emerged over the last eight years since they'd first served together as one of the best medical fraud investigators in the nation.

He just kept that reputation to himself. Only a select few knew that the lanky man nearly as tall as Caine was even a doctor let alone an investigator with the FBI located out of Austin. It had been a position he had fallen into after his younger brother, a physician in Amarillo, had been falsely accused of Medicare fraud by a former senior partner.

Thor had been instrumental in getting Tennyson's name cleared. He'd come across some investigators with the OIG and FBI agencies who'd liked how he'd handled himself.

Medical fraud investigations suited Thor like a second skin. He'd eventually pulled Ten in that direction, as well.

If anyone could figure out the discrepancies in the billing at Barratt County, it would be Thor and Ten Laughton.

"I need it soon. We've had buyers interested in the hospital. But something isn't adding up to me. I want a second opinion before I go making accusations. A man of Ralstone's reputation—there's not a single cloud on his record. He transferred to Finley Creek to work with Allen Jacobson."

"I can't say I blame him. Jacobson's reputation is expanding."

"So you can't go making accusations yet," Ten said quietly.

Ten Laughton was always quiet. Caine was used to it.

"There's something else. I can't make accusations against a Finley Creek physician without damned good reason." Caine pulled out his phone and googled a name quickly.

"Why is that?"

Caine handed over his phone. "Because *that's* the COM of Finley Creek now. If he's known about this and done nothing about it, it won't look good originating with me. And that is a powder keg of problems I'm not ready to open up just yet."

"I owe you one, Alvaro. Otherwise, I'd have to say no right now. But I can't do that to you. A man's brother—that's a relationship you just don't want to screw with."

"Thanks. I was hoping you'd say that." And Caine would turn over the entirety of the audit and anything related to it over to someone who actually knew what he was doing.

He had an entire hospital to run, after all.

Billing was just a small part of it.

Caine felt...itchy. Like he needed to call FCGH and talk to the man himself. Because something major was about to go down.

That was a move he just wasn't ready to make.

Chapter 31

SHE WAS MUCH MORE alert the next day, thanks to an actual full night's sleep. She hadn't slept well the previous two weeks, worried. She should have just gone to Lacy and had the tests requested a week ago. She hadn't had to go through the anxiety this last week.

Fear could be a darned irrational motivator.

Fear robbed you of the future.

She so had to remember that.

Last night's antiemetic in her IV had also made her drowsy. Nikkie Jean had slept *good* last night.

She was halfway back to being Nikkie Jean again. Although she was a very sore Nikkie Jean at the moment, and would be for a while.

She looked at Fin when she led Vincent, the head of security, into her hospital room the next afternoon. "What's going on?"

There was a man dressed in a TSP uniform next to Vincent who looked enough like him to be his son. "I just had a few questions for you, Dr. Netorre. We're trying to figure out who almost hit you."

"Of course." Talking with the police always brought back the memories of that day when she'd been sixteen and first in the hospital.

Not every officer had believed her about the assault, questioning what she'd done to *provoke* Jim's attack. She'd been sixteen and ill—she'd not done a damned thing to provoke the man.

But her father had done one good thing for her back then— he'd turned over security footage of their house. Of the party. Of a drunken Jim making his way in the office where it had happened. Teenage Nikkie Jean had walked into the room perfectly fine five minutes later, alone—but had to be wheeled out on a stretcher ninety minutes later.

Thirty minutes. That's how long it had taken to change her life completely. But she'd not had real help for almost an hour after. Because her mother and the housekeeper had been arguing. The housekeeper had called the ambulance fifteen minutes after finding her. It had taken another forty-five minutes for them to wheel her out of her home. This guy looked rough and terrifying. It was hard for her not to want to shrink away as memories came pouring back in.

"Has anyone had any problems with you in the past month?" the detective asked.

"No. But two months ago I had someone call me. Threatening phone calls. For a few days. But that stopped."

"Nik? What happened?" Fin asked, climbing on the bed near her feet. She wrapped her hand around Nikkie Jean's. "Who was it?"

"Dr. Henedy and Cage lost a patient. Ten years old. I had already spoken with DCS about the foster father. He was angry and started harassing me. Mel had Jarrod Foster—he's a detective—speak with him, and he stopped bothering me. I haven't had any problems since. But...I think he did slash my tires that night. I had two flat tires. I'm surprised I made it to Value as bad as they were." She gave the date. It was a date she would never forget.

That was the night she'd made the baby with Caine.

"We'll need his name," Detective Acardi said.

"I'll have to get the name from the records. I can't remember right now." She'd had so many other things on her mind since then.

"I'll do that," Fin said.

"What about the guy stalking you?" Nikkie Jean asked quietly. Someone had been leaving love letters on Fin's car for over a month now. "Could it have been him?"

"We haven't ruled anyone out," the detective said. "I'm being thorough. What about any recent breakups, love interests?"

"I doubt anyone I've been involved with would do this. And since the last relationship I had was in Pennsylvania and over four years ago and he's married now, that's highly unlikely." Present nonrelationship didn't count.

Caine wouldn't have run her down. And besides, he was distinctive. The driver of the truck was a lot smaller than Caine Alvaro. And Fin would have recognized Caine—and thought he was Rafe.

"We'll be following up on these leads. If you think of anything, let me know. In the meantime…" He proceeded to give her and Fin the standard do-and-don't spiel of protecting oneself from stalkers. The same speech Nikkie Jean had given at W4HAV a dozen times now.

While stalking was illegal, there wasn't a whole lot of recourse available yet.

After the detective and Vincent left, Fin stayed for a while. It hadn't taken Nikkie Jean long to figure out that her friends had come up with a schedule. Fin and Jillian and Lacy and Cherise had all basically ensured that no matter what, someone—a woman— was in her room with her the entire time.

The love and belonging she finally felt had her ready to weep. It was nice to finally have a place to belong.

Chapter 32

DR. HENEDY WAS AT the intake desk when Caine finally made it out of the board meeting. He was the only one around, other than the charge nurse who was busy at the desk. Caine bit back the urge to snarl.

Wallace Henedy was one of the worst surgeons in the department, but he'd never done anything that required discipline. His name topped Caine's list for the Laughtons. There was just something oily about the older man. "Wallace, still here?"

Henedy smiled. "I just stopped by to grab a few files. I'm still officially on vacation. I hit FCGH first."

Caine tried to keep his expression cool. The board meeting had included mention of the same medical group that was considering buying FCGH purchasing Barratt County. It had not been a pleasant meeting. Consolidating hospitals could mean eliminating positions. By up to ten percent. It was not a move he was ready to make just to increase profits.

Not yet. His staff was depending on him. Caine didn't take that lightly.

"Oh?"

"Just to check in, catch up on local gossip. You hear about our drama while I was gone this week? With the assistant COM and our little pediatric surgical resident? Almost lost them both, from the way I heard. Shame, too, what happened."

Caine glanced at the man. Henedy wasn't focused on him, but the files in his hand. "Are you referring to Dr. Netorre?"

"Yes, that's the one. Little Nikkie Jean. Sweet kid."

"No. I haven't heard. She's actually a neighbor of mine. What happened?" Ice coated the back of his neck.

"Someone almost hit them in the parking garage a few days

ago. I swear that structure is cursed, as much trouble as they've had there in the last few months. Still, girls got lucky. Dr. Netorre took the worst hit. They're discharging her today, I believe. Other girl walked away with bruises. Shame. Those girls, neither one of them is bigger than a minute. They could have been seriously injured."

"How badly was Nikkie Jean hurt?" Every instinct he had was telling him to grab his keys and just go. Find the answer to that question for himself. See her, touch her. Make certain she was ok.

The last sight he had of April flashed into his mind.

Bruised, bloody. He'd known from the moment he'd been called to the ER and realized it was her under all that blood that she was never going home to the children again.

And she'd been thirty-three weeks pregnant.

Dalton had had a slight concussion before he'd even been born. His toddler still had the scar from where he'd almost been crushed along with his mother.

No matter what acrimony had been happening between him and April at the time, he never would have wished her suffering on anyone.

He'd held her hand as she'd died. She'd opened her eyes and told him she had loved him at first. And that she did love their children. And always would.

And she'd told him the baby was his and begged him to love the baby like he did the twins.

April had known she was dying, too.

She and her lover had been crossing a busy intersection in Austin and a teenager high on something had run the light, striking the man April had been with first, killing him instantly.

April had lingered for twelve and a half hours.

Dalton had been born two minutes after April had coded for the final time.

Caine forced air into his lungs. It wasn't like that.

Henedy had said she was being discharged.

"Mild concussion. Bumps and bruises, I believe. I'm not entirely certain why they kept her. I peeked in and said hello to her; she seemed alert enough. They've kept everything hush-hush, for some reason. Heard it was mostly a treat-and-street. But since it happened on hospital grounds, maybe that's why. Holden-Deane signed off on it, and they're giving her the VIP treatment from what

I saw. Of course, the girl's pretty well liked over there. Heard Allen Jacobson has been keeping a close eye on her. Guess the wind's blowing that way now."

"I see."

"Yes, Jacobson's got quite the reputation as a player over there. Of course, there's also talk he was involved in all that drama that happened when Holden-Deane and his sister were almost killed in that fire. Jacobson was there, of course. Carried Ariella—that's Holden-Deane's younger sister, the one marrying the governor—right out of the burning building. Pretty girl, that one, too."

Henedy kept rambling. As if he hadn't put it together that any sister of Rafael Holden-Deane was Caine's sister, as well. None of that mattered to Caine.

All he could see in his head was Nikkie Jean.

Hurting. Covered in blood; just like April had been.

Once again, he'd heard too late to do a damned thing about it.

"Dr. Alvaro? Can you step in here, please?" Bryan Mostain asked, motioning to the entrance to the largest conference room. "We have some new information to discuss."

No, he damned well didn't want to.

But Caine didn't do what he wanted. He didn't have the right to worry about her any longer.

Chapter 33

NIKKIE JEAN WAS READY to get out of there. The door to room 403 came open after a sharp knock. Finally. It was time to get a move on—she had an alternate future to plan.

One that included a Mini-Alvaro of her very own. She refused to consider the possibility that something could go wrong. She just wouldn't.

She'd need to get a general contractor out to the house to make repairs and to paint, she'd need to buy a crib and basinet—did people still use basinets?—and she'd just have to get ready.

And figure out what she was going to tell Caine. That was a big one there.

"You with us, Nik?"

Nikkie Jean turned.

Her baby's aunt stood there. "Ready to go? I get to give you the discharge speech."

"What's the speech for unplanned but very welcomed pregnancies?" She looked at Jillian and almost spilled everything. Almost.

She needed to talk to Caine first. She was about to whammy him right upside the head. After she figured out what to say first.

She'd had thirty-six hours to process—she wasn't counting when her head had been hurting too badly to think.

Tomorrow would be soon enough to face the tiger dragon that was Caine Alvaro.

He was going to be furious. She had no doubt about that. And he was going to be a big problem.

He was also going to be a good father. She couldn't forget that.

If he even wanted anything to do with this baby.

He already had three children, as he'd pointed out that night.

There was nothing that said he would want another one. Men did that all the time.

She was the little secret he no doubt didn't want to share.

Even if he didn't want the baby—she did. Nothing was ever going to hurt her baby. She wanted the baby. She would take care of the baby. What kind of a relationship he wanted with the baby was entirely up to him. She would never stand between them, but he would have to make some hard choices over the next eight months.

She was potentially about to change his life forever.

"Take your vitamins, get good prenatal care, and know that you are not doing this alone."

Nikkie Jean impulsively hugged her. She'd tell Jillian and Rafe about the baby—right after she told Caine. Even if Caine wanted nothing to do with this baby, Rafe probably would. He was a wonderful uncle already. She didn't see him and Jillian ostracizing her because of Caine. The exact opposite. Jillian would be her baby's aunt. Rafe, the uncle. That was the next best thing, right?

She'd just build the family she wanted for her baby the best she could.

Her baby would have a family. Some of that family like Rafe and no doubt Ariella would be biological. Others would be from friends who loved the baby, like Annie and Izzie and Lacy. Love. That was what mattered. "Thanks, Jillian."

"Anytime. We pregnant women need to stick together. And no more jalapenos. I'm…speaking from personal experience."

Izzie and Annie came in. Izzie had a stuffed bear in her arms. "We have your things. This came from the PICU nurses. They send healing thoughts and Herbert the Bear."

"Ah, I'll tell them thanks when I'm back on the clock." Right now she just wanted to go. Before she cried. The bear was a soft yellow and perfect for cuddling. The baby would love Herbert.

"Then your taxi is waiting." Annie grabbed Nikkie Jean's bag off the foot of the hospital bed. Annie was quietly good at just getting things done. "Izzie's car is outside, all ready for you."

"I parked in the loading zone and our favorite COM didn't even say a thing. Today is a day of miracles." Izzie shot Jillian a grin. "What did you do to him?"

"We practiced making the next kid before we came in today. It always makes him extremely good-natured—for him."

"Too much information. Way too much information," Nikkie Jean said as everyone laughed. "Ok, I'm ready. But did I ever mention how much I really hate using crutches?"

"Don't worry. Lacy has a chair waiting for you," Annie said. "We're serious about giving you that ride."

She refused the chair. "Honestly, I think I need to practice with these things for a few minutes on flat land. The last thing I need is a fall."

"Good point," Jillian said. "Do you need me to show you how to use them? I got really good when Rafe and I were dating—if you could call what happened between us dating."

"No kidding." She pulled in a deep breath. They'd provided *kid*-sized crutches for her. "I think I can do this. I fell before, during gymnastics practice. I'm sure it's like riding a bike."

She got the hang of it going up and down the hallway. "I'm ready. Let's go before Rafe has Izzie's car towed."

"He wouldn't do that," Jillian said. "He knows I'd punish him. He's terrified of me."

"Smart men are always terrified of even smarter women," Izzie said. "Still, Nik, are you ready?"

"I think so."

"Then away we go."

Nikkie Jean had just rounded a corner when she came face-to-face with the Caine clone. He had a group of men with him—and Fin—that were no doubt the latest potential buyers Fin had mentioned right before everything had went upside down for them. Nikkie Jean rarely paid attention to those kinds of discussions. There were always potential buyers in the wings.

Rarely did they take the bait. Who wanted to buy hospitals that constantly hemorrhaged money? Only crazy people with too much time and too much money on their hands.

Nikkie Jean barely gave them a glance—she wasn't quite as confident on the crutches as she'd let on.

"Nikkie Jean, I'm glad to see you're being released today," Rafe said. His eyes were filled with his concern as he paused and looked at her. "How are you feeling?"

"Like someone almost made a pancake out of me, but at least my brain is back where it belongs. I got a little cloudy headed there. Thanks for the rescue, by the way. Much appreciated." She'd been fighting panic until he'd shown up. He was a good captain. She'd probably never lead a true mutiny against him.

His very presence had made her feel safe. She hadn't forgotten that. He was probably one of the few men she could say that about.

His. Allen's. Possibly Virat's. And Rafe's brother's.

She *had* felt safe with Caine, anyway. Mostly.

"Anytime."

One of the men near Rafe stepped around him sharply. He stepped right into Nikkie Jean's path.

Nikkie Jean fought the instinctive urge to back away from the tall man with sandy-brown hair now laced with liberal amounts of gray.

Nikkie Jean looked into eyes the exact same shade and shape as her own. "Why aren't you in Pennsylvania?"

Where she'd left him. *This* was another one of her bad dreams.

Not today. Not today, of all days. Not when she was ready to put the past behind her and focus on her new future.

Rafe shot her a surprised look. "Dr. Carrington is considering buying the hospital."

"Dannica…" Her father breathed the syllables and stepped forward. "Is it really you?"

Nikkie Jean immediately stepped back, wobbling so much that Lacy put her back on her feet. *"Don't* call me that. That's not my name any longer. It hasn't been for a really long time."

"Nik?" Annie said, quietly. Her hand came to rest on Nikkie Jean's shoulder. Izzie shifted closer, too, the stuffed yellow bear in her arms.

"Dr. Netorre is one of our pediatric surgical residents," Rafe said, obviously trying to defuse the tension. "I take it you two are acquainted."

Nikkie Jean barely heard the words as memories of her childhood slammed into her. All the times he'd practically denied her in front of his colleagues. Or looked ashamed to have to claim her. Her mother had pointed them out to her each and every time.

She hadn't forgotten those moments at all.

Not today. Just…not today.

"She was injured in an accident a few days ago," Rafe said. He tried to motion Jordan aside. But Jordan wasn't budging.

He was just staring. Rudely.

Jordan Carrington had never been that *rude* in her entire

childhood that she could remember.

"I…" Her father started to say something.

"I need to go. Now." Nikkie Jean just couldn't handle this. Not right now. She wanted to run. Run as fast and as far as she possibly could. Which wouldn't be far enough, damn the crutches. "I can't handle this today. Not today."

That was all she had to say to have her valiant protectors springing into action.

Jillian stepped between them, physically blocking Nikkie Jean from seeing her father. "Dr. Carrington, why don't we head up to Rafe's office? I'll send someone for coffee. There's this little shop near the gift shop. They do lattes that are wonderful." She shot a questioning look at Nikkie Jean.

Her father was still staring. At Nikkie Jean. "I looked for you for thirteen years. I am so glad to see you're safe."

"Jordan…I'm not going to talk to you now. I just can't do it. Please respect that."

Her words broke. Her gaze shifted to the man next to her father. "Rafe, please…just…I can't. Not right now."

Rafe immediately took over. He motioned to Izzie to get the wheelchair parked nearby. "Take her home. She needs rest more than anything now. Dr. Carrington, now is not the right time for reunions."

Chapter 34

JORDAN STARED AT HER. He took in every inch of her, from the apple-green T-shirt to the blue jeans and white shoes. *"Dannica."*

She held up one small hand. She had always been so small. Dainty, but fiery. A fighter. That, and the hazel eyes, were the only things she'd gotten from him.

"My name is *not* Dannica."

"Dr. Carrington, how are you acquainted with Dr. Netorre?" Dr. Holden-Deane asked. Jordan just ignored him.

Nothing mattered now but the woman in front of him.

She wasn't a girl any longer. Logically he had known that she wouldn't be when he found her. But in his mind, she'd remained the young girl he had failed.

"Netorre. Your great-grandmother's name." Not his. Not even her mother's. But his wife's maternal grandmother's. Dannica had been *her* favorite. And she had loved his daughter in return.

He never thought to search under that name. Stupid. He should have.

"It's been thirteen years," she said, looking at the women next to her. Two shifted closer to her. The darker-haired girl put a hand on Dannica's shoulder. "I've changed my name twice since then."

"Twelve years, eleven months, and three days," Jordan said, harshly. The hazel eyes widened. She took a step back. *Away* from him.

Afraid. Of him.

No wonder.

He was one of the nightmares of her childhood, after all. And he'd allowed the other one in, too. Had invited him over. Let him right in.

"You always were detail-oriented," his daughter said. She'd

grown into a beautiful woman. But she didn't look well. Terror shot through him.

Just like it had fourteen years ago.

There were stitches in her forehead. Near her left eye. The old injury to her eye had healed, of course. Scarred. A visible reminder of what that bastard had done to her.

Jordan had never been able to look at that scar and not feel the guilt for failing his daughter.

Dr. Holden-Deane put a large hand on her shoulder. "Nikkie Jean?"

"Jordan was married to my mother, Rafe. We've not had…contact…since her funeral thirteen years ago. Even before that."

"I wasn't just married to her mother." He looked at the small crowd of people as they shifted subtly to align themselves with her. With the stitches, and pale cheeks, she looked far too vulnerable. She always had been small and vulnerable. She'd terrified him. "I'm her father."

"So the *birth certificate* said." Bitter fury coated her words now.

"So *I* say." Every day for thirteen years he had told himself he had a daughter. That he loved her; he would never stop loving her. And if he found her again, he would make it up to her. He almost blurted that out right there, but he refrained.

"That's right, the DNA test you had run when I was in the hospital at sixteen told you that, didn't it? I'd almost forgotten." She looked at the darker-haired girl on the left. "I've signed the discharge forms. Let's get out of here."

"Whenever you're ready, Nik."

He wanted to go with her. Or to touch her. To hold her, just for a moment. Like he hadn't since she was two and her mother had told him that she didn't think Nikkie Jean was his daughter, after all. Like he hadn't in the years since. He'd had chances when she'd been a girl. But every time he'd let himself *feel* for Nikkie Jean, his wife would take the girl and leave. For weeks. Months.

Anything to keep him from loving Nikkie Jean as he should.

And he had just let her go.

Carla had wanted to hurt him, and she'd managed with one painful stab right after another. To destroy his heart. For years. He'd adored his baby girl before that day.

But *he* had let that venom and bitterness keep him from his daughter. He'd made the choices. And because of that he had failed his baby girl when she had needed him most. Been too proud, too arrogant, to be the father she had needed.

She hadn't known she could come to him with anything. Had faced weeks of being ill because she'd felt she had no one to turn to. She hadn't trusted him to help her when she had been so sick she'd thought she was dying.

Because he had never let her see just that.

Jordan wanted to hold her. To hug her, just for a moment. Like he should have years ago. Like he never had. Hold her and promise that everything would be ok, that Jordan would make it that way.

Because he was her father, and that's what fathers did. They protected. They didn't cause the hurt, or let the hurt happen. They protected.

Instead, Jordan just watched her leave with the two taller nurses. He rubbed one hand against his heart.

He'd never thought he'd find her again. But there she was. He looked at the chief of medicine. "She's a physician?"

Dr. Holden-Deane hesitated. Jordan hadn't missed how protective the man had seemed of his daughter. "Pediatric surgical resident. She's brilliant. Best I've ever seen. Which is saying a lot. She's got a gift for medicine. She'll go far."

He nodded. She always had been extremely intelligent. But medicine? He'd never suspected she'd ever follow in his footsteps. Fatherly pride warred with the guilt. And concern.

"What happened to her? How did she get hurt? Her condition?" He wanted to know everything he possibly could. He needed to.

If he had had any doubts about buying Finley Creek General, they had dissipated in an instant.

His daughter was in Finley Creek. Living there, working there. Having a life.

Alive.

Jordan closed his eye as elation and relief and joy and love filled him in the instant it finally sank in that it was real. This wasn't yet another dream or false hope.

He'd found her. After thirteen years, he had found her.

Chapter 35

SHE WAS SHAKING SO badly she wanted to puke. Nikkie Jean followed Izzie to her little SUV. Annie was hovering. Just quietly hovering so that she wouldn't be so alone. Izzie was in front, running interference. Protecting. But Annie—quiet, calm Annie—was just walking next to her in support.

The love she felt for these two women who hadn't abandoned her threatened to bring her to her knees. "I love you. Both of you."

Before she knew it, they had their arms around her, too. Holding her up. In more ways than just physically.

Nikkie Jean was crying like she hadn't cried in a long, long time. Right there in the middle of the hospital parking lot.

Somehow, they got her into Izzie's SUV. Annie provided a bottle of water from her bag, and just kept telling her she was going to be all right.

And then they were on the road to Value, and she was telling them how her father had treated her the first sixteen years of her life. The total neglect. How he had ignored her. How he hadn't been there after she'd been raped by his best friend.

How he hadn't said two words to her that first week, and then how he'd only come to her room when people could see him do it.

Because appearances were all that mattered to Jordan Carrington. And that had always been the way it was.

Chapter 36

CAINE LEFT AN HOUR later, escaping the hospital board as quickly as he could. Probably more rudely than he should have. He'd called FCGH twice and asked to be connected to Nikkie Jean Netorre. He'd gotten a voice mail for the surgical department at FCGH. The second time, he'd gotten Dr. Ralstone, who'd offered to take a message once he'd learned the call was personal.

Dr. Ralstone, Caine's prime suspect in billing fraud.

The man worked closely with Nikkie Jean. That didn't sit well with Caine at all.

Caine knew federal regulations would prevent anyone from telling him her condition, so he didn't ask. But he knew where she lived. Caine knew exactly where he was going when he turned the truck onto McGareth Road instead of continuing to his own home. He needed to see her. Just to make sure she was ok. To see for himself that she was in one piece.

As if he had a right. As if someone should have known to call him.

Caine would have been there as soon as would have been humanly possible. If someone had just called him. Just how stupid that sounded wasn't lost on him. He'd been the one to tell her he didn't want the complications she brought. He felt those complications anyway.

Something wasn't adding up. They didn't keep someone for days for minor injuries. She had to be hurt more than Wallace Henedy had told him.

Something more than bumps and bruises had happened to her.

There was a reason they'd kept her for forty-eight hours—he wanted to know exactly what it was. A mild concussion didn't warrant forty-eight-hours observation. Even if it had happened on hospital property.

Visions of April dying kept slamming into him, morphing into Nikkie Jean.

He'd only been with her one damned night. He shouldn't feel like this over one night.

But he did. Caine was almost past the point of fighting it.

He ran over all the possibilities as he made the drive between the hospital and her little bungalow out in the middle of nowhere. She was too damned isolated out there. Anything could happen to her out there.

There was a car he didn't recognize parked next to hers. Caine pulled in behind it.

The front door was opening as he reached the porch. A dark-haired woman younger than Nikkie Jean and dressed in scrubs met him on the steps. "Can I help you?"

She eyed him with suspicion. Another woman with lighter hair and a sweetly pretty face came outside after her. "She's finally sleeping, Iz. She doesn't need any trouble."

The darker-haired woman nodded toward him. "We know you're not Dr. Holden-Deane, so you must be the brother. Can we help you?"

"I'm here to check on her, to see her for myself."

"I just bet you are. She doesn't want to see *you*."

"*Izzie.*"

Chapter 37

LIKE HIS BROTHER, this guy was far too hot for a sane woman's peace of mind. Izzie knew with one look that this was the father of Nikkie Jean's baby. Big, strong, built, intense—he really was like looking at a carbon copy of Rafe Holden-Deane, only he looked far wilder. Dangerous.

Sexier, if one went for the wilder Bohemian rebel pirate type. The guy even wore an earring in one ear.

No wonder Nikkie Jean had fallen for him.

Izzie wasn't stupid; she knew Nikkie Jean. Her friend wouldn't have just jumped into bed with this guy. There had to be some serious feelings there—even if Nikkie Jean hadn't admitted it to herself. "You heard Annie. She's sleeping. She took a pretty hard knock to the head."

"I heard."

"When?" If he cared that much, why had he not been there sooner? Izzie had a hard time trusting men like him. It was obvious this guy was used to wielding power.

It didn't matter. Izzie wasn't budging.

Nikkie Jean was pregnant, and no guy had shown up, until now. Two days in the hospital and no one but her, Annie, Fin, Jillian, and Lacy had been there.

Well, Dr. Jacobson and Dr. Patel and Dr. Ralstone had each shown up for a few minutes on their lunchbreaks, bearing flowers. Jacobson had brought chocolates Nikkie Jean had shared with her and Annie. And he'd sat with Nikkie Jean for a while after his shift had ended each day, too. Dr. Ralstone had brought Nikkie Jean a handheld video game system and pink Legos to play with.

Sometimes she thought his sense of humor was more warped than Nikkie Jean's.

After the doctors had clocked out for the day, Nikkie Jean had been alone.

"Wallace Henedy told me less than two hours ago. I couldn't get here until now. I need to see her." He started to go around her, and into the house.

Izzie wasn't going to have any of *that*.

"Well, you'll have to come back later." She crossed her arms over her chest and shifted to block the door—and Annie. "She's sleeping and we're not waking her up."

"Then I'll sit inside and wait. I'm not leaving until I see her. Just let me peek in on her. That's it. I need to see the damage for myself."

"You're not going inside. Not without permission. Look"—she waved a hand between herself and Annie—"trauma nurses. Her best friends. One of us has been at her side almost every second since it happened. Not going anywhere tonight. We'll take care of her. No worries. No strings. We've got her back. She doesn't need *you*."

He winced when she said no strings. Yep. Nikkie Jean might not have mentioned the guy's name, but Izzie figured it out really quick.

She'd seen users like him before, after all. He might wear Rafe's appearance, but he didn't have the same heart her boss did. That was for sure.

Annie was nicer than Izzie, though. "Dr…"

"Alvaro. Caine Alvaro. I'm in charge of Barratt County."

"Nikkie Jean's got a moderate concussion and contusions. Tissue damage to one leg. We're going to stay with her for a few days until she's able to go back to work. Just so she has company. And so we can keep her resting, instead of pushing herself harder than she should right now. She's going to be ok. Izzie's off for the next two days and can stay with her. I'm sure she'll appreciate you stopping by, but what she needs most is to just sleep. We all know that."

Izzie wasn't about to tell the man that the only thing Nikkie Jean had said about the father of her baby was that he wanted no strings and that she wouldn't be used by a man and then forgotten about. Izzie got the feeling Nikkie Jean thought exactly that had happened. That she hadn't been good enough for this guy. That she hadn't really mattered.

Jerk.

Nikkie Jean was not the kind of woman who entered into sexual relationships easily. She'd said so herself.

In fact, with Nikkie Jean's past, *any* involvement with a man was a big deal. Especially a doctor.

Izzie wondered if the jerk in front of her even realized that. He wasn't happy at not getting his way, but he'd have to get over it. She wasn't budging. Period. She stepped down on the center step and blocked the big guy's path with her body.

He was going to have to go through her.

Nikkie Jean needed people in her life who would stick it out for her. The extent of how much she had been hurt years ago still sickened Izzie when she thought about it. No one deserved to go through what Nikkie Jean had. The fact that Nikkie Jean had made it this far without shattering amazed her. And probably always would.

Nikkie Jean was one of the strongest women she had ever known. And she deserved a man who saw her for the special person she was. Not this jerk who just used her for a good time and then abandoned her.

"Get lost. Nikkie Jean doesn't need *you*. At all."

She waited for the inevitable explosion. If she'd said something like that to his twin, Rafe would have erupted like a volcano.

But this brother was apparently different. He bit back whatever he started to say and stepped off the porch, going backward. The glare he shot her could melt her down to her shoes—and not in a good way. When he was halfway down the sidewalk, he turned and looked right at her. He lifted a hand to his brow for just a second.

A shaking hand. "I just…fifteen seconds. Then I'm gone. I'm not going to beg. But I need to see her."

"She's just peachy, big guy. Just go back to where you came from. You're the last thing Nikkie Jean needs right now, and we all know it. She deserves a man who she can count on, who can be there for her, thick and thin. She's going to be just fine from now on. We'll see she stays that way." But Izzie's tone had softened, and she knew it.

He looked just like Rafe had the times Jillian had been injured. Just like him.

Izzie looked at Annie. Annie nodded.

They were invading Nikkie Jean's privacy, but... "Tell you what. I'll take a picture of her sleeping. I'll text it to you. Nikkie Jean...she won't want someone in her house. Not without permission. It's a really, really big deal for her."

He pulled in a breath and nodded. He was a smart man. He knew that was all he was going to get. Izzie ran inside and took a photo of Nikkie Jean's face and went back out.

It was a matter of seconds to text the image to his phone. They'd gotten lucky. It had appeased the beast. After he stalked off, she looked at Annie. "Wow. I think he's even more intense than Holden-Deane."

Annie nodded, then let out a breath. "I thought he was going to just keep coming. Swallow you whole. Just to get to her. I hope that photo will satisfy him until she's ready."

"Me, too." And they wouldn't have been able to stop him without a massive amount of drama. Izzie would have done it, though, if it meant protecting Nikkie Jean.

She might not appear as vulnerable as someone like Annie, whose shyness made everyone want to protect her, but Nikkie Jean...Nikkie Jean hid the hurt behind the humor so well that most people never saw it.

It was Nikkie Jean's way of hiding in plain sight.

No more. Izzie was going to do what she could to let her friend know that she wasn't alone any longer.

"He hurt her." Annie had that look in her eyes again. She might be shy and timid and easily intimidated, but there was a core of strength and stubbornness in Annie that only showed up when she thought someone was being mistreated. Or hurting. "I think he's the one."

Just like Nikkie Jean.

Izzie hooked elbows with the best friend she'd had since childhood. They headed back inside toward the new friend hurting inside. "Don't worry, Annie. We got this. He won't hurt her again."

"I don't know. If he's the father, I think her trouble with him may just be beginning."

Chapter 38

SHE FELT BETTER the next morning, but nowhere near where she wanted to be. Mostly because she hadn't even made it through breakfast before breakfast was making its way back up.

But this time, Izzie was there to help her back to her feet.

And Annie was handing her a toothbrush. Nikkie Jean wanted to cry. And then she wanted to sleep for a week.

Hormones. Hormones were the answer to why she'd felt so cruddy for the last two weeks.

And then she immediately felt guilty for feeling glad that her life was going to change—because it meant Caine's was, too.

Roller coasters were playing in her mind. Constantly.

The concussion no doubt wasn't helping. Nor was the man she'd seen yesterday that she'd honestly thought she'd never see again. She was so not ready to deal with the emotional maelstrom Jordan Carrington would bring into her life.

She'd almost gotten herself convinced she'd forgotten about him.

Nausea filled her.

It was going to be a long—she did the math in her head—thirty more weeks. Hopefully, the nausea would settle soon. She had about a month to go until she hit the end of the first trimester. By then, maybe the nausea would be more manageable.

She did not want to go on antiemetics again. She'd had enough of those when she'd had chemotherapy.

"You are currently making me glad I'm on birth control. And haven't had sex in eighty years," Izzie said, bluntly. "I can call Lacy or Layla. Have one of them call in something."

"I don't want to do that yet." Layla Kaur, head of obstetrics, had come to Nikkie Jean's hospital room at Rafe's request, and they'd had a chat about Nikkie Jean's concerns.

Layla understood her hesitation with prescription drugs at this point. The more natural her pregnancy, the better Nikkie Jean would feel. Maybe she was being overly cautious—she knew the risks, after all—but Nikkie Jean was scared. And she'd freely admit that to the ones who were with her now.

"So...what's on the agenda today?" she asked. "I'm not just sitting here. I need to do...something. Anything."

If she just sat there doing nothing—even with the headache of doom—she would go crazy, thinking of everything that could possibly go wrong with a pregnancy under the same conditions.

Annie hesitated. "Dr. Alvaro came by yesterday around seven. You were already asleep, and we weren't going to wake you. We didn't think you needed the added strain of dealing with him after...what happened at the hospital."

"Thanks. I didn't. I need time to think." Exactly what she wasn't quite ready to do yet. "I *really* need to think about what I'm going to do about him right now."

"He's the father, isn't he?" Izzie asked.

"Yes. We..." Nikkie Jean led the way into the kitchen. She sank into her favorite chair. Her friends took the other two. She only had the three chairs. Just enough for them. Why hadn't she ever noticed that? "It just sort of happened."

"We didn't even know you were involved with him," Annie said from where she was making Nikkie Jean some scrambled eggs.

Annie had a tendency to mother people at times. Nikkie Jean was still getting used to that.

"I am not. Wasn't. Well, obviously I was involved with him for about thirty minutes. Two months ago, I prepped a boy for surgery with Dr. Ralstone. And he died on the table. I was...upset. And I ran into Caine. I didn't want to be alone. And he figured out that I'd lost a patient. He was just...there. I felt safe with him. Probably because of Rafe and Jillian. I'd met him before—outside of the hospital. I think that mattered. Made me associate him less with a hospital. Made him seem safer. One thing led to another that night, and I lured him to my room, where I—" Nikkie Jean stopped for a moment. No jokes. Not with her best friends. Total honesty. All the way. "We slept together. Then he decided he didn't want more than that. Fast. Pretty much before we were even finished."

"Bastard," Annie said, more hotly than Nikkie Jean had ever

heard her speak before.

"He thinks he has good reason. He has three other kids that he's raising alone. And they are beautiful. They look just like Ari, especially his daughter. And Rafe. I think that is why I trusted him so easily. Because of Rafe being one of the few men I do trust. I know myself well enough to see that. Caine says he isn't ready for a relationship right now. And we were careful."

"Maybe this kid is meant to be?" Izzie put her hands on Nikkie Jean's shoulders and looked at her. Nikkie Jean just looked back. Izzie's brown eyes were wet. She was such a softie, Izzie McNamara. "You said it yourself: the odds of you getting pregnant were super slim, anyway. Let alone odds of a condom breaking. We all three know that doesn't just happen all the time. What fraction of a percent of the population does that happen to, anyway? I don't know, but it happened to you. There had to be a reason for that. I think the kid is a miracle. Whether *he* sees that or not."

Nikkie Jean nodded. She'd had the same thoughts. "I feel exactly the same way."

"He was worried about you. For someone who doesn't want a relationship, he was really worried. He looked just like Rafe did every single time Jillian was brought into the ER hurt a few months ago," Annie said. "I think he cares about you. No matter what he said before. He didn't have to show up here last night. If you had been here alone, or there hadn't been *two* of us to stop him, he probably would have stormed right in and hovered over you all night. You'd have trouble getting rid of him. He was truly worried."

"Somehow, I don't think so. I don't know why he would have shown up here, though." Nikkie Jean pulled in a deep breath and made her decision. It wasn't fair for her to be here with people who knew about his baby—when he didn't. "I have to go tell him. Today. No matter what, he deserves to know about the baby. As soon as possible."

"What time does he leave the hospital?" Izzie asked.

"I think around five. I've passed him on the road a few times around then." For the last two months, she'd deliberately look away whenever their paths would cross on the highway. Somehow, he'd always ended up a few car lengths behind her for the seven miles from the highway to his turnoff three miles from her house.

"Then you spend the rest of the day resting and taking care of yourself and Baby. If you behave, we'll drive you over there. Be there if you need us."

It sounded like a plan. Besides, her head hurt. Dealing with Caine Alvaro was the last thing she wanted to do at the moment, thank you very much.

Chapter 39

CAINE STEPPED OUT of the hospital after one of the most useless and time-wasting board meetings he'd ever sat through, and there she was. Nikkie Jean was waiting on a concrete bench right outside the main entrance.

He'd almost missed her sitting there. Until she spoke. "Hey, Alvaro."

"Nikkie Jean…" His first thought was concern; she could have been there as a patient again. After a half-second's thought, he discarded that idea. She would have gone back to her own hospital with her little guard dogs driving her.

She was paler than he was used to seeing her, and from the way she moved, she was agitated. Frightened of something.

And still hurting. He studied her quickly, there were visible bruises and stitches. His hands itched to pull her close and just hold her. Make certain she was all right. Carry her to his truck, take her to his home, put her in his bed, and take care of her the way she deserved. Fix her with all the skills he possessed.

Like he hadn't been able to do with April.

He would have given anything to save his children's mother that day.

"We need to talk, Caine."

She wasn't as bubbly as he was used to her being. And she was shivering. In July. He could almost touch the nerves running through her.

There would be only two reasons she'd be here today. One, she had bad news about his brother or sister. Two, there was something else she had to tell him. Something that only she could tell him.

Caine took one look at her, did some counting backward.

"You're pregnant."

"Damn, you're good. Confirmed it with a quantitative hCG. And ultrasound. Lacy and Layla—my doctors wanted to be certain the cancer I had when I was sixteen hadn't returned and thrown off the tests. It's real. I'm pregnant. I never thought I could be, but I am. Guess the striped condom had magic powers. Or you're just super potent."

The next words damned him, and he knew it the minute they slipped out. "And you believe it's mine."

The hurt in her eyes was unmistakable. Instantaneous. A shutter fell over her eyes and she stiffened, pulled away from him without even moving. Closed herself off in a heartbeat. But there was no *surprise* in her eyes. As if she'd expected his doubt. "Since I've only slept with one man in the last four years, I'm pretty certain it's your baby. You know, broken stripey balloon? Remember that? But hey, you want to deny it ever happened, that's fine with me. I'll just tell everyone I used a donor. Of course, the kid will most likely look like Rafe, so people will assume…but…I'll just tell Jillian and Rafe all about that night—and what you want to do about it. I'm sure Rafe will volunteer to do the daddy-kid things the baby may need in the future."

"I didn't mean it like that. Not at all." He'd meant…hell, he'd just flashbacked to the moment April had told him Dalton was on the way—and most likely wasn't his.

He'd wanted more children for years. She'd known that and had used it as a weapon. Many times.

But Nikkie Jean was not April. He had to remember that.

"Here." She slapped a familiar-looking photo against his chest. He took it. And checked the estimated date of conception printed in the corner automatically. He ran his finger over the little black shadow that was a human life. His child. Nikkie Jean's child.

Their child.

"I didn't mean it like that. I thought you said you couldn't get pregnant." He'd spent six-plus months not knowing if Dalton was his. Only to have the baby born prematurely and needing him—whether he'd been Caine's child or not. That had left a lasting impression. Yet he knew instinctively that this baby was his. Nikkie Jean was not April. She wouldn't play a man like that. Not her. It wasn't in her DNA. "I need time to think. To decide what to do."

For the children. For himself. And for her.

"*You* need time to decide. I know what I'm going to do. You can visit on weekends if you want. Then when the baby is older, he or she can visit with you. You need to understand something. I don't need anything from you. And neither does this kid. I was told when I was sixteen that I'd never have children, Caine. That the surgery and ovarian cancer had destroyed that hope. Almost completely. My father made that as clear as glass. Until this week, I believed that wholeheartedly. I only have one ovary. And one fallopian tube. And they were only partially functioning when I was a teenager. Adjuvant chemo did a number on them after. I was told they wouldn't be functional past the age of twenty-five and I'd eventually need them removed. That doesn't matter now. What does is that this baby is going to grow up differently than I did. Loved. If you want to be a part of that, I won't stop you. I'm not going to force you to do anything you don't want to. This baby will be taken care of and loved: I promise you that. Period. And because I have a code of honor I live by, I figured you deserved to know as soon as I was out of the hospital. Consider yourself informed."

She'd obviously practiced this speech a few times. It didn't have the same free-flowing Nikkie Jean feel that her chatter usually did.

He doubted she realized that told him exactly how she was feeling. He was starting to understand how this woman was programmed. She spun and stalked across the parking lot as much as she was able on crutches.

She wasn't very good on crutches; she was going to end up hurting herself worse.

Like an idiot he just stood there and watched, rain pouring down over him and thunder rolling in. Instead of following. Instead of protecting her.

His baby was growing inside Nikkie Jean right now.

The mere idea threatened to send him to his knees from emotions he couldn't quite define yet.

Caine called her name, but she either didn't hear him or she was ignoring him. He suspected it was the latter.

He'd just screwed up by not saying the right thing to her. Again.

They had just changed everything—for everyone. He needed time to process. She'd had several days, at least.

He held the ultrasound photo close, protecting it from the rain blowing in under the portico. Experienced eyes studied the little black blob for a moment longer. It was a good-sized fetus. No surprise; considering how big Caine was himself.

Resolve filled him.

It was time the two of them had a serious talk about what had happened. And cleared the air of exactly what he'd wanted to say to her for the past two months.

She was going to listen to him for once.

Caine hurried across the parking lot. He'd follow her home. Make certain she got there safely. Then they'd go inside and talk. Figure out what they were supposed to do next.

He hadn't even asked her if she was ok. Healthy. If she'd been sick, or had any other issues from the pregnancy over the last two months. April had been horribly ill with the twins and had resented him the entire time. He didn't have a clue if she'd been sick with Dalton. Or how she'd felt about their youngest.

He wanted to know everything about Nikkie Jean and the baby now.

He knew one thing. The last thing he would ever do was let a child of his grow up out there thinking their father hadn't wanted them.

Caine knew exactly how that felt. And he would never do that to a child of his own. No matter what the circumstances of that child's conception.

Even if Dalton hadn't been his, Caine would have loved him just as much as he did now.

He still didn't know with one hundred percent certainty, although there was a high likelihood he was. April very well could have been lying when she'd been on her deathbed.

He pulled out of the parking lot and followed Nikkie Jean.

Chapter 40

CAINE HAD BEEN BEHIND them the entire way. Nikkie Jean knew it was him; the big jerk. She'd half convinced herself that things would be different. That he wouldn't turn out to be just like her father had.

Her entire childhood had been littered with her father's doubt. The arguments between her parents when she'd been too young to understand them had stuck in her mind.

Her father hadn't wanted her. He'd made that very clear, from the first time she'd heard him say it when she'd been four or five.

She'd always been unwanted.

What he'd said the day before didn't erase that. Make her believe he'd ever cared.

But it was the first time in her life her father had told *anyone* that Nikkie Jean was his daughter and not looked away when he said it. He'd been almost fierce about it.

Only when she'd been sixteen and her mother had ordered a DNA test done had he finally stopped throwing it up to her mother that she might not be *his*. After the results had proven her mother hadn't lied, that she was just as legitimate as her older brother Dathan, had her father even tried to have a relationship with her.

After it had been far too late.

Nikkie Jean should have known better about Caine. She'd seen that exact same doubt in her father's eyes every time he had looked at her.

Her baby would never go through that pain of rejection. Not for a moment.

Caine may not want anything to do with his biological family, but she was friends with them. She could take her child around whomever she wanted. Her baby would have a family. No matter what happened with the baby's father.

Izzie parked. They'd not said much on the drive, but they'd all known he was there. Following.

"Go home, Iz. Annie. I'm going to talk to him. We're going to work things out." She pulled in a breath after she said it.

It was the exact opposite of what she wanted. She did not want the big, terrifying dragon in her cave again.

"You don't want us to stay?" Annie asked when Izzie protested.

She'd just told her only real source of a safety net that they could leave her with the one man she feared the most. Well. Emotionally feared.

She didn't have a *physical* fear of Caine Alvaro, despite being the size of a mountain.

"No. I can handle Caine Alvaro on my own." He hadn't screamed or raged at her. Or glared at her with the type of stony silence her father had given her mother. There was that.

He hadn't been so angry he'd frightened her. Not at all.

Nikkie Jean didn't know what to think of that. If he'd shown anger or disdain, she would have known how to respond. Could have predicted what would happen.

She couldn't predict Caine.

That both thrilled her and terrified her to her hot-pink-striped painted toenails.

"We'll go. To Lacy's. If he threatens you or scares you, you call us. We'll come with Lacy and Travis and make him leave. Even if we have to bring Travis's ranch hands to help," Izzie said. "Remember: he has no right to touch you. None at all. Keep your phone in your pocket. Text us right away."

She stood in her yard after her friends pulled away, until he killed the engine and opened the door. Nikkie Jean started toward the steps of her front porch. She was up two of the five before he was even out of that truck of his.

She looked back.

He'd caught up to her; no surprise with her on crutches. He was so close she could almost touch him. Nikkie Jean stepped up another step.

And lurched forward as the wooden step buckled beneath her.

Chapter 41

CAINE GRABBED HER. One arm slipped around her waist, and he caught her. He pulled her against his chest and to safety.

The crutches fell to the ground. Her head narrowly missed hitting the wooden handrail. By an inch. He lifted her up into his arms, fighting the sudden rush of adrenaline. Fear. She felt so damned breakable in his arms. "You ok?"

She drew in a shaky breath. "Yeah. Thanks. The step broke. You can let me go now. I don't like men behind me like this."

She'd made that clear that night, too.

He turned her quickly.

Small hands crept up his shoulders. Like they had the last time he'd carried her. Seven weeks and two days ago.

He looked down. The gaping hole in the step was hard to miss. She was lucky it hadn't broken her leg long before. "Has it been weak?"

"Not that I've ever noticed."

He lifted her over the steps completely. "Use the side steps until this can be fixed."

"Aye-aye, captain." She eyed the step, her brow furrowed. "I don't even have the tools to do it. I'll ask someone at work if they'll loan me some. Rafe will know what I need; I'm sure of it."

His damned twin would not be doing *anything* for Nikkie Jean if Caine had anything to say about it. She was his responsibility now.

He'd be out there first thing in the morning to fix the step himself.

Her house was older, a bit shabby, but she had mentioned having someone making repairs before she could redecorate completely. He'd check it over himself in a few minutes. Make certain it was safe for a pregnant woman. "No lead paint here, right?"

"Not that I know of. Thanks for your concern, but I'll take care of making sure my house is safe for the kid, Caine."

"I'll do the same at mine. It's already babyproofed."

It was the first time he'd said anything about the baby aloud. He followed her into the house.

She flipped on the light, illuminating the small living room. The kitchen was visible behind it. It wasn't a large house; he suspected it had once belonged to a ranch hand or something, from its location and proximity to some of the other larger ranches in the county. He thought the W-Deane Ranch was somewhere nearby, too. It would be a nice little house once she finished remodeling.

It already felt like Nikkie Jean. Warm and welcoming and loving. He felt completely out of place now.

He hadn't before.

She'd decorated with brighter colors. Girl colors, Everett would call them.

And owls. There were owl knickknacks and figurines everywhere. "You like owls."

"They were gifts. From my friends. Jillian told me I looked like an owl once. The joke continues. I figured just go with it."

"Jillian."

"Your sister-in-law. Trauma nurse. She's pitching in our softball game Saturday. Rafe's concerned. She's pregnant, too, you know. A week more than I am. Our babies will be the same age. They'll grow up knowing each other. I intend for that to happen, so you'd better get used to it. I plan to make no secret with Jillian, Rafe, or Ariella about my baby. The baby will be their family, too." She shot him a challenging look. Caine ignored it.

"You're playing softball?" She could barely walk without the crutches. She had no business playing ball anytime soon.

"Short stop. I'm good, too."

"You should stop."

She sent him an arch look. One that told him he'd said the wrong thing. Again. "My team is depending on me, Alvaro. I don't let people down when they are counting on me. It's part of the whole honesty and commitment thing I got going on. I should be off the crutches by tomorrow. Jillian's playing."

"That's my idiot brother's fault for not stopping her." He glared down at her. "What if you get hit by the ball? Or fall when running bases? What if you have to slide into a base?"

"Jillian's wearing padding. I'll do the same. And no sliding or diving. Rules have already been given. It's a simple charity game. Slow-pitch. For W4HAV. And I'll have a designated runner. Bum knee after everything that's happened this week, ya know."

It still wasn't enough. Caine knew he was being irrational, but…she had a bruise over her eye. There was an abrasion running up her left arm. She looked like anything could blow her over at any moment. "Get a substitute."

"There isn't any. We're holding onto hope that Bailey doesn't get called in to the TSP. Or Lacy, Fin, or me to FCGH." She shot him a look as she slipped into the kitchen and started rummaging in a cabinet. "Did you really follow me home to talk about softball? To tell me what to do? Because I don't know if you missed the memo, but we've created a little Alvaro-Netorre here." She shot him another significant look—that told him she thought he was being deliberately obtuse.

"Netorre-*Alvaro*." The baby would have his last name. Caine was a traditionalist in that regard.

"Why follow tradition? We could go with Netorvaro and compromise? What's in a name will still smell as sweet, right?"

And she was using sarcasm to keep him away.

She was so afraid of him. He saw it every time she looked at him.

Her cell rang and she grabbed it.

He shamelessly eavesdropped as she spoke to the caller. A friend calling to check on her. After she disconnected, he faced her. "Do they know?"

"Yes, Jillian knows I'm pregnant. She and Izzie handled the blood draws. But they don't know about *you*. No one does. Except Izzie and Annie. They were the ones here with me last night. They headed up the road to Rafe's brother—his other brother, Travis— and his wife. They're waiting for me to tell them you behaved. Jillian's there. She wanted to know if the father of the baby was behaving. But I don't think she knew it was you exactly. She would have called you by name, then. Or that damned Alvaro. Annie and Izzie aren't big on gossiping. We can keep it that way if you prefer. There will be gossip, I'm sure. Especially if the baby resembles you. And…well…Rafe. Which the baby most likely will. I thought Jillian and I could really have some fun with that; if Jillian is willing. She might be. Jillian can be a bit wicked at times."

Some of the chatter was coming back. Caine almost smiled to hear it. Her friend's call had distracted her, relaxed her.

When Nikkie Jean felt safe, she chattered. It hadn't taken him long to figure that out. It was when she went quiet that she was the most afraid. That was when she was trying to do her best to be invisible. To not draw more hurt her way.

"I don't give a damn about gossip." And he didn't. Gossip didn't matter to him in the least. Truth did. And responsibility.

And like it or not, she'd just became his responsibility in every way that mattered. He'd been trying for weeks to apologize to her because he hadn't liked having things end the way they had. And because he hadn't been able to get the woman out of his head. But now? Now he had so much more he wanted to say to her. All of that would have to wait now. They had to deal with the baby first.

This woman mattered to him more than any other had since April. She had even before the baby; that had just tripled. As had his responsibility to her. Caine did not take that lightly. He brushed a hand over her shoulder, just needing to touch her for a moment. To see if she felt real beneath his hand. He had never expected Nikkie Jean.

She stiffened beneath his hand. The look in her eyes was nothing but wariness.

"Sure about that? You're the chief of medicine, Caine. And you screwed around with a woman you're not married to—a lowly resident, at that. We know how people can be around here. It doesn't bother me, but...your position is a bit different." She slipped away from him. "You have to be aware of how it will look at all times. If you want to continue in hospital admin, anyway. I know how important that is for a man like you."

Her words trailed off at the end.

He wanted to stalk her around the kitchen until he had her in one spot. Where he could see her eyes. She grabbed a pair of eyeglasses from the kitchen table and turned her back to him. "I need to take out my contacts. My eyes are burning."

"I'm not going anywhere." He'd already called Henry on his way over and explained an emergency had surfaced. He had hours to spend with this woman.

His greatest wish was that she'd let him hold her through those hours.

He'd spent the last twenty-three hours imagining how badly she'd been hurt. That had had him on edge even before her revelation.

She hobbled into a small half-bath beside the kitchen. When she returned, the glasses were purple-rimmed and twice as thick. She did look like a little cartoon owl when she blinked at him.

"How well can you see me now?" he asked softly.

"Not enough to drive with these, but I have near perfect with the contacts in. I just can't wear the contacts all day. Don't worry. It's only partially hereditary. The rest of it is because of... an old injury. What do you want to do about the baby? Terminating the pregnancy is *not* an option for me."

No. He hadn't even considered suggesting it.

This might very well be the only child Nikkie Jean could ever have. She wouldn't believe him if he said it, but that mattered to him, too. He would never deprive someone of being a parent for his own selfish reasons. "I have three other children I have to take care of. Their needs have to be put above my own. And they've had a few extremely not fair years. I...this will confuse them. It'll take time to get them transitioned to this change. I need to make sure they have that time. But I'm not leaving you to go through this alone, either."

She stared at him for a long time. "Would knowing this baby make things worse or better for them? I don't want to see them hurt by what *we* did. That's the last thing I want. I've been that kid, and I'll never do it to another."

"I don't know yet. Keller and Everett had a hard time with their mother. She struggled with being a parent. She was in the process of divorcing me for a man almost in his sixties. Leaving the children. And she was pregnant with Dalton at the time. But the twins—Everett especially—equated her leaving with Dalton's birth. It took them a while to bond with him and to understand that it wasn't Dalton's fault. I can't undo the progress they've all made together." And he didn't know how to keep that from happening with this baby. He'd only known about the baby for an hour. How was he supposed to have all the answers after only an hour? "You've known for days. Did your guard dogs know yesterday?"

"Izzie and Annie. Their names are Izzie and Annie. They're both ER nurses, but Izzie's also a student. She wants to be a nurse practitioner. It's taking her a while because money for her is really tight. They are the best friends I've ever had, Caine. In my entire life. They were with me when I had the ultrasounds. To make sure…I was afraid it was going to be cancer again. I was sure that's what it was. The two weeks before the hit-and-run…I was sure the cancer had come back. Or I had some sort of infection. Then in the hospital I was afraid that the pregnancy wouldn't be viable. I'd been warned before that could happen. If my eggs had been damaged by the chemo. I needed my friends, and they were *there*. They stayed with me until I knew. After. I had to chase them away." She smiled as she said it. Like she hadn't believed it was possible. "I've never had friends like them before. They stayed with me. With *me*. No one has ever stayed with me. Or for just me. They've already promised to help me however I need them. They're planning to come paint the room I'm going to use as a nursery. To help me."

"I'll be doing that." It was *his* place to be there. He'd be the one painting, and putting together the crib. Just like he had with Dalton, Everett, and Keller. He wanted to be the one to do it all—with her. For her. He wanted her to want that with him. Just how much he wanted to be a part of this woman's life was sinking in. Rapidly. "It's my baby, too."

"I'm not denying that. But…I'd rather we not get dependent on you. Not long term. It would be easier that way when things go south. You do what you want with your house. But this one is mine, and I…I think it's best if we draw the appropriate boundaries before the baby comes."

Nothing had hurt him more since the day April had told him the baby she carried probably wasn't his. He'd been building fantasies of more with Nikkie Jean, and she'd been thinking of ways to freeze him out. It shoved Caine ruthlessly back into his place. Fast. "Appropriate boundaries? For whom? You? This is *my* child, too. And I'm not just going to let you have him and not even try to be there when he needs me. Do you know what that would be like, my child being just three miles down the road? I spent six months away from Keller and Everett with the military. It was the hardest six months of my life, not knowing what was happening to them each and every day."

"Then what do you suggest?" She looked at him and paled, right before his eyes. She trembled and stepped back. Wobbled. Fear coated every inch of her. "You're not getting full custody. I'll fight tooth and nail—and it won't be pretty."

Horror and panic in hazel eyes stabbed right into him. She

shook her head and took another step back. Away from him, wobbling.

"Don't be afraid of me, Nikkie Jean." Caine's hands wrapped around her arms, and he pulled her closer in an instant before she fell. Seeing this woman afraid stabbed him straight in the gut. "I'm not going to take the baby from you. Ever. I wouldn't do that to you. But I will be a part of this child's life. I promise you that. We'll both do what we have to, in order to make this work. Around our careers, and across the three miles between us."

In that instant, Caine made his decision. By the time the baby came, there would be *no* miles between them.

Nikkie Jean would be with him—right where she belonged. He just had to figure out how to make it work.

She shook in his arms. He waited for her hands to go around his neck or his waist or something, waited for her to give him permission to hold her. He wanted to just hold her right now. He needed that connection, and he suspected she did, too.

But she didn't.

Nikkie Jean had drawn into herself. Away from *him*. Shut him out completely, to protect herself from more hurt.

He didn't know what to do—or even what had hurt her on so deep a level that she thought having friends to see how special she was inside was such a miracle that she couldn't fathom why they'd stayed with her in the hospital when she'd needed them most.

Chapter 42

CHERISE WAS THE ONE who brought the letter. Nikkie Jean heard the car coming down the road and hurried to look out the window. Some part of her had expected it to be Caine.

His parting words the night before had been that he would be back in the morning. Well, it was eight thirty and no sign of him.

Just the little two-door car that Cherise zipped around in everywhere like a madwoman.

Nikkie Jean pushed out a relieved breath.

She wasn't ready to deal with Caine Alvaro. Not yet.

Couldn't he just…leave her alone for the next seven months? They could work out the whole shared-parenting details closer to time to actually *be* parents.

Even as she thought it she was being unreasonable.

"Cheri, what are you doing here?"

"I brought you some food in microwavable containers. I know you tend to live on takeout. And I thought that would be tough right now. And…I brought you a letter."

"A letter?" The food sounded good—Cherise often brought her some of her own leftovers when they worked the same shift. Cherise had made a giant-sized lasagna and brought it to the hospital—for Nikkie Jean's birthday.

Jillian and Annie had pitched in for a giant sheet cake.

Lacy and Izzie had provided paper plates and forks. Wanda and Courtney had provided sodas.

It was the first and only birthday party Nikkie Jean could ever remember having.

"From your father." Cherise didn't cherry-coat anything. "He left it at the desk. I didn't want it to fall into the wrong hands."

She handed Nikkie Jean a plain envelope with the hospital

emblem in the corner.

Nikkie Jean's hand tightened on it.

"I'm not sure I want it."

"He wasn't sure you would."

"What did he say?" Cherise would be the type to appeal to her father. He would feel comfortable with her. Cherise was the exact opposite of Nikkie Jean's mother. As far as she knew, her father had always been faithful to her mother, at least.

"He said you were probably not ready to hear what he had to say. That he was the one who let the monster in. Who hadn't protected you." Cherise pulled a white bag from the back of her car. Nikkie Jean limped up the steps—the side ones—aware of her friend behind her. "For what it's worth, he seemed...tortured. Hurting. The man has some serious demons to work out."

A wild laugh escaped. "Him and me both."

"I just promised I'd deliver the letter. But if you want someone to talk to, I'll listen. And it will never go past my ears."

"I know. I'm...I can't talk about him anymore. I already have too much this year, and I'm too raw. Especially after...seeing him again."

"Understood, but I'm here—"

Both women turned to the drive when a familiar large-man truck pulled in.

Nikkie Jean let out an undignified squeak.

Her hair was still down around her shoulders—brushed, at least—and she was in her pajamas. She had not had time to shower yet.

She'd been waiting to see if her stomach would let her move that much yet.

The stomach in question clenched at the sight of the Roman-god look-alike climbing out of the cab.

"Well." Cherise shot her a look, one with clear confusion. "That looks like him, but it's not him."

"Dr. Caine Alvaro. Rafe's twin," Nikkie Jean said, flatly. "Yes. He is. No. Rafe and Jillian don't know yet. We have some things to work out."

"I'll say." Cherise shot her a look of quiet humor. "At least you have great taste in beautiful men. The tool belt over his shoulder just...yeah. I think Wanda's right—we need to do a calendar of just hot doctors as a fund-raiser. It would be a hit."

Nikkie Jean laughed softly. There was no need to ask the other woman to keep this quiet. Cherise was discrete. And Nikkie Jean trusted her.

"Thank you. I just have to figure out what I am going to do with him now."

"I can think of a few things. I'm so glad Vince has the day off today. I think we're going to stay in tonight…"

—

There was a pretty redheaded woman on the porch with Nikkie Jean when he pulled in. He climbed out of the truck as the woman climbed in her little economy car.

Nikkie Jean watched him warily from the front step.

Her hair was down. Long and honey-streaked and stick straight. Pure silk. If he wanted to be idiotic about her, he would say it was pure silk.

The pajamas had llamas on them. Nikkie Jean apparently got joy out of things designed for children. The simple things in life.

How he envied her that ability.

He'd lain awake all night trying to figure out how to make all of *this* work so that all four of the children got what they needed, Nikkie Jean got what she needed and wanted—and Caine got what he wanted.

He wanted this woman in his life, in his arms, and in his bed.

It had all boiled down to just that.

He wanted Nikkie Jean. Now he had to convince her that she wanted him, too. "Hey. How did you sleep last night? Are you ill this morning? Have you eaten?"

She just stared at him. "Poorly. A little. Not yet."

"I brought breakfast. Uncle Henry made omelets for the kids. I had him pack some up for me—and you. And bacon. Do you think they'll stay down?" Did she even *like* bacon? What he didn't know about her was far more prevalent than what he did.

It was an uphill battle he faced.

"I suppose I could eat. Just what are you doing here today? Shouldn't you be spending today with your kids?"

"They think I'm at work. I want to spend the day with you."

"You really think that's a good idea? I might lure you to your doom."

"Lure away." He hopped up on her porch and started into her little house. "I am a willing victim."

"Sure, you are. You're just trying to make the most of this new situation. You're adaptable. Dragons usually are."

"You know many dragons?"

"More than my fair share." She eyed the containers in his hand hungrily. "You know, seducing me with food is extremely lame, right?"

"But is it working?" Caine had had one purpose when he'd asked his uncle to make an extra few helpings. Taking care of Nikkie Jean.

April had gotten so pissed whenever he'd even tried to show care and concern for her with the twins. And she'd already left him after she'd told him she was pregnant with Dalton.

He'd never gotten much chance to pamper a pregnant woman.

He had no clue how to do it.

"It's a good start. A small one...but Jelly Bean is hungry. So hand it over. I'll decide what to do with you after that."

"I can think of a few things."

But now wasn't the time for that.

She put a white envelope on the table between them, then eyed it like it was a snake. She picked it back up and tossed it on the kitchen counter.

"Bad news?" he asked quietly. She'd drawn into herself and shut him out the instant her focus had shifted to the letter.

"Family drama that I'm not about to get into. Ever. With anyone. So why are you here? I think we can print shared-custody papers off the internet."

He shot her a look. "There isn't going to be a need to worry about that. We'll figure out what to do with the baby in a way that works out for both of us later. Right now...we need to figure out each other first."

"What is there to figure out. I'm pretty self-explanatory. I eat, I sleep, I work, and I am fully housebroken. I'm rather uncomplicated."

"Sure, you are. Eat. You need about three hundred more calories than you usually eat for optimal fetal development."

"Aye-aye, captain. Does anyone ever mutiny there on the SS Barratt County?"

"All the time."

—

There was a hot doctor who really knew how to work with his hands fixing her front porch step, while stripped down to the waist in the hot July Texas sun.

Nikkie Jean was having a hard time not drooling like a beagle over an ice cream cone in August.

The man was a Roman god of perfection right there on her porch.

Good thing she hadn't seen that much skin on him in the full light the night they'd made Jelly Bean—or she would never have ever let the man leave her bed.

Sexual hang-ups or not.

Wow.

If Rafe looked even half as good, no wonder Jillian had captured him as soon as she could.

She definitely needed something to distract herself from *him.* Before she did something stupid; like go out there and taste him right there in the middle of his chest.

Caine didn't have a lot of chest hair. He just had a bunch of glistening muscles that she wanted to touch. Again and again.

If fire ants weren't a problem, she'd just go out there and…

Nikkie Jean reined herself in. Quickly.

It was official. Caine had moved from the category of generic male doctors to be avoided to extremely hot man she wanted.

She didn't know whether she should be happy to be having healthy lustful thoughts for a man—doctor or not—or appalled because he alone had the power to rock her entire world now.

Still, it was three million degrees outside. The man had to be hot.

She should at least offer him something to drink.

Her hand landed on the white envelope from her father.

Just like that, ever healthy thought she'd been having about one male doctor shifted into stress and pain over another.

What on earth did he possibly think he had to say to her now?

Nikkie Jean ripped open the letter before she let herself be afraid of it any longer.

There are no excuses for what I did, nor for what I did not do when you were a child. Or when you were ill and hurting…

She read the rest of the cryptic note in disbelief.

An apology. That's all it was. A simple apology and a request to be able to talk with her again.

When he returned to Finley Creek.

He would be staying in Finley Creek for the foreseeable future in order to oversee the purchase of Finley Creek General and Barratt County General hospitals by the corporation he had formed with her brother three years after she'd left.

Her father was going to be the new owner of her hospital. And Caine's.

And because of the baby and Caine's right to be a part of that baby's life, Nikkie Jean couldn't do the one thing that she most wanted to do.

Run.

Run far from Finley Creek and the nonfather she had never wanted to see again.

But she just couldn't do that now.

As Caine came back inside and told her he had to be going to take his daughter to a birthday party in town, all she could think about was how she just couldn't face any of this right now.

Nikkie Jean shut down the instant Caine had left.

She just couldn't deal with anything other than the baby right now. She just couldn't.

Chapter 43

REECE DETERRO WAS the head of pediatrics for Finley Creek County General. He was also well acquainted with the younger of the two men across from his desk. "How can I help you out, Ten?"

"We need information on some of your staff," Ten Laughton said. "We've come across some inconsistencies in some records at one of the hospitals some of your physicians have been affiliated with. We need to do some comparisons."

Ten had already shared his new career information with Reece. It hadn't exactly surprised him.

What Ten had been through had been pretty low on the part of a man Ten had thought he could trust. "Anything. You know my records are an open book—with a warrant. And nothing against HIPAA."

"We thought you'd say that." Ten's older brother Thor whipped out a document and handed it to Reece. "Here's the warrant. And exactly what we are needing."

"I'll have my assistant get this together."

The three men listed on that warrant would have some serious explaining to do.

Billing fraud in this industry was taken very, very seriously.

And with good reason.

Sixty billion dollars a year was estimated to go to fraudulent practices within the medical industry. That wasn't something to sneeze at.

Chapter 44

THE MESSAGE FROM Dr. Priario, chief of medicine of Finley Creek County, came at the worst possible time. Wallace wasn't prepared to respond.

Sweat beaded on his brow as he looked at the memo. Someone wanted to speak with him regarding billing practices for his department—at Finley Creek County Gen.

County was his *safe* zone.

He had only padded the accounts there a few times. It wasn't worth it, otherwise. Most of the County patients were there as lower-income patients. Overbilling them wouldn't result in much of anything. And it would just jeopardize his position. Federal insurance programs paid special attention to charges. They didn't like to pay out even a penny more than they had to.

He'd always been careful with patients records. He'd known carelessness was stupid. If he brought attention his way through HIPAA violations investigations, everything else would come to light. He couldn't let that happen.

No. The few times he'd overbilled the federal or state programs through County, it had made him so sick with worry for days after he'd finally decided not to do it at all.

The staff room door opened, and Nikkie Jean hobbled in. "What are you doing here, honey? You should still be at home resting."

"I've been resting for two days, Dr. Henedy. I'm not doing anyone any good driving myself crazy. At least here I can go over files for Rafe. He's asked me to help with the audit for the years before I was here."

"Can he do that?" Of course he could. He was the COM. He could do just about anything he wanted.

But Nikkie Jean—Nikkie Jean was as sharp as her father had always been. Far smarter than Wallace was; Jordan had put him to shame in every class. If there was something Wallace had missed, Nikkie Jean could very well find it.

"He's Rafe; do you think anything will stop him?"

"No. Probably not. Dr. Alvaro at Barratt County is the same way." The girl jolted.

Wallace reached out to right her on the crutches a little better. "How long are you on the crutches?"

"Two more days. I have plans for next Saturday. I will not be wobbling my way around then." A rush of determination went through her eyes.

Sometimes, it was hard to look at her eyes.

He was lusting after Jordan Carrington's daughter, after all.

He'd gotten an email from Carrington that morning. Well, it had been a forward from a friend of theirs in Wyoming.

Jordan Carrington's daughter had been missing for thirteen years. Now she'd been found. In Texas.

Nikkie Jean Netorre was most definitely Dannica Carrington.

"Don't you have some family you want to visit for a few days? Take it easy? Rest?"

She was such a little thing. Her mother had been, too. Her father wasn't overly tall, Wallace had about two or three inches on him, but Nikkie Jean's mother had been small.

They'd had an affair when Nikkie Jean had been two.

Carla had brought Nikkie Jean with her once. She'd slept in Reggie's bed while her mother and Wallace had…entertained one another. He had never forgotten that day.

She had been the only woman he had ever been involved with who had ever had children. Her body had shown the signs. Not something he'd found attractive. They hadn't been together again after that day.

He'd wanted excitement—not someone's mother. He'd told Carla that very bluntly.

Nikkie Jean was most definitely Jordan's daughter—she favored him more than she did her mother—but Jordan had known how unfaithful his wife had been.

No doubt that had greatly hurt him.

It was one reason Wallace was careful not to let Jennifer know about his own indiscretions.

The last thing he wanted to do was hurt Jennifer.

"I would rather be working. Even if that means reading over printouts from the last ten years. I really hope Rafe remembers I need the big letters on my homework."

"That's right, you do. Well, good luck to you. I'm going to escape before I'm roped into helping with this herculean task he's assigned you. Have a good evening. And make certain someone escorts you out tonight. It may still be light out there, but that doesn't mean it's safe."

"Have a good night."

"I…wouldn't mind staying for coffee, if you want company." And then he would pick her brain to find out exactly what it was Dr. Holden-Deane had assigned her to find. Because there was a reason she had been asked. There had to be.

"I'm good, but thanks. You'd better escape while you can."

Chapter 45

CAINE WOKE THE Saturday after he'd fixed Nikkie Jean's front steps more than determined.

He had plans.

Everett had a traveling baseball game in Finley Creek. Caine arranged for his son to go home with a teammate, and then contacted Keller's friend's mother.

It was easy enough to arrange a playdate with Marly Hiller, the mayor's eight-year-old daughter. Keller did better in one-on-one situations with other girls; playdates were his best solution.

He dropped her off at Marly's, then drove his sons to the Finley Creek athletic park.

He had intended to leave Dalton with Henry, but Henry had mentioned having a date with the man who ran the local auto repair shop. Caine wasn't about to impose on his uncle today. Henry so rarely had time to himself any more. Not since school had let out for the summer.

After Everett's game, Caine was going hunting.

Nikkie Jean was playing elusive now. Running from him before he could hurt her. He was starting to figure out exactly how that woman operated.

Her hurt was going to be his biggest obstacle. Her fear.

Something in that letter she'd read the other day had compounded that hurt and fear to the point where he'd known that anything he said or did would just make her hurt worse—or be missed while she internalized whatever it was she had been feeling.

He'd given her her space, when that had been the absolute last thing he'd ever wanted.

Everett was quiet on the drive until they were halfway there. "What's the matter, Daddy?"

"Just thinking about daddy things. Why?"

"You keep looking at us, especially Dalton. Like we've done something to get in trouble. But he's too little to get into trouble."

"Nobody's in trouble." And he *had* been looking at the boys. Wondering what another brother or sister would do to their world. Dalton would probably never remember any difference, but his elder two would. They were old enough to be angry and resentful at such a life change again. That wasn't something he could just overlook, and hope would resolve itself for the best. "I'm just thinking."

"About what?" Sometimes his son didn't understand there were things he didn't need to know about. And he pushed. Insatiable curiosity, that's what Henry called it. Said Caine had been the exact same way at that age.

"A friend of mine. She's going to have a baby. And I'm worried about her." And just how to get her where he wanted her. A rush of anticipation went through him; Caine was a primitive caveman at heart.

Hunting his female was bound to get him...wired. Ready.

Impatient.

"Is she sick? Like Mommy was? Dalton made her really sick before she went away."

"I don't know. I didn't ask." All he'd get back in return for his morning and afternoon phone-call attempts over the last five days had been the same damned two-word text each day:

Baby's fine.

That was it.

As if the baby was all he cared about. His fault for giving her that impression.

He had no idea what to do to change it. "Would it bother you if she brought the baby over sometimes? Well, a lot, actually." Like every night after she left the hospital. Finley Creek Gen had a day care within the building. Barratt County didn't.

She could take Dalton and the baby to the day care every day with her, and he'd drop Keller and Everett off at the school on his way in the opposite direction. Henry could pick the twins up at dismissal.

That would give Henry a break during the day, too.

Or they'd hire a full-time nanny to help with the younger two during the day. There was an apartment in the back barn. With some remodeling it would work for a young, college-aged, live-in nanny. Or an older woman who had downsized. But he suspected Nikkie Jean would want the younger two where she could check on them during the day.

"Why would she? Is she your girlfriend? Uncle Henry thinks you need one."

"Does he?" The man was the only relative he had on his father's side that he wanted anything to do with. Henry was his father's younger brother, and had retired from the Houston Children's Library about the time that April had died. He was about the only one Caine had ever trusted with the children fully. Henry had been a godsend when the baby had been born. "And she's not my girlfriend; not exactly, at least not yet. She might be soon. I want her to be."

If he had his way, she would be.

She was the mother of his fourth child. But he wasn't quite ready to tell the children that yet. It had been five days since she'd basically asked him to leave her home. Told him that she needed time to think about what *she* wanted now.

He'd vowed after April that he would never be involved with another woman until well after Dalton had graduated high school. He didn't want his children caught between him and a stepmother. That wouldn't be fair to them. But he doubted Nikkie Jean would ever do anything to hurt his children. Of that, he was certain. No; she'd adore them. And they'd grow to adore her.

No. It was him she terrified. His world she had the power to destroy. All she had to do was tell him he wasn't the kind of man she wanted in her arms again.

Her rejection would sting him far more than even April's had done.

He'd known months after the twins were born that he hadn't truly mattered to his wife; just like he hadn't to his father and biological mother. He'd let those wounds callous over years ago. He had mattered to his uncle as a child, and he had mattered to the twins. He had family.

But Nikkie Jean had zoomed right past his defenses and lodged herself so tightly around his heart, he almost swore he could feel it hurting.

She wasn't about to let him close enough to show her that.

But Caine had never given up easily.

"Why would she bring the baby? So Uncle Henry could babysit? Keller would probably like that. If it was a girl, anyway. So she could put it in dresses and necklaces. But I think Dalton might be jealous of another baby around."

Dalton babbled something around the fist he had shoved up by his mouth.

A girl.

One who looked like a cross between him and Nikkie Jean. Dimples like Nikkie Jean's would be a distinct possibility. Or maybe a girl would look just like Keller. He smiled. A girl would be nice. One just as bubbly as her mother.

But without the constant shadow of fear in her eyes. What had made Nikkie Jean so afraid? That had to be the first question he answered.

"I just thought it might be nice. She's really nice. You've met her before. The same day you met Ariella and your...cousins." He bit back a wince as he said it. He'd been careful since that day not to talk about his biological sister too much. The children already had pestered him and Henry about the past.

Questions Caine hadn't been ready to answer until they were older.

How did he tell his children that his father had abused him simply for existing? His children were not quite old enough to understand that. All they knew was that he hadn't had a great childhood. That his father had been a cruel man. Caine and Henry had kept it at that. Until the children were old enough to understand. But Ariella had brought questions from the children that had surprised him at how astute they were.

"I guess. I mean, it's just a baby, right? Not as fun as a puppy. I'd rather have a dog instead of another baby."

Well, that wasn't going to happen. Not yet.

The baby was a reality. Caine would have to tell them soon. *After* they had a chance to get to know Nikkie Jean a little better.

The last thing any of them needed was the children resenting her or the baby. Caine was just going to have to figure it out. Fast.

He'd start by finding Nikkie Jean. It was the first day off he'd had since two days before he'd learned she'd been hurt. He was going to spend it with her. No matter what he had to do to make that happen.

Chapter 46

THEY DRESSED HER UP in extra catcher's gear they borrowed from the opposing team. Between the two teams, they had five players in the first and second trimester of pregnancy. And a lot of catchers' gear. Lacy insisted, as did Izzie, and all the rest. She and Jillian and Lacy—the actual catcher, who was not pregnant, that anyone knew, anyway—looked interchangeable when they came out of the dugout.

Nikkie Jean turned her hat backward so she could see well. One issue with her eyes involved tracking and lower field of vision, even with the contacts. The prescription sports glasses weren't the best for field of vision, either. "Let's do this!"

Lacy looked at her, a warning on her face. "No diving, daredevil. You've had a concussion recently, as well. You probably shouldn't be playing, honestly. No diving, no reaching, no sliding, no falling, no anything. Same for you, Jillian Anne. As head physician of this team—"

Lacy held up her hand when Fin and Nikkie Jean both protested. "As self-appointed head physician, the two of you are not to do anything even remotely dangerous. And the two of you especially need to be careful, considering your positions on the field."

"Bailey and Annie—cover the inside of the mound as much as you can," Mel added. "Try to stop the ball from getting to the little chicks."

Nikkie Jean nodded. She understood exactly what Lacy wasn't saying.

Everyone on the team knew about the baby. She'd told them in the dugout. She'd been congratulated and hugged the instant it became known. Her friends were happy for her.

That mattered.

The game went well. There was only one time she had to stretch more than she was comfortable with, but she was able to grab the ball and toss it to Bailey, the deputy she'd worked with at the motor vehicle accident, who was playing third.

Bailey's own father had almost let her die just a few months ago. Bailey was still trying to process that.

She and Nikkie Jean had talked about their fathers at W4HAV once, when it was just the two of them in the lounge. The charity was designed to help women in all stages of recovery from violent attacks.

She liked to think she was at the point where she could be a guide for those whose hurt was newer. Nikkie Jean had made a point of helping run the Tuesday night therapy groups when she could. She'd made a point of keeping an eye on Bailey since she'd first started coming to W4HAV.

Nikkie Jean had assisted Rafe in the emergency surgery that had initially saved Bailey's life months ago.

Fathers…could be so problematic.

Nikkie Jean shoved thoughts of the men who really didn't want her out of her head and focused on the game.

The people who did care about her were counting on her now. And *that* was what was important.

Not Dr. Caine Alvaro—or Dr. Jordan Carrington.

Chapter 47

IT WAS GOING TO JUST be Caine and Dalton for the rest of the afternoon. Unless Caine's hunt went according to plans.

He carried his youngest toward the restrooms. A diaper change was in order before they searched for Nikkie Jean. And quickly.

Caine rounded the back of the restrooms when he was finished with his son and almost slammed into the last man he'd ever wanted to see.

He stared.

An identical face—minus the long scar that bisected his eyebrow—stared back. The other man scowled and cursed partially—before stopping abruptly when he noticed the boy in Caine's arms.

Dalton erupted into sobs. Caine looked down at him and bounced him. When Dalton was upset, everyone knew it. His son wouldn't stop until he got what he wanted.

He'd gotten that trait from Caine.

"Well," Rafe said.

It was hard to think of him as Dr. Holden-Deane now that he'd gotten a close look at him. The hair was shorter. The guy had the smaller scars Nikkie Jean had mentioned. But other than that, there was no denying this brother that he didn't want. "So. You do exist."

"Apparently, so do you. He's a beautiful kid, with a healthy set of lungs there. I heard you met Ariella and the kids. She confirmed you weren't a figment of anyone's imagination."

"Yes. She's a nice woman. I'm not sorry to have met her." And he wasn't. She seemed exactly what she was—a nice young woman about to marry Texas's favorite politician.

"She's over there. Playing softball with her friends." His twin nodded toward the field farthest from all the others.

"Nikkie Jean's over there?" Like a magnet, his gaze went in the direction his twin pointed. "I'm...looking for her today."

"Dr. Netorre? Yeah. Nikkie Jean's...on the team." The other guy practically growled it. He'd tensed, and his fists had flexed.

"Then that's where I'm headed. I understand your wife's playing today?"

Suspicion hit the man's eyes. "She is. Does Nikkie Jean know you're here?"

"Not yet. But she's not going to avoid me any longer. I've been trying to get ahold of her for days. She's stealthy when she wants to be." She'd even stooped to taking the backroads behind her house to avoid passing him on the road.

He'd seen her take the turn off one day and do just that.

Nikkie Jean was one hell of a little schemer at heart.

Caine wasn't about to forget that. He smiled; he was looking forward to the challenge that woman presented.

"You know her well?"

"You might say that." He wished he knew her even better; now...he wished he had a better answer. He wished this child had been conceived under better circumstances than her just wanting to forget a loss. He wished she felt proud enough of what had happened between them that everyone who was close to her at all knew that *he* was the man who'd fathered her baby.

"The baby's yours?"

"Yes."

His brother's expression darkened. For a minute there, Caine thought he was about to get slugged. Rafe felt protective of Nikkie Jean; that told Caine one thing. Rafe and his wife would be in the new baby's life—probably from the beginning. Which meant...Caine would have to make peace with how he felt regarding this man with the exact same face. "Where the hell have you *been*? She's been terrified and not letting anyone see it, but those of us who care about her haven't missed it for a second."

"She didn't bother to have anyone call me," Caine said, flatly. The idea of how frightened she would have been sickened him. His son was finally settling down, alternating between chewing on his favorite teether and Caine's shoulder. Caine shifted him to his other hip as he and Rafe started toward the far field. "Now she's practically been hiding from me, and with what's going on at Barratt

County, I barely have time to shower, let alone chase her down on *her* off time. She's not making it easy. Nikkie Jean's stubborn."

"No kidding. She's also very vulnerable. I'd hate to see her hurt again."

"Who in the hell said I'd hurt her? That's the last thing I want to do."

"Never said you would. And hell, she's the mother of my future niece or nephew, apparently. Jillian has already been making plans for joint birthdays and holidays. Once she finds out our children will be cousins, there will be no stopping her. You might say I have a vested interest in making certain Nikkie Jean is ok. And healing."

"I don't want a damned thing from you, or the rest of them. But I know she and your wife are close. I'm not going to do anything to jeopardize that for her. Them. But I'm not looking for siblings in my life right now. Or really ever."

His twin snorted. "Neither was I. Now they are everywhere. My brother—adoptive, just for clarification—is marrying my sister—biological, again for clarification. I can't escape our mother's children, even if I continued to try. I did at first." His expression darkened. "Ariella's as dear to me as my other brother's wife. Or any one of Jillian's sisters. Dearer. And there's not a damned thing I won't do to keep her from getting hurt again. By anyone."

Caine understood the warning, loud and clear. Rafe was giving him a message, loud and clear. "I'm not a damned monster out to hurt as many women as possible, you know. I just want *my* woman to stop running from me so we can deal with the future head-on—together. Before the baby comes."

"Never said you were. But I wasn't too keen on finding my biological siblings. I'm still not. And I did some idiot things that hurt Ariella, *and* my wife. I'd hate to see someone else do the same thing. So just consider that a friendly advice from a…brother."

Caine didn't respond. He knew what this brother was saying. But he made his own choices. "I'm here for Nikkie Jean only. I told her not to play today. It's too damned dangerous so soon after her injuries."

Rafe snorted. "I told Jillian the same damned thing."

"When's she due?"

Rafe told him. He did the math quickly, based on the date on the ultrasound photo he still had—in his pocket. He'd made a copy, as a reminder of what he still needed to do. Until things were settled between him and Nikkie Jean, that photo was not coming out of his wallet. Except when he needed to look at it and remind himself of what really mattered. "They're not that far apart."

A little more than a week apart. The babies were going to be born within days of each other, most likely. Hard to miss a coincidence like that. Their children would spend their childhoods growing up together.

No matter what Caine had initially thought about his biological siblings they were in his life now. He didn't see that changing any time soon.

Rafe shook his head. "No. They're not."

"Nikkie Jean, she's been ok this week? All she'll give me is a quick snotty text each morning and evening saying she's fine."

"She's fine. We made sure of it before we released her. I signed off on her charts myself. If I had known you were the father, I wouldn't have let her leave. Jillian and I would have taken her back to our place for a few days, at least. Hell, we offered anyway, and she turned us down."

"She wasn't alone. She had friends with her. Both brunettes. Pretty women, younger than Nikkie Jean. Short, dark-haired snappy one and one who looks like the world's sweetest kid sister. Guard dogs."

"Izzie McNamara and Annie Gaines, no doubt. They're the ones that match those descriptions. They're close; well, as close as Nikkie Jean lets anyone get, anyway."

Caine would have said something, questioned this unexpected source of information even more, but he had more pressing matters. Vocal ones.

"Dad, Dad, Dad! Two!"

Dalton babbled at the other man, no doubt seeing what Caine did. It was hard to ignore what was right in front of him. "Well, we've met now. Nice to know you."

He wanted to find her. See her for himself today.

"I have questions. About you. I don't want to, but I do. Jillian's insistent that I deal with my biological family, and I'm starting to agree with her," Rafe pointed to the far field. Apple-green T-shirts were visible in the distance. "That's where they are. It's a charity event."

"What for?"

"W4HAV. Ari created it."

"I've heard of it, but I can't recall what exactly it does." There had been flyers up around the county and in the hospital lobby. He hadn't looked too closely.

"Each and every woman involved in W4HAV has been the victim of some sort of extreme or prolonged violence and trauma. Every woman on that field for the green team. And that is just far too many. W4HAV provides services, shelter, and counseling for the women who need it. Group therapy, life-skills training, and just basic connections to others who understand."

"And Nikkie Jean goes there?" Caine's words dropped low as what the other man was telling him registered.

It wasn't just a failed relationship making her skittish. It was something far more.

Rafe's face tightened, told Caine there were secrets Rafe knew that Caine didn't. Yet. "Yes. She goes there and she volunteers there several times a week. That's one of the founding principles the charity runs off of. They help each other heal. Nikkie Jean, her two friends, my wife, *our* sister, and all of my sisters-in-law, as well."

The ramifications of the other man's words had him looking at the women with new eyes. As a physician—and one who'd spent time overseas in war zones—he was no stranger to trauma. Or its aftereffects.

He stayed with the other man until they came to the fence next to the right-field line. A woman waved. Rafe waved back.

"That's Ariella."

"She's doing ok? I remember seeing what happened on the news." He winced when his sister missed the ball. She grabbed it off the ground and tossed it in to the second-base player. It fell three feet short.

"Healing. It had to do with drug trafficking. But she and Katie are getting counseling. At W4HAV. Ariella is the driving force behind it; and it's already helped so many women. FCGH even refers female trauma victims to them for services. Barratt County might keep that in mind. Marc adores her. It's easy to do."

"My daughter. She reminds me of my daughter. Keller looks just like her, same complexion. Same build. Same eyes. Same smile and even jawline. It was like a punch to the gut when I first saw her. I know exactly what my daughter will look like in fifteen or twenty years now." And that had had him opening up to the possibility of knowing *her* at least. Caine didn't think he'd be able to ignore the connection. Not now that Keller had seen it for herself.

April had apparently liked pointing out that Keller hadn't looked like her at all. April, who had been beautiful, blond, and sophisticated, had made their daughter feel the exact opposite. At five. He still hadn't gotten over the fury that had caused.

But there was this woman right there who was an older version of his daughter. One who had done something important to help others.

Ariella had changed the world with what she had done.

He could think of far worse role models for his daughter than Ariella and Nikkie Jean. Far worse.

"Yeah. We all resemble each other, so far. I'd like to meet the kids sometime."

"I'll think about it. My, our, uncle lives with me. Helps take care of the children." He'd not talked to Henry about the others. But Henry knew about Rafe. Now. He hadn't always. "He and our father weren't close. But he was always in my life. He wants to meet you. When you are ready."

Rafe looked at him for a moment, then down at Dalton, who was gnawing on Caine's shoulder. "I'm not certain what I'm supposed to do with you. We needed to meet eventually. I'm glad it was here, instead of at some damned benefit or function for the hospitals. That would have invited more questions I don't want to have to answer."

"No kidding." It would have been awkward for all involved. Caine had no doubt his brother felt the same way about his personal life and the hospital as Caine did.

The two shouldn't intersect.

"That's my wife on the pitcher's mound." Rafe's voice softened when he spoke of her. He pointed to the redhead winding up to pitch. Directly in the line of fire. One wrong line drive and she could be hurt.

As could Nikkie Jean.

He'd never found softball terrifying before, but now? Caine knew he was acting like an idiot. He knew the odds of something happening to her out there were extremely slim. Slow-pitch softball was one of the safest sports in existence.

He found Nikkie Jean easily, even if she hadn't told him she'd be on short. Small and wiry and quick. It perfectly described her.

She was wearing a catcher's vest loose over her front so it dangled low over her abdomen. She had her cap turned backward. The sports glasses looked like goggles. Hot-pink ones. He'd never seen her in the same pair of glasses two times in a row.

She was heckling a player from another team and grinning. Looking too damned adorable for his peace of mind. Caine smiled, just watching her for a moment.

It was nice to see some of the Nikkie Jean he had met that first night returning. He had been afraid he'd chased that woman away.

His gaze shot to the redhead on the mound. She also wore the extra padding. "How can she pitch with that on?"

"Pure stubbornness."

"Seems there's a lot of that going on at Finley Creek Gen."

"You have no idea."

In another life, if they had been raised together, he might have actually liked this twin of his. But now... "I don't know what I am supposed to say to you."

"Welcome to the club. I had this plan when I first got the letter. I wasn't any happier about it than you were. I'd decided to stay the hell away from all of them. So I decided to track down the woman who wrote the letter. Tell her just stay away. That's the woman in the dugout yelling orders, by the way. Barratt's wife. He's a big backer of the hospitals that his family founded. You'll meet him eventually, no doubt. I found her redheaded hellion of a sister instead."

"And now? Your theory of how to deal with this?"

"No reason we can't be friends, is there? The siblings I've met have been good people. People I'm actually proud to know. I wasn't so certain that would be the case when all of this started."

"How many are there?"

"That's the question we're still trying to answer. We didn't even know our sister, Pen, existed until recently. She's sixteen and a sophomore at FCU. We're old enough to be her father. Hell of a kid. Simon's thirteen now. We think there may be one or two still out there younger than Simon. Zoey is raising Pen. She's twenty-eight and looks just like Ariella. Paige is in St. Louis and with the FBI. She's got Simon. Luc's the eldest. He's Lucas Technologies and a real pain in the ass. Runs the whole thing. There are leads on three or four more of adult age. But nothing is confirmed. She bred like a rabbit. And there was at least another set of identical twins, but we've not confirmed that yet. Brynna, my sister-in-law, found evidence she made a business out of it, taking fertility drugs when needed. Acting as an illegal surrogate some of the time, and then there was the flat-out baby selling. She sold Ariella to her own father for one hundred grand. I went for two hundred fifty. I was four days old."

"I wasn't so lucky."

"You were raised by our biological father?"

"Dumped on him. I had a heart defect. I was in NICU for the first three months. He took me home after that. Apparently, he gave her fifty grand to keep her mouth shut about some of his not-so-great activities, and he had to take me off her hands. He should have given me up. He wasn't exactly father-of-the-year material."

"I'm sorry. Hell, I'm not even certain which of us is older. My adoptive parents weren't exactly forthcoming about who they bought me from."

And there was a world of history in what Rafe had just said.

"I am, baby brother. According to the birth certificates I found when the old man died." Some of the resentment he'd felt for the twin that had supposedly had a better life lessened. "What kind of people buy babies illegally?"

"In my case, ones who thought a second child made a nice looking accessory, as long as there was a nanny to take care of it, and they could abandon all their children when the third child came along."

Dalton blew a raspberry at this new uncle he'd never met. Then giggled and reached. "Hold Dalty."

Before he knew it, Caine was handing his son over to the closest relative the boy had other than the twins and Caine himself. The impact of that wasn't lost on him. "He's my youngest. Nineteen months old. Name's Dalton."

"Ariella said you had twins the same age as Katie."

"Keller and Everett. They're off with friends today. Everett just left with a friend of his. Keller's in Value with her friend from school. Dalton and I were heading out to lunch. After we commandeer one Nikkie Jean Netorre."

"Have you known her long? Nikkie Jean's a favorite at the hospital. Patients just love her."

He could see why. She was the most animated player out there today. "She needs to take it easy. Not be hopping around like that."

"I've seen her doing cartwheels and backflips in the cafeteria. This is tame for Nikkie Jean."

Pregnant women weren't made of glass, by any means. But…that was *his* pregnant woman out there. It made a difference. And she was still recuperating.

He wanted to stalk out there and get her. Make certain she was safe. He felt like a damned caveman.

"Nikkie Jean always does everything enthusiastically. Including gluing my office door shut once. And various other things I can't prove but I'm ninety-nine percent certain were her."

"This thing between us is new. But if I had known she had been hurt, I would have been there. Even before she told me about the baby."

His brother excused himself to return to his family. Caine didn't know what to say. He had no doubt that they'd meet again someday. He knew where his brother was if he ever wanted to find him. Not like Rafe was all that hard to find.

He held Dalton on his hip and watched the woman who had changed his world with just a few terrifying words. Compared her to the estranged wife he'd buried nineteen months ago.

People were drawn to Nikkie Jean. Cared about her. And she made a point of encouraging them when she could. Of being supportive—and kind. To everyone. He recognized some of the players.

Her guard dogs were out there in left field and on first base. The sheriff's deputy played third. Played very well. His brother's wife, a damned good pitcher, was at the center of the action.

His sister was in right field. Poor thing had no business playing softball. That was evident. But she tried. Caine couldn't help smiling as he watched her, thinking of how strange genetics actually were.

Keller's resemblance to her aunt was uncanny. Caine broke out in hives whenever his daughter got close to any kind of sports equipment. Keller just wasn't meant to be athletic. Apparently, neither was this little sister he didn't know yet. He found he was actually starting to want to.

Caine smiled as he watched her, this sister he'd never known about until recently. His smile fell as the announcer plugged the charities represented again.

The knowledge that all of these women were there because they'd been deliberately hurt by someone sickened him. His sister. His sister-in-law. The guard dogs.

Nikkie Jean.

After the game, there was hugging and high-fiving among Nikkie Jean's team. She hugged his sister and his sister-in-law, both. She did a little victory dance that sent the catcher's pad wiggling in an interesting way. Another woman laughed and congratulated her.

On the baby or the win? Nikkie Jean patted her extra padding and grinned, and he got his answer. Unlike the last woman to have his baby, *this* one was happy about it. His gut tightened at that thought.

This woman carried his child; he liked that idea, caveman that he was. He would be tied to Nikkie Jean forever now.

Nikkie Jean was the life of the party, and she kept up the enthusiasm for the rest of the women surrounding her.

Rafe's words came back to him when she turned and looked toward the rest of her teammates.

Women who were all victims of violence and trauma. Trauma. She was on that team because of *trauma*. What in the hell had happened to her?

He wanted to know every detail of her story.

"Dalton, we have some questions to ask of that woman. Let's go get her." Caine rounded the fence with purpose. Nikkie Jean was not about to escape him today. Or hide from him like she had been. He might not have all the answers, but he wanted the right to try to find them.

That woman out there was going to make one hell of a mother—fun, loving, kind, encouraging, and compassionate. He wanted that for this baby. Every child deserved that. The baby Nikkie Jean carried would have that from the beginning. Would be far luckier than Caine had been, or his three eldest were now. With time, hopefully he could give them exactly that. With her. It was time he got everyone used to that idea.

He and the children and this new baby were a family. Nikkie Jean was going to be a huge part of that, too. It was time they figured out how to make it work—for all of them.

His children weren't ready for her *yet*. But he would get them there. Caine knew he had worked to do to make sure they were before their brother or sister made their way into the world. There was no time like the present to get started.

Caine was going hunting. He had his woman to catch.

Chapter 48

MOST OF THEIR TEAM was heading to a favorite diner to celebrate the win. Only Margo and Bailey had other commitments after. No surprise, Margo had flown in specifically for the game to fill in for another player. And Bailey had no other ride. Nikkie Jean had offered to drive the other woman, but it was obvious that the welcoming nature of the group was overwhelming Bailey a great deal.

Plus, there was a tall, handsome sheriff waiting to take Bailey home. One dressed in worn jeans and FCU T-shirt that had nothing to do with the TSP.

Sheriff Addy wasn't on the clock now. And the way he was looking at Bailey made Nikkie Jean go all gooey inside.

Nikkie Jean planned to grill her friend on that relationship first opportunity she got.

She walked off the field with Annie and Izzie, chatting with her friends as she did. Izzie stopped walking, her eyes widening.

Nikkie Jean followed her gaze.

And there was Caine. Walking right toward her.

He stood glowering at her, surrounded by people she had no doubt he wanted nothing to do with. His son was chattering at people walking by.

"Don't worry. We won't leave you alone with him," Izzie whispered.

Annie just grabbed her hand.

She appreciated their support, but Caine was her problem to deal with. Not theirs. "I'm ok. I'm not sure why he's here."

She wasn't going to walk over to him. That was exactly what he wanted—his prey to come to him. So that he could play with her.

Damn her hormones; that thought wasn't as terrifying as

she'd thought it would be. She wouldn't mind a little more playtime with Caine. Under the right circumstances, of course.

The man was made for faded jeans and BCGH T-shirts that made his shoulders look just a little wider than the brother's standing next to him.

Shoulder to shoulder with Rafe, she saw the differences. There was just something *more* about Caine than his brother. Hands down.

Jillian saw Caine then. And she was fearless. She stalked right up to Caine and put her hands on her hips. She looked ridiculous with the catcher's gear still in place and the apple-green T-shirt clashing with her hair, standing between two almost-identical men who towered a foot over her. "*Well*. Look what the cat has dragged in this morning. Yet another one. And it's a clone this time!"

Caine shot her a look. Nikkie Jean waited for him to say something cutting to his sister-in-law, just like Rafe would have done before everyone realized what a softie he actually was. It didn't come.

"You always this sassy, little sister?" There was challenge there—but humor, as well. Caine's temper wasn't as trigger-happy as his brother's, apparently.

Yet she wouldn't exactly say he was *tamer* than Rafe, though.

"Better believe it. You should get used to it. How old?"

Caine smiled at Jillian. "Thirty-five and a half. Aren't I just the cutest little thing?"

Jillian snorted, then softened when Dalton chattered at her and clapped his hands. Reached for the bright-red hair. "Not as cute as *he* is. He's absolutely adorable."

"Of course, you'd say that, Jillian. He looks just like Rafe did at that age," the governor said from nearby. He held out a hand to Caine. "Marcus Deane. Ariella's my fiancée. Rafe's my brother."

The way he said his fiancée's name made a woman gooey inside, too. Caine's sister was a very, very lucky woman to have her man love her like that.

"Caine Alvaro. This is my youngest, Dalton." Caine barely looked away from Nikkie Jean long enough to introduce himself to the governor of Texas.

These were some of the most observant people Nikkie Jean knew. They were going to notice just where Caine was staring. One and one were quickly going to add up to three here. And fast.

"Nice to meet you. And Dalton." Marc was good at soothing awkward moments. But it didn't matter.

Caine was intent. And he was prowling. Hunting.

Nikkie Jean stopped walking. She fought the urge to scurry off in a totally different direction.

Izzie looked at her. "You ok?"

"I don't think so. He's up to something. I suddenly feel like a little pygmy owl with a falcon on my tail here."

She'd seen Rafe look at Jillian just like that before. And not always in a good way. Rafe and Jillian had had some epic battles in the ER, after all. Battles Nikkie Jean had witnessed. Nikkie Jean was smart enough to learn from others' experiences.

"We can distract him," Izzie offered. "While you take off. If you run really fast, you can make it home, grab your things, and head to Mexico. I heard Mel say the new Barratt-South Padre is open now, too."

"I think it may be too late," Annie said. "He's coming this way. And he's very determined."

Sure enough, when she looked up, Caine was stalking straight toward her, the mini-version of him riding on his hip.

"At least we know one thing," Izzie whispered. "Your baby is bound to be beautiful."

"No kidding." He was close enough now that she had to acknowledge him. "Alvaro."

Dalton babbled at her and waved. Then kicked his feet to get down. Caine lowered him to the ground, trapping the little boy between them, Izzie, and Annie.

Her friends weren't going anywhere. And she knew it.

"Nikkie Jean, *sweetheart.*" He reached for her. She tried not to flinch, but she must not have been successful. He tensed. His hands went to the straps of the chest pad instead. Oh, nice move, Alvaro. Make it look natural. "Was this thing even long enough?"

"It covered enough. I am fine." She never would have risked the baby on anything that she considered truly dangerous. Slow-pitch softball wasn't that risky. Especially if caution was taken. And it had been—almost every time the ball had come her direction Bailey had been there first. But he wasn't there to talk softball. Far from it. "What are you doing here?"

"Everett had a game on another field that ended an hour ago. He went home with friends."

"And your daughter?"

"With the Hillers. Dalton and I stayed to wait for you."

People were moving away. Except Izzie and Annie, who were listening to every word.

He slipped the straps free and caught the padding when it fell away. He looked at Izzie and held it out on one hand deliberately. "Here, Guard Dog Izzie, you can deal with this."

Her friend took it after shooting him a glare.

He scooped his son up, then wrapped his free hand around Nikkie Jean's arm. Capturing her. "We need to talk. *Now*. I've been trying to catch you for days."

She almost thought the man meant literally.

Well, now she was caught.

Nikkie wanted to pull away but didn't. Not in front of these people. Caine wouldn't want to look like a jerk in front of his family. That would just make him angry at her, and she couldn't deal with that right now.

But the last thing she wanted to do was be somewhere alone with him. Not with him looking at her like he was. His toddler wasn't exactly much of a barrier between them.

In fact, the kid had his hand wrapped around one of Nikkie Jean's braids and was using it to pull her closer to his father.

Little devil; he really was his father in miniature.

Nikkie Jean wanted to hold him again. Just for snuggles.

She looked at Annie for help. Annie expertly extricated the captured hair. Dalton wasn't that much younger than the youngest little boy Annie would hopefully be adopting soon.

Izzie stepped between them. "Nikkie Jean has plans."

"She'll need to change them."

Well, that was bound to set everything off. Especially Izzie. Nikkie Jean intervened quickly when she saw the younger woman bristle into full-out protective mode. "Caine, we're going to lunch to celebrate. Mamaw's Place. Almost the whole team."

"Then I'll drive you. We'll come back and get your car after. I'll follow you home afterward. We can have that talk."

He wasn't taking no for an answer.

Chapter 49

HE KNEW HE'D RAILROADED her, but Caine would ask forgiveness later. They couldn't resolve anything if he couldn't pin her down long enough to get a discussion actually started.

Dalton babbled at her and then reached for her. The instant he did, Caine handed his son over. He wanted her to know his children. He wanted them to know her.

It would make things easier on everyone in the long run when he finally convinced her to move in with him in a few months or so.

She was easy, natural, with his son. She snuggled him close and kissed his forehead. So damned beautiful his teeth rattled with how hard he clenched them. He wanted her to kiss him next.

His sister said something to her, reaching out and patted Dalton's back. Dalton grinned and waved at the woman who had the exact same smile. "Kell, Kell, Kell!"

Even the baby saw the resemblance, apparently. He looked at Ariella. "It's the resemblance to his sister. He adores her."

As his sister laughed and talked to Dalton, a sense of *rightness* went through him.

He'd moved the kids to a small town so they could have these very kinds of days. Little league games, connections. People who knew the kids' names when they saw them.

He hadn't expected some of those people to be his siblings, but he might be able to adjust to that. He'd just run into aunts and uncles his kids didn't even know they had. Talk about serious connections.

If he wanted to make them. It meant getting out of his comfort zone, but hell, he hadn't had much of a comfort zone since having children, anyway.

Neither of the two he'd met so far had seemed like bad people.

They'd seemed...family oriented. His sister's future children were racing around the grass toward the playground under the watchful eye of the actual governor of Texas and an older redheaded man Caine didn't know. His twin's firecracker of a wife was right there in the midst of the crowd. Caine suspected he'd like her quite a bit if he got a chance to know her.

But it was Nikkie Jean that he wanted his children to know. She was talking with another redheaded woman, who stood clutching a forearm crutch and leaning against a man as tall as Caine but thinner. The man looked vaguely familiar, but he didn't know why. It didn't matter.

It was the woman in the center of the crowd that Caine wanted.

His body tightened with the thought that he wanted Nikkie Jean in more than just his house—he wanted her back in his bed, too.

Long before the baby's arrival. It wasn't shared custody he was after. And it never had been.

It was Nikkie Jean—all the ways he could get her.

He waited until the grounds man crossed the parking lot on the riding lawn mower and then unlocked the passenger door of his truck. He lifted her, still holding his son, into the passenger seat. "Stay there. I'll come get him through the other side and get him in his seat."

She just nodded. Her friends had taken her mitt and bat when he'd shown up so her arms were free to hold his son. She seemed to enjoy that and Dalton was eating it up as well.

Caine made quick work of dealing with Dalton. Then he turned toward the woman he'd basically commandeered. She sat staring at him out of hot-pink sports goggles. He bit back a grin—and suppressed the urge to lean over and steal a quick kiss, just like his son had done before she'd put him in his car seat. "You fastened, sweetheart?"

Her eyes narrowed with suspicion when the endearment slipped out. "Yes. And I am not your *sweetheart*. I'm your baby incubator-slash-former-one-night stand. That's about it. Best if we just keep things in the proper perspective here. Not confuse anyone."

He snorted. "I think you're a bit more than that. And you're the closest thing to a sweetheart I'm ever going to have again."

Or want. A primal rush of emotion shot through him. This was the woman he wanted; Caine would do what he had to in order to make that happen.

"You're weird, Alvaro. At first you want nothing to do with me—" She shot a look at Dalton. "Other than that one-nighter thing, anyway. Which, while I'm sure was pretty good, I'm not so certain now it was so awing and inspiring to the point of us repeating it. I'm not really certain why you want to. You took off so fast last time I thought I must have had onion breath. Now, you show up here. In front of my friends. Your own brother and sister. Even the *governor* knows what you did now. You can't keep me a secret any longer. You just shouted to everyone that you're responsible for getting me pregnant. I've not told anyone who the father is. It was kind of like supposed to be the mystery of the year at FCGH. I was enjoying having my spies collect all the rumors." She shot him a pointed look that Caine just ignored. He guided the truck out of the parking lot and onto the highway. "I heard there is already a betting pool. Money's on Allen Jacobson, by the way. He bet a thousand dollars on himself! Cage Ralstone bet five hundred on himself, too. I didn't realize I got around so much. All proceeds go to W4HAV. Payable by check, cash, or money order. Fourteen people put Rafe in as a wild-card vote. Can you imagine what they'll think when the kid is born looking like…Uncle Rafe? If you just stay quiet, we can make life really difficult for Rafe and Jillian. I can play the other woman wronged. Jillian and I could play wrestle over Rafe in the lobby. Maybe with Jello!"

"Hardly. I'm not hiding that that's my child growing inside you. I'm damned proud of it. I won't hide it. Any more than I could hide paternity of the one in the backseat. I'm going to be there for my children, Nikkie Jean. All four of them. Period. I needed to see you again. You'd better just get used to me being around. No more avoiding me or holding me off with cryptic or snotty little text messages."

—Dude, your spawn is incubating just fine. Now let me go back to sleep.

At seven thirty the night before. Caine had just burst out laughing—startling Dalton who'd been in his arms—and then had to explain to Henry and the twins that his friend Nikkie Jean had sent him something funny.

He'd never realized how easy frustration could be communicated through text before.

He'd just asked if she'd had dinner yet or wanted him to bring her some spaghetti. And tuck her in bed. He'd hoped she'd extend the offer.

"Well, you've seen me. Now what? I'm real. Not a nightmare you can just wake up from. Can't get away from me now."

Snark. It was right there. But so was the fear. Nikkie Jean was afraid of what he was going to do. "Now? I buy you—and Dalton—lunch. And we spend some time getting to know each other. Outside of the one-nighter thing. The way we should have that night. And that next morning. I'm sorry I ran. You scared me."

"No kidding. I'm big and fierce."

"It was how you made me feel."

He should have spent the entire night with her. The next day, too. Make her understand that he did care about her. If that hadn't worked, he should have been out there that first day after that he could.

He shouldn't have left her feeling like what had happened between them hadn't mattered.

Because he wanted to know what made her afraid. What made her happy. What made her sad. What made her...love.

She was as different from April as a woman could get. He wasn't too thick-headed to see that.

He'd seen it that night, too.

And *that* was what had sent him running into the night. The potential of what he could feel for her.

He'd run, and those feelings were catching up with him anyway.

It was those fates and their plans for him again.

Caine decided then and there to let those fates catch him. This time.

"Rafe and Ari will be there. You might actually have to talk to them again." She gave him a wide-eyed, snarky look. The woman was trying to distract him from what needed to be said between them; Caine was wise to her ways now.

When she was frightened or anxious, Nikkie Jean tried to push people away with snark. Just like she used chatty humor when she was comfortable.

She went from one extreme to the next. Like she was too uncertain of where her emotions truly belonged.

"I'm a big boy. I'm sure I'll be fine. I may even send them

Christmas cards this year."

"Gee, I'm sure they'll appreciate it."

"You always use sarcasm when you're nervous?" Of course, she did. He was starting to figure her out. Nikkie Jean Netorre used humor and her bubbly personality to deflect people away from the insecurity underneath. Now he had to figure out what had made this beautiful, kind, intelligent, absolutely amazing woman not realize exactly who she was. Because something had. Caine understood the aftermath of trauma when it was right in front of him. "I don't have any family, Nikkie Jean."

"What?" She looked at his son pointedly. "Yes, you do."

"I have my children and a sixty-year-old uncle who isn't in the best of health. That's it. My so-called father is dead. My mother, I have no idea what happened to my mother. And I don't plan on asking. She abandoned me in a hospital incubator when I was two days old because I wasn't as good as Rafe. In reality, I think she couldn't sell a defective baby, so she just walked away. That's what my father told me my whole life. That my only worth to my mother was how much she could sell me for. I went for a fifth what my identical twin did. That...stayed with me. Making me feel second best for years. It took a while to get over that and my wife choosing other men—some of them twice her age—over me just pounded that in. I have never mattered to someone to come first except my uncle. And my father often separated us just to be an asshole. But my children—all of them, will know what they mean to me. My children have no one but me and my father's brother. The people back there that we don't yet know. And now you. I want my children to know you most of all. Because I want you to mean something to me, too. And I...want to mean something to you. Like I haven't anyone else before."

She was silent for an extremely long time. "My father never thought I was his, and he made that fact very well known. Every time they disagreed on anything one or the other of them brought up my paternity. As a weapon. They married because she was pregnant with my older brother. They stayed together for him. I was...the leftover. Like rotten meatloaf. *My* kid will never feel the way I did."

He hid a wince. There went any half-baked idea of them getting together for the sake of the baby he might have been formulating. Now he wouldn't even mention that as an option.

Nikkie Jean needed to know that he wanted her for her. Not because of their baby. Now he had to figure out just how to make her see that.

"I need to get to know them, for my children. And I need to do it before I expose Keller and Everett to them. Just to be sure."

"They're some of the best people I have ever met, Caine. I promise you that. The things I've watched them go through over the past six months have been horrifying. But they love each other and won't ever hurt your children. Or you."

"They'll be our daughter's family, too."

"Daughter? You have magic powers or something?"

He hadn't realized where his thoughts had gone. Since that morning conversation with Everett, he'd pictured the baby as a girl. That had only deepened when he'd watched his sister playing softball. He would love a little girl with Nikkie Jean's smile. The darker hair and eyes he possessed would be more dominant, but the smile—he hoped the baby had her smile. "Just thinking ahead. I'll love whichever we get, but I know Keller will want the baby to be a girl. She already feels outnumbered."

"I bet she does." Nikkie Jean stared out the window for a moment.

"I hope she has your smile. Or he. I'm happy with either."

"What are you going to tell them?"

"I don't know. That I've met a woman I care about and we've made a baby together. I've also started mentioning you—as a friend. So you won't just appear out of nowhere. They know where babies come from."

"It'll shake up their whole world. What if they resent the baby? I can't do that to them. Or to the baby. I just can't. I've lived like that, and I can't do it. Especially since it's built on a lie. Babies shouldn't hold up *lies*, Caine. It's not right."

He heard the well of hurt in her words. "It's not. But that happens in reality anyway. It took me a year to get Everett and Keller bonded with Dalton. They blamed the baby for their mother wanting to leave us. She left me two days after she learned she was pregnant. She told me the night she left. I didn't see her again until the day she and her lover were brought in to my ER. She died that day, leaving me with a premature infant I didn't know whether I was the biological father of."

It was the first time he'd ever said that aloud to anyone other than Henry.

But if he wanted Nikkie Jean to trust him, he was going to have to open up to her first.

"I just want to focus on getting through this pregnancy. Staying as healthy as I can. Because all I want is for this baby to have a chance. If you tell your children about the baby and something happens, what would you say then? I'm terrified that something will happen."

Her broken whisper went straight through him. No wonder her defenses were up. This entire journey had to be nothing but a massive roller coaster for her right now. "We'll do everything we can, sweetheart. And no matter what happens, I won't leave you to go through it alone. I'm sorry I've left you alone this week. I shouldn't have. Even with your little snark texts. We'll figure it out somehow. I promise. For all of us. I'm not leaving you to face this alone again."

The look she shot at him stabbed right through his gut. Because it told Caine one thing.

Nikkie Jean didn't trust a word he had just said. And it was his own damned fault.

Chapter 50

HIS SISTER-IN-LAW commandeered Dalton the instant Nikkie Jean carried him into the diner. Dalton wanted nothing to do with his father at the moment, instead being fascinated by Nikkie Jean and the other women around him, who kept stopping by to talk to Nikkie Jean and eye Caine with curiosity.

Dalton was eating up the attention. Caine, not so much.

He kept a watchful eye on his son as he was passed between Caine's sister-in-law and new sister, but he was grateful for the extra sets of hands to entertain the baby—while he focused on the woman with him.

He was going to follow her home. They were going to talk. It was as simple as that. He still had four hours before he had to drive into town to pick up the twins.

He and Nikkie Jean would talk, then maybe he'd convince her to go with him to pick up his older two. They could take the children to the diner.

Give the children a chance to get to know her, and her them.

Afterward, he'd take her back to his house with him. Introduce her to his uncle.

He'd never introduced a girlfriend to them before.

Nikkie placed her order, quiet in a way he didn't like. He shifted closer. "You've not been sick, have you?"

She nodded. "Every day for over three weeks. Usually clears up by noon. Usually. Allen shifted my schedule to later in the day. Dr. Jacobson. He said it's for Jelly Bean. That's what he's calling the baby."

"Do you have a good obstetrician?"

She nodded. "Same one as Jillian. She's affiliated with Finley Creek. And she does high risk. Layla Kaur."

He'd heard of the woman, but they'd never met. "I didn't realize you'd be high risk."

"I just don't want to take any unnecessary chances. Layla handles both high-risk and average pregnancies. And she's someone I know well enough to trust."

Because she was terrified. He could see that. He leaned down where he could whisper in her ear. "We'll be fine, sweetheart. I promise."

She looked up at him. "But there are never any guarantees. This is probably my only chance to carry a child, Caine. What if something happens?"

He twisted his fingers in hers. "It won't."

"I wish life worked like that."

—

Nikkie Jean would not let herself be a clichéd overemotional pregnant woman. She forced back the tears and smiled at Jillian when she said something about the little boy looking just like his father.

Just like his Uncle Rafe, too. That was no doubt what Jillian meant.

Jillian's child would no doubt look a lot like Dalton or the twins. Caine pulled her to a booth near the back, after grabbing a high chair from the corner. He retrieved his son from Rafe, who had somehow ended up with him, while she waited.

It was odd seeing him with the little boy. He was so comfortable being a father. He knew what he was doing. Far better than she did, apparently.

The new baby would probably slip seamlessly into Caine's life. He was just that confident at being a parent.

"Come home with me today. See my place. Talk to me."

"We can work out details after the baby is born." Nikkie Jean pulled in a deep breath. He didn't want her. She knew exactly what he wanted. And he was confident enough to think he was going to get the baby. She just happened to be the packaged deal he was stuck with. No matter what pretty words he used. "I…don't think anything else is a good idea. We both know this isn't going to go anywhere."

She knew that. And it was better that she remembered that.

No one had ever stuck with her long term. He definitely wouldn't. He'd wanted one night in her bed and that was it.

Caine was a good father right down to his toes, and he wanted their child. She was just a means to an end for him. She *had* to remember that.

Literally, she was just the incubator.

"How in the hell do we know that? It's obvious there's something there to work with—or we wouldn't be expecting the baby in the first place."

"We had a one-nighter after a pretty crappy day for me. I don't normally do that, in case you're thinking otherwise. And now we're dealing with the consequences. It's not like I'm the love of your life or anything."

He wasn't hers, either.

Caine was definitely not like the sweet young man who'd shown her that sex didn't have to be a nightmare. The three times she'd had sex with Cole had probably helped her in that one regard. She'd needed his soft touch and kindness. His love. He'd been more nervous than she had. The fun and play they'd engaged in had helped her feel more in control than she had in months back then.

With Caine, it had been about having someone's arms around her just for a little while. A human connection at a time when she'd needed that most.

Until he'd rejected her when they were finished. So soon she'd known the truth.

Sudden nausea hit her.

She stood. "Look, just…I'll keep you informed of the pregnancy's progress. Ultrasounds, that kind of thing. But let's not pretend there's ever going to be any more than a joint custody kind of thing. We'll be like divorced parents without the marriage between us. Think how much time and money on couples' counseling we'll save. But right now…just…I don't want to see you anymore. I just…can't deal with…I just can't."

Nikkie Jean looked for the best avenue of escape. And found it.

Izzie and Annie were watching her. Waiting. She nodded to her friends and they stood. Annie had three white takeout containers in her hands.

They already *knew* she needed them.

Izzie had her keys in one hand and a belligerent look on her face. Izzie was ready to take Caine on right now.

Nikkie Jean hurried over to the people who had never rejected her. "Let's just go. Please. Hurry. Before I do something stupid, like cry in front of everyone."

Chapter 51

HE HAD JUST SCREWED UP. He didn't have a clue how. But he had.

Now he had to figure out how to fix it. Dalton grumbled in his arms, wanting put down. Caine obliged. He couldn't stand there staring after her forever. He turned, and looked into a face identical to his own.

His twin had witnessed the whole exchange, no doubt. And heard every word. "Well? Any ideas how I can get through to her?"

"Nikkie Jean's got a reputation for being very skittish with men. Especially physicians," his twin said, quietly. "I've been very careful when speaking with her not to invade her space too much. The first time I was less than three feet away she nearly jumped out of her skin. Her hurt runs deeply. As does the fear."

"She wasn't afraid of me." Now he wasn't so sure. Had she not been so upset that night, would they have ended up in bed together? He didn't like the sour taste that thought left in his mouth.

"How did you meet?"

"She came into the ER. And I met her a few times in town." He wasn't going to discuss her with her damned boss, even if the guy was his twin brother. "We have some things to figure out between us."

"I know the feeling. Jillian and I—we met at a time when she was healing from some significant trauma of her own. Hell, we both were. And it wasn't easy in the weeks after we met. We both almost died, my brother Travis and his wife also. Then what happened with Marc and Ariella. Trauma, it changes people. I don't know Nikkie Jean's full story, but enough to know that it wasn't something most people would have come out of so strong. But she did. Triumphed. But there are still scars."

"We all have scars." He looked at the baby in his arms as some of his own wounds came flooding back. Yes, they all had scars.

"Some heal better than others."

Caine wanted to go after her. Force the issue. Demand the answers they both needed.

Rafe was a fast source of information, a step toward the goal of getting what he wanted. Caine would take that step no matter how much it rankled.

"We'll work things out between us."

"I have no doubt that you will." His twin smiled. "But you should be aware. Jillian has already told me that she is one hundred percent on Nikkie Jean's side, no matter what. Said that *that* is what Nikkie Jean needs most of all. Someone who can put her first, where she belongs."

"I'll keep that in mind."

"You do that." Rafe's expression hardened. "And you should know—when she was injured and I asked her if she wanted me to call you, she said no. Said that *you* thought she wasn't good enough for you. So whatever you've done to make her believe that, good luck in fixing it."

Caine bit back a curse. He'd known he'd done some damage with his stupidity, but that wasn't what he'd intended at all. Not good enough for him? Hell, she was probably *too* good for him. "That's the furthest thing from the truth. If anything, I'm not good enough for her."

"I know that feeling, too. Good luck. I think you're going to need it."

Chapter 52

FOR TWO DAYS, THE man invaded her brain at every possible opportunity. Nikkie Jean ruthlessly pushed him out. Fortunately, the people at W4HAV knew how to keep things relatively quiet. No one knew about Caine except Lacy, Fin, and Jillian. Well, along with Annie and Izzie, who were quietly supportive.

Jillian and Lacy were far more vocal. Jillian had hugged her and made a point to tell her that their babies would always be family and that Nikkie Jean couldn't escape her.

Family was everything to the Becks, Jillian had said. And had said that Rafe was thrilled to be getting another niece or nephew to pamper.

The man had started out as a pediatrician, after all.

They were acknowledging her—even if they weren't quite acknowledging Caine.

Jillian had also told her that Rafe was open to contact, but wasn't too thrilled with the idea of it. But Rafe wasn't thrilled with the idea of finding any of his mother's missing children.

Jillian had hinted there was more to the story than what Ariella had shared at W4HAV. Far more. And that Rafe and the others were willing to meet with Caine if he was ever ready. As if Nikkie Jean would ever talk to him about that subject.

Apparently, they'd both come from crappy home lives. Something they had in common. She wished her baby would have grandparents, but that apparently wasn't in the cards.

Well. Unless she counted Cherise and her fiancé Vincent. Cherise had made a point of telling her she was volunteering herself as a grandmother substitute.

Even though there was only fifteen years between her and Nikkie Jean.

Nikkie Jean had gotten all watery-eyed again. No wonder—Cherise had already given her a little yellow and green blanket she'd knitted. Jillian had received one just like it.

It was going to take some getting used to. Nikkie Jean was better at being at the fringes of social groups. It was easier to slip away when she was feeling overwhelmed that way.

But once the baby came, she wouldn't do that. Her baby would be a part of a community. Even if she had to build that community by stepping outside her comfort level.

Her baby would have brothers and a sister. Her baby would have cousins, including the three boys Annie was adopting. There were going to be actual aunts and uncles—something she hadn't ever had before—and there would be a mother and a father who loved the baby.

Of that, she had no more doubts.

Caine had gotten the softest look in his eyes when he'd spoken of the baby. And he'd been wonderful with Dalton.

She could so easily see those big hands of his cradling an infant. A girl, like he'd mentioned.

Damn him; he wasn't even there and she was starting to want to see him. Actually…almost…yearning to see him.

Just what had he done to her?

Nikkie Jean started across the parking lot instead of continuing to her car.

She needed W4HAV, needed someone to talk to about the man she couldn't get out of her head. She covered her stomach with her hand. "Baby, Mommy will figure this out. Somehow. Because I can promise you this—I don't think Daddy will ever go away."

Which meant she was going to have to deal with the attraction she felt for the man, before she did something completely insane.

Like actually think she was brave enough to *try* with Dr. Caine Alvaro. She really was going crazy.

Chapter 53

CONNIE WAS GETTING clingy. Wallace didn't know how much longer he could drag out the inevitable. Movement caught his attention, and he looked. Nikkie Jean, walking through the parking lot and talking to herself.

Heat flashed through him.

Had she seen who he was with?

He didn't want someone at FCGH seeing him with Connie and gossiping. It would be too easy for it to get back to Jennifer.

Wallace knew exactly how to keep his affairs from making it back to Jennifer.

He hoped Nikkie Jean hadn't seen. She was the last woman he wanted to know about Connie besides Jennifer.

He forced himself to breathe and relax. She probably hadn't seen him. Seen *them*.

Nikkie Jean had poor vision at a distance. She'd told him that herself. A damned fine surgeon, and she saw well enough close up with glasses and contacts, but he should be too far away for her to see exactly what it was he was doing. Or even who he was.

Jennifer's words from the night before ran through his head. *You always screw up anymore, Wallace. Why should this be any different. Just fix this. Just do it. I don't care how.*

Now, Jennifer was obsessing over how much damage had actually been done to her *campaign*.

Wallace thought she was gasping at ghosts, but she was the strategist in their relationship not him.

Dr. Holden-Deane's new audit of every department in the hospital was going to reveal some things Wallace wasn't proud of. As was Alvaro's. Rumor had it Alvaro had hired hound dogs to dig for every blip in every department. And he was starting with

Wallace's. It was a possibility they'd find exactly what Wallace didn't want found.

Maybe Jennifer was right; maybe Wallace's entire future—*their* entire future—truly was at stake.

If he lost that, and he couldn't secure a position on any of the other hospital boards, Jennifer's goal of him attaining a chief-of-medicine position would be gone.

He understood why she wanted him in a position of such authority. He did. Her entire platform was that she was a natural leader who understood *the people* far better than billionaire Turner Barratt, who had just fallen into the position when the previous mayor had died of a heart attack and Barratt had been appointed in his place.

Wallace would have to think of something.

He'd disappointed Jennifer so many times in the past; he didn't want to do so again. Not now, when it was so important to her.

Jennifer had never wanted anything more than she wanted this. He had to do what he could to make it happen for her. It was what a man did when he loved a woman as much as Wallace loved his wife.

Wallace slipped into his sedan and left the parking lot, head full of worries and ways he could fix things for Jennifer, aware of Connie's car behind his as she pulled out after.

Chapter 54

NIKKIE JEAN BREATHED a sigh of relief when she recognized Jeremy Tolvert, one of the county's TSP deputies, as the man waving her down from the middle of the road this time. She really needed to find another route home, apparently.

She didn't know him well, but he and his wife attended the same church where she'd worked a recent clothing drive with W4HAV. She'd spent the day with his wife working the intake. And had liked her quite a lot. "Jeremy…what's happened?"

"I thought that was your car, Doc. We need help. MVA. We got fifteen down at least and only two ambulances nearby. Sheriff and Bailey are just up ahead."

"Let me pull over." The least she could do was help stabilize people before they were transported to the hospital. It would be Barratt County. It was closer. But if there were that many injured, no doubt FCGH would take some of the overflow. She'd most likely get called back in anyway.

She grabbed her phone, called Wanda the ER intake nurse to let her know to just be prepared, and then grabbed the small first aid kit from her trunk. Within two minutes she was following the deputy toward the lights. And the smoke. "Air ambulance for FCGH on its way?"

Jeremy, a man a few years younger than Nikkie Jean, nodded. "Clay already called for it. But, Doc, I don't know if it'll be enough. I've never seen such blood."

Nikkie Jean grabbed her bag and ran.

—

The wreck must have happened just minutes before he came up on the scene. Caine pulled his large 4x4 off the road where it wouldn't obstruct the rescue vehicles, and he grabbed the bag he carried everywhere. Some lessons he'd learned in the military would never be forgotten.

People were out of their vehicles, attempting to give first aid to those who needed it. Or helping others out of the vehicles and out of the way.

Caine didn't bother with anyone already up and moving—he headed straight to the sheriff's deputy.

With this number of cars involved, there would be more serious injuries near the epicenter. Caine scanned the vehicles, looking for a familiar dark-purple Jeep.

It was too dark to see for certain.

Her schedule had been shifted back a few hours, she'd said. She was most likely still at her own hospital. The deputy in charge looked at him. "Dr. Caine Alvaro, head of Barratt County General. I'm here to help."

"I don't know. There are too many."

The sheriff was shouting orders from about one hundred feet away. The deputy was struggling to not get overwhelmed. To not let the panic show.

Caine made a decision.

He'd seen more field experience than this man; far more. This wasn't the first disaster scene Caine had been on, either. "Get someone to form a triage area over there, away from the vehicles in case of fire. Those cars in the middle. They still have people trapped?"

The young deputy, probably just out of school, nodded. "We're trying to get the ones out that we can. Before anything ignites. Make sure you're not in one if it does. That's what the sheriff said."

"Listen, it's going to get worse before it gets better. *Don't* let anyone see just how scared you are. You're their source of confidence out here tonight. That uniform is all the strength you need. Lean on it. You've got this. No one is doing it alone out here."

"Yes, yes, sir. I'll remember."

Caine took off toward the center of the crushed vehicles. It was there that the worst of the injuries would be.

The man inside the first truck was gone. It was obvious with one look. But the car nearby—there were people working next to it.

Pulling children from it. And shouting about fire.

Caine ran toward them it just as the sheriff's female deputy, Nikkie Jean's friend who'd played third base, lifted a little boy from the car.

Another woman slid out behind the child, barking orders.

Caine took one look at the glasses and the pretty face. The blood on her scrubs. Terror shot through him.

She was supposed to still be at her own hospital.

His hands went under her arms, and he pulled her free of the car. "Where are you hurt?"

She looked up at him and shook her head. "I was on my way home. Came up on it a few minutes ago."

"Me, too. Be careful out here. Watch for glass and don't fall." She and the deputy had a first responder working with them. But it wasn't enough. He wanted to carry her out of the way where she'd be safe. But every pair of hands out here could mean life or death out here. Her hands and his, especially.

The last place he wanted her was on the scene of a massive trauma event. He didn't want her anywhere near here.

"I can handle myself. Just go, Caine. Hurry; I'm going with that kid and his family."

The deputy was there, yelling about someone with burns. "Go! Don't worry about me! I can take care of myself!"

Caine took off.

When he next looked up, Nikkie Jean was gone. It took him ten minutes to learn she'd taken off with one of the ambulances. Most likely with that little boy she'd pulled free.

That didn't help him feel any better.

He found her again when he made it back to his own hospital. She was in his ER, giving orders to his staff. Some of his tension lessened. "Taking over, Netorre?"

"Sorry, not sorry."

"Status of the MVA patients?" Caine wrapped one hand around her elbow and kept her from disappearing. And just to touch her, reassure himself that she was safe. He looked at Jakob, his charge nurse on duty. "Children first?"

"Two kids are in critical, but it looks good. Three others are in stable. A few were treat-and-street, thank whoever you want to thank. Seven adults are in critical but good. Some of them are damned lucky you and Dr. Netorre were out there tonight, sir. Good thing you left when you did."

And not a moment before. If he'd left five minutes earlier, he could have been one of the ones on the stretcher.

Him or *her*. He looked at Nikkie Jean. She wore scrubs with rainbows and what looked to be candy-colored ponies he was all too familiar with. Scrubs covered with blood. "I'll take it from here; you sit and rest. Jason will get you some clean scrubs. Some juice and crackers."

"Thanks on the scrubs; I'm going to stay a while. My Jeep is still out alongside the road, and I'm not exactly certain how I'm getting home yet. And those kids we pulled out tonight? I want to stay until I hear how they are doing. Their parents are in your exam rooms now. They'll need someone to keep them updated on their kids. Or I may get called in to FCGH. One of your ambulances is doing a transfer there in the next hour. I'll hitch a ride."

It was the life of a surgeon, to be called when needed. Especially pediatric and trauma. Nikkie Jean would *always* run the risk of being called in at a moment's notice.

"Sit. Rest. I'll run you home myself on the back roads as soon as I can."

Chapter 55

NIKKIE JEAN SPENT SEVERAL long hours in the waiting room, helping comfort the loved ones who had started trickling in twenty minutes after Caine had disappeared into the surgical ward. Nikkie Jean looked like she knew what she was talking about; people needed that. Especially tonight.

People had died on that highway tonight.

When Caine finally emerged, he had changed into standard blue scrubs that made his shoulders look ridiculously wide.

She blinked. He looked just like Rafe right there.

Except for the dragon tattoo.

It was twenty minutes past midnight, and he looked as exhausted as she felt.

The people in the waiting room were watching him. Her. He nodded at them, quickly. "Your son came through just fine."

She listened as he gave the couple the information they needed. They left to speak with his charge nurse, and he looked down at her. He reached out a hand for her. It surprised her so much she took it and let him pull her to her feet.

Then she was in his arms, and he was hugging her. Nikkie Jean's arms snaked around his waist, and she hugged him back. She kind of needed that right now.

Either one of them could have died tonight. Kind of hard to miss.

He felt real and strong, his heartbeat right beneath her cheek. She just clung to him for a moment.

"I'll give you that lift now."

"Thanks." She waited until he spoke with the charge nurse, then followed him outside. The parking lot at Barratt County Gen was a lot smaller than that at Finley Creek.

He led the way to his 4x4. He unlocked the door and opened it.

There was an aftermarket handle installed that made the climb in a lot easier. But he gave her an extra hand up, lifting her into the belly of the beast. "Thanks."

"The truck comes in handy where I live."

"Do you get flooded in?"

"It floods to the north of us, but I have a few alternate routes into town I can take."

She fastened her seat belt as he circled the front of the truck.

It was a mostly silent ride. When they pulled into her drive, he parked right in front of her porch. "Stay there. I'll help you down."

She wasn't quite ready to be alone with what she'd seen just yet. But that didn't mean she was about to invite Caine into her inner sanctum again.

She probably weighed a third of what he did. He'd lifted her far too easily that night. She'd be stupid to remember how his hands had felt. To want that again.

"Thanks. See you around, Alvaro."

"You really think it's going to be that easy? We are finally alone. No toddlers or your guard dogs around."

"What do you mean? There's not much else to say."

"No?" He shifted closer, until he was crowding right into her space. "You scared the shit out of me tonight when you slid out of that car. *Nothing* has ever scared me more except when Keller had to have her appendix out a year ago."

"It was a pretty rough night." Her breath came out in a gulp. "I wasn't certain you weren't in the middle of it. I kept looking for your truck."

"The first thing I did was look for a purple Jeep."

Caine's hands went around her waist. Nikkie Jean found herself in his arms again. Hers slipped around his neck.

She just wanted to breathe him in. "It…was just random. People were just in the wrong places."

"I know."

"I've never…I've always been in the hospital operating rooms. I've never seen them still seat belted in. I had to get him out. Bailey…Bailey was just a little too big to fit, but I could. He was so little." And his mother had been screaming. Nikkie Jean had had to force the woman to just *move* so Nikkie Jean could help him. Tears slipped from her eyes. "His mother was screaming. So terrified. I've never loved anyone like that, Caine. What if I can't with the baby?"

"You will. You'll love our baby so much. I...when I first held the twins, my world changed. Completely."

"And Dalton?" His shoulder was so strong. How had she ended up with him carrying her again? She couldn't remember. "Was it the same with him?"

He stiffened. Nikkie Jean tensed. And pulled back to look at him.

"Caine?"

"She told me he wasn't mine," Caine said, harshly. Nikkie Jean froze. "We separated after she told me she was pregnant and the baby wasn't mine. I didn't see her again until the night she died."

"What?"

"She came to the house twice to visit the children, with my uncle there. She stayed less than an hour each time. April was finished being a mother."

And Caine's hurt was right there in his words. Nikkie Jean's hands flexed on his shoulders. "Tell me."

He shuddered, actually shuddered, beneath her hands. "We were separated. I had full, uncontested custody. She wanted to start over again with her sixty-year-old lover who was ready to retire and take her everywhere. Pamper her like she deserved. She didn't want a husband who'd started as a lowly military doctor. Not enough prestige."

And that had hurt him. She knew it instinctively. Caine...he was the type to have become a physician to *heal.* To help.

Like she had.

Never for the money; and she'd known a few physicians who were in it for that very reason. Medicine was very, very lucrative. "I'm sorry. That must have hurt."

"More than anything I had ever experienced. But more than that, how could she not want our children? That was an answer I didn't get...until the end."

And that end had not been pretty. She just knew it. "You can tell me. I'll listen. Sometimes it does help to talk. I know that from years of therapy."

His hands tightened on her as he stepped up on her porch, over the steps he'd fixed himself.

No one had ever fixed anything for her—not unless she paid for it first.

"Do you have your keys ready?"

"Yes." She gave them to him.

Somehow he managed to get her door unlocked without even jostling her.

Then they were in her house again. Just the two of them.

Nikkie Jean didn't feel so much as an ounce of fear. Not for this man. Not now.

He carried her to her couch. Then she felt herself going down. He'd sat down, with her right in the center of his lap.

Nikkie Jean had never been carried around by a man in her life. She kind of half thought she liked it. "Caine? What happened to your wife?"

"Hit-and-run." His hands tightened on her. "She was thirty-three weeks pregnant."

A surprised curse escaped. "I am so sorry."

"I was the assistant chief of trauma medicine. I was called in before they realized who she was. The man she'd left me for had been killed on impact. But April…he'd managed to push her out of the way slightly. But he wasn't a strong man, and she was a taller woman. She was still hit. She landed on her abdomen. Dalton…he had a slight concussion before he was even born."

Nikkie Jean wrapped her arms around him and just hugged him. "I'm so sorry."

He used those strong hands of his to shift her slightly. Nikkie Jean didn't care. She just wanted…to comfort. To help erase the pain she heard in his voice.

"I'd stopped loving her long before that. He wasn't her first affair. But I…we had two children together. Children who deserved their mother. I've learned since that she wasn't always kind to our children. I wish…I wish I had left her earlier, but then I wouldn't have Dalton, Nikkie Jean. And I will never regret him."

"How could you? He's…perfect. Wonderful."

"He's my son. He was from the moment they performed an emergency C-section and delivered him at less than thirty-four weeks. It didn't matter that I didn't think he was biologically mine until almost three months later. Dalton was my son, and he needed me. I…April woke. She was awake long enough to know they were going to take the baby. And that she most likely wouldn't survive. She coded on the table two minutes before our son was born. She never got to see him."

Tears flowed over her cheeks. Tears she also heard in his

voice. Caine *had* loved his wife. Once. And he loved their children.

He cleared his throat. "It took me a while to forgive her. She told me at the end...she just didn't feel like she could be a good mother. A good wife. She needed someone to take care of her, not the other way around. And she had to leave the children before she did any more lasting damage. She'd been married before; to an older man, then, too. But she had loved me."

Nikkie Jean just nodded. What was she supposed to say to the sheer amount of pain in his words? She didn't have a clue. But she hurt for him. So much.

"She'd just never thought she'd measured up to what I needed, to what kind of doctor she thought I was. But I didn't see any measuring up. I just...I'm not sure I loved her the way she needed to be loved from the beginning. By the time I realized that, we had two toddlers and a life I didn't want to destroy. I tried my best to be the husband she needed. But I was always going to be second best to the memory of the man before."

"Oh, Caine. I don't think it was you that was second best. It sounded like that was how *she* felt about herself."

Nikkie Jean pressed her face against his heart again. He was just that much bigger. Larger-than-life. Intimidating and intense.

But she *knew* in that moment that those large, strong hands of his would never lift in anger to her, or anyone smaller or more vulnerable. She just knew it.

Caine cared about people just too darned much.

Nikkie Jean pulled back and looked at him for a long, long time. And then she leaned forward and kissed him.

Kissed him just to comfort.

—

Caine fought the urge to just crush her against him and hold her. It had been the first time since Dalton's birth that he'd fully shared what had happened that night. Henry knew some of the story. But not all.

Not that Caine had sat next to his dying wife and promised to take care of all three of her children for her. She hadn't known if Dalton had been Caine's either.

But he had promised. And he had held her hand until the moment they took her away for the emergency C-section.

He'd been forced to watch from the window. And he'd known the moment she'd died.

He'd known.

Nothing.

He sat there for a long time, kissing Nikkie Jean. Some of the anger he'd felt toward April dissipated.

She'd just…been doing the best *she* could, trying to measure up to ideas that she had. Trying to be who she needed to be in order to find peace with herself.

It had just been rotten fate that had led to her death before she could find that peace.

He pulled back. He needed to finish the story. To tell her *why* she'd meant so much to him from that first moment.

"I…Dalton was in NICU for three weeks. I signed the birth certificate, gave him the name she'd chosen—Dalton was her maiden name—and took him home when the time came. And I had a DNA test done."

Nikkie Jean stiffened against him, then visibly forced herself to relax. "Did it matter, though?"

"Not for a moment. He was mine from his first breath. I never opened the results, Nikkie Jean. They're still in the safe in my home office. I doubt that I ever will."

"He's your son, biologically. He has to be. He looks just like you."

"He does. And he is my son. I don't *care* what those results say. He's my son because I say he is. Period."

"I wish my father had said the same," she said in a small, broken voice.

Caine's hands slipped around her back, then dropped to rest lightly on her ass. "What do you mean?"

"My father wanted nothing to do with me until I was sixteen, fighting ovarian cancer and recovering from his medical partner raping me. He never claimed me as his daughter—until the DNA test my mother requested from the hospital where my father worked came back showing I was his kid, after all."

Caine's hands tightened as what she said sank in. "Dear God."

"Yeah, I know, right? He had a single sheet of paper saying I actually was his spawn, so I was supposed to forgive him everything and just let him in my life. I recently got a letter from him. Apologizing. Said a father should protect his child and he'd failed. No kidding."

She'd been raped.

By a physician.

Caine's hands trembled. What was he supposed to say now? "Sweetheart—"

She stiffened. "Don't get all freaked out, Caine. We both know everyone has scars. Some are just deeper than others."

"I know."

"I didn't tell you to make you go all freaked."

But someone had before. "You're not the first rape victim I've known, Nikkie Jean. Or childhood cancer survivor. You are, however, the first one I've made a baby with. Our conversation will be a bit unique because of that, right?"

"At least, you haven't just stood up and walked away. The second guy I was with—willingly—said he couldn't deal with damaged goods. Hightailed it out of my apartment like his shorts were on fire. I guess he didn't want his own *goods* to be damaged by association."

Caine cursed that bastard's antecedents. Vocally. "He didn't deserve you."

"No kidding. That's ok. He was such a fail in the bedroom I don't think I was missing much." She was holding herself stiff, her arms over her midsection. Defensive. Frightened.

No wonder. Opening old wounds after a night like they'd just had was bound to make them both feel more than a little raw.

"He was an idiot, Nikkie Jean. There's nothing *damaged* about you. No more than there is anyone else who's experienced a trauma. Of any kind."

"You and I know that. But he didn't. But he was young. Hopefully, he's learned his lesson. Or some enterprising little witch has turned him into a toad."

Jokes and little quips. She was feeling unsettled and insecure again. Caine loosened his grip on her immediately. "I'll listen. If you want to tell me. If not…I'll just hold you. As long as you will let me."

"Maybe, Caine Alvaro—" Her breath hitched once. Her fingers toyed with the V-neck of his scrubs. "Maybe you're just a far better man than the ones I've known."

"I'm not sure I am. I just…I'll never deliberately do anything to hurt you. Ever."

"I know." She just looked at him from those eyes of hers. Eyes that always saw straight into his soul. "And that is what makes me so terrified of you. You…can make everything about my world change."

"And would that be a bad thing? Change isn't always

necessarily *bad*."

"No. But in my experience, it can be. It always has."

"Nikkie—" His cell buzzed, jerking both of their attention to where he'd placed it on her end table.

He cursed and grabbed for it. He checked the screen. The curse got louder. He answered, curtly. "Henry? What is it?"

He listened for a long moment. His gaze shifted to Nikkie Jean. "I'll be there as soon as I can."

After he disconnected, he turned to her. "I…damn it, I hate to do this right now."

"You have to go."

"Yes. The twins. They are both vomiting and feverish. Henry's not great with the kids when they're sick. He starts to panic." Caine let his hands linger on her back. He brushed another kiss over her forehead. "I…will see you again, soon."

"Of course, you will, Alvaro. I pop up when a man least expects it."

"And that's one of the things that fascinates me about you. Just remember that. No woman has ever fascinated me more."

Chapter 56

HIS UNCLE HAD LEFT A light on for him. Caine appreciated it. His ranch that he'd bought with insurance money from April's policy wasn't in the best of shape yet, and the driveway had a tendency to wash out a bit during heavy rains. He'd been meaning to get a security light put up, but hadn't managed that yet, either.

And sometimes there were bikes and toys left right in his path.

He hurried up the steps out of the rain, his mind not on the horrors he'd seen earlier—those would probably hit him just as he was crashing—but on what Nikkie Jean had told him.

Caine knew enough of trauma and its aftereffects to know it wasn't going to be easy. Healing never was.

Hell, he'd finally felt like he'd started to heal from what had happened when he'd found his wife dying in his own damned ER.

Healing was a lifelong battle. And it could reshape a person's entire life.

He'd wanted to hold her and tell her that he wished he could go back and fix everything for her. All of it. But no one could fix the past. They could just listen and be there for the now.

He couldn't erase what had happened to her—any more than she could erase what had happened to him.

All they could do was try to build a better future together. Caine wanted the chance to try.

He stopped in the first bedroom on the right.

The female he should be worried about wasn't where she was supposed to be. Caine fought off panic, Nikkie Jean's words earlier running through his own head.

A father was supposed to protect his children.

Caine forced himself to calm down. He suspected he knew exactly where Keller was.

And he was right—she'd made her way to the bottom bunk in her twin brother's room. Keller was a sensitive little girl. And when he wasn't home, easily frightened. He covered her with the special blanket she'd dragged in with her. It had pink-and-purple ponies on it, her only concession to girliness.

Sometimes, he wondered if maybe living in an all-male household wasn't doing Keller a disservice.

He didn't even think his daughter owned any dresses.

Why that worried him at the moment, he didn't know. The things Nikkie Jean had told him about how her mother had been inconsistent in her life. How she hadn't had anyone to help her navigate the teen years and had been so confused all the time? He didn't want a similar anxiety for his daughter.

A father was supposed to protect his children.

He crossed the hall into his youngest's room. Dalton still slept in the fetal position every night. He was a good-sized, sturdy kid. He was built like Caine had been as a child. Caine studied this child he'd considered a gift from the first time he'd held him. Dalton did resemble Caine more than the others.

He checked each of his children quietly. Fever-free. Probably something they'd eaten hadn't sat quite right. They were sleeping peacefully now.

Everett was a taller kid, as well, but he was thinner than Caine had been. Keller was tall, thin, and delicate.

Sometimes, he was afraid she'd break. She was the kid he worried about most. He couldn't imagine how Nikkie Jean's father could have denied his daughter for sixteen years.

The love Caine felt for each of his children sometimes threatened to take his breath away. It was just that strong.

If Dalton hadn't been his, it would have devastated him at first. But his son had still needed him. From the very first moment he'd held Dalton he had loved him.

He didn't think that would have changed no matter what was printed on that sheet of paper in the safe.

Nikkie Jean's hurt stabbed right through him.

His thoughts were heavy when he left his youngest's room after checking for fever, and headed toward his own. It didn't matter how late he got in at night, breakfast always came at seven. He had the weekend off, except for quick check-ins, but that didn't mean he'd get to rest.

Better get what sleep he could, while he could. If the children were coming down with something, Caine was going to be extremely busy in the morning.

Caine stretched out in his bed and tried not to let the nightmares he'd seen haunt him. Tried not to let Nikkie Jean's.

Tonight had made things crystal clear to him.

Five minutes earlier on the highway and Nikkie Jean would have been in one of those cars. And he would have found her there. His world would have shattered in an instant if he'd lost her and the baby tonight.

A thousand times worse than it had when April had been in his ER.

Whatever feelings he had for Nikkie Jean at first, they'd already shifted into something deeper. Something lasting. Something stronger than even what he'd had with April. He wasn't going to give that up. But he would have to do things right. For everyone. He couldn't rush her. He couldn't rush the children. There would have to be things he worked out with her. So that she'd always know she'd be safe with him. The last thing he wanted to do was hurt that woman.

It was a long time before he slept.

Chapter 57

SHE REFUSED TO LET HERSELF think about the man who looked just like the one staring down at her. Once Nikkie Jean returned back to work the day after the MVA, she forced Caine from her mind. She wasn't going to think of him right now.

She just felt like too much chewed up raw hamburger after what had been shared between them.

She'd given him all of last night in her head. And had dreamed about how those strong perfect arms had felt around her. That dream had morphed into an oddly familiar-looking dragon flying through the Value, Texas, sky, slaying all of her enemies with a single claw.

Enemies that looked like her father and like the man who had raped her years ago.

Ridiculous. Enough was enough.

She had to get back to normal. Had to. Last night had felt too right, the way he had held her while she'd cried. And told him everything.

The last man she'd told everything to had gone loony tunes on her afterward. He'd alternated between being angry with her—and trying to coddle her with kid gloves.

Nikkie Jean hadn't needed that.

Their relationship had fizzled less than a month later, because Scott hadn't been able to handle her *baggage.* He'd been only a moderate improvement over the one before who thought she'd been damaged beyond repair, not even fifteen minutes after she'd told him why she wasn't ready for sex that fast.

The FCGH chief of medicine was still all grumbly. Maybe he needed a fifteen-minute break with Jillian or something.

Rafe had come into their department, within the throws of

what could only be referred to as his warpath mode.

Someone, and she suspected it was Dr. Henedy, had flubbed up again.

Rafe was looking for the answers. Answers no one had, except Dr. Henedy.

Nikkie Jean did the only thing a sane woman could do when he questioned her. Interrogated her, third-degree style.

She shrugged and tried to run for the hills. Behind his sister-in-law. He adored Lacy, after all. When that didn't work, she covered her stomach with one hand, and put her wrist to her head. Maybe there was some uncle mercy in there somewhere?

"Oh, Lordy me, I feel faint." She shot him a grin. "It's the baby, sur-uh. It makes me forgetful...bad genes from the fath-uh, after all..."

It didn't work.

But she was *almost* certain his lips had twitched. That happened a lot since he'd hooked up with Jillian. She sent him an innocent smile again. "Yes, Dr. Holden-Deane, sir? Can I help you today?"

He shot a look at Allen. "Do they always misbehave in here?"

"Every day. But what can we say? They're the patients' favorites."

Rafe shot her a look. "If you see Dr. Henedy, remind him that I want to speak with him. Immediately."

"Will do." And she'd just make a point of avoiding Dr. Henedy. More than she usually did, anyway.

He was getting a bit...creepy. She didn't want to complain to Allen or Rafe—yet. But if he didn't stop just *watching* her, she would have to consider it. Something odd had been in his eyes the last time they'd encountered one another in the parking lot.

He always seemed to be waiting in the parking lot, no matter what time Nikkie Jean left for the day.

"And Nikkie Jean? Behave. No more shaving cream in other doctors' lockers." He shot her a grin that sent an unexpected pain through her heart. For Caine. Rafe looked just like his brother then. She just wished Caine had found Rafe sooner. Wished he'd had some sort of better support system years ago when he'd lost his wife. Caine hadn't deserved to have to face that all alone.

She looked at Lacy and winced. She'd helped, but it had been Lacy's idea. "What is he talking about? I never put *shaving* cream anywhere."

Lacy just shrugged innocently. "Travis says he's always had odd fantasies."

Rafe's look intensified. He held up a hand and rolled his eyes toward the ceiling. "Behave. *Both* of you. At least for one week, ok? Until after this billing audit is off my plate and the buyers from Carrington are settled. Consider it a challenge. Lacy, see that she eats something healthy for lunch. Have to combat those bad genes from the father somehow. Get back to work, both of you."

She was almost convinced he was smiling when he left.

Someone bumped her from behind, and she turned, forcing herself not to squeak at the contact. Looked into gray eyes and an extremely handsome face. Smelled his subtle cologne.

"He might be fooled by your innocent act, but I know who it was." Allen leaned down and whispered in her ear. "And there will be payback."

She shot him the most innocent look she could. "I don't have a clue what you're talking about."

"Of course not. But since you and Lacy apparently have the most free time today...I'm sure maintenance has cleaning rags ready. Happy lunch."

She waited until the man had walked out, then turned to her partner in crime. She high-fived her accomplice. "Nice to see him smile again."

"It is. People have been tiptoeing around him long enough. That's the last thing Allen needs. He needs to have a normal again."

"Completely agree." Allen was a friend; not a close one, but she cared about him. "Come on. We have *whipped* cream to clean up."

"Let's do it. Then I'll buy you lunch, like Rafe ordered. We need to think of what to do with Allen next," Lacy said. "Shake him out of it."

"I think he needs a woman. A woman as opposite from that pharmacy tech as possible." Allen was lonely. That pharmacy tech who'd hurt him had done some serious damage. And the poor guy had lost both of his best friends around the same time. "Someone genuine and kind. Who isn't so mercenary."

He was guarded now in a way he hadn't been before. She knew what that was like far too well. She knew the hurt trauma could cause up close and personal, after all.

"You volunteering? I think you'd give him gray hair, Nik. And don't you have a big, snarly COM of your own?"

"Mine's not as snarly as Jillian's. He's just…more hurt…than Rafe, I think." Caine and Rafe had very different temperaments, in a lot of ways. Unexpected ways. Caine was far more…sensitive. And hiding his own deep dragon wounds. It made her feel a bit more than protective of him. "And I'm not so certain he's *mine*."

Although it had felt right all snuggled up against him on her couch last night. She had to remember not to read too much into that though.

The phone call about his children could have just been a convenient excuse for him to escape—even if it had come at nearly one thirty in the morning.

"Not to mention, I'm going to be busy for the next eight months, followed by eighteen years after that. How can I juggle being mommy and being doctor *and* being with a man like Caine Alvaro?"

"Totally understand. So who can we throw at Allen to take that look out of his eyes?"

"I'm not sure." Nikkie thought about it as they went to work cleaning up their mess. "Annie?"

Lacy shook her head. "He's too brotherly with Annie."

"And she'd probably run for the hills if a man like Allen even looked at her." Annie wasn't just uncertain of men. She was extremely shy. A man with Allen's confidence and, well, *charisma,* would terrify Annie. And overwhelm her. "Fin was my first thought a few weeks ago, but I think Virat might object to that now."

Lacy smirked. "No doubt."

"Izzie?" She discounted that as soon as she said it. She and Lacy both laughed for a long moment after that one. "No. I have a feeling they'd fight constantly. She *really* doesn't like male doctors."

"For good reason."

Izzie had had some trouble with a former chief of medicine.

Nothing had come from it at the hospital. But the man had been arrested shortly after. On prostitution charges. Stemming from a sting on Boethe Street.

Izzie's uncle was with the TSP, and often patrolled Boethe Street. Nikkie Jean had put things together rather quickly.

Most physicians were good people. Nikkie Jean knew that. But there were always a few buttheads in the bunch. Just like in any other profession.

It was the first time that thought had actually occurred to her.

Allen's trauma was far different than Nikkie Jean's had been, but he'd still been betrayed. Hurt in a way that there was no simple bandage for. And that was why she'd do what she could to help him.

Caine had his own share of trauma to heal from. And a part of her thought that maybe *he* wasn't quite as far along on the journey as she was.

His pain had sounded so raw last night.

Her phone buzzed and she read the text quickly.

"Apparently, I have to go as Allen's plus-one to Ari's wedding. He says it's his revenge."

"Weren't you planning to go anyway?"

"Of course. I'm helping oversee the guest book and the ushers. Apparently, I'm destined for Guest Book Greatness."

"I think you're Allen's safety date."

"I'd be up for a just-friends evening with Allen. But that's it. He looks like he could really use a friend. And I just don't have enough of those."

She texted back a quick reply. And said yes.

"I don't think any of us do."

Chapter 58

ALLEN WAS STILL SMILING when he walked into the entrance of Barratt County Gen an hour after he'd left Finley Creek County Gen. It had been a while since he'd had anything like that to laugh about. Once he would have told Jess about the prank, but not now.

That wasn't possible.

But at least he was able to get through half a day without thinking about her and what had happened. Or Logan and Banks.

The day had gone too well for him to let old nightmares resurface.

He had a follow-up patient who'd somehow ended up in Barratt County. He wanted to check on him, and since he was on his way to Garrity to pick up his sister Shelby after she'd ridden home with a classmate two days ago, he figured now was as good a time as any.

He rounded the corner near the information desk and stopped short as he almost slammed into a familiar face. "Rafe."

"Caine." The man wore jeans with his suit coat. Not something Allen would expect of Rafe. Other than that...almost dead ringer. "His twin."

Once Allen looked closer, it was obvious. The scar was rather distinctive. "I apologize. At first glance..."

"I know. We're identical. Can I help you?"

Allen held out his hand. He'd gotten the message. "Dr. Allen Jacobson, Finley Creek Gen. Head of surgery."

"Caine Alvaro, COM."

Allen wasn't lost to the similarities—or the coincidence. Rafe hadn't mentioned having another brother. And Allen had known the Deanes for years. Curiosity filled him, but Allen kept his mouth shut. Their private life was none of his business. "Nice to meet you. I'm just passing through. I have a patient in your ICU. Mr. MacHeney."

"He mentioned he was under your care. Dr. Henedy is handling his care here."

The conversation turned to the patient, and Allen was impressed. Alvaro knew his stuff and knew what was happening in his own hospital.

But then again, so did his brother. Rafe was a damned gifted physician and always had been. And a fine administrator. He suspected this brother was extremely similar in that regard.

When they were halfway to the ICU unit, Alvaro looked at him. "You have white foam of some sort on your cheek. It looks like a fingerprint."

Allen lifted his hand, and sure enough, his face was sticky. "Whipped cream. Dr. Netorre...that little brat."

"Nikkie Jean?" The other man's expression shifted in an instant. Allen's hackles rose.

"That's her. She kissed my cheek before I left. Little troublemaker. I knew she was up to something. She almost always is. She filled my locker with whipped cream this afternoon."

The man's lips twitched. "She did? Why did she do that?"

"The same reason she glued Rafe's office door shut a few months ago. Or ordered pizzas for the PICU nurses and told them to bill Rafe's wife. She ordered two hundred rainbow balloons for the pediatric cancer ward—charged them to Dr. Patel after he'd switched her lunch order to one with jalapenos. She's incorrigible. Nikkie Jean can be a handful. She's also one of the best pediatric surgical residents I've ever seen."

"And she kissed you?" If possible, the man's expression darkened. "Why?"

"We're...friends." He knew what that implied, but he didn't give a damn. Some protective urges were rising, and Allen knew it. "About Mr. MacHeney?"

He wasn't going to stand there and discuss Nikkie Jean, a woman who was far too vulnerable to men like Caine Alvaro—men like Allen used to be—with a stranger. For all her humor and playfulness and friendliness, Nikkie Jean kept a distance between herself and others.

One that spoke of more hurt than Allen wanted to think about.

Allen didn't like to speculate about the people he worked with, or the people he was starting to care about, but there was something in the other man's eyes when he spoke of Nikkie Jean.

Something that Allen just did not like.

Possession.

"Let's get Henedy down here, see what he has to offer."

Chapter 59

WALLACE WAS SWEATING. He just hoped the other two men attributed it to the July Texas heat. He'd been paged from his office to the third floor where Dr. Alvaro and Allen Jacobson had been waiting.

He'd always been a bit nervous around authority figures. And his boss at Barratt County was definitely an authority figure. He'd reamed Wallace four times in the six months or so that he'd been chief of medicine. The last thing he need was Dr. Alvaro turning the full force of his fury in Wallace's direction.

Allen turned to him, soliciting his opinion. "We'll need to build a team, quickly. Do the surgery at FCGH. I want both Dr. Netorre and Dr. Deane to assist. It's not pediatric, but the technique is the same, and I don't believe either have seen it enacted. And I'm comfortable with the two of them in my OR. Wallace?"

"I'm fully on board with those two little ladies assisting. Remarkable girls, and damned fine surgeons."

Dr. Alvaro's shoulders tensed. Wallace studied him.

"I've been trying to get ahold of Dr. Netorre this afternoon. I'm not having any luck."

Wallace had no idea why Caine Alvaro would be wanting to talk to Nikkie Jean. He hadn't even known the two were acquainted.

Unless it had something to do with Carrington. The sweating intensified.

If Jordan Carrington put things together…

Allen checked his watch. "She's most likely still assisting in surgery. She had a long one today. And it wasn't going to be easy. I actually should go, check on the department as a whole. Rafe has been on everyone lately."

"The audit at FCGH is supposed to finish next week?" Wallace asked.

If Holden-Deane and Alvaro started discussing the two hospitals, and the two audits, they could eventually put things together. If they involved Nikkie Jean and her father, it was possible Jordan could trace records back twenty years or more. Jordan had those kinds of connections in the industry.

And if he put it together with Miranda...

The men were both sharp as tacks. Probably sharper than Wallace was. If he had failed to cover his machinations even once...one of the two brothers would find it.

And that would bring the entire house of cards toppling down, blowing lost in the wind.

The man who'd been Wallace's roommate in medical school had just been arrested for Medicare billing fraud in Wyoming. It was making the news nationwide, as that man had been a noted speaker and researcher. And thief.

Wallace didn't want to be painted a thief by association.

What he had done wasn't theft. Not really.

At one point, Jennifer had ordered him to cultivate those relationships. She seemed to have forgotten that fact. Now, all he had to do was cleanse and purge his files. That's all, Jennifer had said.

As if it was that easy.

All that was in the computers somewhere, Wallace knew it. Barratt County might be quite a bit behind compared to Finley Creek Gen, but they weren't in the Dark Ages.

If Alvaro's audit found even a single mistake in Wallace's files, it could destroy everything.

Jennifer was panicking.

She'd said there were things Wallace didn't know about. And he would just have to trust her the way she was trusting *him* to clean this mess up. Fifteen particular files had to be erased, and Jennifer had given him very clear instructions to just get it done. Then get through the next seven days or so without making waves or drawing attention his way. She was trusting him, she'd said.

"Starting the final portion Monday. Rafe is wanting to finish with surgical and anesthesiology. Give it a deeper review." Allen's face tightened. "After everything that's happened."

He shot a look at Dr. Alvaro. But the other man didn't seem to be paying much attention to Wallace.

"Totally understand. I'll finish up here, then make my rounds at FCGH." If he hurried, he'd maybe make it back to have a short word with Dr. Netorre. Tell her he'd checked on the patients she'd helped rescue in the motor vehicle accident. "The surgery? I have an opening tomorrow at ten a.m."

Allen nodded. "It's probably best to do it as quickly as possible. But I want to wait, give the antibiotics time to work on the swelling. Ten should work just fine."

Allen excused himself. Wallace was ready to find his own office and get started on what he needed to do, too. "I'll see you tomorrow at ten, then."

"That works," Dr. Alvaro said before Allen left. "Jacobson? Do me a favor? Tell Nikkie Jean she'll be seeing me soon."

Wallace bit back a curse. The last thing he needed was Alvaro putting things together with Nikkie Jean. If she was in contact with her father, and *he* chimed in, the house of cards wouldn't just fall apart, it would be completely destroyed. There were things Jordan Carrington probably knew about that could be very, very bad for Wallace. Things that could ruin everything.

Chapter 60

"WE'RE GETTING CLOSER," Thor told Caine over lunch a few days after the MVA. "We'll have your answers soon."

"Anything standing out?" To be honest, Caine hadn't had much time to think about the audit and its ramifications.

He had had three sick children and a sick uncle recovering from what he strongly suspected had been food poisoning to focus on. They were finally back up to near-full speed. The children were all cranky from having been cooped up too long, but Caine finally felt like he could take a breather.

Maybe.

He still had one Nikkie Jean Netorre to hunt.

The woman was avoiding him again.

It hadn't surprised him. She had a habit of retreating every time something significant occurred.

The night of the MVA had been something significant between them, and they both knew it.

Her text responses had changed in tone since then, too. Some of the snark was gone. And *she* had actually texted him first for the past few nights.

Conversations. Not just two- or three-word responses.

She'd wanted to know how the children were doing, how Henry was.

How Caine was.

He'd wanted to know how *she* was. Whether she was resting. What she was craving. Just anything he could ask her.

But that was one thing—pinning her down to actually *see* him again was another.

He hadn't quite figured out what to do about that yet.

"You with me, Alvaro?"

Caine tuned back in. "Sorry. Got distracted. I have a lot on my plate right now."

"No kidding. I'm heading over to Finley Creek to do some poking around. I'm not so sure this Ralstone is the guy you're after. There are a few others with discrepancies that might be more…fruitful avenues to pursue. Can you give the guy over there a heads-up? I don't want to step on any toes."

"Let me make a call. I'll get you in the door with the COM."

"Oh yeah, the long-lost twin. So how's that working out for you?"

Caine shot him a look. "None of your damned business."

"Hey, you helped me save my little brother's ass from the fire. I figure I owe you one for that. If that means poking into your business, then I am all up for it."

"He's halfway decent. Good friends with the woman I'm involved with."

"Oh? Tell me about her."

"Not yet." Thor was worse than any gossip he'd ever seen. Always wanting the goods. But he wasn't ready to talk about Nikkie Jean fully yet. "She's over there, in pediatric surgery. Works directly with Ralstone and some of the other men on that list."

Thor swore. "Then I'll make sure not to make any waves. Keep your lady as safe as possible."

"See that you do. Or I'll finally have to kick your ass."

Chapter 61

WALLACE WATCHED HER AGAIN, just a few hours after he'd left Barratt County. Nikkie Jean Netorre was scurrying across the parking lot. She did remind him of a little mouse at times. He was pleased to see that she was moving a bit better than she had been.

She'd tossed the crutches aside pretty early on. She was just stubborn enough to think she didn't need them. He was glad to see she was doing ok.

He hadn't seen Nikkie Jean much since his return from vacation. But he'd found himself thinking of her while sitting on the beach with Jennifer. He hadn't anything else to do with his time. He'd left everything back at the hotel to spend the time with his wife. Jennifer hadn't been that interested. At least not in him. Her cell phone had gotten more of her attention than he had.

Wallace had tried not to let that sting. Was it so wrong to want his wife's attention on him for the one week they had had together in years? Reggie had paid a pretty penny for this trip for their anniversary.

Wallace hadn't wanted to pick a fight with his wife. Not there on a public beach.

The young woman nearby with her husband and two small children had looked a great deal like Nikkie Jean. Wallace had watched her from behind his sunglasses. Poor woman had her hands full, with two young children under four. The husband didn't seem that engaged. But the woman handled things well. She was pretty, warm, welcoming. Very sexy in that real woman way.

Wallace had enjoyed watching her. It had brought Nikkie Jean to his thoughts. He'd thought about that woman for several hours. So long he'd forgotten to reapply sunscreen.

His skin had twinged for three days after that.

Nikkie Jean sent a leery look around the parking lot. Wallace sped up. He hated that she was as afraid as she was. Rumor mill had it that something extremely traumatic had to have happened to the girl to make her that skittish of men.

Wallace had seen it himself. She avoided being alone with every man in the building except patients, Rafael Holden-Deane, Virat Patel, and Allen Jacobson. And even the last two were rarely. The only man she truly seemed to trust was Dr. Holden-Deane.

Probably because he was *safe* due to his obvious fascination with that little redheaded vixen nurse of his.

Nikkie Jean wouldn't be alone with Wallace at all.

He had his suspicions why. He couldn't remember all the details—he and Jennifer had had moved away a few years before it had happened—but he vaguely recalled there being an assault of some sort in the Carrington home.

He'd seen sexual assault victims before. That was one of the things the rumor mill had speculated on.

Wallace frowned as he thought about that. Nikkie Jean was such a little thing. It would be easy for someone to overpower and hurt her.

To have it happen in her own home like the rumors had said—it was horrific. It made him feel even more protective of her. No wonder she was so frightened.

He'd overplayed his hand a few months ago. Since then, she'd avoided him at almost all costs. But there was no way he was going to let her cross that back parking lot near Boethe Street alone. Cherise, the nursing supervisor, had been mugged in that very spot. "Dr. Netorre! Wait for a moment!"

She turned, shooting him a weary look. She had her bag clutched tightly in one hand, and her phone in the other. No doubt it was ready to dial 911 at a moment's notice. Not that it would do much good back here. The TSP was almost notoriously slow at responding to this section of Boethe Street.

Which had never made much sense to him—the city was less than fifty thousand people. It wasn't like this area was as bad as an inner-city block. He and Jennifer had started their married life in Philadelphia—that city was much worse than little Finley Creek.

It was just Boethe Street.

She waited for him but he easily sensed the fear. He cursed himself lightly for his rush to show her his interest last time. Nikkie Jean

Netorre needed a slow-and-steady courtship to get her past her fears. He knew that.

He'd just always been so impatient. Especially with beautiful women. But his attraction was waning, being replaced with something else.

Something more protective. Almost paternal. He almost felt like he owed Jordan something; the man had gotten Wallace through medical school after all.

"Hello, Dr. Henedy. I believe Dr. Holden-Deane was looking for you a few minutes ago."

"Yes. He found me. Questions about billing over five years ago. I'm having one of the admins locate the files. I believe we're updating the billing system, finally. It should have been done…five years ago."

Wallace refused to worry about what would be found. The excess charges he'd been including on each bill added up to less than four percent. He wasn't stupid. But that four percent had gone straight to his own bank account through the years. It had paid for his son's education and every luxury Jennifer had wanted.

It had never directly affected his patients. Wallace wouldn't do that to the people he helped.

But the insurance companies would have had to keep excellent records to be able to find his little hobby. No matter what Jennifer thought.

Wallace just had to get through the next nine days. Then he should be in the clear. And be able to do some better creative accounting after this audit ended. "I'm glad to see he's moving Finley Creek into the twenty-first century. A few decades late, but…"

She smiled, some of the tension leaving her shoulders. "He's a great COM."

"Much better than Daniels." He almost winced as he said it. Dr. Daniels had been a friend of his. Maybe Daniels hadn't been the smartest when it came to women, but he'd been reasonably efficient at running the hospital. What he'd done to some of the nurses couldn't be condoned though.

"I didn't work here then," she said, still eyeing him nervously.

"You really shouldn't walk out here alone. Let me walk you to your car."

"Thank you. I usually walk with Izzie and Annie, but they're both still on the clock again."

They started across the parking lot. Wallace made a point of not looking at how closely she still clutched her phone.

It didn't matter that she knew him—many women were attacked by men they knew, compared to those that they didn't know. And she already knew he was interested in her. His foolish mistake.

"So how did Annie's protest go? I asked my wife if she'd heard anything about Boethe Street, but she hadn't." A lie. He hadn't mentioned anything of the sort to Jennifer.

He'd learned a long time ago to *never* mention women he worked with to Jennifer.

That was one thing she didn't want to know. Even the knowledge that there were female physicians in his department had infuriated her.

He'd never understood why. He'd always been careful to keep his little distractions quiet.

He'd never want Jennifer to know that he'd found sexual satisfaction elsewhere. That would just hurt her.

He remembered the first time she'd ever asked him if she was enough for him in bed. She had been twenty. He'd been an older twenty-five and felt so mature. So protective.

He'd been her first and only.

Of course, she'd been enough for him.

Until she'd stopped caring whether they had sex together or not.

"I'm always glad to walk you, or anyone else for that matter, to your car at night. I can't forget what happened to Lacy Deane and Logan Lanning out here. Nor what happened to Cherise. I wouldn't want my wife walking across this parking lot at night. I'm hopeful the mayor's initiative will make a huge difference in this part of the town." He would just keep mentioning Jennifer, make Nikkie Jean see that he didn't mean *her* any harm. He was just a harmless family man, looking out for the young women in his department.

"As long as it doesn't keep evicting people who have nowhere else to go," Dr. Netorre said. "There's my Jeep. Thank you for the escort, Dr. Henedy. It's appreciated. I can't always see that well in low light. Thanks again."

"No thanks necessary. I was already heading this direction.

I'm a few spaces up. Get in and lock your doors, ok? I'll stick around until you're out of the parking lot."

She nodded and hit the button to unlock her door. "Good night, Doctor. And thank you for the escort."

Wallace knew when it was time to pull back. He deliberately put space between. Make her feel safe; that was his goal.

"Have a safe trip, Dr. Netorre. I need to be going. My wife and I have special plans this evening."

"Enjoy."

She practically dove into her Jeep.

Wallace bit back a smile at how nervous she was.

He waited until she pulled out before heading up the aisle to his own SUV. It took him a moment to remember that he hadn't asked her about her association with Dr. Alvaro. He'd wanted to go fishing, see just how close she was to the other man.

Movement to the left of his car had him pausing.

"Wallace…"

He recognized the voice. She'd always had a voice like smooth sex.

Connie Addis stood next to his car for the second time in less than a week, her eyes following Nikkie Jean's little purple SUV as it pulled out of the parking lot.

"Is that my replacement?" There was a hard edge to her voice that he didn't like. But Connie always had been insecure. "A little young. What is she? Fifteen?"

He had tried to break things off with her two months or so ago. After he'd first walked Nikkie Jean to her car. Connie wasn't taking his hints. The calls and emails were one thing, but she'd taken to showing up at FCGH and County. Without being asked.

She was becoming more of a problem. And Wallace couldn't handle the stress of Connie on top of both Rafael Holden-Deane and Caine Alvaro.

"I'm not replacing you, Connie. But it was always meant to be temporary. I told you that up front, going in." Wallace kept his tone firm. He'd played out this scene at least two dozen times over the last twenty years. He could handle her, despite the rest of the stress flooding his life.

"Maybe I'm not ready for things to end. I'm…in love with you, Wallace. I have been since the moment you walked into the ER my first week at Barratt County."

She was only thirty-two, attractive but not stunningly so. Tall and curved in all the right places. There was another man out there for her. Wallace was just an interlude while she waited.

Wallace almost told her that, but he refrained. Now wasn't the time. He hated it when they developed feelings for him. Hated it. He always warned them not to do that.

He loved Jennifer; he always would.

Connie's hand wrapped around his arm, and she pulled him closer. She pressed her lips against his. Just as Nikkie Jean's distinctive Jeep made the final turn out of the parking lot.

Wallace winced.

No doubt Nikkie Jean had seen the exact thing he didn't want her to. Again. And she'd been far closer this time.

He pulled back. "I love my wife, Connie. I've told you that before. What you and I had was special, but not as special as what I have created with my wife."

"Maybe I'll tell your wife. Let her decide whether it's time you left her or not. Or told Dr. Alvaro just what you've been up to through the years at Barratt County. I've seen your journals. You really shouldn't leave them in your messenger bag when you come to my apartment. I might get curious. I might learn things. Eighty thousand dollars for an appendectomy? For shame."

Desperation. It was in her voice.

It had always turned him off. "Connie…"

"I…I think I may be pregnant, Wallace. What am I supposed to do now?"

Well, hell. What was Wallace supposed to do now? This was the last thing Jennifer needed. He had to clean up this mess, somehow.

Even if it meant just giving Connie what she wanted for right now.

He pulled her into his arms and kissed her, feeling the inevitable stirring of his body as he did so.

Maybe he wouldn't end things with her just yet.

Chapter 62

CLEAN UP YOUR MESSES. That was what Jennifer had yelled at him the last time they had argued. She'd meant with the hospital billing issues. He'd made the mistake of confessing all to her, about the money he'd been siphoning from the insurance companies for two decades.

The money hadn't mattered to her, she'd said. Making certain that it didn't come up before the mayoral election she was running in soon was what mattered.

Public perception. That was what mattered to her now, rather than Wallace's career. Just where he ranked in priorities for Jennifer wasn't lost to him. So why in the hell was he in this position for her again?

He lifted Connie's body as quickly as he could.

He had to find a way to get rid of her. Without anyone seeing.

There were TSP deputies out everywhere, patrolling during the approaching storms like they always did.

Her head lolled back, long, blond-streaked brown hair falling over his elbow. It was nearly the same shade as Nikkie Jean's. A moment of regret hit him.

He hadn't meant to kill her.

And she had slapped him first. He hadn't meant to call her Nikkie Jean. That had been his first mistake. She'd had a right to be angry. She hadn't had the right to hit him. Or to call him the things she had.

He hadn't meant to squeeze her mouth as hard as he had. To cut off her air. He'd just wanted to cut off the viperous words she'd been hurling at him before some of her neighbors heard through her thing apartment walls, even while her hands had been reaching for him.

He'd just squeezed too hard. Too long.

And he hadn't been able to revive her. If he had, there would have been obvious brain damage.

He'd stopped trying to revive her after that.

Wallace had sat by her naked body and cried. For hours. Until he'd gotten ahold of himself.

He hadn't meant to do it again. To kill another woman he had cared about. It had just happened. He'd sat there until he'd convinced himself of that.

And then he had had to get to work.

He knew enough about DNA to know he had to do something to erase his presence from her body completely.

It would take water. Bleach. And lots of it.

Now he had her wrapped in a blanket that had been in his trunk. For those times they'd been together in his SUV. That blanket would have to be completely destroyed.

He'd liked the excitement of it all.

But he would have to vacuum it out. And he had to get rid of her body somehow.

He thought about burying her somewhere, like he had Miranda in Pennsylvania all those years ago. He could drop her in a cave somewhere in Barratt County. There were many such caves in the northern part of that county.

But that would require knowing where to find one that wouldn't be accessible to anyone easily. He didn't have time for that. He had to act soon.

The idea that Connie's family and friends—she wasn't extremely well liked at Barratt County, but she'd worked there for three years and she'd be missed—would never find her remains didn't sit well with him.

They deserved to bury their dead.

And Connie deserved that dignity, as well.

He'd enjoyed her. He truly had.

It had been an accident. He'd just held her down too hard.

There were scratches on the inside of his wrist where she'd clawed at him. He should have backed away then.

He had tried that once. But she had kept yelling.

And then she'd threatened to report him to the police. For a minute there, he'd jolted back in time. To Miranda.

To what the cost would be if that every came to light.

His hand had tightened on Connie again.

Just to teach her a lesson. That had been all. It had been an accident.

He drove around for several hours, her body bundled up tightly in the back of his SUV, wrapped securely in the entire roll of trash bags he'd found beneath her kitchen sink.

Wallace just kept driving.

Until he could see the flooded waters of the Value Reservoir in the distance.

Chapter 63

WALLACE STARED AT NIKKIE Jean Netorre as she and Allen walked toward him, deep in conversation around noon the next day. Allen had his hand on her shoulder. Comforting her.

The news he'd received from one of the gossiping nurses just a few minutes ago had flat-out floored him.

Nikkie Jean was pregnant.

Just like Connie had claimed to be.

Wallace bit back the anger again. She hadn't been pregnant. He'd had a vasectomy fourteen years ago when Jennifer turned forty.

If she had been pregnant, the fetus hadn't been his.

He tried to fight back the feeling of betrayal.

Connie had cheated on him. And had been looking for him to take care of her and her baby.

Had she thought he was an easy mark?

Someone had fathered Nikkie Jean's baby, as well. He somehow doubted a resident who was barely thirty and career-driven like Dr. Netorre would have visited a sperm bank. No. She'd gotten close to some man, close enough to have sex with him.

Even as skittish as she was.

He wondered who it was.

It could have been Jacobson.

The two were certainly together quite a bit, and Jacobson had a habit of dating women in the hospital openly. He'd had been integral in getting the no-fraternization policy of the hospital changed from absolutely not tolerated to permissible with a waiver from human resources. He'd argued people should be free to be involved with whomever they wanted, whether they worked together or not. It had been a reasonable argument.

If Jacobson hadn't pushed for that while acting as the assistant COM with Daniels, then Holden-Deane and his little redhead wouldn't have been allowed to remain working together now.

Nikkie Jean wasn't as skittish with Virat Patel, either. But that surgeon was involved heavily with Finley Coulter. Dr. Coulter was a good friend of Nikkie Jean's. No, he doubted they'd be as friendly if Dr. Patel was the father. Cage Ralstone—he was friendly with Nikkie Jean.

As was Rafael Holden-Deane.

But he doubted that man would look away from his redheaded nurse long enough to see another woman. At least not yet.

It could be Ralstone's, he supposed.

This job was a high-pressured one. Wallace certainly wouldn't blame a man for looking for a little excitement—or a way to blow off steam.

He just hoped Nikkie Jean hadn't seen him with Connie last night.

If she had...

Once it became known that Connie was dead—and he wasn't an idiot, it would come out eventually—people would start to talk.

If Nikkie Jean put it together, she could pose a very real problem. All he could hope was that Nikkie Jean hadn't seen enough to identify Connie.

It had been low light. And Nikkie Jean had vision issues, after all. Wallace could be making mountains when molehills didn't actually exist.

He hoped.

Nikkie Jean could become a bigger problem than he was ready to face just yet. Wallace would just have to watch and see what happened. Then he'd make a decision about Nikkie Jean. If that girl ever figured out just what it was she had seen, Wallace could be in even deeper trouble than he imagined.

If she ever spoke with her father about Pennsylvania that trouble would just compound.

Miranda had worked as Jordan's assistant, after all. She and Jordan Carrington's wife had been extremely close friends.

If Jordan remembered...if Nikkie Jean put it together...if Holden-Deane's audit revealed more than Wallace wanted...if Alvaro's did...If any of them put any of it together, even just small parts, *all* Wallace had worked toward would fall completely apart.

Wallace's hands shook.

He didn't know if he was going to be able to make it nine more days. He didn't even know if he was going to make it to tomorrow.

Chapter 64

SHE HADN'T PLANNED on going with a man. She'd been asked to handle the guest book for Ariella and the governor's quickly planned wedding, and she'd been honored to say yes. Allen had said that was fine when he'd told her she had to be his plus-one at the wedding as payment for her latest little prank.

She'd countered with the fact that it had been Lacy's idea.

He'd absolved their friend from culpability far too easily. And then he'd told her the truth—he didn't want to go around Ariella and the governor's families alone. Not after what had happened before. And he wanted a friend to go with him.

Lacy had privately told her that the people in his social circle outside of the hospital had practically dumped Allen after everything that had happened with the man's former friends.

She had had to say yes. She couldn't let him face those people alone.

Not that Ariella and Marcus Deane were monsters. Far from it.

Besides, no one wanted to go to a wedding alone.

Now she stood next to a tall, handsome man and was *not* looking forward to going inside.

Her baby's family was in there. And she had no idea what the people in the church were going to think.

They knew just exactly who the father of her baby was, after all. Maybe they'd think she was just an interloper now. It was never too late for them to reject her, after all.

"Nervous?" Allen asked.

"I shouldn't be. I mean, they are just *his* family. That's all. And I was friends with some of them first. Hopefully they won't forget that. And I don't think he'll be here. Way too soon for that. I think."

Allen shot her a confused look. "Excuse me?"

Heat hit her cheeks. Her friends from W4HAV may know who the father of her baby was, but that didn't mean FCGH did. "You don't know, do you?"

"No."

"Caine Alvaro, Rafe's twin. I really don't want to see him today. So I'm hoping I won't."

"He's Jelly Bean's father?"

She closed her eyes. "How did you know?"

Once it got out, it was going to blaze up and down the halls of FCGH that the father of Nikkie Jean's baby ran the smaller hospital nearby—and was the identical twin brother of the COM. Talk about soap opera.

She was about to be the star of the show.

"The way the man looked when he spoke of you. Just for a moment. I know when a man wants a woman. And he wants you. Badly."

"Well, he's not going to get me. That's for sure. No-doctors rule for a reason." Although, she wasn't just seeing him as a doctor any longer. He was Caine and would always be. Even if he drove a garbage truck for a living instead of ran a hospital. He would be Caine.

The man who understood what it was like to be as hurting as she was.

For the most insane moment, she half hoped he would be inside today.

She'd never had hour-long text conversations with a man before. Not like she'd had with him two nights ago while he sat up rocking a sick toddler at one a.m.

She'd wanted to just drive over there and cuddle the both of them.

That was what had her completely terrified right now, thank you very much. Getting deeper into him than he got to her.

Like her mother had said, Nikkie Jean ran the men in her life off eventually. It would no doubt happen with Caine, too.

"Well, there goes all my dreams."

Nikkie Jean shot him a quick look. His smile told her he was just teasing, but the look in his eyes...now she wasn't so sure. "Allen..."

"I'll be here, anytime you—or Jelly Bean—need me. Friends.

Consider me a pseudo big brother. Shelby says I'm pretty good at it. Most of the time. And I'm more than willing to be an uncle. Kid can never have too much family."

Nikkie Jean surprised herself when she hugged him.

She seemed to hug Allen a lot lately.

"I would like that very, very much."

"So...should we get in there?"

"Probably. Lacy told me to be here an hour early with the rest of the wedding party."

"I'll find a quiet place to wait for you." He smiled down at her.

"I'll need to find a seat at the back once everything is about to start," Nikkie Jean told him. She hadn't had a date for Jillian and Rafe's wedding. Just Annie and Izzie. The three of them had sat together and sighed over how beautiful Jillian had looked and how absolutely perfect Rafe had been in his tuxedo. He hadn't been scowling that day.

But tonight, she had a beautiful man right next to her. And no matter that it was Caine's family who'd be surrounding her, Nikkie Jean was going to enjoy herself.

A friend had found happiness. Nikkie Jean was going to celebrate that. No matter what.

—

Caine did not want to be there. But his uncle had been the one to find the invitation to the governor's wedding in the mail. Henry had been beyond excited. And when Caine had explained just how the governor was related to Rafe, and who the governor's fiancée—who the media absolutely loved—actually was, Henry had insisted that Caine and the children attend.

The invitation had had three smaller invitations included for the children individually from their new cousins—who would be having a party at the Barratt after the main reception.

Caine wanted connections for his children, Henry had pointed out. Now was his chance to start making them.

The children had been excited, especially Keller.

She'd spoken frequently of the aunt she'd met and had asked when they were going to meet again. And if Keller could visit her sometimes.

Caine had felt the ropes tightening around him with every

question. He was going to be meeting these people. Whether he was ready or not. Now was the time.

He would meet them, and then he would find the woman he wanted in the crowd. And she would be there; he had no doubt of that. He wasn't about to let her escape again.

The wedding chapel was bound to be a large one; they would just find a place near the back.

"Daddy, look! There's the church!" Keller yelled, more excited than he'd seen her in a long time. She had been a terror from the moment the invitation had been opened. It had taken an emergency trip to the Finley Creek Circle Mall to find the perfect dress to help settle her down.

Keller had never before cared what she wore. And never had she cried and begged him for a pretty dress. Caine had felt completely out of his element. It had taken two hours of the mall before he'd found what she wanted. He'd tried to get Henry to take her, but his uncle knew even less about little girl dresses than he did. His daughter was a very beautiful girl, and he wanted her to know that.

He didn't know how he was going to survive puberty. And it was just around the corner. "I see it. You don't need to yell."

"Do you think Aunt Ari will like my dress?"

He doubted Ariella would even notice the niece she'd only met once. "I'm sure she will. But she's going to be very busy today."

"I know. But…" She pouted for a moment. "She's so beautiful. And she looks just like *me*."

"That she does. But I think you are prettier." His daughter was quiet, shy, and a little bit self-conscious. He'd never figured out why. Maybe it was growing up in an all-male household. Or maybe it was something that had happened with her mother—both the twins were well old enough to remember when Caine had been deployed and April was the primary caregiver.

All he knew was that Everett had told him that sometimes Mommy was mean to Keller. Caine had never figured out exactly how. Or why.

He wished he had. He wished he could help his little girl see the beautiful being that she was. Somehow, he got the car parked and all three kids inside out of the rain. Keller was worrying about her hair and dress getting wet. Six months ago she hadn't cared about her appearance at all. Now…it was all she thought about.

Being as pretty as the other girls.

She was going to drive him insane someday. Once they stepped inside the church, the twins went quiet.

"There are a lot of people in there," Everett said.

"Are we supposed to go in here?" Keller asked.

Caine followed the sign with his eyes. "That way. Avery/Deane wedding."

He shifted Dalton on his hip and pointed. Everett clutched the diaper bag closer like a shield. None of his kids really liked large crowds.

Hell, neither did Caine. Only Keller seemed happy to be here today.

Caine was just waiting for Dalton to start screaming in the midst of the ceremony and disrupt everything. That would be one way to get Nikkie Jean's attention—and drive her running toward the nearest hills. "Let's go. Find a seat."

—

She was just speaking with one of the ushers—Ariella's brother-in-law—when she heard them come in. Everything echoed in the old church, especially the sounds of a babbling toddler. She smiled at the elderly woman who had just asked her how old she was now and when she'd graduate—high school—and turned to the next set of guests.

Her breath backed up in her throat. A squeak escaped.

The usher, Mick, looked down at her. He was just as big as Caine and Rafe. Just as handsome with warm-brown hair and blue eyes. He was married to Ariella's older sister, and they'd met before at Jillian's wedding. "Are you ok?"

"I just...was not prepared to see him today for some reason."

Mick looked toward the man who had just entered. Caine hadn't seen her yet. She half thought about slipping behind Mick and hiding. "Any particular reason why? I know why I'm not too keen on seeing him."

"Let's just say...that..." Well, it was going to get out there sooner or later. She lowered her voice. "Caine and I...made a baby together, due in seven months or so. But that's still on the down low. I just really don't want to see him right now."

"Congratulations, I've been told I make a great uncle. And too late. He's noticed you and heading your way."

"Do me a favor? Arrest me or something. Book me for the…next eight months or so? That might give me time to come up with a plan."

"The FBI doesn't quite work that way." Mick gave an almost feral grin. "I'll introduce myself. That should handle your problem."

"Thanks. I really appreciate it. You have the hero thing down pat, right?"

"I've been working on it. Welcome to the family."

He stepped in front of her.

—

There was a man in a tux, equally as big as Caine, blocking his path to the guest book. Rather, the guest-book attendant. The man held out his hand—to Keller. He gave a little bow to Caine's daughter and smiled. "Right this way, miss. I'll show you to your seat."

"We're on the bri—"

"I know. I'm married to your younger sister, Paige. She's inside with our sons."

Caine turned his attention more fully on the other man. "Caine Alvaro. These are my children, Everett, Keller, and Dalton."

"So are you our uncle then?" Everett asked. "Like Uncle Henry is our dad's uncle?"

"That's it exactly. I'm married to your father's sister. Our sons are your cousins."

"Cool."

"We need to take our seats. The wedding will be starting soon," a woman said from directly behind Nikkie Jean. "Nik, you can probably find…your date…inside."

"Thanks, Mel." Nikkie Jean shot a quick look at Caine. One that told him she was about to escape.

"Nikkie Jean, we will talk later."

She shot him an innocent look. "Really? I can't imagine what about."

The redheaded woman behind her snickered.

Caine just glowered. He wanted to go to her. Touch her for a moment.

But his brand-new brother-in-law was directly in his way.

"I think you know exactly what about. Everett, Keller, let's go take our seats."

Everett started inside. But Keller, little turncoat that she was, was too busy preening to pay attention. Nikkie Jean noticed.

"Hi. Are you and your brothers feeling better?"

"You're Daddy's girlfriend Nikkie Jean!"

"Am I?" Nikkie Jean shot Caine a pointed look. He just sent a benign look right back. "That is the prettiest dress I've seen today. And your hair! Absolutely gorgeous. Would you like a flower to tie in it? It'll match those on your dress perfectly."

Keller was in heaven. Caine just watched as Nikkie Jean slipped a flower free from the arrangement and handed it to his daughter, with a sweet, genuine smile.

Yes. A little girl who looked like Keller but with Nikkie Jean's smile…he would be beyond thrilled.

Just what that meant for them all was starting to sink in.

The brother-in-law was waiting. Caine followed him to the pew in the middle of the church. "Family is this way. Rafe and Jillian are both in the wedding today. My wife, as well. Her sisters Pen and Zoey are helping watch the children."

"Thank you." What in the three hells was he supposed to say to this guy? Caine hid his unease by shifting his youngest son in his arms.

"I get it. My wife spent years alone on the streets. All of this is hard for her. But I don't think she'd change a thing about the way things are happening. Enjoy the wedding. Say hello and then get out of here if you want. Trust me—they'll all understand."

"Thanks. I'll keep that in mind."

Fortunately, the guy had led them to a pew directly behind two dark-haired young women and a bunch of children. Caine settled the twins and slid into the pew. The woman nearest him turned and looked at him.

Caine tensed.

"I'm Zoey. This is Pen, my—our—sister. And this is Mikey, our nephew."

Caine took a look at the baby she held. He greatly resembled the one in Caine's own arms, but was about half Dalton's age. "This is my son Dalton. Everett and Keller."

Keller had apparently lost all shyness completely. "You look like me, too!"

The teenager turned, as well. She had blue hair and the same shape eyes as Everett.

Caine felt chains of bonds he didn't really want tightening around him. "Hi. I'm Aunt Pen, if your dad says you can call me that."

"Daddy?" Keller turned toward him, pleading in her eyes. Keller, who had built huge families out of the few dolls she had for years.

"Of course. Hello, Pen. Zoey. It's nice to meet you all."

"You, too." There was a wariness in the older sister's eyes. One that told of its own stories. "I'm with the TSP out of Garrity, you?"

"I'm the chief of medicine at Barratt County General Hospital in Value."

"I'm in college. At FCU," the young girl said. His sister. He had almost twenty years on this child, yet there she was. Looking at him expectantly. The last thing Caine knew how to be was a big brother to a teenager with blue hair.

She intimidated him almost as much as his own daughter.

"What are you studying?"

"I don't really know yet. I haven't made up my mind what I want to do. I'm considering social work. Or maybe something with Luc's company. Do you know Luc yet? He's our oldest brother and does all sorts of cool things." The teenager was a bubbly one, that was for sure. She and Nikkie Jean would probably find a million things to chatter about.

"He's Daviess Lucas, of Lucas Technologies," Zoey said quietly. Caine recognized the name and the company and bit back a wince. "He's in the wedding party. His wife is an attendant, as is Mikey's mother."

"I've heard of him." Caine looked at this quieter sister. "Just how many of *us* are there?"

"At last count, eight. There are possibly four more that they are trying to track down. But the birth—our mother—used aliases, we think."

Dalton babbled loudly, reminding Caine of where they were. "I see."

"We can talk later. I'll tell you what I know," the quieter sister said. She was far more reserved than the younger girl. Wary. Caine understood.

Nikkie Jean often had that same expression in her eyes.

"Thanks." He hadn't felt an immediate connection with these people—with the possible exception of his twin—but he did feel pulled.

He couldn't deny that.

"Daddy, can you put the flower in my hair?" Keller asked. Caine shifted Dalton to the pew beside him.

"Come here." One skill he had yet to develop was fixing Keller's hair appropriately. A flower was likely to crumble if he tried. But he did the best he could.

"Where did you get such a pretty flower?" Zoey asked, with a smile an exact match to the one on Caine's daughter. Keller looked more like her aunt's child than she did Caine's.

That was hard to miss.

"The lady at the door gave it to us. Her name is Nikkie Jean, and she's a doctor. Our cousin Katie says she's really nice and plays with real American Girl dolls. I don't have one yet. I heard her tell uncle...I don't remember his name! I heard tell him she wanted him to arrest her and hide her from Daddy for eight months. But that's weird, because she's going to be Daddy's girlfriend."

"I see." Zoey shot a look toward the back of the church. Caine didn't turn around. Of course, that would be something Nikkie Jean would say.

His favorite little scaredy-cat was hiding from him. He'd have to flush her out during the reception.

"Nikkie Jean and I—are involved." That was all he was going to say in front of his children and to a stranger. "She's trying to avoid me today."

"Can he arrest her?" Everett asked, intrigued. He looked toward the back of the church.

"He could. He's with the FBI. But I don't think he would."

"Unless she robbed a bank?" Everett had a fascination with all things crime and law enforcement. He'd been a police officer and a detective for the last two Halloweens.

Zoey smiled again. "Unless she robbed a bank. Then I can arrest her, too. But I don't think Dr. Netorre would do that."

"Unless her other boyfriend did it and she's keeping a secret," Everett said, almost with glee. His son did have an active imagination. "He looks like the kind of person who would rob a bank. I'm going to be a policeman when I grow up. With the TSP. I'll arrest him. Then she can be Daddy's girlfriend."

Caine rolled his eyes to the ceiling.

"I'm with the TSP."

"Cool. Can I see your gun?"

"No. I'm afraid not, but…" She reached into a small purse and pulled out a badge. She let his son hold it.

Everett's face showed his fascination—and a bit of hero worship for this new relative. He reluctantly handed it back to Zoey when Caine prompted him.

"We'll see if Paige, she's another aunt, has her badge today, too. She's with the FBI."

"That's awesome. Can we arrest Nikkie Jean's other boyfriend, though?"

"Not unless we catch him doing something wrong."

Caine couldn't help himself. He had to see who this other boyfriend was.

Allen Jacobson.

Of course.

Chapter 65

"DON'T LOOK NOW, BUT I think we're being watched," Allen said.

Nikkie Jean barely avoided looking toward Caine. "I know. I talked to him a moment when he came in."

Allen slipped an arm around her and hugged her closer, just for a moment.

Nikkie Jean didn't tense. When she realized that, she looked at him, elated. Apparently, she really did trust Allen. She shot him a smile, a deep, heartfelt smile. "Thank you. For being my friend. I haven't had much of them. Especially men."

"That's a shame. A good friend will stay with you through thick and thin. You can count on me, Nikkie Jean. I promise."

"I know. And that is what makes you so great. Did you know, until I came to Finley Creek the second time, I had one close friend? And we had lost touch when I was sick, when I was sixteen. My fault. I pushed her away. I pushed everyone away. And then there were Annie and Izzie. I think they'll stick with me. If I don't do something to push them away, too." She shot a look to where the two of them sat midway back on the bride's side. They'd made plans to meet up at the reception. There had been no way Izzie would sit that near Allen.

Allen turned toward her. "Listen to me. A true friend sticks even when you push them away. That's the way it works."

Tears hit her eyes. She would have said more, but the music changed. The first attendant started down the aisle; she thought the blond may have been one of Caine's sisters-in-law he hadn't met yet. She couldn't remember how many he had now.

Allen held her hand for the longest time. While it was comforting, her skin didn't sizzle the way it did every time Caine touched her.

Nope.

It was just Caine who made her feel that way.

It would probably *always* be just Caine who made her feel that way.

She was definitely in way over her head now.

—

The children's reception happened after the cake had been served. The bride's eldest brother—a billionaire from St. Louis who looked a lot like Caine and his twin, only thinner—had hired a private entertainment company to provide just about anything the child guests wanted to do. There were even care workers for the number of smaller children.

He was reluctant at first to send Dalton, but his son wanted to follow Everett and Keller. Pen had taken Dalton for Caine and promised to stay with him for a while. Technically, she'd told him, she was still a child. She wanted to spend some time with her nieces and nephews, then she'd join the adults for the rest of the reception.

He hadn't wanted to deny them the fun the other children were going to enjoy. The governor's daughter had sought the twins out personally.

Without his children as a barrier, Caine had no excuse.

He had to meet his brothers and sisters on his own. Like the adult he was.

But first…the mother of his fourth child was hiding from him. And he was going to change that.

He stalked her around the reception room. It was the finest the Finley Creek Barratt had; that was evident.

The bride, sweetly shy and obviously well-loved by everyone, had made a point of saying hello to him.

That had broken the flood waves—within minutes he'd been introduced to the siblings he hadn't met yet and their families. His biological mother's children ranged from a teenage boy, who greatly favored Everett, to the billionaire a few years older than Caine and his twin.

Successful people. No failures among the lot of them. Even his youngest sister, Pen, was a high achiever who'd graduated high school at the ripe old age of fifteen and immediately entered college. Simon, the teenage boy of around thirteen or fourteen, had skipped a few grades and now played varsity basketball.

They spoke politely with him, but no one was too pushy. Caine appreciated it.

Especially since most of his attention was on watching Nikkie Jean—and that damned Allen Jacobson—where she sat three tables away.

Every time he stepped over in her direction, someone else would materialize to talk with him.

It took him a moment to realize that someone was doing it to him deliberately.

He just had no idea who was orchestrating it. Whoever it was, they were very good at it. And enjoying it. No doubt Nikkie Jean's feminine little hand was at work in it.

Someone nudged him lightly.

He turned and looked into the light-brown eyes of his redheaded sister-in-law. "You keep staring at her, people are going to figure it out, you know."

"Figure what out?"

"How you feel about her. I'm sorry about my sister Mel, though. She's been helping Nikkie Jean avoid you, I think. Mel's evil like that. She gets perverse pleasure from messing with people."

"I don't think I've met her."

"I'm sure you will eventually."

"Nikkie Jean's been avoiding me. And we have things to discuss."

A look went through Jillian's eyes. "Yes, she's probably avoiding you. You probably scare her to the bottom of her toes, you know. I'm just surprised with her history that you were even able to get close to her at all, let alone make a kid."

"I know." Her story hurt him every time he thought about it. Hurt him for her sake.

No doubt she was feeling unsettled after having told him about the assault. Afraid of what his reaction would be. And Nikkie Jean needed to hide from the things that scared her at first. Until she could work her way through them in her own way.

Caine wasn't so certain he was all that different in that regard. He'd taken off from her that first night like his own shorts were on fire. All because of how immediately she'd made him feel.

The band was churning up. Dancing would start soon.

He was going to get Nikkie Jean in his arms and away from that damned Allen Jacobson no matter what he had to do.

Other boyfriend, his ass. Nikkie Jean was Caine's. It was just taking her a while to see that.

"Just...take it from one who knows her well—the forceful-hunter routine, one you apparently share with your twin, by the way—will not work. It'll terrify her. For darned good reason. She'll run and keep running. It has to be Nikkie Jean's choice to come to you. Otherwise, you'll never—"

"I get it."

"I'm sure you'll figure it out, big guy. In your own time." She shot him a wicked grin of her own. Yes, he could see why his brother had gone for her. "I'll help you out. Allen owes me a dance. Hate to see Nikkie Jean playing the wallflower. Get over there, while you still can."

Caine did just that.

Chapter 66

ALLEN KNEW WHEN THE man who looked like Rafe stalked over to their side of the reception hall that Nikkie Jean was in some serious trouble. Alvaro was on the prowl.

Nikkie Jean was the man's chosen rabbit. "He's coming for you."

"I suppose I should probably let him catch me," Nikkie Jean said. "Otherwise, the man will make a real scene."

"I could keep him away." Somehow. When a man looked at a woman like that, keeping him away was probably easier said than done. "You could hide in the ladies' room."

"Oh, a sign on the door would not keep him away."

Nikkie Jean almost sounded glad of that. Allen took a closer look at her face.

Nikkie Jean's cheeks were pink. She was chewing on her bottom lip lightly—and her eyes were actually sparkling.

She was excited by the fact that Caine Alvaro was hunting her like an antelope. "Unless you want him to catch you?"

The red in her cheeks darkened. "Well…he has caught me before, Allen. And I never thought I would be excited by that. What am I supposed to do?"

Allen just stared at her for a long time. "Do you care about him?"

Nikkie Jean nodded. "Very…much so."

"And he cares about you." All one had to do was look at Caine Alvaro's expression as he watched Allen dance Nikkie Jean around the dance floor to see that.

"I believe he may actually…" Nikkie Jean pulled in such a deep breath Allen could almost feel it. "Yes, Caine cares about me."

"And you trust him."

"I…do. Probably more than I have any man in a long, long time. It was fast, sudden, and it was real. I *trust* him."

"Then you go to him, and you grab him with both hands, Nikkie Jean. And you make sure he knows exactly how you feel. Don't risk losing that—for anything." He spun her lightly.

And then he stopped dancing and passed her off to the man who had come up behind them.

"Dr. Alvaro, I believe this dance may just be yours."

Allen gave her to the other man then walked off the dance floor.

Alone.

Chapter 67

IZZIE WAS CLOSE ENOUGH to see Nikkie Jean dancing with Dr. Jacobson and chattering away. She didn't quite understand why Nikkie Jean was such good friends with him, but she respected that Nikkie Jean was.

Someone came up behind her, and Izzie turned in her chair. "Hey. Welcome back."

Annie had her foster son, Syrus, riding on her hip. At twenty-two months old, he was the definite baby of Annie's little family. Annie rocked him gently. She was such a beautiful mother. "He was fussing. He doesn't understand what's going on, and he's tired."

Annie rocked her son until his eyes drifted close. "Sol and Seeley are having a blast."

"I'm ready whenever you are." Ariella was her friend, of course, but Annie needed a break. Her friend just pushed herself too hard sometimes. "I do want to talk to Nikkie Jean first."

"I think he loves her," Annie said in a soft voice. "Look at how he's watching her."

Izzie looked over at Nikkie Jean. Allen Jacobson held Nikkie Jean close to his own chest. But it was the man behind Nikkie Jean that Annie meant.

He was staring at Nikkie Jean with a longing that Izzie had no difficulty interpreting.

Dr. Jacobson spun Nikkie Jean right into Dr. Alvaro's arms, then gave a funny little bow.

And stepped aside. As if he approved of the other man.

"Men are so weird, Ann. Especially men like them."

"I don't know. Look at how he's looking at her."

Izzie pulled her attention away from the jerk that was Allen Jacobson and looked at the gorgeous pirate that held her other best friend so close it looked like they were one being.

Nikkie Jean weighed a third what he did. Less. Yet he was holding her like she was made of glass. And the way Nikkie Jean was looking at him…it melted something in Izzie just to see it.

"They are so…mismatched."

"He's holding her like she's the most precious woman in the world. I don't think there is a better match than that."

Annie always had been the wisest woman Izzie had ever known.

Chapter 68

"WHY DIDN'T YOU TELL ME before? I could have done something to help." Jennifer practically hissed the words at him as she paced around the surgeon's break room Monday afternoon. "How do you know it's buried well enough to survive two audits?"

"I don't. Except it has this long. Hell…" He wrapped his hands around her arms. Jennifer had always had the softest skin. Yes, she might have put on some weight in the last ten years, but it suited her. "My departments have been audited before. I refuse to panic."

She looked perfect. She always looked perfect to him. Big dark eyes that sucked a man's soul right in, the perfect chocolate-brown hair that was never out of place anymore.

When they'd first met, her hair had hung to her waist and had been completely natural. The softest silk he had ever touched.

Now it took routine visits to the stylist and half a bottle of hairspray to make it look like that.

He leaned down and brushed his lips against hers. When was the last time he had kissed his own wife?

Wallace couldn't remember.

Jennifer was always so busy—it almost felt like their paths never crossed any more. They even had separate rooms. She said it was because of his snoring, but Wallace had wondered.

"What are you doing?" She practically squeaked the question, like she had the first time he had ever kissed her.

"I love you, Jennifer Rose. That has never changed in the thirty years we have been married."

"Has it been that long?" she asked quietly, calming against his chest. "It wasn't that long ago we were eating macaroni-and-cheese with hot dogs in Philly."

"I know. We've been through quite a few things together,

Jenny. This…this is just a bleep on our radar. We have bigger things to focus on, Madam Mayor."

She smiled, like he had known she would.

He had faith in her. She'd get the election; provided the voters voted with common sense instead of picking whichever Barratt was in the running.

Barratts did rather own the county. And the one south of them. Barratts were just about everywhere.

"You always have been a flatterer, Wallace. I believed you, once."

He smiled at her, his hand brushing against her cheek. "Go home. I'll be there in a few hours. We have a surgery scheduled tonight that I need to observe. I'll bring us a late dinner. We can sit in front of the fire and just talk together. Like we used to."

They hadn't had time for much romance in years.

Wallace really missed that.

The door to the surgical break room burst open.

Wallace jerked around. He'd thought he'd locked it.

He tensed, seeing Nikkie Jean. The look on her face wasn't good.

She hadn't seen them. Instead, the girl dashed to the restroom near the back.

"What on earth is wrong with that girl?" Jennifer asked.

Wallace squeezed her arm and turned back toward his wife. "Never mind her. The girl is newly pregnant and not having an easy time of it."

"Who is she? She looks very familiar."

"That's Jordan Carrington's daughter. Do you remember her?"

"Jordan and *Carla* Carrington? From Philadelphia? What is she doing here? I thought their daughter was dead. Didn't she have—"

"Ovarian cancer; yes. But she recovered. From what I understand, she left shortly after her mother' s funeral."

"How on earth did she end up here?" She shot him a suspicious look. "Did you have something to do with it? Did *you* bring her here?"

"Of course not. She doesn't even realize who I am. I don't intend her to. But then again, she was what? Eight or ten the last time we saw her? I believe Reggie had been invited to her brother's birthday party." The last thing he wanted to do was discuss Nikkie Jean with his wife.

He never discussed beautiful women with her. She was so insecure in that regard that he had learned years ago not to do that. And she'd always been jealous of Carla Carrington, even though they'd been good friends.

"And now she's pregnant. I wonder if Jordan knows? You don't suppose he's this mysterious hospital buyer, do you?"

Wallace thought a moment. It was possible. Carrington Medical Group was expanding deep into Texas. "I don't know. It's possible. I haven't spoken to him in several years. And even then, it had been through email."

Wallace and Jordan Carrington had attended medical school together. Their wives had been friends. Their sons had attended the same schools from day one.

"You should make the association known to her. If her father is buying the hospital, that might work in your favor. Especially if he decides a new COM is in order. Especially at Barratt County." She'd never been too happy that Wallace had been passed up for that position for what she believed was a no-name former army doctor who had no connections.

Well, Alvaro most likely did have the connections now. Wallace had seen the photos of Dr. Alvaro at the governor's wedding reception. Photos of all of the guests were everywhere, thanks to the *Snotty Garlic*.

"I don't think so. I've heard her mention several times that she's estranged from her family. I don't know any of the details, but I don't want to make it awkward for her while she's a resident here." Best to direct her away from Nikkie Jean. Before Jennifer's jealousy was triggered.

The door opened again, and that dark-haired fireball nurse friend of Nikkie Jean's was there, no doubt looking for her. Wallace waved a hand toward the restroom. The nurse disappeared after Nikkie Jean. "But it's not her I care about right now. It's you. Go. Relax. I can't wait to get home and hear about your newest strategy. I have always loved your mind, sweetheart." He leaned forward and brushed his lips across her neck. "And your body."

He looked over his wife's shoulder as Nikkie Jean reappeared with her friend. Poor girl looked horrible. Wallace suppressed his grimace. He never had found pregnant women attractive.

Chapter 69

CAINE BIT BACK A STUPID smile when he thought about the rest of the wedding reception and how he had felt that night when Allen Jacobson had been paged to the hospital.

Jacobson had asked him personally to drive Nikkie Jean home.

She hadn't protested.

He hadn't crowed, like he'd actually wanted. Caine had behaved himself. Mostly.

He'd wanted to pull her over to a table by themselves and share wedding cake with her while they talked.

She'd been commandeered by guard dog Izzie instead. Guard dog Annie had had a sleeping toddler on her shoulder. The sight of the little boy the same age as Dalton had jolted Caine back to reality.

It had been past the time that he retrieve his own children, ensure they had a bit of the cake he'd promised them, and take them home himself.

Nikkie Jean had helped him do just that, carrying Dalton to the car and chattering with the twins.

Caine had ensured the twins were climbing into the rear of the cab, then lifted Nikkie Jean and Dalton in like he had before.

He'd let his hands linger. Until reality had set in with one simple question.

"Dad, is Nikkie Jean your new girlfriend yet?"

Leave it to his son to ask a question at the exact wrong time.

Caine hadn't known how to answer.

Nikkie Jean had, though. As she'd looked right at him. "We don't know yet, Ev. Your father and I are still figuring things out."

Figuring things out? No. Caine knew exactly what it was.

Nikkie Jean texted him again.

She was accompanying guard dog Annie to city hall for a

meeting with the mayor.

She would text him later, at ten o'clock. He was required to wear clothes. Mostly. She'd texted he could take off his socks. Nothing more.

Caine promised to do just that.

"Hey, Alvaro, tune back in. We have a problem."

"Thor? I'm sorry. I didn't realize you were here already." Time to focus back on the hospital around him.

He had a job to do, after all.

"What's the problem?"

"One of your nurses has just been reported missing. And she was having an affair with one of the suspects on your list. A Dr. Wallace Henedy. Same guy was linked with a nurse who went missing fifteen years ago. From Philadelphia. Not saying there's a connection, but…the guy's name is on your list—and the one I got from your brother last week. Care to tell me everything you know about him?"

"Who's missing? And what do you have already?"

Wallace Henedy, who was no doubt with Nikkie Jean right now.

Chapter 70

WALLACE FOUGHT THE NERVES. What he was about to do was more than just wrong. It was beyond criminal. Highly unethical and far worse than padding a few insurance bills.

But he needed the answers. He'd received an email from Jordan Carrington directly, stating that he hoped Wallace was well—and they needed to talk.

Privately. And as soon as possible.

No doubt Carrington was starting to put things together.

All he needed to do was see the report of Connie's body being found—it had, near the reservoir, washing free during the recent rains—and linking her to the hospital where Wallace worked.

Jordan was smart enough to put it together.

Caine Alvaro had just called, told him he needed to see him in his office as soon as he could.

It was almost word for word what Rafe Holden-Deane had said to him just three hours earlier.

They all wanted him right now. None of them sounded the least bit happy.

And Jennifer had just called him to tell him—she wanted a trial separation. *Before* the end of the FCGH audit. Because if the audit showed something unfavorable, she wanted some distance from him.

Jennifer wanted to leave him.

He *had* to know what had been found. Now.

Nikkie Jean was the only answer he could think of. *She* was the only variable he could ever hope to control.

And she was connected to every one of the other men involved in some way.

Even Dr. Alvaro.

He hadn't missed the fact that everyone was speculating about just how Nikkie Jean and Dr. Alvaro had met. Most thought Jillian had introduced them.

He supposed it was possible.

Alvaro was the father of her baby. Jordan Carrington was coming to Finley Creek. Both COMs wanted to speak with him.

And rumor at County said that Dr. Alvaro had brought in the FBI. To ferret out *fraud*. That someone had been stealing from Barratt County.

But worse, the TSP had put out notice that they were looking for a vehicle matching Wallace's—in connection with Connie's murder. Wallace didn't know how much longer he could do this.

He needed information.

Hopefully, this was the safest way for him to get them. He'd get what he needed from Nikkie Jean, then ensure she was found in a safe place. He'd even carefully researched what he was going to do so that it presented the least amount of harm to her and her unborn fetus.

All he wanted was her in his control and incapacitated so he could ask her a few questions.

Like if she'd seen him with Connie. Like if Alvaro was turning him into the FBI.

If her father had ever mentioned Miranda Plattin. He'd just...scare her into talking. Then he'd leave her somewhere she would be found.

Unless her answers revealed too much.

"Dr. Netorre, your tea. Dr. Deane, a latte, extra cream. Patel, straight up black." Wallace continued passing out the drinks. The now-empty small plastic vial burned a hole in his pocket. It had been so easy to do. Now he just had to be patient.

Lunch would be over in minutes, then they were free to return to their departments for the rest of the shifts.

But his shift ended as soon as this meeting was over.

And then he had to make it to Barratt County to meet with Dr. Alvaro within the next three hours.

That should give him plenty of time to get what answers he needed from Nikkie Jean.

He couldn't fight a battle when he couldn't see exactly what weapons his opponents possessed.

Nikkie Jean's shift ended when Wallace's did.

He'd already told his nephew to alert him when Nikkie Jean stepped into the parking lot.

He'd simply told Ray that he had a private matter to discuss with Dr. Netorre that he didn't want anyone in the hospital to overhear.

Ray had nodded, distracted by whatever it was that went on in Ray's head. It was hard to figure out just exactly what that was.

Ray had always frustrated Jennifer.

He had been a good boy, really. Trauma had had an impact on him from the time he had been only seven. Wallace had tried to be as much of a father to him as he could. It hadn't been easy. But he loved Ray. Almost as much as he loved Reggie. They were *his* children.

Wallace had raised his wife's nephew to the best of his own ability.

To his satisfaction, Nikkie Jean downed the iced tea quickly. She picked at her food, though. He'd noticed before that she was fighting the NVP quite a bit lately. And not just in the morning.

Poor thing.

Her obstetrician needed to put her on some sort of antiemetic. Nikkie Jean was too thin to lose that sort of weight so early in her pregnancy. Dehydration was also a concern. Although, he doubted that Caine Alvaro was letting much slip past him when it came to her. Alvaro wasn't the type to miss anything with the woman in his life.

The anesthetic he'd slipped into her drink wouldn't harm her long term. It would just make her easy for him to control, to question, and then she'd forget ever seeing him. She'd most likely forget the entire day's events. Everyone would most likely assume she'd just fainted from high blood pressure, resulting in a seizure. It was rare, but it could happen.

And it could cause memory loss.

That's what he was counting on.

And if her answers to his questions revealed anything she didn't need to know, he'd do what had to be done. He wouldn't want to, but there wasn't anything Wallace wouldn't do to protect his family.

Even if it meant harming Nikkie Jean.

Chapter 71

NIKKIE JEAN GATHERED her bag and laughed at something Lacy was saying, but she wasn't paying extremely close attention. She was starting to feel light-headed again. Woozy.

Hormones or blood pressure, she wasn't entirely certain yet. Pregnancy was playing ping-pong with Nikkie Jean's body lately; that was for sure.

Lacy asked her if she was fine. Twice.

"I'm ok. Just a little woozy. Jelly Bean didn't like the onions today."

"Quit eating so many onions. Go home. Take a nap."

"I'm on my way downtown to meet Annie. She's meeting with the mayor about his initiative, and I told her I'd go with her. Give her moral support."

She liked the mayor. She'd met him before.

He'd asked her for coffee once, but she'd turned him down. He was too big, too powerful, too forceful. She'd liked quieter men. It was safer that way.

Of course, Caine was all of those things, too. And she'd now freely admit she liked him just exactly that way.

Otherwise, he wouldn't be Caine, the man she half suspected she was falling in love with.

"Take it easy when you get home. If you need a ride in tomorrow, give me a call. I'll swing by."

"I'll do that." Right now, she just wanted to get to Annie, help her friend, and then get home.

To sleep for about a week.

Pregnancy was making her body do all sorts of strange and unusual things. She'd never eaten tomato-and-onion salad before—at least not and liked it, anyway.

Nikkie Jean forced herself to shake it off.

There was no way she was going to drive feeling like this. That would be stupid. If her blood pressure dropped, she'd end up passing out behind the wheel. City Hall was only six blocks up the street. Not Boethe, which ran behind the parking lot and the hospital, but Main Street, which ran parallel on the other side. It wasn't quite five o'clock; she had time to hoof it to the mayor's office to meet Annie before her five-fifteen appointment.

Nikkie Jean started across the parking lot as Lacy went in the opposite direction, toward W4HAV.

It took her a moment to realize someone was calling her name. She turned.

"Dr. Henedy…" She didn't know what to say to him. He hadn't asked her out again. She might have even imagined he'd meant more than he'd said last time. But…he was saying something to her. There was concern in his gray eyes.

Her eyes started to close. Nikkie Jean tried to fight it. Panic rushed in, giving her enough adrenaline to take a few more steps. Something…something wasn't making sense.

His hands came up. Wrapped around her arm. "Hey, honey. I've got you. It's ok. I'll get you back inside. You'll be safe. I promise you'll be safe with me. I won't let anything hurt you."

He helped her into his car. Nikkie Jean wanted to protest. This wasn't right. Something wasn't right. She was in the front seat of his car. He was next to her.

She shouldn't be in Wallace Henedy's car.

The hospital was right behind him. She shouldn't be in his car. Fear for her baby flashed like lightning through her.

Nikkie Jean's hand tightened on the door handle.

She shouldn't be in anyone's car.

Especially now.

She pulled in as deep a breath as she could and pawed at the handle.

There was a stop sign up ahead. They were eight blocks from the hospital now, two blocks past city hall. If she couldn't make it to the hospital, Annie was at city hall. Annie and the mayor. Annie would help her. The mayor would.

She had to get to Annie. She had to.

Chapter 72

WALLACE COULDN'T BELIEVE IT. He stared at her as she stumbled down the sidewalk, almost falling into traffic at one point.

He had been stupid. He should have fastened her in. He could have belted her arms in as well. Hell, she was so small he could have wrapped his necktie around her arms and subdued her so easily that way.

But he hadn't.

She stumbled through the crosswalk, barely missing getting hit by a two-door economy car.

Damn it. They were close enough to two different hospitals.

If she made her way to one, she might still be lucid enough to tell who had drugged her. If she stumbled into traffic and was injured or killed, there might still be enough drug in her system to show up on tox screens.

And he was no doubt the first suspect. He'd delivered her tea, after all.

He had to make his original plan work.

He yanked his car over to the parking spots parallel to the sidewalk and jumped out. He could see her in the distance. Stumbling. Toward the rear entrance of the ER, off of Main Street.

If he chased her, someone would see him. They could put it together.

Wallace forced himself to stop. To think.

He couldn't chase a drugged woman down Main Street. That would just bring complications he didn't need. Unless he was the one to "find" her.

He would be the hero. Everyone loved Nikkie Jean. They'd circled around her since word of her pregnancy had spread and were treating her like the darling of the hospital.

Wallace started out of his car, following her a good distance back and at a reasonable speed. The rain made it easy to do without getting noticed.

She stumbled to the ground just as the air siren sounded.

People screamed. At first...he thought it was because of Nikkie Jean.

And then Wallace looked over his shoulder.

And prayed, as he ran toward the nearest building, that he would survive *this* monster bearing down on them all.

He hurried inside, remembering the young woman he had drugged after it was far too late.

Chapter 73

IT WAS A WARZONE. Reece DeTerro stared at the destruction that stretched from the parking lot of County Gen to as far as the eye can see. There were going to be injuries. And there were going to be dead.

He was halfway between Finley Creek County and city hall when he got his first real look at Finley Creek General.

The front entrance, where the ER had once been, was total destruction. At least three floors were completely exposed.

If anyone had been in that part of the hospital—and it was likely that they had—it would have been devastating.

He hoped to high heaven the COM had evacuated everyone to a different part of the building.

He cursed and picked up his pace. His plan had been to head to his own hospital and be ready—every available physician would definitely be needed in this kind of disaster—but no. FCGH would need him more.

He was jogging across the parking lot of what had once been a bodega but was now a pile of debris when he saw the woman.

Reece almost missed her. If she hadn't been wearing florescent pink, he never would have seen her.

Reece went to his knees next to her, giving her a quick visual inspection. Her hair, long and wet, hung in limp braids. There was blood on her temple. A quick check revealed it was relatively minor. But something had struck her.

Rainwater ran over her in a continuous stream, soaking her more and more. Her face had been pressed next to the sidewalk.

Directly in the runoff. Damn it. She most likely had a chest full of filthy floodwater. She could drown in that. That was the only reason he had risked turning her over in the first place.

"Miss, can you open your eyes?" He waited. No response. He lifted her eyelid and checked her pupil. No reaction. He checked her vitals.

Her breathing was slow, raspy.

Someone somewhere was missing this young woman. From the cartoon bunnies on the scrubs top, she worked pediatrics. But not in his hospital. He should know; he headed the pediatrics department at County.

He hoped to hell she hadn't been sucked out of the Finley Creek Gen building and flung this far. They were at least three blocks from the entrance to Finley Creek General. That would have been one hell of a ride for someone to survive.

Thunder cracked overhead.

There was no way in hell he was going to be able to leave her here while he went for emergency help. He looked up. There were more clouds building, fast. No. Reece wasn't leaving her there. The woman turned her head, a whimper escaping. She was small and young. Probably no more than twenty-two or -three. A nurse, most likely.

He had a special place in his heart for pediatrics nurses, considering what all they went through on the job.

He lifted the scrubs top, looking for swelling or any obvious signs of internal injuries. Scrapes and contusions, but nothing concerning at this point.

Thunder rolled overhead. He leaned over the woman. A pretty one, he'd bet. When she wasn't soaked through to the skin and pale as a ghost.

"Hang on, little darlin'. I'm going to get you someplace safe and dry." He slid one arm behind her back, careful of her neck. He didn't think there were any spinal injuries, but you never knew in these types of situations—his other arm went beneath her knees. Hot-pink scrubs. Those damned scrubs had been what had caught his attention.

She turned toward him, obviously seeking warmth. It reassured him somewhat. No spinal injury. Just out. A rush of tenderness and protectiveness went through him. He'd always been a sucker for small and vulnerable like this. Poor kid. "Hang on, baby. I'll get you somewhere warm and dry real soon."

She didn't weigh much. She could have been picked up by the storm and lost in the wind far too easily.

Someone, somewhere, was going to be missing this girl soon. He did one more visual check of the area, making certain he hadn't missed anyone else.

The closest hospital was FCGH. No doubt she belonged there. Well, he would get her there as fast as he was able.

Chapter 74

WALLACE RECOGNIZED THE hot-pink pants the instant the man in a black T-shirt and ragged jeans came hurrying through the parking lot. Sweat immediately formed on his brow. He'd hoped she'd be missing for a while longer. And that when they found her, she'd be dead. She'd have just been taken to the local morgues for later identification, and been considered a victim of the storm. Lost in the tornado.

Then he wouldn't have had to blame himself at all. The storm would have done it, taken care of her for him. Then the entire situation would have been out of his hands. Divine intervention.

Now that she was back, he had to make a show. And hell, he didn't truly want Nikkie Jean hurt. He'd just wanted answers. And wanted to clean things up for Jennifer. If he made things *right,* she'd come home where she belonged. "Where did you find her?"

"Reece DeTerro, chief of peds at County. I found her about four blocks from here, in a damned puddle. She may be a nurse here. I don't think I've seen her in my department before."

"She's one of ours. Pediatric surgical resident," Wallace said, shortly. The man laid her out on the gurney they were using as an exam table. "Nikkie Jean Netorre. Clocked out a few hours ago."

"Shortly before the storm? I don't know how long she was in that puddle. Or how much she breathed in."

Wallace immediately made a show of checking her vitals, as if she were any other patient. "I've got her from here."

Cherise, the nursing supervisor who had been working on Wallace's team, leaned over Nikkie Jean. "Nikkie Jean, sweetie, open your eyes. Time to wake up."

Cherise checked her pupils. "She's unresponsive."

Wallace did the calculations. The anesthetic should be

wearing off soon. Wallace knew exactly how long it tended to take. He'd hoped to have finished with Nikkie Jean by now.

But with the way Cherise was hovering already, that wasn't going to happen tonight. "We need to get her inside. Get her hooked up to the monitors. Full panel. How far along is she again? Possible to hear the fetal heartbeat?" Cherise would know, even if Wallace made it look like he didn't.

"Eleven or twelve weeks. We may be able to hear the heartbeat with Doppler."

Wallace shook his head. "Better with ultrasound."

"Jillian has one over in the next tent."

He did a cursory examination, as the man who'd found Nikkie Jean slipped out of the tent.

"No sign of outward injury. Except the scalp laceration. Most likely a concussion. But I don't like that she's unresponsive." Chances were good she wouldn't recall a damned thing. Wallace forced himself to remember that. "Strap her down. We'll get her over to Rafe and Jillian. Move on to the next."

"But—" Cherise started.

Wallace held up a hand. "I know. It's Dr. Netorre. But tonight, we can't afford to spend too much time with any one patient. I suspect she's just hit her head, and is going to be out for a while. There are no signs she has internal bleeding or anything other than a hit to the head, and probably a drop or rise in blood pressure. She was in the storm, probably saw it coming right at her. I'm more concerned with potential water in the lungs. We'll get her to Courtney, get a full scan. See what's going on. In the meantime, let's just get her where she can be monitored. I want to start her on antibiotics to prevent infection. Cephalexin should be safe enough for the fetus."

He checked her pupils again. Still no real response. He frowned. He had given her a heavy dosage, yes. But she should be waking up by now. Of course, he may have miscalculated. It was an experimental drug, after all, and based on knowing the patient's weight. She'd lost some weight in the last few weeks. Hey may have overestimated. With a knock to the head and pregnancy, she may just be out for a while longer than he thought.

It shouldn't have caused any harm to a developing fetus, but the amnesia afterward had been what he had wanted. He forced himself to take a deep breath. That amnesia was more likely with a concussion. And trauma.

Nikkie Jean wouldn't remember what had happened at all. He just had to play it cool. And take care of her like the physician that he was.

She wouldn't remember a thing. "Nikkie Jean, open your eyes."

To his surprise, her eyes flickered open. "Caine? Where are you?"

"No. It's Dr. Henedy, Nikkie Jean. You're at the hospital again." He nodded at Cherise and pointed toward the exit of the tent. He waited until the redhead was gone to lean over the woman on the bed. "Do you remember what happened?"

"I was supposed to meet Jillian..." Her eyes closed again as her words slurred off. "My head hurts. Was going to talk to Jillian about the babies. Cousins...Caine..."

Wallace patted her hand, not knowing what else to do. He couldn't exactly cover her mouth and smother her here. Someone could walk in at any moment, even if it would be far too easy.

Nikkie Jean would never be able to put up a fight.

He didn't know if he could do it. Not with her just lying there so helpless. And the autopsy would reveal she'd been suffocated, if he did. No. He had to wait.

Drugging her and tossing her body into the Value Reservoir if necessary had been one thing. But to do it right there, with her so...helpless...as his patient? That was a line Wallace just couldn't cross.

Even to keep his secrets.

He just couldn't do it. He'd sworn an oath to never hurt a patient. He took that seriously.   Just like he did the oaths he'd made on his wedding day.

The curtain flap opened again. A familiar pair stepped in.

Jillian immediately went to the head of the gurney. "We will take her across the parking lot. Get her inside."

"She came in unresponsive, but was able to answer me when I spoke to her a few minutes later. She said she was meeting you soon."

"That was yesterday. Tonight, she was supposed to meet Annie downtown."

"She was found near city hall," Wallace said. Two more orderlies came in, and Jillian started giving orders. Wallace just shook his head. The redhead was getting too big for her britches at times now that she was married to the head of the hospital. But at least he could say he'd rarely heard her be wrong when it came to patient care. She would have made a damned fine doctor instead of a nurse. Or a drill sergeant. "It's raining. We'll need to move fast. I've radioed ahead. We're handing her off to Hannah once she's inside."

Wallace just stepped back. Jillian knew exactly what he was supposed to be doing. If he stuck around too long, people would wonder why.

He just hoped to hell the drug, one that was reputed not to show up in the bloodstream immediately, worked as well as it had been touted to. He really needed her not to remember what had happened before the storm.

Chapter 75

CAINE SAW MORE PATIENTS after the storm than he had in the previous four months combined. It wouldn't be the first time he'd run a hospital when he'd been injured. Nothing other than Mother Nature could compare to a hospital in a war zone. Henry and the children were fine, and the truck could be repaired. The hail damage over the top of it would be fixed. But his family—they were all safe.

For a moment there, he hadn't been certain he would be able to get Dalton inside.

Caine shoved those memories aside as he finished up with Bailey, Nikkie Jean's little deputy friend. She'd injured her leg when the TSP vehicle she and the sheriff had been riding in had been blown off the road.

Dalton was fine. His family was fine.

But his heart had yet to start beating again.

He still hadn't been able to locate Nikkie Jean. And it had been hours since the storm. He checked the clock quickly. Almost four in the morning. And he still hadn't heard from her. Or found her.

He'd tried, every second he could. Nothing.

And calls weren't going into the Finley Creek Gen switchboard. Cell services in the area were down for the time being as well. Rumor had it half the towers had been hit directly.

He needed to know where she was. He needed to get to her.

But he was in charge of this hospital and people were counting on him.

Never had he felt so damned torn in two.

"Caine, phone." JoLyn handed him the main line almost frantically. She'd been trying to get calls out to everyone necessary, to make certain they had enough ambulances and support staff to send to other areas, if requested. Barratt County had been hit, but what they were hearing said it was nowhere near bad as Finley Creek County had. "It's Holden-Deane, at FCGH. Hurry."

Caine grabbed it quickly. "Rafe? Where's Nikkie Jean? I can't find her. Tell me you have her and she's safe."

"Do you have any beds? I need to transfer people out. Make room for more critical," his brother asked instead. *"We'll...talk...about Nikkie Jean in a minute."*

Caine checked the list. There had been something in his tone... "I have room for fourteen. Five of those are in my critical ward."

"Good. I got three stable but guarded coming your way."

"You all doing ok?" Obligation and caring he hadn't realized he'd feel made him ask. "The rest of our...siblings?"

"Ariella fell on the stairs, getting the kids to the basement. Some tissue damage. Scared her husband. Everyone else is relatively unscathed. It's not even storming in Garrity, so Zoey and Pen are fine. You?"

"Caught on the road with the children. Barely made it home in time to get them all inside. Everett needed stitches, but he's ok now."

His brother swore. *"Glad to hear you're doing ok."*

"I can't find her, Rafe. And I need to." Even Caine heard the panic. He'd never panicked like this in his life. He'd always had to be the one in charge in a crisis. "And I can't leave here to go look for her."

"I have her here, Caine..."

"But?"

"She was found outside after the storm. She'd been out there for at least a few hours. We don't know what happened to her before. She woke a few minutes ago, but doesn't remember anything that happened. And now she's under again."

Sheer fear had his blood freezing, his lungs fighting to work. "How badly is she hurt?"

"Mild concussion. Quite a bit of fluid in her lungs. She was found in a damned puddle, unconscious. We're watching for infection, and she's a bit banged up. We're trying to figure out why she was out when she was found. There's no signs of impact injuries, no concussion. We have her on fluids to prevent dehydration and are watching for complications from the

concussion, but it's a minor one."

"The baby?"

"Seems ok at this point. Strong, steady heartbeat visible on the ultrasound. No signs of early fetal distress."

Caine closed his eyes as relief hit him for the baby, chased by fear for Nikkie Jean. "I'm coming for her, Rafe. I'll be there as soon as I can leave here. I'm coming as soon as I possibly can. You make certain she knows that if she wakes before I get to her."

"She's in room 403. I'm not going anywhere until you get here yourself."

Chapter 76

DR. JACOBSON WAS A real jerk when he had his mind made up about something. It didn't matter. It wasn't like she was going anywhere anyway.

Not with Annie and Nikkie Jean still there. They'd both woken a few hours ago, but it was obvious they were hurting.

And scared.

Especially Nikkie Jean. She kept saying she had to get away. And looking for a dragon.

Izzie feared she was having nightmares about what had happened to her years ago.

No one knew if Nikkie Jean's house was still standing, but she and the baby were going to be ok. Annie had woken frantic, worried over her foster sons.

Izzie had already thought about that and had had one of the orderlies who had been injured but still stayed around to help track down Annie's mother.

Annie's mother was fine and demanding to know when Annie could make it home—even though their home was seriously damaged—to help take care of the three boys, who were just too much for Annie's mother to handle.

Izzie had her opinions on that. Annie had been *raising* her mother since Annie and Izzie had been all of twelve years old. The least the woman could do was watch Annie's children while Annie was in the hospital injured. They'd started off as Annie's mother's foster children. Not Annie's. But now they were Annie's everyway but by blood.

She wouldn't let it matter—*she* was there for Annie and Nikkie Jean. No matter what.

She grabbed some spare scrubs and headed back toward 403.

She was going to take a shower, then clock in. See if she could do some good around the place. It was still an all-hands-on-deck callout right now.

She rounded the corner and passed Cherise and Hannah, the nursing supervisors who'd basically glued themselves to the hospital since the tornado hit.

Hannah's arm was in a sling, but she was still game. Her three-year-old daughter was down in the basement day care.

Their people pulled together in times of crises. They always would.

He was there, too.

Izzie would just ignore Allen Jacobson as long as she could. To think she'd actually thought the guy had become a nicer person since everything had happened. Wrong. He was even more of a dictator than he had been before.

They'd cut off all travel to Finley Creek unless it was vitally necessary. No one was getting in or out without permission. Not until this passed. She'd have to stay where she was, anyway.

The doors to the ward burst opened.

A pirate wearing biker leather and a gold earring walked in. One with massive shoulders and an attitude of "get out of my way" around him.

Everyone just kind of paused for a moment. Izzie stared, even though she'd seen him a few times before. Some men were just like that.

It was the way he carried himself. No one was standing in his way. She doubted even Allen Jacobson could stop him.

Maybe Rafe could. But *that* would be one even match to watch.

Dr. Alvaro had a bandage over one eye, and the hair was a total mess. It suited him. He was definitely a wilder version of his twin; that was for sure.

But dear gravy, he was hot.

No wonder Nikkie Jean had lost all reason when he'd looked at her.

Everyone just stared at him.

"Can I help you?" Cherise asked.

"Dr. Alvaro," Izzie said, stepping forward. She strongly suspected she knew exactly who he was looking for. "About time you showed up."

"Rafe just managed to get a call through to my hospital. I've come for Nikkie Jean."

Of course, he had.

"She…"

"Room 403?" He barely looked at anyone other than Izzie. He was far more intense than his brother. Izzie never would have thought that was possible.

But, *wow*, to have a man like that come for her…would be absolutely amazing. If Izzie was in to that kind of cheesy-romance thing.

If he just wasn't a doctor. Or so forceful and masculine and dominating…yeah, Izzie knew her own limits.

But no wonder this guy had gotten through Nikkie Jean's defenses.

Someone walked up behind her and put a hot hand on her shoulder. She yelped like a wimp.

"Izzie, I don't think you've been discharged yet. I know I haven't signed off on it."

No. Technically she hadn't been. But Izzie had been making her own decisions for a long time.

And now *he* had her hostage.

She thought about squirming beneath his hold, but Izzie wasn't going to give him that satisfaction. The jerk should have other people to worry about besides her.

So what if they'd ridden out a tornado wrapped up in each other's arms—*that* had been coincidence. It didn't give him extra rights to control her or anything. The man needed to just leave her be.

She looked up over her shoulder into gray eyes. Allen Jacobson was tall. A few inches shorter than Dr. Alvaro, but still quite a bit taller than Izzie. Broad shouldered, and strong. Rugged good looks that he just didn't deserve.

It made her feel a little too vulnerable stuck there between the two ridiculously large, beautiful men. Beautiful, dominant, not-take-no-for-an-answer, used-to-getting-their-way men. "Stuff it, Jacobson, I'm just grabbing clean scrubs so I can take a shower before I'm paroled."

"Nikkie Jean?" Alvaro demanded again. "Which way is 403?"

"She's in here," Jacobson said. "We've had to put three to a room. Izzie went AWOL."

"And Annie is still sleeping. So don't wake her up." Izzie trailed after the two tall men, after shrugging at Cherise and Hannah, who were both making wide eyes at the back of Holden-Deane's twin when they should have been reorganizing the temporary ER intake desk.

No surprise. It wasn't exactly common knowledge around the hospital that the man even existed. Yet there he was—shouting to all that could hear his words that *he* was Nikkie Jean's lover.

And he had come for her.

There was no way Izzie was going to miss this. If Nikkie Jean woke and didn't want him there, Izzie was ready to call Vince and having him removed.

No matter what the consequences were. But somehow she didn't see that happening.

Because Nikkie Jean had been asking where Caine was in her sleep, too.

As if she expected him to be there somewhere.

Now he finally was.

Chapter 77

"JUST TELL ME HOW she's doing." Caine stepped closer to the bed. One small hand was wrapped in plaster. It was the same one he'd sewn up the first time he'd met her. The other had tubes taped in place. There was a bruise over her left eye. Near the scar. "Her glasses and contacts?"

She'd wake nearly blind. In a hospital room. Afraid. Worried for the baby.

"Lost the glasses in the storm. We haven't been able to get out to her house yet. To see if it's still standing," Izzie said.

"It most likely isn't," Caine said harshly. She'd lost them in the storm. And hadn't been able to see clearly without them. Just how vulnerable Nikkie Jean was slammed into him. Again. "It was right in the path. Mine took some damage. I barely got the children inside in time. The storm headed toward her place next." His voice broke. He'd known the storm had been headed right toward where he'd thought she'd been. Either her house or the highway. Her hospital.

She hadn't stood a chance; and he'd known it.

Just how much she'd meant to him had been as clear as the lightning flashing through the small ground-level windows near where he'd huddled with his children and uncle. And prayed.

"I'm sorry."

"Nikkie Jean's place is three miles down the road from mine. The storm hit my place first." And the radio and news said it had only gathered steam before hitting Finley Creek next.

Her hair had been washed and braided. She had in My Little Pony ribbons. Who had done that? She had an oxygen tube in her nose. He checked the monitors. Her stats were right where they should be.

He could have lost her. Lost the baby. Before he had even had them.

"She's mostly just resting, Dr. Alvaro," Jacobson said. "And we're watching for bacterial infection or pneumonia. She had quite a bit of water in her lungs that concerned us for a while. She'd been knocked out and landed in a puddle. But she should make a full recovery."

"Our baby? That'll be the first thing she asks about when she wakes. I need to know what to tell her. If I need to…prepare…"

"The baby is fine," her friend said. This time there was compassion in her words. "I stayed up most of the night next to her. We checked the Doppler twice. At first, the heart rate was a bit sluggish. The second time everything sounded fine. Not a single blip on her monitor. This is Nikkie Jean's kid. You think it's not already stubborn enough to stand up to a tornado?"

He was barely aware of what was said between the two after that. He just stared at Nikkie Jean for the longest time.

Caine wasn't going anywhere. Everett, Keller, and Dalton were safe at the house right now, with his uncle. He'd get someone out to cover the windows on the house as soon as he could. But his number one priority at the moment was the woman still sleeping in the bed he sat by. His number two priority was their child.

He slipped one hand over her stomach. It was the first time he'd ever felt the proof of what his child was doing to Nikkie Jean's body. She'd only just begun to show at all.

Emotion built up in his throat, making it hard to breathe for a moment.

Her eyes flicked open, and she shifted.

Whimpered, in a way destined to destroy him. "Nikkie Jean, sweetheart. It's ok. Everything's ok."

"I…Rafe? I can't see you. Where's Jillian? I'm supposed to meet her in fifteen minutes. Balloons…" And then she went back under again.

She came back out of it twenty-five minutes later. This time her eyes were clearer when she looked at him. But she was looking past him a bit, with unfocused eyes. "I need my glasses."

"They have your contacts in solution in the drawer. But your glasses were lost in the storm." He brushed his hand down the arm with the IV tube stuck in it.

"*Caine.* I know your touch." She turned toward him. "I was wondering when you'd get here."

When. Not if.

"Yes. Caine." Always Caine. And from this moment on he would be doing his damnedest to be there when she needed him. No matter what. "Damn, Nikkie Jean, you scared me again."

"You...sorry. I don't remember what's happened. I was...working. Then...I'm here. A car... Did I get sick again?"

"Do you remember the storm?" Traumatic head injuries could bring memory loss; he knew that well enough. And where she'd been found...there had been concrete and debris near her. Jacobson had said another physician from County had told him.

She'd been found and rescued by a stranger.

The debt he owed that man would never be forgotten.

Chapter 78

WHEN SHE OPENED HER eyes, all she saw was a blur. She assumed that blur was Caine. She had heard him before she'd opened her eyes. It was either him or Rafe, and there was a dark-green shadow on the arm resting next to the rail. And she knew…

"Caine?"

"I'm here, sweetheart. You're in the hospital."

"What's going on? Why am I here?" Fear for the baby shot through her and her hand shifted to her abdomen.

"Do you remember the storm?"

"No." She couldn't remember much of anything. Just walking across the parking lot. In the rain. She thought she had talked to someone…after that. Nothing, except someone with strong arms carrying her. Someone not Caine, but who had promised to keep her safe. "How badly am I hurt?"

"Mild concussion. Contusions. Abrasions. Superficial cuts. You were unconscious when a Dr. DeTerro from County found you. He brought you here. You've got a hairline fracture in your wrist. But it's a minor break and should heal within the month. You've wrenched your knee again. Some bruised ribs. And bruising on your neck."

"How long was I out? The baby?" She fought the panic as someone moved nearer. Without her glasses on, Nikkie Jean couldn't tell who it was. Until she saw the bright-red hair. And the green scrubs. "Our baby?"

"The baby is fine, sweetheart. Jillian's going to take you down to radiology for another ultrasound in a few minutes. Just to make sure everything still looks good now that it's been more than twelve hours since the last one." Caine's hand covered her stomach. "They've started a betting pool to see whether our baby or Jillian's is bigger. I think she just wants to see if we're winning or they are."

She would know his touch anywhere. But she needed to see his eyes, to make sure he wasn't lying to her.

"I wish I could see you."

"We've got someone searching for your prescription. We'll get you something soon," Caine said.

"I have spare glasses in my locker. Surgical break room."

"That solves that problem," Jillian said. "We'll get Allen or Virat to grab them. You'll just need to provide the combination."

"Not locked. We never lock the lockers in there. No need." She closed her eyes. It was easier to do that than deal with the blur. "When can I go home?"

"Sweetheart, I don't know when they'll be releasing you. A tornado hit while you were out in the parking lot, and the streets aren't open right now. We're stuck here in Finley Creek for a while. But I'm staying right here with you. And your guard dogs are both here." There was a hesitation in his words she couldn't interpret yet.

"The kids? They ok?" If they weren't, there was no way he'd be with her. Nikkie Jean knew that instinctively. But he needed to be with them. Not her. But she needed to know they were ok.

"It frightened them. We were on the road when it hit, but they are ok now. I had to put stitches in Everett's arm, but he is fine. Says he's going to tell everyone a bad guy did it. My place took some damage, but it's still standing and habitable." He leaned closer. She felt him brush his lips over her forehead. "I could have lost you, Nikkie Jean. It's never going to happen again. You and Jelly Bean are coming home with me. We'll figure everything else out together."

She wanted to say more but was just too tired to form the words. They'd given her something, despite the risks to the baby. She didn't want that. Not again. She forced her eyes open and tried to look at him. "No more sedatives. Not for the baby. No matter the risk. Understand?"

"Understood. You just rest. I'm not going anywhere."

"Make sure the baby is safe, Caine. *Promise me.* You're the father. You tell them for me. No meds. We don't want any drugs, not for our baby."

"I promise. Nothing will hurt our baby." His fingers spread over where their child rested. "I'm watching the monitors, too, sweetheart. Everything looks fine. I will take care of you. I promise."

Of course, he would. He was Caine; there probably wasn't anything he couldn't handle. Nikkie Jean let herself float into the ether, at peace knowing Caine was there to make sure everything with the baby was going to be all right.

Chapter 79

WHEN SHE OPENED her eyes the final time, Nikkie Jean could focus on the world around her. Well, as much as she could without her contacts and no glasses. She tried to sit up in the bed.

Pregnant women had to pee frequently. She was definitely no exception. There were no wires hooked up to her, except the ones she would have expected. So no more peeing through a tube, at least. Someone was next to her bed. From the size, coloring, and green blob on one arm, she had a good inkling who it was. "Caine? What are you still doing here? You should be home with the kids— or off running Barratt County."

"Waiting for Sleeping Beauty to wake up. I was about ready to try the kissing thing. My daughter assures me a kiss from the prince works every time. At least, she did when I talked to her an hour ago and told her you were still sleeping. I'm supposed to kiss you so you will wake up. I thought that sounded like a good idea."

"You are no princess, and the last thing I am is a prince." She paused a minute as what she'd said sank in. "Wait a minute. Reverse that. My brain is like scrambled eggs right now. The baby?"

"Fine. Jillian's been checking with Doppler. Everything sounds fine. She's coming back on her lunch break to try again. She's determined. Apparently, Jelly Bean and her baby—which Jacobson has named the Kidney Bean—are going to grow up together as lifelong friends, best cousins, and pseudo twins."

Tears hit her eyes. "I'd like that."

"None of that." He placed a tissue in her hand. "I have glasses right here." Those followed the tissue. She slipped them on, and he came into focus. That's when she realized where she was again fully.

"I'm not sure how I got here, but I'm tired of waking up in this room. I am starting to think it really is cursed."

He hesitated.

"The baby is ok?"

"The baby is ok. But it's you we were worried about. What do you remember?"

Before she could answer, someone knocked. Jillian poked her head in. "Good, you're awake. We need to talk. And…I brought this."

Jillian had a Doppler in her hand. "Lacy and Layla and I were talking…about genetics. Lacy has the theory that since my baby is apparently bigger than average for some strange reason—" Jillian shot the man behind her a look. "There's a chance yours might be as well. Layla wants to take you to Courtney and get a pretty picture again. I'm not sure why, probably just for science. I think we're the hospital experiments here."

Caine laced his fingers with hers. "Dalton was almost an eight-pound baby at thirty-three and a half weeks. The twins were each over seven pounds. Everett was closer to eight, at thirty-seven weeks."

"Big for twins," Jillian said quietly.

"Do either of you know how much you weighed at birth?" Nikkie Jean asked. Both men stiffened. Ok. She'd found a powder keg there.

"I have our original birth records," Caine said. "We were both over six pounds. I was closer to seven. Maybe. It could have been reversed. We were baby A and B on the original records."

"I'd like to see them some time," Rafe said.

Caine leaned forward. "The birth certificates list us as Caine and Abel. Clever, weren't they? Our birth parents weren't exactly parents of the year, Nikkie Jean. I'll tell you the story sometime later."

"Yeah, I know how that feels myself. So…" Nikkie Jean had more important things to worry about than what happened thirty-six years ago; she wanted to see that Doppler monitor in action. She wanted to hear for herself. "Bigger-than-average babies seem to be the norm here."

"Same for their siblings' children. Luc and Payton's baby, Patrick, weighed almost nine and a half. Paige's Mikey weighed almost ten—and was twenty-three inches long."

"Ouch. Ouch. Ouch," Nikkie Jean said, eyeing Caine and Rafe

like they were the overly large devils they were. "Too bad these guys didn't come with warning labels."

Caine just shot her a hot look—one that had her remembering that she hadn't exactly protested what they'd done that night.

Far from it; she'd lured him to his doom easily and willingly, after all.

"No kidding, right?" Jillian motioned for her to lie back on the bed. She went to work with the monitor. "So how do you feel today?"

"Honestly? Other than the always-with-me morning sickness, I feel fine. I'm just…not certain how I got here." She'd heard enough the last time she'd opened her eyes to figure out that a storm had hit. But the details were more than just fuzzy to her. They were nonexistent.

Caine leaned forward as Jillian fiddled with the settings. His eyes were trained on hers. It would take Jillian a moment to find the baby, if the machine could pick it up at all. The room was silent until…

"There. Found the Jelly Bean."

A steady *thump, thump* sounded from the monitor.

Tears sprang to her eyes. Nikkie Jean's gaze shot to Caine's. He had the dopiest grin on his face. His fingers were wrapped around hers.

His eyes met hers. For a moment, Jillian and Rafe disappeared. And it was just her and Caine. Connected.

Jillian let them listen for a few more minutes. "So…my niece or nephew sounds just fine. But I bet he or she is hungry right now?"

"Definitely. I don't remember eating anything since—" She frowned. "I don't remember. I don't remember anything since yesterday afternoon. I think it was yesterday."

She fought back the panic. She shouldn't have lost that much time. Not for the little scratch on her head. She didn't even have much of a headache. "Did I hit my head again?"

"We don't know," Caine said. His fingers slipped around hers and he squeezed. Some of the panic receded. "You left the building, according to what Izzie said, to go meet Annie at the mayor's office. You never made it. The head of pediatrics from County actually found you on his way to County after the storm."

She didn't have a headache. Not like the last time she'd been in the hospital. "I don't feel like I hit my head."

"You have a small bruise right here." Caine brushed the area over her right temple. "But no concussion. The wound didn't even require stitches. It's more like an abrasion or road rash."

"What's the last thing you do remember?" Jillian asked, quietly and calmly. Nikkie Jean looked at her friend and pulled in a deep breath. Whatever had happened, she was safe now.

"There was a meeting at lunch—with Rafe. I walked in with Lacy and Allen. After that…blank."

"It's possible you did hit your head and, combined with the previous concussion, you just don't remember," Rafe said, with a soothing tone in his voice. "Or you simply fainted and bruised your head when you fell. And rode out the storm where you landed. Or the trauma has caused you to block it out. We've seen that happen before. We have no real way of knowing unless you can remember later. Which, with a blow to the head, isn't all that unusual."

"I—" She tried. She truly did. But all she remembered was walking down the hallway with Lacy right before the meeting started. "I think…I remember…Dr. Henedy? Was he there? And a woman? A nurse?"

Jillian nodded. "Dr. DeTerro actually found you on the sidewalk, Nik. He carried you to us. Wallace Henedy was working a triage tent in the parking lot. He and Cherise were the ones to originally treat you."

"The lunch meeting ran to about four thirty. The storm hit after that. You were found and admitted less than ninety minutes later," Rafe said. "After Wallace and Cherise checked you over and determined you were stable, Jillian and I brought you here."

"But what happened in between?" Anything could have happened to her. Nikkie Jean fought the panic that brought.

"Only you can tell us that," Caine said. "But it doesn't matter. What matters is that you are safe." He leaned closer and brushed a kiss over her hand. "You're both safe right now."

All at once, what he'd told her flashed through her head. How he'd had to sit with his wife as she died, knowing she'd never see their son. Nikkie Jean flipped her hand over and cupped his cheek.

"We're all going to be ok."

—

He'd only been gone a few hours. He'd been there when she'd opened her eyes around noon. She'd just watched him sleeping for a few minutes before drifting off again, reassured that he was safe. That she was. That the baby was. He'd been gone the next time she'd surfaced. No doubt to captain his own ship.

But Izzie had been there in his place. Now Rafe stood looking down at her.

"I'm giving you a clean bill of health—well, Dr. Kaur is. She asked me to stop by and give you the message since she was paged to an emergency twin delivery fifteen minutes ago. You are fine. Jelly Bean is fine. And you are being released."

To go where?

Izzie had confirmed what she'd suspected. Her house had taken an indirect hit. Her roof was damaged, and the back part of the house had taken structural damage. Izzie had taken photos for her. It was fixable, but she wasn't going to be living there for a while. She'd gotten lucky it hadn't been blown to smithereens. The tornado had cut a swath right over Caine's house and straight toward hers.

They'd both gotten incredibly lucky.

"I need to find a place to stay. Need to call the Barratt or something." She wasn't too attached to her house. Not really. She'd certainly moved before.

But this was the first place she'd purchased with her own money, earned with her own work.

Maybe she was more attached to it than she'd thought. Tears burned her eyes behind the pink sports glasses that she'd had in a tote bag in her locker. She'd left them in there, and Izzie had retrieved them for her so she would be able to see.

"You're coming home with me."

Nikkie Jean wrapped her fingers around the hand he'd touched her with.

She'd like that very much.

She wasn't quite ready to let him go just yet.

If she ever would be.

Chapter 80

THEY LET HER OUT JUST after nine that night, twenty-two hours after the storm had first hit. An odd discharge time, but Nikkie Jean understood. They needed the bed. And she was well enough to go home.

Well, to Caine's home, anyway.

He pulled into the driveway of his house. The lights were on, but the kids should be asleep.

It looked different in the middle of the night. Less welcoming.

Every joint in her body ached. She was exhausted and not exactly in a good place in her head right now. "I can't do this right now."

"Do what?"

"Think about this. I just want to sleep." And cry. She wanted to be alone so she could cry.

"Then I'll carry you inside. You can be asleep in a few minutes, I promise. I have your prescriptions in my pocket."

She nodded. There was acetaminophen in there somewhere. It was all she was going to take. Well, in addition to the vitamins, anyway.

"Stay there. I'll come lift you out."

She didn't want that. She wanted to be able to stand on her own feet with him. To not be the least little bit vulnerable. But that wasn't happening. Nikkie Jean couldn't even get in and out of his truck right now without assistance.

Caine's hands practically scorched her skin when he lifted her out. He sat her down on her feet just briefly. Then he scooped her back up—far too easily. She sighed.

He must have felt it. "It'll be ok, sweetheart. No matter what I have to do to make it that way. I promise."

Nikkie Jean rested her head against his broad shoulder as he carried her inside.

"Here you ar—" An older man with wild white hair, tan skin, and brown eyes waited in the kitchen.

"Hello," Nikkie Jean said softly.

—

Henry was staring at Nikkie Jean, obvious confusion on the man's face. No wonder. Caine hadn't said much to him about what had happened. He just hadn't had time. "Uncle Henry, meet Dr. Nikkie Jean Netorre. She's going to be staying with us for a while."

"Nice to meet you, honey. How did you hurt yourself?"

Nikkie Jean nodded. "I...this is awkward. I was hurt in the storm."

"I'm sorry, honey. Let's get you comfortable. Then I'll get one of the guest rooms ready. There are two."

"The one that connects to mine, Henry. There's something you need to know." Caine wasn't one for wasting much time. Especially now. He'd come too damned close two damned times too many to waste time any longer. "Nikkie Jean is pregnant. The baby is mine."

His uncle just stared. And stared. At the two of them. Nikkie Jean was so tense in his arms it was a wonder she hadn't shattered. Caine just tightened his arms around her.

"You're serious."

"Very much so." Caine brushed a kiss over her head without thinking. Gradually the tension left her body. "I need to get her settled, Henry. She's had a rough few days."

"Of course. Welcome, little honey. I'm Uncle Henry, and anything you need at all, you come to me. Let me get you some extra blankets. Do you have any clothes with you, or do we need to find you something to wear?" Henry started buzzing around, gathering what he thought Nikkie Jean would need. Just like he'd suspected his uncle would. His uncle was a natural-born nurturer. Henry was the only reason Caine had survived to adulthood; Caine had often thought that before. "You can sleep in one of my nephew's shirts tonight. Tomorrow, you can get me a list of anything you need, and I'll go get it for you."

Henry did exactly what Caine had expected. He fussed. His uncle had never married. The man Henry had been in love with had died in the military almost forty years ago. He'd never had a family other than Caine and Caine's children.

Henry had not been overly fond of Caine's wife, and the two had grown apart then. But after she'd died, leaving Caine with a premature infant to care for, Henry had come running to help.

Caine adored the older man. And he suspected Henry was going to adore Nikkie Jean.

Nikkie Jean thanked him. Caine heard a significant sniffle the instant Henry took off down the hall. His arms tightened around her. "Hey, you ok?"

"He doesn't have to go to so much trouble for me."

"He wants to." Caine wanted to. He wanted to be the man to do whatever Nikkie Jean needed. Or provide it.

He wanted this woman in his arms to *need* him. Him. He wanted to be the focus of her world for a while.

"I—I could have gone to the hotel. Or to Rafe and Jillian's. They offered." She shot a look at him. There were tears on her cheeks. "They told me...no matter what happens between us, that they consider me family now. Me and Jelly Bean. Rafe even gave me a hug."

"He did, did he?" He'd hug her. Hold her however she would let him.

"I...only have Izzie and Annie. As my family. And now I have Rafe and Jillian, too. You're lucky you're part of their family, Caine. Very lucky to have them, just waiting for you to let them in."

"You have *me*. And I'm considering letting them in, as you said. I can't...close myself off any longer. I...hell, Nikkie Jean, I told myself at April's funeral that I wasn't going to let another woman in like that to hurt me, to hurt the children. But you...slid right in. As if you were meant to be there. If I believe in the fates—which I'm starting to—then it's the way it's supposed to be."

"The baby will have a family. A real one. Like I didn't. That matters, Caine." Her head rested on his shoulder. She was trembling in his arms, going limp as he stood there, giving Henry time to get her room ready. "I'm glad you're letting me in. And that I'm letting you in, too."

Within seconds, Nikkie Jean was sound asleep in his arms. He tightened his hold, feeling like *he* mattered to her now. Like he could make a difference for her. Like he'd just been existing for the last two years, waiting to find her.

Caine brushed a kiss over her head. "You matter, sweetheart. I can promise you that. Now it'll be up to me to show you just how much."

He carried her to the room right next to his. If it had just been him and her, or even him, her, and Henry, he would have walked straight to his room and put her in his bed.

Where she belonged.

But there would be time for that later. He'd need to ease her and the twins into the idea. He wouldn't rush any of them.

Henry was waiting, the blankets turned back. "Ah, little thing fell asleep already?"

"She's had a rough few weeks. And morning sickness hasn't been easy, either."

"I didn't realize you had a woman, Caine. I thought the children were just fixated on a friend of your sister's."

"That's her. We...met several months ago. Things happened. The baby...was a shock. A surprise, for sure. But one I'm so damned thrilled about."

"And now you're getting another child. You planning on doing the right thing with this little lady?"

He knew exactly what Henry meant. His uncle had some definite old-fashioned ideals at times. "I'm planning on it. But I screwed up with her months ago. I don't know how to fix that."

"Now your little honey there is skittish?"

"That's a good word for it."

"She going to be good for the kids?"

Caine nodded. Of that, he had no doubt. "She's a pediatric surgeon, Henry. And has one of the biggest hearts I've ever seen."

"Then you'd best be careful not to crush it." Henry looked down at her as Caine lowered her to the bed. "She's very small. As young as she looks?"

"No. That, she's not. She's thirty." He removed Nikkie Jean's glasses. She wasn't wearing the contacts. "She's stubborn as a pack of mules, too."

"Then I guess you'd better plan to out-stubborn her."

"I guess I will. I'm looking forward to it."

"Glad to see you're back among the living, boy. I was starting to think you would close yourself off forever. Good to see that you aren't."

"I wasn't, until she came barreling into the ER one night." And he'd been there, almost waiting. As if that was exactly where he was supposed to be.

Chapter 81

WHEN NIKKIE JEAN OPENED her eyes the next morning, Caine was leaning over her, and the three most beautiful mini-Alvaros were standing next to him.

"Good morning," he said in a rueful tone. "I was planning to let you sleep, but Dalton wandered in here. And Keller followed him. They seem to think I brought Sleeping Beauty home with me."

"That is such a lame story," Everett said. "All the princess does is just sleep."

Keller gave her a shy smile. "I like Belle the best."

"I bet you do. You're just as pretty as she is," Nikkie Jean said. This was one of the most awkward mornings of her life. "Hi, guys."

"Dad says he wants you to be his girlfriend, and we're not to do anything to scare you off. So I can't push Keller off the roof again. Or anything like that." Everett gave her a challenging look. But one that had the same wariness she'd seen in his father's eyes.

No wonder. With what Caine had said April had done to her own children, they'd view any woman Caine brought home as a possible threat. "No. Probably not. Why were you on the roof, and did you use proper rock-climbing equipment?"

That had the little boy looking at her closely. "No. She was supposed to be the hostage so I could rescue her and arrest the bad guy."

"It was the shed roof, sweetheart. Eight feet off the ground. But she sprained her wrist." Caine sat down on the bed next to her. "How do you feel today?"

"Rested. My head is finally clear. I'm a little sore, but I could probably go into work today and be just fine."

"Not happening. You're going to laze around like the princess while we take care of you."

Dalton squirmed and pulled himself closer to the bed. Caine

reached down and lifted his son.

Right into her arms.

Dalton babbled at her and clapped his hands.

He was such a beautiful child. They all three were.

"We've made breakfast. Daddy is going to carry you into the kitchen," Keller said. "Uncle Henry told him he had to be romantic, so you'll stay with us."

"Do you want me to stay with you? I mean, I'm not going to be in the way?" Nikkie Jean asked, looking at the twins.

Caine was watching her with them, a tension about him that she hadn't missed.

"I don't think you'll be in the way," Keller wrapped a hand around Nikkie Jean's. "Do you want to see my room? I have dolls in there. I don't have a lot of dresses for them."

"I like to make doll dresses sometimes. I'll show you how."

Everett rolled his eyes. "Dolls are for girls."

"Not necessarily just girls. And your sister is a girl." Nikkie Jean sent him a grin. "I'm a girl, too. I like ribbons and nail polish and toe rings."

"That's yuck." He shot her another look; one that was one hundred percent identical to his uncle's at his most curmudgeonly. "I guess you can stay. If you promise to be nice to all of us. Including Keller."

"I promise to always be nice to all of you. You have my word. But be forewarned; I liked frogs, but I don't kiss them. Snakes, I'm reasonably ok with as long as they don't rattle. And...I have pet snails in my locker at work."

He stole her heart when he gave her a shy smile.

Dalton stole the show when he crawled up next to her and sat—directly on her chest. Nikkie Jean let out an oomph and laughed.

Caine's eyes widened, and he snatched his youngest up quickly. "He didn't hurt you?"

Dalton's lower lip wobbled, no doubt from his father's quick movement. Nikkie Jean's heart melted.

Every bit of fear that had clung to the back of her mind dissipated and just flew away. Right there, looking at them. She reached for the toddler again. She wanted snuggles. If she could get away with it, she'd snuggle the twins, too.

And definitely, their daddy.

"I'm perfectly fine, Caine. Exactly where I want to be."

Chapter 82

NIKKIE JEAN HAD HER work cut out for her—getting both Caine *and* his clone to approve her returning to work took more finagling than she'd expected.

Well, Rafe was the only one with the true power to stop her and they all knew that. But Caine was hovering. Being an overprotective expectant father, Henry had told her.

Henry had told her that Caine had tried to coddle and pamper April when she'd been pregnant with the twins—and the other woman had sliced him up and ridiculed his concern.

She'd been a fiercely independent woman who hadn't wanted to rely on—or be responsible for—anyone other than herself.

Caine was the exact opposite; he thrived having people to care about. She was starting to see evidence of that for herself. At home, the man was far more relaxed than she ever would have expected. At home, he was comfortable fixing things with his hands, playing with Barbies and Duplo blocks and Hot Wheels, and wearing worn T-shirts with Yoda and Bart Simpson printed on them. Caine had a nerd side that she found absolutely beautiful.

He was a far cry from the man who ran a hospital and made hard decisions every single day.

He seemed to love being with *her* just as much as she was being with him.

She spent one week at Caine's and knew she never wanted to leave.

Henry was almost as bad about coddling her. Talk about overwhelming. But she finally felt like she'd found a place to belong with the Alvaro men and Keller.

But a week off was long enough to sit around doing nothing. Nikkie Jean hadn't sat down that long for thirteen years.

Since the storm, Lacy and Virat and the others had been pulling double duty. She had to do her part. It was time to go back to Finley Creek.

She just had to get her super-hot, super-sexy, super-good-at-sneaking-in-kisses-after-his-children-went-to-sleep jailer to give her a clean bill of health. Without it, his evil twin wasn't letting her return to the hospital.

Rafe had actually told her via text that she could only return to work when Caine gave her the one hundred percent A-OK. They'd double-teamed her. Perfectly.

"Well, I'm going back. And you aren't going to stop me," she finally told him. She waited for him to explode, to tell her that wasn't happening.

That if she left, she wasn't welcome to come back.

"I will drive you in and pick you up when you're ready. I'm off for the next two days—other than some meetings with Rafe concerning some billing issues the audit revealed."

Well, that fizzled. "It's a deal."

"Want to seal it with a kiss?"

"I'd like that very much, thank you. Now, lean down here." It was so easy to *play* with this man. Like she never had the opportunity to do before. Nikkie Jean was finally learning how to enjoy that.

She was also getting tired of the constant petting. It was time the man started delivering on the promises those hands and lips kept giving.

But just how to get him *in* to her bed was proving more difficult than Nikkie Jean wanted to admit. It wasn't like she had a lot of practice seducing hot COMs, after all. Maybe she needed to ask Jillian for some pointers. Because Nikkie Jean was determined.

Caine Alvaro was going to be hers. As soon as she could figure out how to make it work.

Chapter 83

WALLACE KNEW IT WAS coming to a head. He was due in Rafe Holden-Deane's office at five p.m.—in fifteen minutes. To enumerate his sins, no doubt. Wallace knew what was going to happen.

He'd met the two investigators from the FBI that morning. They'd asked him so many questions he knew they were on to him.

It was just a matter of time before they arrested him. Before they ruined everything.

Took his world from him.

But no; he'd done that. By not doing what Jennifer had asked of him.

Clean up your own messes, she'd asked. And he couldn't even do that.

They'd released a sketch of the man last seen with Connie over the news that morning.

Combine that with him working at the hospital, the matching vehicle, and he was most likely going to prison soon. All Nikkie Jean had to do was see the sketch and put it together.

There were friends of Connie's in all the hospitals; they were crying and making a show of caring about her—more than they had while she'd been alive—and passing that flyer out to whoever would look at it.

It was just a matter of time.

Nikkie Jean was as smart as a whip, after all.

They would come for him soon. It was just a matter of time. And not just for billing fraud.

He was a murderer. He had been for fifteen years.

It was time he admitted that to himself. He was a murderer. And that knowledge was going to ruin the world for his wife and son.

Tears built in his eyes as he thought of Raymond.

The boy was gone, victim of the storm.

While Wallace had been treating Nikkie Jean, Raymond had been dying from being crushed by debris in the back parking lot. He'd died with coworkers around him, not family.

He...Wallace had tortured himself all night, thinking of Raymond calling out for his uncle to at least be with him in his final moments.

Stupid. Raymond had been hit in the head. He hadn't known what was happening. He had just been...gone.

Wallace shoved the grief away ruthlessly. Jennifer had barely looked at him at the funeral that morning. Like he should have been able to do something to fight against Mother Nature.

Ray...he was supposed to be in the security office. Not out in the storm. He wasn't supposed to be out in the storm.

Wallace sat in his sedan and watched people crossing the parking lot as first shift came to a close.

There were nurses everywhere, of course. Like there always was.

The little fireball who had always reminded him of Jennifer crossed in front of his parking space.

There was a small woman in purple scrubs walknext to her.

Wallace studied Nikkie Jean as his hand fiddled with the small gun he'd carried in his glove box for years.

It had been Jordan Carrington's gun once.

Wallace had won it off of him in a card game when Nikkie Jean was probably all of five years old.

The irony wasn't lost to him.

That gun was going to end it all. Because he couldn't stand to see the shame in Jennifer's eye when she looked at him.

He would not expect her to associate herself with him any longer. Not with her plans for her future. Reggie's plans for his.

They didn't need Wallace.

He'd royally screwed everything up. He had to do something to end this. Without putting a stain on Jennifer's good name.

He had to think of something.

Nikkie Jean was laughing, looking beautiful and happy—and healthy. Wallace said a quick thanks to the man upstairs for that.

He had never meant to hurt that girl.

Wallace climbed out of his sedan. Before he left this world, he had some explaining to do.

Some forgiveness to ask for. And then...then he would make it all end. For all of them. Jennifer deserved that much.

Clean up his own messes. That's what she'd said.

And that was what Wallace was going to do.

Chapter 84

HE'D PASSED THE GOVERNOR'S wife and her gaggle of bodyguards as he'd crossed the parking lot toward the women's charity that Nikkie Jean was always talking about. Wallace didn't pay the Texas first lady any mind. He had one thought only.

He needed to talk to Nikkie Jean and make things right. Make her understand that he'd just wanted answers during the storm. He hadn't meant to leave her out in it.

And he wanted to make things right for Connie.

It was the least he could do.

He opened the door to the building. From what he knew, the charity took up the bottom two floors. Allen Jacobson and Cage Ralstone rented office space on the third now. There were a handful of other offices on Jacobson's floor that were still available for rent, since the recent fire and rebuild.

There weren't a lot of people in the lobby of the charity. Wallace waited until they went about their business in various other directions.

He had no business with them, after all.

Just Nikkie Jean.

He put the gun in his pocket. No sense scaring anyone. Not with as many problems as the women in this charity reputedly had.

Nikkie Jean's little firebrand of a friend was working the counter. She looked up at him, surprise on her delicate Tinker Bell face.

She really did remind him of Jennifer thirty years ago.

Jennifer.

Who wanted to leave him.

Before Wallace realized he was doing it, he pulled the gun free and fired. Twice.

Nikkie Jean's little friend hit the ground and didn't get up again.

He just stood and stared at her. She looked so much like Jennifer there.

Nikkie Jean screamed from behind him. Wallace spun, the gun rising toward. He hadn't even realized she was in the room.

"I didn't mean to do that." He started to tell her. But she wasn't listening.

She'd fallen to the floor next to her friend.

Who opened her eyes and stared at Wallace with all the accusations he couldn't make against himself. Dark eyes.

Eyes just like Jennifer's.

How was he supposed to clean up his mess now?

But she didn't say a word to him. "Run, Nik. Get out of here."

"No! Don't move. Just don't move. Nikkie Jean, we...need to clean up this mess. We have to clean up our own messes."

Chapter 85

WALLACE HENEDY HAD LOST IT. Nikkie Jean fought the panic. They were trapped. And Dr. Henedy wasn't about to let them out.

Her hands went to work, trying to determine whether the bullet was still inside. Izzie just kept staring at Dr. Henedy.

Blood welled. Rapidly. But not as much as could well. "I don't think it hit the brachial."

She hoped. If it had, Izzie only had a handful of minutes before she bled out. "I need something to tie off the wound."

"There's a string on that sweatshirt hanging there," Izzie said, steadily.

She wasn't panicking.

But then again, Izzie didn't panic over much of anything.

"Why did you do this?" Nikkie Jean asked, grabbing for the sweatshirt. Dr. Henedy was pacing in front of them. Between them and the only way out besides the windows.

They were trapped. And he still held the gun.

"For Jennifer. I love her."

"Your wife told you to do this?" She yanked the sweatshirt off the nearby hook and used the string to tighten a tourniquet around Izzie's shoulder. As best she could. "To shoot Izzie?"

There was another entrance wound. And that meant there were two exit wounds on the back.

Izzie required immediate attention. She needed a surgeon. One with an operating room and a team of assistants and nurses. She needed the best. That meant Allen or Virat or even Rafe, who had dual specialties in surgery and pediatrics.

"I need to get her across the street." Somehow. Even if she had to strap Izzie to the desk chair and roll her across the parking lot. "Wallace, you have to help me help her. *Please*."

"You're a damned surgeon. Stop the blood." He shot her a wild look. "We have to clean up our own messes, Nikkie Jean. That's what we've got to do. You know what to do here. Now do it."

Chapter 86

WALLACE HAD MADE A SERIOUS miscalculation. He had never meant to shoot anyone. Especially that little nurse there. She just sat, watching him from tear-dampened eyes. Watching him like he was a monster or something, as he locked the double doors that led to the women's charity.

"Nurse...how old are you?"

"Twenty-five." She almost breathed the answer. Hadn't he heard somewhere she was asthmatic or something? Just like Raymond had been as a boy.

Grief welled again.

"The same age I was when I meant Jenny."

"Your wife," Nikkie Jean said flatly. "What is she going to think about this?"

"I don't know. I don't think she's going to care any longer. She asked me for a separation an hour ago."

"I'm sorry," Nikkie Jean said. "That must have hurt."

"It did." Wallace watched her for a moment. Such an odd little cross between Jordan and Carla, but so pretty. "You'll need to pull it tighter than that. Clamp it off a bit better."

If the bullet had hit the brachial, that girl was as good as dead. He looked at her again. "I'm sorry. I never meant to involve you."

"Well, you did." The little fireball shot him a glare. "What are you going to do to make it right?"

"There's not a whole lot I can do. You're probably going to die. I hit you twice." And that was a shame. She was such a pretty little thing, too. Should have had her entire future ahead of her. He told her that. "You and Nikkie Jean both. But Nikkie Jean always was. As pretty as her mother."

Nikkie Jean didn't even look at him. She was too focused on

finding bandages in the first aid kit. It looked like it was a well-stocked one. No surprise, considering that Nikkie Jean, Lacy Deane, and that little dynamo Fin Coulter spent so much time in this building.

Wallace had never been inside. It was a charity for women, after all. Word had it all who went there had been hurt in the past.

That was such a shame. These were sweet girls, after all. Well, the fireball wasn't exactly sweet. But she was a pretty thing like all the others.

She looked like a kid sitting there.

Wallace just studied her as Nikkie Jean did her best to stop the bleeding.

If he and Jennifer had had a daughter, she might have very well looked like Nurse Izzie, with the short-cropped, dark hair and the big brown eyes.

Jennifer's eyes had always stared straight through his soul. But at Raymond's funeral, they had been absolutely blank.

She'd looked right through him.

Wallace's hand clenched on the gun. He had four bullets left.

He should just shoot them both and then himself. Just end it all.

Make it better for all of them.

Chapter 87

CAINE WAS HALFWAY ACROSS the hospital parking lot after his meeting with Rafe and Thor. It had gone about as poorly as he'd expected. Cage Ralstone had vehemently denied any wrongdoing.

Said there had to be a mistake, that he'd followed HIPAA's laws to the absolute best of his ability. There was no way he'd ever do anything to jeopardize his patients.

Caine had to admit—he had believed the man. And so had Rafe.

Rafe had mentioned that there had been doctored records in his hospital before. Records that had had his own sister-in-law's signature on them. During a time when she'd been on medical leave. And he hadn't been fully satisfied with the explanations all those months ago.

Rafe admitted he could have missed something.

Whoever was responsible for the billing errors, they were involved with both Finley Creek Gen and Barratt County.

That only left four names.

Three of those names were in Nikkie Jean's department. Rafe wasn't any more thrilled than Caine was.

As he'd pointed out, he had a sister-in-law in that department. And Nikkie Jean, who was as good as a sister-in-law already.

Caine had agreed with that point.

They needed to get the snake out of Nikkie Jean's playhouse, before someone else got hurt.

He texted her; she was supposed to be across the street while he met with Rafe. Then the two of them together were going to retrieve Dalton from the drop-in hospital day care on the lowest floor. Dalton had started day care at Finley Creek Gen two days ago; and was loving it. The twins had finally agreed to do the back-to-school shopping with Caine and Nikkie the next morning; then they had back-to-school teacher conferences. Both the twins had invited Nikkie Jean to attend with them.

Just like Caine had planned. They'd already started building the routine that everyone had needed.

Caine wanted Nikkie Jean.

He started out of the building, intent on finding her.

He could see W4HAV with its familiar apple-green logo right there across the street; the destroyed ER was between them.

He'd find her and guard dog Izzie and help them blow up balloons or paint posters or whatever they needed. Then he was taking his woman and his son home to the rest of his family, where they belonged.

Chapter 88

ALLEN WAS JUST LOCKING up his office when he heard the first sounds. He suspected what they were within seconds.

He hurried down the stairs. His office was directly above the women's charity where Lacy, Jillian, and Nikkie Jean spent so much of their time.

Sometimes abusive husbands had found their way there; even in the short time the charity had been open for business.

He always kept an ear out for problems downstairs. He had ever since a man had set the old building on fire and nearly killed him, Rafe, Ariella, and Jillian.

Allen learned from the past, that was for sure.

Never had there been gunshots before.

Allen pulled out his phone and quickly called 911. The TSP was operational again after the storm, but they were still stretched thin.

Just like every other group dedicated to helping others—the storm had tasked every resource available.

He hurried down the stairs toward the front office of the W4HAV. It was past six now. None of the medical offices in the building would still be seeing patients. And the rest of the offices on the second floor had closed, relocating to the larger building next door for a better price. Travis Worthington-Deane, Lacy Deane's husband and the landlord of the building, had been trying to clear out the second and first floors for the charity his wife and sisters-in-law were so involved in. They were planning to expand rapidly.

Allen was most likely the only one still on the third floor.

So that meant whatever was happening, it was happening at W4HAV. Nikkie Jean, Jillian, or Lacy were probably there. One of them usually was this time of night.

He wasn't about to leave one of them in trouble.

Allen wasn't stupid. He crept up to the glass doors and peered inside.

To see Wallace Henedy brandishing a gun as he loomed over Nikkie Jean.

Ice shot straight through him.

Allen didn't have a clue what to do next.

And then his gaze landed on the woman next to Nikkie Jean.

And the rapidly spreading blood.

Chapter 89

NIKKIE JEAN FOCUSED ON stopping the bleeding. Everything else had to be secondary at the moment. She was 99.999 percent certain the bullets had missed any major arteries. If it had, Izzie would have already passed out by now. "I don't think it hit the arteries, Iz."

"That's good," Wallace said. "You'll need something to close the wound for now. There should be needles in that kit."

Nikkie Jean had already pulled them out. "The bullets exited cleanly. Nothing jagged. But you'll definitely have a cool scar or two. Everett will want to see."

"I'll have to show him." Izzie was staying calm. Probably calmer than Nikkie Jean. But Izzie had just *seen* more. Most of Nikkie Jean's work was done in an operating room. With schedules and supplies and routine.

Nothing like this.

And she didn't even know why. "Can you put the gun down, Wallace? You're making me really nervous here."

"Is there any lidocaine in there? You're going to want to put something on her before you set the stitches. Otherwise, she'll be hurting too much to stay still."

So helpful. Gee, she never would have expected it out of him. "Why did you want to shoot...us?"

"I didn't. Just wanted to talk." He was pacing—in front of the only real exit they had. There were windows with a fire exit—but they were clear across the lobby. Forty feet away.

And locked up tight. Ariella's oldest brother was a stickler for security. The man designed security tech for a living after all.

There were exits at the rear, but those were out of reach, too.

She was just thankful that she and Izzie were the only ones in the building now. Ariella and her brother Luc had joined Jillian outside just moments before Wallace Henedy had burst in. Otherwise, all of those big, strong, *armed* bodyguards would have been right there.

Nikkie Jean hoped Ariella had forgotten her purse and sent one of those armed guards back for it or something.

Izzie had lost far too much blood.

"What about?"

"Questions. The storm. And about the past. What you know."

"I don't know anything about your past. Why would I?"

"Because I had an affair with your mother twenty-eight years ago and with your father's assistant fifteen years ago. And I know he's coming out here. If he puts it together, I'm not going to be able to give Jennifer what she really wants."

"What is that?"

"To be mayor. To be someone she thinks is important."

"What does that have to do with my mother?"

Nikkie Jean couldn't think of anything else to do but *talk*. She had to either get the gun away from him—or get herself and Izzie out.

Somehow.

She had no idea how to do either.

"This is your father's gun, *Dannica*. I won it off of him when you were around five or so. I was in and out of your house for years. I'm surprised you didn't recognize me."

"I've forgotten a lot of my childhood. Shut it out on purpose. Can we at least put her in the hallway? Where someone can get to her? I'll stay, right here." She stitched up the smallest injury as quickly as possible. Izzie gasped, but didn't cry out.

She didn't seem to have the breath to.

Izzie was extremely asthmatic, especially in times of physical distress. And one bullet had most likely hit a lung. She needed help; fast. "I think it's punctured a lung. She needs to be across the street."

"Don't be ridiculous. I'm not letting go of the gun, and you are far too small to lift her. It wouldn't be good for you or the baby."

Why did he care about that? Unless he hadn't meant to hurt her. But how that was supposed to help her, Nikkie Jean didn't have a clue.

"We have to do something. Maybe we can put her in the desk

chair? Roll her out? Wallace, we're *doctors*. We made a vow to help people. Patients. Well, do something."

"Yes, we did. Didn't we?" He stepped closer. Until he was looming over where she knelt next to Izzie. He held the gun steady, then reached down.

His hand wrapped around Izzie's. "Stay there," he ordered Nikkie Jean.

He yanked Izzie to her feet.

Izzie cried out.

Then Wallace was dragging her toward the door.

Nikkie Jean tried to follow.

He turned the gun toward her and fired. Nikkie Jean covered her stomach and hit the ground as Izzie screamed again.

Chapter 90

WALLACE RECOGNIZED THE man in the hallway the instant he yanked open the doors. It was all over now. Allen Jacobson would bring the cops for sure. If he hadn't already.

Jacobson was a smart man, after all.

And he'd seen…Wallace with the gun.

It was all over now for him. Jennifer would find out.

Hell, of course, she would. Wallace had just shot a young woman, after all.

He'd had some stupid plan of shooting himself and somehow making it seem like Nikkie Jean was responsible.

Like he'd frightened her and she'd shot him with her father's gun.

The logistics of it hadn't made sense even to him. But Wallace just hadn't been thinking straight. Not since the storm.

Not since Ray. Not since Jennifer had said she wanted a separation.

Not since he'd failed to get the answers he sought of Nikkie Jean.

Wallace had failed at a lot of things lately.

Hell, he'd been failing at them for fifteen years. "It is all Miranda's fault."

Wallace had the girl in his grip. Nurse Izzie, such a little fireball. She didn't weigh much. Skinny. She smelled like soap and antiseptic and…blood.

He might well have killed this girl already, too. Just like Miranda and Connie. Only this one hadn't done a damned thing to him. Except be a little sharp-tongued when he'd made mistakes.

Clean up your messes, Wallace. Just clean them up.

Then deal with little Nikkie Jean.

He shoved the nurse. Hard. Straight into Jacobson's arms. Boy always had liked dark-eyed brunettes, after all. Might as well give him this one.

Then he raised the gun.

And fired again. Right at Jacobson. Not to hurt him, but to make it clear. Jacobson wasn't coming in for Nikkie Jean.

He slammed the glass doors shut and turned the deadbolt quickly. Leaving himself alone with Jordan Carrington's daughter.

Chapter 91

ALLEN CAUGHT IZZIE, JUST as the bullet singed past his arm and embedded in the wall.

She cried out against him. Weakly.

"How many times were you hit?" he demanded. He needed to see, but there wasn't time for that.

"Nik's in there with him. You have to get her out." She was struggling to breathe, but she forced the words out. "Three. He shot me three times."

Big, dark eyes filled with terror looked right into his soul in that moment.

"Has she been shot?"

"No. Not yet. I don't think he wants to hurt *her*. He mentioned her parents. He knew them."

Allen had to make a decision.

Izzie had been shot—three times by her own count. Allen couldn't just stand there and let her bleed to death.

He could hear sirens in the distance.

It could have been an ambulance for the hospitals nearby. He just hoped to hell he was wrong.

There was no way he could put Izzie down to go save Nikkie Jean.

He had a decision to make and he knew it.

Allen carried her down the hall to the back stairs as fast as he dared.

Chapter 92

CAINE HEARD THE SHOTS. He'd heard enough shots in his life to know exactly what they were. So had the man next to him. Caine didn't care. Nikkie Jean was over there. In that building somewhere. He ran. No one was running out of the building. Nikkie Jean and her friends would be running out of the building if they could. That thought blazed across his mind. She was in there.

Thor grabbed for him and nearly jerked him back. But Caine was bigger. "Stop! Use your head, man!"

"Nikkie Jean is in there."

"And so is a gunman. We wait for the SWAT units."

"The TSP building took a direct hit last week. They're short-staffed." He wasn't waiting. Not with Nikkie Jean in there. "Nikkie Jean is in there. I'm going to her."

She needed him. His every thought was on the woman inside that building.

Allen Jacobson met them in the lobby, a familiar dark-haired woman in his arms. Guard dog Izzie looked dead. That was Caine's first thought.

And if she was hurt—Nikkie Jean was nearby. Izzie was almost fanatical about knowing where Annie and Nikkie Jean were at times. Nikkie Jean had shared bits of the other woman's story. Caine was warming up to her. They had the same goal after all. Protecting Nikkie Jean.

"Jacobson, where's Nikkie Jean?"

"Henedy has her in the lobby."

"Is she hurt?"

"No! But he's used four bullets. I don't know how many he has left. I got to *go!*"

The woman was turning blue in his arms. "Go!"

Chapter 93

NIKKIE JEAN FORCED HERSELF to stay present for this. If she checked out like her mind was telling her to do, she would probably die.

She would…and so would her baby.

Nikkie Jean was going to do everything in her power to make certain that didn't happen.

She wanted Caine. She wanted to see Caine hold this baby like he did Dalton. She wanted to help save Izzie. She wanted to be there when Annie adopted her three little boys.

She wanted to go to a parent-teacher conference for the first time. To buy clip-on earrings and purple nail polish and to learn about Minecraft and zombies.

Not sit there and listen to a madman expound about things she didn't have a clue about. "I…let me go, Wallace. I need to go be with Izzie. She's my best friend. She's going to be scared."

"I need to clean up some messes first, Nikkie Jean."

"What messes?"

He motioned for her to sit down. She did. Against the wall nearest the windows.

She just needed to see that light.

Henedy was blocking her path to the lobby doors. There was no way she'd be able to outrun him—or a bullet.

The window might be her best option. Why not? It had worked for Rafe and Jillian all those months ago.

Chapter 94

CAINE TOOK ONE LOOK through the glass doors. Nikkie Jean huddled near the window, Wallace Henedy paced in front of her, clutching a revolver. Most likely a six-shooter.

Thor peered inside from the opposite door frame. "Six-shooter. How many did your pal say?"

"Four."

Two bullets left. Unless Henedy had brought more.

"We have to get her out of there." He could see the fear, the panic, on her face. She had her arms crossed over her stomach, over the baby.

Caine forced his own panic back. She was alive right now. That mattered. That meant there was hope.

"There's got to be a rear entrance. It's still early; it may not be locked."

"Which means I can get it. It might take me some time."

"I'll buy you that time. And then you get Nikkie Jean out."

Two more bullets.

If that gun discharged, Caine meant for it not to be in Nikkie Jean's direction.

"Go. I'll cause a distraction out here."

The glass-pane doors wouldn't provide protection, but if he could get Henedy to shoot at one, Caine could get himself inside.

To her.

He forced himself to wait, to give Thor time to get to the back of the building.

Henedy turned toward Nikkie Jean more fully, the gun in his hand aimed in her direction. Caine wasn't waiting any longer.

Caine slammed into the glass doors of the charity that Nikkie Jean loved so much.

Chapter 95

"CAINE!" NIKKIE JEAN yelled for that damned Alvaro the instant she saw him. She rose, no doubt to go to him. Wallace grabbed her by the arm and yanked her back.

He wasn't stupid. If Alvaro got inside, there would be hell to pay.

Part of the reason he was in this mess was because of Caine Alvaro's damned forensic accountant investigator, or whatever the bastard called himself.

Wallace fired. Right at the big son-of-a-bitch.

The glass shattered.

"Caine!"

She clawed and twisted and fought to get away from him to her lover.

Wallace just yanked her off her feet. Her back slammed into his chest. His hand tightened over her waist, right over the slight thickening where Alvaro's baby rested.

Damned bastard had ruined all of his plans.

Wallace didn't know how to clean up this mess now. He jerked his hand from her waist and wrapped it around her shoulders, just to hold her still.

Nikkie Jean screamed, a blood-chilling, curdling wail that had him dropping her right there on the floor. Never had he heard a sound like it.

Chapter 96

CAINE SAW THE opportunity, and he took it. Nikkie Jean was on the floor, curling up around the baby.

She was shutting down. He knew that.

It didn't matter. What mattered was that there was one bullet left.

And Wallace Henedy was too close to the woman he loved. Caine dove for the other man. He was younger, stronger, larger, and had more to fight for.

Caine wasn't going to let himself think about losing.

His hand wrapped around Henedy's gun hand. He used his own shoulder to barrel into Henedy's chest.

They went down.

The force of Caine's blow sent the other man sprawling.

The gun discharged.

Fire shot through Caine's chest, but he ignored it.

Nikkie Jean was screaming. Yelling his name. She was back on her feet now. "Get out of here, Nikkie Jean!"

Henedy swung. Missed.

And he just kept coming.

Chapter 97

CAINE SLAMMED HENEDY to the ground, the gun fell out of the other man's hand. Nikkie Jean kicked it to the far corner.

Her eyes stayed trained on the men. Caine stood up, staggered. Blood was blooming on his chest.

"No!" Henedy dove at him.

Caine stumbled. He shouldn't have. He was bigger, stronger. And he'd been shot. Caine was hurt. Panic built again.

The two men rolled on the floor.

When the men rolled again, Nikkie Jean didn't think. She just jumped. Landing on Wallace Henedy's back.

"You leave him alone!" She sank her teeth into his neck.

He howled and tried to throw her off of him. Nikkie Jean may have been small and a bit battered, and nauseated as hell ninety-nine percent of the time now, but that didn't matter.

What mattered was that this man had tried to take the people she loved away from her. And that was just not going to happen anymore. Nikkie Jean's hands went for his eyes. She clawed. As fiercely as she could.

He just kept howling. Like a rabid animal. Her knees tightened around him.

This time, *this time,* she was the one attacking from behind.

And she was going to make it count. Nikkie Jean grabbed a handful of salt-and-pepper hair and yanked with all of her might. She was determined to win this time. It was her turn now. She was fighting for the man she loved.

Chapter 98

HE COULDN'T SHAKE HER off. Not and fight the big bastard, too. Wallace shifted his attention from escaping Alvaro to keeping Nikkie Jean from gouging out his eyes.

Such a fierce little wildcat, she was. Fighting for the man she loved.

At one time, Jennifer would have fought for him, too. But he had ruined that. Jennifer *knew* about his affairs. And had known from the very beginning.

For thirty years, she'd lived with his betrayal, she said.

And she'd stopped loving him a long time ago.

With a roar just from the anguish that caused he reared up, shaking the small woman off his back like a fly.

Nikkie Jean went flying, to slam into the wall five feet away.

She cried out.

Both men froze. Alvaro turned frantic. His hand went around Wallace's neck.

Wallace kicked him in the balls. Alvaro went down. Wallace grabbed for his only avenue of escape. He yanked Nikkie Jean from the floor.

She yelled and screamed and kicked. Wallace couldn't help himself; he shoved her away again.

Alvaro was back on his feet.

Wallace saw the huge fist coming at his face far too late to avoid it.

Alvaro's punch connected.

Wallace went down—and didn't get up again.

He just laid there on the floor of the charity designed to help women heal, and bawled like a baby, sobbing out his wife's name over and over.

It was over.

He'd never be able to clean up his own mess again. He stayed there until hands of a stranger yanked him from the ground and cuffed him.

Other hands were there to help Alvaro to his feet.

The man's twin was carefully lifting little Nikkie Jean into his own arms, promising her he'd take care of her, and the baby she was pleading him to protect.

The baby. Wallace had forgotten about Nikkie Jean's baby in the heat of the moment. He hoped he hadn't harmed the baby. He wasn't that much of a monster, was he?

He was. He was. It was time he finally admitted it.

All of this was his own fault. He'd failed. Wallace tuned everything out from that point on. It didn't matter.

He'd lost what mattered most.

Chapter 99

CAINE'S ARM WAS ON fire, and every bone in his body ached. He didn't care. He could hear her crying. He forced himself to turn. "Nikkie Jean?"

And there she was.

Rafe had her. Carrying her protectively. "How badly is she hurt?"

"Bumps and bruises," Rafe said. "You're hurt worse. I'm going to take care of her. I promise that. You just get that shoulder taken care of."

"Dalton's still in the day care."

"We'll take care of him." His twin looked at him. Nikkie Jean was still sobbing in Rafe's arms. But her eyes were on Caine. Fear was written all over her.

"I can carry her." She'd be afraid. What this had done to her—beyond the physical—they'd have to get through the trauma from this, too.

"Not right now, man," Thor said. There were TSP detectives flooding the room. Caine just ignored them, and Henedy's broken wailing for his wife. "You're bleeding pretty badly. Let the twin get your girl. I'll watch over her, too."

"Caine," Nikkie Jean said firmly. "You do what you are told this time. This is *my* hospital you're going to. My rules."

Her eyes were...steady. Calming. She was resting in Rafe's arms, but she wasn't crying any longer. She was ok.

No matter what happened from here on out, she was ok. "Yes, ma'am."

Thor groaned. "Now she's got him hen-pecked already."

—

"Who are you?" Nikkie Jean asked as Rafe carried her across the parking lot and Vince Acardi's son helped Caine.

Caine was walking at least. Talking. But the blood on his shoulder was spreading.

"What's it the ladies are saying now? I'm his *bestie,* sweetie. Who are you?"

"I'm his…Nikkie Jean."

Caine and Rafe both laughed. Rafe grinned down at her, then looked at the big man in a plaid shirt she'd never met before. "That's about the only way to describe her."

"Damn, Caine. This one is peanut-sized. What does she see in you?"

Nikkie Jean looked at the man she loved. "Everything."

Caine stopped walking. His brother stopped, too.

Caine leaned over and kissed her. Just once, right on the forehead.

The most perfect kiss of all.

"Rafe, Izzie?" Nikkie Jean asked, as fear for her friend resurfaced now that she and Caine and the baby were safe from Wallace Henedy. "How is she?"

"Allen handed her over to Cage and Virat. I don't know anything at this point."

"Then hurry. Get Caine help and…just get us there."

"Hang on, baby. We'll do that."

Chapter 100

HE TRIED TO BLOCK OUT everything that had happened while Dr. Kaur set the stitches in his arm. Allen wouldn't let himself worry about Izzie and what was no doubt going on in that operating room.

She'd been gasping for breath when he'd carried her in. And the blood loss...

"She's with Cage and Vir," Fin said, after peeking her head in. "And Wanda went in with her."

"Any updates?" Layla asked. "What happened across the road?"

"TSP is over there now." Allen heard the fear in Fin's tone.

No one knew what condition Nikkie Jean would be in when this all ended.

Allen waited impatiently until she set the last stitch and applied the bandage. He yanked his shirt off his head and tossed it toward the biohazard bin. "I'm going. See if I can help."

"Allen..."

"Layla, that's Nikkie Jean over there. And Henedy worked for me. I need to be there."

Someone yelled out orders, just outside the exam room curtain. Allen jerked it back. Rafe was there, Nikkie Jean in his arms. She was moving and talking and crying.

And alive.

Thank God.

"Go, Layla. I know she's your patient."

The OB didn't hesitate.

Dr. Alvaro walked at her side, being supported by a big man Allen didn't recognize. There was blood all over Alvaro.

"Allen!" Nikkie Jean yelled when she saw him. "Where's Izzie?"

"Virat has her on the table now," Fin told her. "I'm going up to wait for word."

"So am I," Allen said.

"Stay with her, Allen. Please? Just take care of her for me?" Nikkie Jean turned those big hazel eyes in his direction.

"Of course, I will. I'm not leaving this hospital until I'm sure she'll be ok."

"Thanks."

Lacy and Dr. Peno, one of the ER doctors, sprang into action, taking Dr. Alvaro in one direction.

Layla Kaur took Nikkie Jean in another.

Allen headed toward the OR.

Epilogue

CAINE WATCHED HER sleeping for the longest time.

They were in the same room as last time. It was remarkable how that room somehow always seemed to be open when needed.

The OB had decided to keep Nikkie Jean overnight, as a precaution.

She hadn't taken any direct hits to the abdomen, but she'd been knocked around. His fists balled up as he thought about that bastard Henedy and what he'd done.

What he could have cost them.

Izzie was one floor down, in critical but guarded condition. Mostly from complications from the asthma. One bullet had nicked her lung. The other had passed through fatty tissue and done moderate damage to her liver. She'd had to have part of her liver removed, but she would heal. The third bullet had passed through her outer arm to lodge in Allen Jacobson's shoulder. It had grazed the bone, but the man would make a full recovery.

He sat in the room with Nurse Izzie now, refusing to leave.

He'd made a promise to Nikkie Jean—that's what Fin had told them when she'd stopped by to check on them. Whether Izzie wanted him there or not, he wasn't leaving.

Izzie hadn't woken long enough to say one way or the other what she wanted.

Her uncle was out of town. She had no one else except Annie, who was recovering somewhere Caine had no idea, and Nikkie Jean. The people she worked with.

He knew what it was like to be that alone. No more. Izzie had a family with him and Nikkie Jean whenever she wanted it.

"You're supposed to be in bed," a voice said from behind him. "Yours. Not hers. Trust me. Those beds aren't big enough for two people."

"She could sleep on top. She'd fit."

"Yeah…don't try it. Personal experience here."

He looked at his twin. At the sleeping little boy Rafe held.

Henry was keeping the twins at home for the night. But Dalton…Dalton was going home with Aunt Jillian for his first official sleepover.

Caine's world was never going to be the same again.

He was damned glad Nikkie Jean had blown into his ER that night. She'd brought the wind with her.

Brought hope and life and everything.

He wrapped the fingers of his good hand around hers. It rested over their baby.

Right where it should.

Caine leaned in and kissed her once, as his twin brother settled his sleeping son in Caine's lap around the sling he'd have to wear for a month or so. The damage had been minimal, thanks to a small caliber size and him being a larger-than-average man.

But he would need to heal.

They all would.

But they'd be healing together.

.

Also available,

Lacy, Jillian, and Ari
get their own happily ever afters in

the

Finley Creek: General

Trilogy

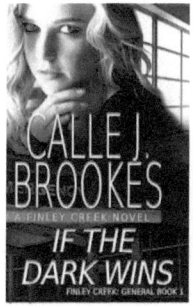 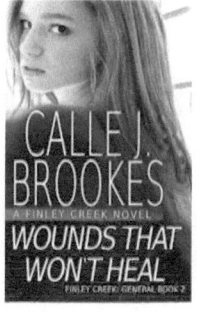 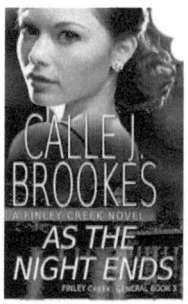

Coming Soon!

Annie and Izzie get their own stories in

Walk Through the Fire

&

We All Sleep Alone